MW00389516

PRAISE FOR PAUL BLACK'S NOVELS

2-Time WINNER for science fiction
Independent Publisher's Book Award.

Multiple GOLD and SILVER medalist for science fiction,
ForeWord Magazine's Book of the Year.

WINNER for science and general fiction
London, New York, Midwest and Hollywood Book Festivals.

WINNER for genre fiction
Writer's Digest Magazine's International Book Award

"Science can be a boon to humanity. *The Presence* is a science fiction thriller set in a future where reality is something manufactured by corporations. Sonny Chaco is charged with finding something that resembles law in this world. As he tails one billionaire CEO who may have made those billions with a bit of foul tactics, he finds that the reality-manufacture industry is more tumultuous than he could ever hope, and that throwing in some romance only complicates the complicated. An EXCITING READ that should prove HARD TO PUT DOWN."

~ *Midwest Book Review*

"*The Presence* is fast-paced thriller, full of smart, interesting characters and suspense. You'll think it's one thing, but it's something else entirely!"

~ *Writer's Digest Magazine*

"It was a FAST READ and I enjoyed the trip that it took me on. It's one of the better hard Sci-Fi books I've read in a long time, and Paul Black is an author I'm looking forward to seeing more from!"

~ *Jordan Mason, themoviepool.com.*

"An exciting read that should prove hard to put down."

"Author Paul Black brings a fresh look to the near-future fiction-writing genre."

~ *PearlSnapDiscount.com*

"*The Presence* is fast-paced and WELL WRITTEN. Paul Black pulls futuristic tech into a believable and seamless world."

~ *Darcia Helle, author Quiet Furry Books*

"Dallas writer Paul Black makes his first foray into the world of science fiction with *The Tels*. It's a HIGHLY ORIGINAL novel set in the near future and IT MOVES AT LIGHTNING SPEED. Mr. Black has quite an imagination and puts it to good use. The MIND-BENDING PLOT centers on Jonathan Kortel, who is approached by a shadowy group called the Tels, who covet his telekinetic gifts. The ENSUING ACTION IS BIZARRE enough to read like something straight out of The X-Files."

~ *Steve Powers, Dallas Morning News*

"(*The Tels*) is WRITTEN SO SPLENDIDLY, at times I forgot I was reading science fiction — with the emphasis on fiction. The characters are realistic, and the hero is someone you relate to, worry about and wonder if he's going to be able to cope with the reality that is set before him. This is definitely ONE OF THE BEST SCIENCE FICTION NOVELS I've ever read... the BOOK IS REMARKABLE."

~ *Marilyn Meredith, Writer's Digest's 11th Annual Book Awards*

"...*Soulware* was a BRILLIANTLY EMBROIDERED STORY, mixing science and fiction in a plausible and entertaining way...I absolutely LOVED THIS BOOK!"

~ *Ismael Manzano, G-POP.net*

"A riveting science fiction novel by a gifted author."

"This story by Paul Black is as STRONG AND WELL WRITTEN as any of the stories of my heroes: Robert Heinlein, Isaac Asimov, Andre Norton, or Anne McCaffrey. He is one of those writers that we who worship this genre look for every time we pick up the novel of an author who is new to us...The CHARACTERS COME ALIVE for you. You feel right along with them. You can believe the decisions they make. And best of all, nothing is clear-cut and simple. The story brings us to a strong ending while leaving us with the desire for more...I recommend *The Tels* to every lover of sci-fi. Good work, Paul! Welcome to my bookshelves!"

~ *John Strange, thecityweb.com*

"Paul Black's ENGAGING PROSE promises big things for the future...."

~ *Writer's Notes Magazine*

"...a GREAT READ, full of suspense and action...."

~ *Dallas Entertainment Guide*

"A RIVETING science fiction novel by a gifted author...*The Tels* would prove a popular addition to any community library Science Fiction collection and documents Paul Black as an IMAGINATIVELY SKILLED STORYTELLER of the first order. Also very highly recommended is the newly published second volume in the *Tels* series, *Soulware*, which continues the adventures of Jonathan Kortel in the world of tomorrow."

~ *Midwest Book Review*

"...there's a grittiness and sensuality that pours out of every word..."

"Black rises above the Trekkie laser tag spastics found in your typical sci-fi novels resting on the grocery store racks. His sensibilities broaden from machine gun testosterone to discreet fatherhood, from errant sexuality to wry humor. HE DELIVERS A CHARGE OF VENTURE RARELY FOUND IN FIRST-TIME WRITERS. And *THE TELS* HITS THE MARK as a solid adventure serial, leaving you hanging for the next publication."

~ Brian Adams, Collegian

"*The Tels* is an ADDICTIVE READ from first-time novelist Paul Black, a promising new storyteller on the sci-fi scene. He manages to capture the reader in the first ten pages. He introduces us to a set of intriguing characters in a totally believable possible future. There is a grittiness and sensuality to his writing that pours out of every word in the book. Whether it's his description of the preparation of a good meal, the seduction of a beautiful woman, or a fight to the death, *THE TELS* HAS IT ALL. Even people who don't read sci-fi will want to read this book. The action is great and would make one hell of a movie. Is Hollywood listening? Paul Black has a winner on his hands. I can hardly wait for the next installment."

~ Cynthia A., About Towne, ITCN

"*Soulware* doesn't miss a beat as it continues Jonathan's story, the story of his quest to find out exactly who he really is and why the Tels are so interested in him. The ending makes it clear that there's more to come, and readers who crave their science-fiction with a hint of weirdness can look forward to the next book in the series."

~ Steve Powers, Dallas Morning News

For Holly

Much affection

Paul

Other books by Paul Black

The Tels

Soulware

Nexus Point

The Presence

The Samsara Effect

NOVEL INSTINCTS PUBLISHING
Dallas | Santa Fe
www.novelinstincts.com

ISBN: 978-0-578-17190-6
1. Fiction / Science Fiction / High Tech 2. Fiction / Near-Future 3. Thriller / Suspense

Library of Congress Control Number: 2015917735

Printed in the United States of America.
10 9 8 7 6 5 4 3 2 1

Cover photo: Paul Black Design

First trade paperback edition.

This book's text is typeset in Adobe Garamond 3, 11 point / 18 point.
Its page numbers and chapter heads are in Bureau Agency, and some titles
are in Trade Gothic Bold Eighteen Condensed.

A DILLON BRADFORD NOVEL

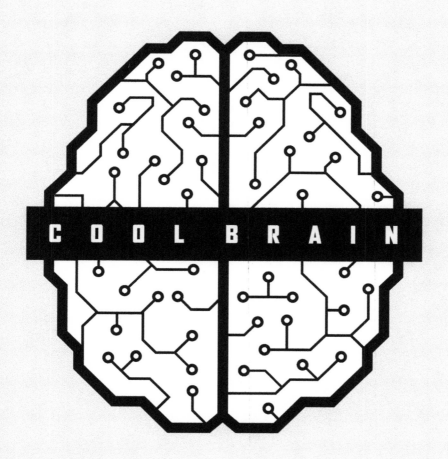

COOL BRAIN

PAUL BLACK

NOVEL INSTINCTS
Publishers of fine genre fiction and non-fiction.

Part 1: Bitch Slapped

1. You knew, didn't you?

The client's right eye narrowed, forcing his already deep crow's feet into a suspicious canyon of scrutiny.

"He loves the new logo," my 20-something junior account manager said.

Cyndi was the daughter of the CMO of Ewing Laboratories, one of our largest accounts. Heavily bronzed and pierced in all the wrong places, she had been forced down my throat by a shitty economy and my need to make payroll.

I didn't have the heart to tell her that the Eagle Energy brand identity we had spent the better half of the first quarter retooling was dying a slow death on the conference room table. And it didn't take my 20 years in advertising to render that verdict. The dance of contracting muscle in the client's right eyelid was the giveaway.

"Mr. Bradford?"

Cyndi leaned on my desk, having turned away from the monitor that dominated the far wall of my office. Thanks to the hidden cameras in our conference rooms, we were watching my firm's two top creatives squirming in their Dolce & Gabanas. Their genius was being sized up by what I could only call the biggest asswipe ever to grace my company's client roster. He and his 10-month-old alternative energy start-up had been valued, pre-IPO, at $120 million. He was, as my partner was fond of reminding me, a gift from God. I shot Cyndi a doubtful sideways glance. "What?"

She arched her eyebrows in a girlish way that had probably worked on her daddy since she was a kid. "Tommy and Isato have busted their asses on this identity. It's brilliant!"

Although I hadn't confirmed it yet, Tommy likely had been sleeping with her for the last month. The act of leaning onto my desk, along with a sweater whose neckline plunged far south of corporate correctness, had deposited the better part of Cyndi's cleavage in my direct line of sight. Since her forced employment six months ago, Cyndi's flagrant brandishing of her assets had worked well on the junior art directors. But that was the extent of her sway.

"Tommy and Isato have a long night ahead of them," I replied.

I returned my attention to the monitor. Tommy, defending the brand strategy, was clearly at the end of his creative rope. His body language – especially his hand gesture, a kind of defiant karate chop – signaled the remoteness of any hope for compromise. The client slowly folded his arms across his chest. I muted the sound.

"You knew, didn't you?" Cyndi said. She conveniently leaned a little closer. "It's like you can read his mind."

Yes, I wanted to say, I can, but not in some bullshit, Uri Geller-like way. The talent I wielded was the real-meal-deal. *X-Files* kind of stuff. It was wonderful and unnerving – and also monumentally profitable. I'd like to say I had been struck by lightning or taken by aliens. The truth was more prosaic. Something changed in me at puberty: one day I couldn't hear people's thoughts, the next I could. In case you were wondering, no, it isn't like a psychopath who hears voices in his head, then goes off and butchers 20 women. What I do is more like eavesdropping on a conversation at a crowded party. I let their thoughts *in*. With concentration, I can pick up most things. "Most" is the operative word. I wouldn't want to listen to everything. You have to pick and choose. Listening to all the crap that rattles around peoples' minds will distort your view of humanity and make you one cynical son-of-a-bitch.

I gave Cyndi another doubt-filled sideways glance because Mr. $120 million, while flippantly dismissing three months of hard creative work, was actually more concerned with getting the stripper he had met last night up to his hotel room after dinner. Thoughts of her tits and cell number kept tumbling around inside his head like sneakers in a dryer, which probably explained why he had been nervously thumbing his iPhone inside his pants pocket. Between sick fantasies about her, he'd reminded himself to check with his CEO about a phone conference with their Chinese head of sales who, by the way, happened to be the son-in-law of the energy minister. He'd also called Isato a faggot, praised Tommy for having some balls, and surprisingly, was considering us for another brand creation. Something about a new aviation motor that would revolutionize the industry. I hadn't picked up on its details because his iPhone had vibrated, Cyndi was brandishing her cleavage, and I'd been distracted by the 426 other voices that made up my brand agency, CoolBrain.

"Dillon," Cyndi purred. "I bet I can read your mind."

I had sweaters older than this girl. What could she hope to accomplish with this bad Lindsay Lohan act? I considered listening in on her thoughts, but what could I learn that she hadn't already revealed by her dress, words, and actions?

What the hell, I thought. *I'll give a listen.*

Cyndi's attention moved to the monitor. As Tommy and Isato folded down the presentation equipment, her mind flashed through a fragmented collage of thoughts, starting with her dinner last night with Tommy and ending with collecting her clothes after they had sex. She was frustrated with Tommy's lack of skill and wondering if I could give her what she needed. Her eyes shifted to me. *Jesus.* I didn't need her bullshit in my company, and I certainly didn't need my best employee distracted.

"I seriously doubt that," I replied.

Cyndi straightened and squinted her eyes into a cliché of concentration. She even put a finger to her temple. After an excruciatingly long second, she finally declared, "You're thinking of taking me to dinner, right?"

"Close," I said, and graced her with half a smile.

"Really?"

No, I thought. *You're fired.*

2. Back at ya.

In an area the size of Dallas/Ft. Worth, there are about half a dozen people with my ability. At least, that's what I've found to be true. Roughly one in every 400,000, and they're usually rich, or powerful, or both. Listening in on people's minds makes navigating business a whole lot easier.

"What did Hampton say when you told him about his little girl's new position in life?" Derek Hoffman swirled the olive in his Stoli martini with a little too much panache. He had been CoolBrain's head of account service and my business partner from the beginning, 12 years ago. He was one of the few people I knew who was actually a native of Dallas. He'd married his high school sweetheart and I once heard her think, on a double-date before they had moved in together, that she was going to take him home and sop him up like a biscuit.

I was from Chicago, and even though I had been in Texas for more than half my life, I'd never really warmed up to some of these precious colloquialisms.

Derek had blown up when I told him I was firing Cyndi. I assured him that we wouldn't lose the account, and agreed to call the client and break the news. Truth was, I had listened to the client's thoughts the day he broached the idea of sending over his daughter. He seemed to understand her limitations and was going through the motions just to appease his wife.

"I don't need to remind you again that Ewing Laboratories is our second largest account," Derek said, with another swirl.

I finished the last of my Dalmore, neat, and eyed myself in the bar's mirror. "I didn't fire her."

"Really?" Derek swiveled to face me and leaned onto the bar with one elbow. "You aren't scared of her old man, are you?"

"Daddy sees through his little girl's bullshit."

"But?"

I turned from my reflection. "But Hampton's account is important—"

"And you swallowed your pride and did what's good for the company." He pointed and a little of his drink sloshed over the rim of his glass. "That's the Dillon I like to see."

Thomas "Red" Hampton was a bull of a man. A decorated ex-Navy surgeon and former advisor to President Bush 41, he was CEO of one of the nation's largest privately owned pharmaceutical groups. Screwing with him was a lesson in tactical warfare, as several of my creatives had discovered the hard way. He'd founded Ewing Laboratories in the mid-1980s and had sardonically named his company after the main character in the old TV show *Dallas*. He claimed it sounded important, and besides, didn't everyone know J.R.? A PR firm had brought in CoolBrain to rebrand the company. They had tried in vain to dissuade Hampton from continuing to use the name. In one heated discussion, the head of the PR firm had ended up screaming at Hampton, citing that no under the age of 50 would have any idea who J.R. Ewing was. When asked what I thought, it didn't take any special powers to come up with the answer. I told Hampton the name had a certain cachet, and I assured him that a focus study would probably reveal a lot of residual equity for the image of J.R. Ewing. The PR firm lasted one more week. CoolBrain became Ewing's brand agency of record.

Derek set his drink down and removed the mini lightsaber that was its swizzle stick. "I would have missed Cyndi." He slid the last olive off and popped it in his mouth.

"You would have missed her tits," I said.

A knowing smirk crept across Derek's mouth as he chewed. "I heard Tommy's team is going to be Red Bulling it tonight."

"They can handle it."

"Think we can mine any more work out of Eagle?"

It was my turn to cultivate a smug grin.

"What?" Derek asked. "Another one of your hunches?"

"Let's just say I have a good feeling about this."

Derek knocked back the rest of his drink. "Jesus, Dillon, how do you predict this stuff? I'm the new business guy, and I can't gauge dick in this economy."

"Sixth sense?"

"God, teach me, please?"

"Love to, but I've got to run." I threw down a Jackson, turned to the mirror behind the bar and passed my fingers through my hair.

"What's her name tonight?" Derek followed my twenty with one more.

"Kadin."

"You like her, don't you?"

I adjusted the knot in my Zegna and faced him. "I do. She's smart, sexy without being too Dallasy, and she makes me laugh." Truth was, Kadin was all of those, but she was also a member of a group of friends who shared my special ability. We met irregularly, usually on Fridays. In a world of millions of detached voices, a little quiet went a long way. We couldn't eavesdrop on the thoughts of another person who had the gift. It was like dead air, which meant meeting in a group gave us a respite from the noise inside our heads. I can't exactly explain what it's like to have this ability, but I can say it's nice to be around your own kind.

Derek came off his barstool. He slipped his suit coat on and tugged at his shirt cuffs. "You're really into her, aren't you?"

"I don't know," I said, truthfully.

Derek shook his head. "Dillon, you're almost forty, and you've never had a steady girlfriend. Life isn't getting any longer, you know? She's a great girl. Don't lose her."

Maybe Derek was right. I did like Kadin, maybe more than I wanted to admit. But the fact that I couldn't read her thoughts was both refreshing and scary. I had tried to get serious with a couple of girls, but it never worked out. Truth was, after a lifetime of listening to people's thoughts like God Almighty, I knew too much about the two-faced human race. It was rare to find someone who didn't lie almost constantly, either to themselves or others. I used to listen in to see if a person was bullshitting me or not. Believe me, you don't want to know the stats. God, there were times I just wanted to be free from the noise in my head. Even though I had taught myself how to shut it all out, the tumult was always there, hovering like a giant swarm of bees.

"I'll try not to. Later, man–" A gentle tap to my right shoulder cut me off. Derek's deadpan didn't give me a clue as to who was behind me. Probably an ex-girlfriend. I turned cautiously into the voluptuous force of nature that was Cyndi Hampton.

Her dark red lips parted into an impish little smile. "Now what are you two button-downs doing in a place like this?" she asked.

Piss Off was one of the last vestiges of a seedy, tragically hip Dallas neighborhood known as Deep Ellum. In the '80s and early '90s it had been a thriving Mecca where underground bands like the New Bohemians and Tripping Daisy gestated before launching into the majors. Once littered with fashionable restaurants and trendy boutiques, it suffered a massive collapse when Dallas's developers created safe, clean destination zones with tony names like West Village and Uptown. Deep Ellum, once the only place in Dallas for anything remotely resembling a New York experience, was a shell of its former self. And Piss Off was now the place for the late night tat-and-pierce crowd to sip cheap drafts and tap their black-nailed fingers to exhausted alternative music.

It was also a couple of blocks from our building, which we bought just before Deep Ellum's death spiral began. That's a great example of what I was referring to when I said sometimes I didn't get the whole conversation.

"It's our office away from office," I replied.

I tried to keep my eyes from leaving hers, but Cyndi was dressed as if she were headed to the set of some cheap soft porn shoot. The top she wore looked like an Elizabethan corset had mated with a military flak vest. It presented her cleavage on a crisscrossing, riveted lacework of black braid and brown leather cups. Her long legs were wrapped in black fishnet, and they flowed from a matching riveted leather miniskirt into what I could only categorize as six-inch stiletto military boots.

I lifted my eyes, and she met my scrutiny.

"Shit," Derek said, eyeing his wristwatch. "I have to run. You all have a great weekend."

Before I could say goodbye, he was wedging his way through the bar crowd toward the front door.

"Can I join you?" Cyndi asked.

I nodded. "I'm surprised I haven't seen you here before."

As Cyndi mounted Derek's barstool, I pushed the two twenties up to his empty martini glass.

"I usually get here later, when the music starts." Cyndi hooked a heel onto the stool's lowest rung and crossed her legs. She tugged at the hem of her miniskirt, but it didn't help much.

"Us button-downs are gone long before then." I motioned, and the taller bartender ambled over. He scooped up the money and Derek's empty glass.

"Something for the lady and another one for you, Dillon?" he asked.

"Yes and yes." I leaned toward Cyndi. "We've been following Jimmy for years. He makes the best martini in Dallas."

Jimmy preened, then took a chrome cocktail shaker and held it behind his back. He grabbed a 12-ounce glass and flipped it over his shoulder and caught it with the shaker. He finished with a flourish to a neat row of ice-filled martini glasses that were waiting to be made into someone's fantasy drink. Two girls at the end of the bar, dressed in cheap business wear and well into happy hour, gave Jimmy demure golf claps.

"Alright," Cyndi said. "One Monopolowa, three olives."

"Dirty?" Jimmy asked.

"Very," she said.

He spun the shaker on his palm and began working his magic.

"So tell me, Dillon." Cyndi swiveled to face me, and the boot of her crossed leg bumped against my calf. It rested there like a flirtatious volley on a first date. "How did you know Tommy and Isato's presentation was crashing?"

"Who wants to know?" I asked.

She flashed her smile again, and its usual girlish seductiveness was on full display. "Just an eager newcomer. My father says you're one of the best presenters he's ever seen. I want to learn how you do it."

"It's nothing special," I lied. "I just have a knack for reading body language. That's all."

Jimmy set our drinks down, and then sidestepped around one of the barbacks to the two girls who had golf clapped.

"You're being modest." Cyndi took a sip and savored.

This girl was working it. I took a drink and waved her compliment away. "No I'm not. It's easy to do."

"Show me."

"Pick someone out."

Cyndi scanned the bar like a cat searching for prey. "Him," she said, discreetly pointing to a dark-haired club type perched at a highboy against the far wall. His date, dressed not too unlike Cyndi, seemed utterly bored.

I shook my head. "Too far away."

Line of sight was important, but with this many heads it's hard to listen in when someone is over 40 feet away. There was just too much interference to get a good focus on an individual brain.

Cyndi scanned again, and her attention settled on a distinctly out-of-place yuppie couple at another highboy. They were about half the distance as the other couple and seemed oblivious to anything except each other.

"What about her?" she asked.

"Sure, I can see her better."

I scooted my barstool closer to Cyndi's. She had turned to observe the couple and I leaned in behind her ear. The perfume she was wearing smelled expensive and floral, and was in severe conflict with her urban clubwear.

"Okay," I said. "Watch her body language, and try to read her thoughts."

Cyndi twisted and looked at me like I was crazy.

"Not literally." I gestured to the couple. "Come on, give it a try. Just watch for the clues."

I put my arm on the bar and Cyndi relaxed against it.

"See how they're both leaning into each other?" I asked.

I focused my mind on the pretty blonde's mouth. I don't know why I do this, but it works for me. There's something about the mouth, the sensual way it moves, that acts as a connection point to a person's mind. I channeled all my concentration, and the ruckus of Piss Off ebbed away like a wave on a beach.

"Yes," Cyndi said. "But people do that when they're really into each other."

We watched for another moment, and I realized Cyndi had nestled her shoulder into the crook of my arm. It was a little awkward, because after all she was probably at least 10 years younger.

What the hell, I thought and scooted closer.

The pretty blonde was thinking about their future – a ridiculously big home in Southlake, with kids and soccer practice and all the trappings – probably what they were discussing at the moment. He was doing most of the talking, which was good because when someone is talking they're usually just thinking the same thing. But the girl's thoughts abruptly shifted from her suburban fantasy to the last time they had had sex, and her right toes, which were fully exposed by a simple strap sandal, began gently rubbing the guy's calf.

Cyndi turned her head slightly. "She's thinking about–"

I shooshed her, and she stiffened.

"Sorry," I said.

She relaxed back against my arm.

The girl thought that the last time they had had sex he hadn't been satisfied with her performance, and she told herself that tonight she was going try a technique she had read in *Cosmo* and rub at the base of his scrotum while she went down on him. She even considered fingering his–

"She's thinking about marrying him," Cyndi declared.

A laugh coughed out of me. Cyndi twisted again, and I gripped her shoulder.

"I'm wrong?" The look of failure on her face was kind of cute.

I pointed. "She has a ring on."

Cyndi jerked back, and her shoulders slumped with resignation. "Now how did I miss that?"

I gently pulled her close and whispered, "She wants to have his children, and raise them in a big house in Southlake."

"How do you know that?" Cyndi asked quietly out of the corner of her mouth.

"Her toes are getting awfully frisky with his calf, and she's rubbing the edge of her glass with the tip of her finger. Besides, see the way she's looking at him. Love or lust?"

Cyndi cocked her head. "Love, I think."

"She's still rubbing her glass."

"Oh, lust—"

Suddenly, as if she could read our minds, the pretty blonde looked over. Cyndi and I quickly spun back to our drinks.

"Oh shit, I think we were caught," she said, stifling a laugh into her martini.

"Who cares?" I took a large pull from my Scotch.

For a long moment we sipped our drinks in silence, letting the energy of Piss Off swirl around us like lost phantoms from a secret subculture.

"So it's all body language, eh?" Cyndi asked with a raised eyebrow.

"That and twenty years of selling people on concepts they wouldn't usually buy into."

"Tell me about that," she said.

I shrugged.

"There's that modesty I've come to admire," she said, mockingly.

"Branding," I said, "is a tricky business. People come to you to develop a certain kind of experience. A certain kind of cool."

"Would you call yourself a cool hunter?"

"That's kind of a dated term, but in a sense, yes, among other things. My specialty is identities."

"Logos?"

"An identity is more than a logo. It's the essence of a brand. It's an icon or look that distills the concept down to its simplest form. It can be an attitude or a feeling a consumer gets when they think about a product or service. It's a combination of many factors, all cooked down into a succinct message. Identities are the heart and soul of a product. And when you create a great one, it's magical."

It was refreshing to talk at such a base level. Concepts that were ingrained into me like instincts were fresh and new to Cyndi. She was hanging on my every word, and we were now leaning into each other, just like the cute couple we had been analyzing.

We both seemed to realize our posture and retreated to what was left of our drinks.

"Well." I glanced at my wristwatch. 7:12 p.m. "I better get going."

Cyndi straightened, alarm pouring into her face. "Really? I thought we could go get some dinner. I want to learn more about how you run your business."

"I'd love to, but—"

Her expression melted into frustration, then she started laying the bedroom eye thing down like I had seen her do with the interns and Tommy.

Cyndi slid off the barstool and stepped close. "Come on," she said. "I'll treat."

I'm sure she would. There was a time when I would have taken Cyndi up on her not-so-subtle offer. Treated her to a great dinner at Terilli's or Abacus, then up to my condo. And if I was lucky, breakfast on my balcony.

"Cyndi," I said, "there are some folks waiting for me at home. Maybe another time?"

"Can I come?"

I smiled. "No. These are old friends, and you'd be bored."

Cyndi pulled a face as I hopped off my barstool.

"Leaving so soon?" Jimmy asked, wiping the rim of a fine-stemmed wine glass.

"Got to go," I said.

I laid two fifties onto the counter.

Jimmy whistled. "Dillon, come on," he said. "You only had two drinks."

"Get theirs." I pointed to the yuppie couple we had studied. They were still engrossed in each other.

Jimmy nodded with a knowing grin.

"Come on," Cyndi urged. "Inquiring minds want to know."

Jimmy folded his arms and rested them on the bar. He motioned us close.

"They're architects. Work in the same firm," he said in a low tone, like anyone could actually hear him over the din of the bar. "They're married, but not to each other. For the last two years they meet here every other Friday and paw all over each other. Then they leave, hand in hand, and go do whatever they do. I've got a buddy who works the bar at the Palomar Hotel. He says that's where they end up." He raised his hands and mocked quotation marks. "Working late."

The Mercedes CLS was an incredible car. Its unique body styling was equaled only by its interior perfection. Subtle, gauged European leather merged with hand-polished cherry wood in what could only be described as a cocoon. Did I love this car a little too much? Maybe. But next to meeting with the group, it was the best thing for keeping the voices out. Distance was a factor, but if a person was, say, standing on a corner and I wasn't going too fast, I could pick up what they were thinking. Usually these detached fragments weren't anything, but sometimes they would startle me, like being tapped on the shoulder when you were lost in thought.

I was now piloting the Merc through what was arguably the prettiest part of Dallas: Turtle Creek, once the address of choice, now home to expat Californians. Indecently tan and toting rat-like furry dogs, these creatures of the Left Coast had bought up the best views in many of the luxury high-rises.

The boulevard I was navigating shared the same name as the area. I lived on the top floor of The Terrace, one of the tonier addresses. Across the hall lived a couple from Long Beach, who actually commuted back and forth each week. Dallas, they were often pressed to admit, was the way L.A. used to be before the gangs—

Fucking rich bastard.

A gruff voice cut through Miles Davis's *Summertime* and carved deep into my skull. Its echo resonated with all the truth of a migraine.

"*Jesus.*" I squeezed the wheel and tried to will the voice out of my head. The Merc warned me that I was too close to the curb. I jerked the wheel and noticed the light had changed to red. "Shit!" The braking system lived up to its claim. I skidded to a stop with only the tip of the Merc's grillwork protruding into cross traffic. A white F-150 moved slowly through the intersection. The driver's girlfriend flipped me off as it passed, which is when I spied a pair of bright chrome bull nuts hanging from the hitch. The guy's thoughts were as crude as his vehicle, but not nearly as ugly as his girl.

My cell rang. It was Kadin.

"You on your way? Everyone's here."

It required a second to excavate a response. My mind was still recovering. "Yeah," I managed.

"You don't sound too enthusiastic."

"I'm okay. I just had a weird feedback." Feedback was our group's slang for a stray voice that cut through the clutter. Usually they were banal thoughts you could shrug off, but what I just experienced was different. I had to find the source. The light turned green, and I swung the Merc around and headed for the spot where I'd been punched. Silence. Had I lost Kadin?

"I had one last week," she said finally. "A little girl in a stroller. Very profound."

"You'll have to tell me what she said when I get there."

"Are you looking for who did it?"

"Yes."

"Don't be too long. Marcus is going Tea Party on me again."

Turtle Creek was an actual creek. Both it and its namesake boulevard bounded a beautiful park named after General Robert E. Lee. There was a huge statue of the man on horseback with a soldier at his side, as well as an exact duplicate of Lee's home in Arlington Cemetery, only smaller. I spotted a dark figure among the burr oaks and Arizona cypresses. I slowed to a stop and put on the emergency flashers.

What do you want? It was the same voice. The pain was excruciating, and bit into my nervous system with the ferocity of a pit bull. I lowered the front passenger side window.

"Hey, you!" I yelled, leaning over the center console.

The figure walked into what little glow emanated from the corner's mercury vapor. He looked homeless, probably in his fifties. The play between light and shadow bisected his tall frame. He pointed, jabbing his finger at the Merc.

"Yeah, you," I repeated.

The man stepped forward, and the shadows fell away. In the gloom he looked like a thin, mangier Kris Kristofferson. He had on a dark blue jacket, a white button-down shirt, fairly clean jeans and a pair of Nike running shoes, retro style with the bright yellow swoosh.

What do you want, dipshit? His "voice" sounded like it had crawled from under one of the bridges spanning the creek. This time, it didn't cut so deeply, and the pain was about half as intense.

"Look, I know what you're thinking," I said, not caring. "Just talk—"

I know what you're thinking, too, asshole.

Impossible. The digital clock in the Merc's dash segued to 8 p.m. I didn't have time for this. "Really? Then what am I thinking right now?" *If I had a gun,* I thought, *I'd put you out of your misery.*

The man exposed a heavily bleached smile and pointed again, but this time his first and second fingers mimicked a gun barrel. He cocked his thumb, then jabbed the air like he'd shot me. *Back at ya, motherfucker.*

3. Simple demographics.

"God, Dillon, you look like you've seen a ghost."

I didn't know what I'd seen. The bum's Dirty Harry impression was unnerving. After he'd faux shot me, he blew the smoke from his fingers and stuck them into an imaginary holster somewhere under his jacket. If he had the gift, how did he know what I was thinking? It had to have been just a lucky guess.

"I need a drink." I brushed a kiss across Kadin's cheek.

She and I had been dancing around what we had termed a "speculative" relationship, although lately it felt like I was falling for her. We discovered one another on a return flight from Europe two months ago. I say "discovered" because that's what it feels like. If my guesstimate was correct, there weren't many of us on the planet, so discovering someone was always weird because, after all, you were meeting a human who had moved up a peg on the evolutionary ladder.

When I met Kadin Bolek, we both had aisle seats. She was two rows up in the inside seating section; I was near the bulkhead. Most of the passengers were sleeping, and our lights were the only ones on. When people sleep, their dreams come at half volume, and sometimes they can be entertaining. Kadin and I had both burst out laughing simultaneously. Neither of us was watching a movie, and after the third time it happened, she turned and stared right at me. We had been listening to the same dream. Usually, when you look at someone, their thought volume jumps. I don't know why. Marcus – one of our group's oldest members – is a neurosurgeon, and he thinks we have the ability to intercept the neurotransmitters that leap between neurons. So when Kadin – who, by the way, is a gorgeous Polish beauty with light green eyes, dark curly hair, and a big endearing smile that exposes just enough gum to make her completely approachable – planted her best "who the hell are you" stare, my brain went quiet. It startled me. She picked up on it, too, and smiled that smile of hers, like the one spreading across her face right now.

"Dillon, honey?"

"Yeah?"

"Where'd you go?"

"It's been a busy day. Sorry."

"Come and entertain our guests."

Even though she had been in the U.S. for half her life, Kadin still had an accent, and it got to me every time. She took my hand and led me into my living room. I had given her a key two weeks ago because she lived in Frisco, a distant suburb closer to Oklahoma than downtown.

"Ah, there you are," Toby said, standing. "The hardest working man in advertising."

Tobias King was the first guy I'd met who had the gift. At the time, 14 years ago, he had just retired from the pro tennis circuit. Because he knew what serve his opponents planned, he had one of the best returns in the business. We had speculated that Agassi might have had the gift, but neither of us had ever gotten close enough to confirm.

"No," I said, loosening my tie, "just the most beat up." Kadin handed me a Scotch and sauntered into the kitchen.

"We have a mixer tomorrow at noon. You should come out. Lots of good hitters."

"I just might."

"Dillon!" Dr. Marcus Fitch was our group's elder statesman. Near retirement, he liked to bestow his worldly advice on all his "neuros," as he called us.

"Lose anyone today?" I joked.

"Not yet." Marcus was clearly deep into happy hour. "Kadin said you had some bad feedback today?" He was laying his fatherly voice on me.

I looked into the kitchen and glimpsed Kadin before she disappeared behind the open door of the Sub-Zero. "Yeah, I guess. I don't know."

Marcus scrutinized me through his shaggy eyebrows. "Well, either you had one or not."

"I had one, but it wasn't bad," I lied. "Just some homeless guy bitching at the world."

Marcus nodded as if the answer met with his approval. Our happy hours used to be relaxing, but of late I had begun to find them tedious. Maybe I was getting too comfortable with our group's silence. Or maybe I had become addicted to the world's white noise.

"Doc, I've always wanted to ask you something."

"What's that?"

"When you're operating on someone – inside their head – do you ever, you know ... indulge?"

Marcus's scrutiny tightened. "It wouldn't be ethical."

"Oh, come on." The Scotch was beginning to take the edge off. I took another sip. "You've never once listened in on their thoughts?"

The furrow between his eyebrows relaxed. "Most of the time a patient is unconscious, so there's nothing to hear."

"Yeah, but I thought a person had to be awake during brain surgery."

Marcus hesitated. "Sometimes, yes."

"And you never snuck a listen?"

Marcus took a slow pull off his beer.

"Ah ha," I said. "Just as I thought."

Marcus stepped closer, his expression burdened with a pain I'd never seen before. "When I was in 'Nam," he said, his voice low, "I helped many young men die." He looked across the living room to the row of windows that faced the skyline. His attention lingered, drawn by memory, still hunkered down in some God-forsaken jungle helping a poor teenager through the last seconds of his life. "I listened in once," he said, still staring.

"And?"

He turned back and shook his head. "Dillon." His hand went to my shoulder. "There are some things we're not meant to hear. That's why I never indulge."

I felt a pat on my back, and Christopher Banks stepped to my side. On his arm was a gorgeous Asian woman. A spike of anger cut through me. Bringing someone new into the group without consulting the members was way out of line. But Chris had issues with rules.

"What's Doc doing, bitching about the President again?" Chris was a litigation lawyer and fairly new to the group. Toby had brought him in. He worked for one of those downtown, multi-named firms. You could see his building from my balcony, and he often pointed that out after I had told him our building was in Deep Ellum.

"No," Marcus said, opening a polite distance between us. "We were just talking about the Mavericks' chances."

"Waste of breath." Chris turned to me. "Dillon, I want you to meet someone."

It crossed my mind to say something intelligently rude about smuggling in someone who hadn't been vetted, but the woman thrust out her hand in a way inconsistent with her delicate poise. I looked into her eyes.

Silence. Good.

"Dillon Bradford," she announced, as if she were someone I should know. Her voice was throaty, pure Lauren Bacall. Both she and Chris looked like they'd stepped straight off a Ralph Lauren set. Her dress hugged the curves of her body with an elegance found only in women comfortable with their sexuality. Without doubt, this Asian beauty had it going on: the exotic-skin belt perfectly balanced on hips probably shaped by a personal trainer, hair cut in a short bob that accentuated her slim jaw line, and sublime makeup that staged a pair of eyes that concealed anything she might be thinking. "Chris has told me a lot about you."

I hoped the look I shot Chris didn't reveal the depth of my irritation. "Nice to meet you," I said, taking her hand. "Ms...?"

"Debra Lao." She returned her hand to Chris's arm.

"I knew you wouldn't mind if I brought Debra," Chris said with an edge of arrogance.

"Sure, why not?" I was pissed. "It's always good to discover one of our kind, right?"

"I met Debra, of all places, at Dr. Mary's."

Dr. Mary Collings was chiropractor to the stars. Her walls were adorned with framed accolades from singers like Lyle Lovett and several Dallas Mavericks. And she was a genius at relieving pain. I had turned Chris onto her.

"As soon as I saw Christopher, I knew," Debra said.

"Knew what?" Marcus had opened the distance and was now leaning against the back of my Smink couch. Toby had joined him.

"I'm sorry, dear. This is Dr. Marcus Fitch. He's a neurosurgeon." Chris gestured. "And this is Tobias King."

"You were on the tour," Debra noted.

Toby brightened out of his gin and tonic haze. "Yes, I was."

"I love tennis."

"Do you play?"

"When I get the chance."

"Then you should come out to my academy. I'll give you a lesson."

"Tobias is now coaching kids to be future Federers," Chris said.

"So, what did you realize when you met Chris?" Marcus pressed.

Debra looked at him like he'd asked the dumbest question ever. "That I wasn't the only one."

"No worries there," I said and took a rather large drink off my Scotch.

Chris jumped in. "Dillon believes there are about one of us in every 400,000."

I swirled what was left of my drink around the walls of my glass. "Simple demographics. Plus or minus 10 percent."

"That's mostly cities," Marcus added. "Who knows what the numbers are in rural areas?"

"So tell me, what do you do when you're not getting adjusted or watching tennis?"

Debra Lao burned her almost pupil-less dark eyes onto me like an acetylene torch. "I'm in pharmaceuticals."

"Really? My firm does all the marketing for Ewing Labs."

"I know," she said. "I work there."

4. The Borg wears Prada.

"I thought you took that well tonight." Kadin rucked a leg over my hips and nestled her head against my chest. We were cocooned in my bed's 1000-thread count, and the faint smell of alcohol mixed beautifully with her sweat.

"I wanted to kill Chris for bringing Debra unannounced," I said, stroking her hair. "Where does he get off?"

"Don't let him get to you." Kadin yawned and snuggled closer. "So, am I staying tonight?"

"What do you think?" I kissed the top of her head.

After a few moments of holding each other, her breathing changed to soft snoring, and I gently untangled myself from her naked body. I had downed four Dalmores on virtually an empty stomach over the course of the evening.

The bum's words kept playing in my mind, but at the moment I was focused on trying to abate the bedroom's spinning. I had been drunker on many occasions. This was more of an annoyance. I edged my left foot onto the floor, which helped, but only a little. God, I hated going to sleep when my brain was still partying. The faint sound of my iPhone's marimba ring made me flinch. It was late. It might be someone from Isato's creative team. *Fuck.*

Padding to the kitchen, where my cell was charging, felt a little like the time I had gone on a cruise. The ship's movement was almost imperceptible until I focused on it. Then, every step became a battle to keep from puking. The incoming number said BLOCKED. Probably one of Tommy's or Isato's interns, given the task of waking me to find out if I could push back the nine o'clock meeting on Monday. Or worse, ask me to come down to the shop and pull them out of their creative dive.

"This is Dillon Bradford."

"Hello, Dillon. This is Debra Lao. Did I wake you?"

My cell said it was 10:34 p.m., but it felt later. Did I give her my number? "Not at all. Did you leave something here?"

"No." She hesitated. "I was just wondering if you wanted to meet for a drink."

Are you shitting me? "Right now?"

"Yes, unless you're already headed to bed."

It took a fuzzy second to process her request. We hadn't talked much during the party because I couldn't stomach another minute with Chris.

"To be honest, Debra—"

"I'd like to talk some business. Chris isn't with me."

Doing business late on a Friday night wasn't that out of the norm, but usually it started with drinks and dinner, and finished with more drinks. If I could squeeze additional bucks out of Ewing Labs and make our second quarter, then I'd meet with this Debra Lao anytime she wants. Beside, I wasn't even close to being sleepy. Maybe we could meet somewhere I could get something to eat. Earlier, before Marcus and Chris had sucked me into one of their political-debate vortexes, she and I had briefly chatted about developing an addition to their website that could support Ewing's white papers.

"Okay then," I said. "But I have to eat something before I drink anymore."

Her laugh was cultivated, like it had its own pedigree. "How about Stage Left? They serve appetizers all night."

"Give me fifteen minutes."

"Good. I'll meet you there."

I pocketed my cell, crept back to the bedroom, and knelt next to Kadin. She was balled up in the sheets, drool on her pillow.

"Baby?" I brushed a strand of hair off her forehead.

"Yeah?" she said, barely surfacing. Her eyes opened slightly. "Everything okay?"

"I have to go down to the office to review some concepts. We have a huge meeting Monday morning. The team is working late, and they want some guidance." Kadin was used to my middle-of-the-night work hours. I didn't like lying to her, but sometimes it was just easier to be like the rest of the world.

She moaned and tucked her pillow closer to her head. "Don't stay too long."

"I'll be back in a couple of hours. I'll make you breakfast."

"Promise?"

I kissed her forehead. "Promise."

Dallas didn't have a true theater district, but if it did Stage Left would be the place you'd go after a show. At least, it was trying its best to embody that Broadway spirit. Almost everything here came from somewhere else, just like its inhabitants. But instead of being tucked around the corner from some veteran theater, Stage Left was sandwiched between a Tommy Bahamas and an Italian gelato shop in West Village. Not that I was complaining. It was five minutes from my condo, and driving was already a bit of a challenge.

Debra Lao waved girlishly from a semi-circular corner booth. Her juxta-position of high style and adolescent enthusiasm was intriguing. A low glass coffee table separated her from the rest of the bar crowd. On it were various Mediterranean appetizers, and she was well into a tall, frosted, three-olive mar-tini. A Scotch stood sentinel, waiting for me. She stood as I approached, and I realized she was sporting attire like she had come from a rave. Five-inch pumps elevated her to my face, and she wore a black slitted dress that bared dark shoul-ders and firm cleavage upheld by either a custom bra or expert surgery.

"Hi, Dillon." She stuck out her hand in a crisp, corporate manner.

"Hello again."

Debra's grip was firm like before. My dizzy buzz was wearing off, and I was beginning to regret agreeing to come out. I sat at a politically correct distance, which was hard to do in this curved booth. She scooted over until our thighs pressed together.

"Sorry." I inched away and eyed the hummus.

"You said you were hungry, so I took the liberty of ordering."

"This is perfect." I scooped up a generous mound of hummus with a wedge of pita. "Where'd Chris go?" I asked, chewing.

"He was too wired from that conversation with your friends and needed to go meet up with some of his buddies. He can be so darn opinionated."

"Chris is pretty self-winding." I took a sip from my drink. "Tastes like Dalmore. Thanks."

"I thought that's what you drank."

Debra moved closer. The sides of our thighs were touching again. Her hy-per-short dress made it a little awkward, but it cleared my addled brain a bit.

"Bandage dress?" I took another drink, this time savoring the single malt.

"Excuse me?" she asked.

"That's a Hervé Léger. He created the look."

"You know your labels."

"It's my job to."

"You know, Dillon, there's more to life than cool hunting."

"But Ms. Lao ... cool is life."

Debra, ignoring my sarcasm, leaned over to get a pita chip. The top of a tattoo made an appearance above the low-cut dress, and I averted my eyes to the tray of dolmas. I grabbed one and started eating.

"I did it on a dare," she said, focused on spreading some kind of chutney onto the chip.

"What?!" A tiny bit of lamb flew across the table.

Debra grinned and bit into her chip.

"Excuse me." I wiped my mouth with a cocktail napkin. "I thought you couldn't listen in."

"I saw you look. It's okay. I'm proud of it." She turned and seductively pulled the left edge of her neckline away from her shoulder. A masterfully rendered dragon tattoo, about the size of an Oreo, was poised to strike her nipple, which, thank God, remained hidden under the delicate pattern of her dress's fabric. The dragon's tongue wrapped its body, and its eyes were crossed like an iconographic Asian screen print.

"It's beautiful." I let my eyes linger.

She adjusted her dress back onto her shoulder and picked up her drink. "I had it done in Hong Kong. All the best artists are there. The dragon is the embodiment of yang. The male side." She took a long sip.

I was speechless after her theatrical vignette. "So, Debra," I stammered, "we never got to talk much about Ewing Labs. How long have you worked there? What do you do?"

She started to answer, but a little of her martini dripped from her lip as she pulled the glass away. Debra wiped her chin with her finger in a fashion that couldn't have been sexier.

"I've been there for three years," she said. "I'm in research."

"Really? Which division?"

"Neuroscience."

"Which campus is that? We've photographed in every building."

"Not in this one."

My radar went up. There wasn't a department we hadn't documented either in video or still. Which one was she talking about?

"We do research mostly for the government," she continued. "Secret-squirrel stuff. Our labs are out past Canton. We share space with TR Com. They're a big defense contractor."

"Never heard of a department based out there."

"You wouldn't. Red likes to keep us secret."

"Until now."

"Well, you'd learn about us eventually, so I don't think there's any harm in telling you." She turned and drilled her attention into me. "Besides," she said, "it's not like I'm going to give you the access codes to the lab, right?"

I took another sip from my Scotch. "You said you wanted to talk business. How can CoolBrain help your department?"

As Debra went on about a series of white papers she wanted to have launched on Ewing's website, I found myself wondering how I would lick the dragon if given half the chance. I usually wasn't the kind of guy to play around if I considered myself taken, especially with a client. And if I was falling in love with Kadin, I had to cool my playboy ways. But I was a sucker for powerful women, and right now, Debra Lao was leveraging a good deal of hers in my direction.

"So, what do you think?" she asked.

I snapped back into pro-mode. "I think CoolBrain could do a great job for you. We already know the brand. Hell, we created it. We know your mission and your message, and we have all the assets to create the weblink. We could do it with our heads tied behind our backs."

Debra leaned in and pressed all of herself against me. "You're cute when you're selling."

"Um, thanks." I tried to inch away, but the edge of the wall stopped me. I had girls come on to me before, plenty of times, but there was intensity about Debra that was both intoxicating and a little scary. Her hand dropped to my thigh.

"Are you and Kadin an item?"

"Kind of. Yes."

One of Debra's beautiful eyebrows rose slightly. "Doesn't sound like it to me."

"Well, I've only known her for a couple of months." *What the hell was I doing?*

Debra inched closer and edged her exquisite cleavage against my arm. "Dillon? Can you guess what kind of client I'm going to be?"

Fuck it. I leaned into her advance. "One that will need lots of personal attention?"

Debra's full lips brushed my cheek. "Daily," she purred, then pressed her lips against mine.

We kissed for what seemed a minute. Her eyes were closed, but mine were wide open and searching the bar behind her for I don't know what. She pulled back and took me in. It was then I realized that her hand had found its way to my crotch, and the tip of her finger was gently playing with the head of my manhood through my pants. I hadn't wanted to wake Kadin searching for a fresh pair of underwear and had left the condo going commando. I was quickly getting aroused.

"H-hey, there." Debra's finger had flicked just the right way, and I stumbled through the words. "I thought you wanted to talk business." She flicked again and I sucked in a breath.

"I do." Her eyes narrowed to tight slits.

I glanced around the bar. No one was bothering to catch our little show. Our eyes met again. She leaned in, but I gently pushed her back. "Hold on, Debra. You're beautiful and all but–"

You want to lick my dragon, don't you?

Her voice resonated so clearly, I thought our minds had merged. I gripped her shoulders. "How can you do that?"

Debra lowered her chin and grinned. *I can hear your thoughts.* Her eyes went to my crotch. *But I don't need the gift to know what you're thinking.*

This was impossible! I moved her hand off my pants.

I've only been able to link with one other person my entire life. Debra's fingers began tracing the line of my jaw. *Until now.*

I couldn't believe what I was hearing, and was on the verge of being completely sucked in. "How can you ... I mean, how can *we* hear each other's thoughts?" I felt myself being drawn into her erotic energy.

Her lips touched mine again. After a moment of kissing, she pulled back and blinked. *Come back to my apartment, and I'll show you.*

I thought about Kadin. Breakfast. Our Saturday together. But I was fascinated that Debra and I could hear each other's thoughts. I had to know.

You'll be back in time to make Kadin breakfast. She giggled. *Or at least pick it up on the way.*

What the hell kind of X-Files *porno had I fallen into?* I thought.

Debra's hand squeezed my inner thigh again. *One that you'll never forget.*

■   ■   ■

I had tried not to think about Kadin or what a shit I was, for fear of Debra picking up on it. It wasn't my usual MO to gallivant around with women I barely knew. But I was drawn to Debra Lao, and not because she was sexy. The idea that I could hear what was in both our minds was just too enticing.

On the walk from West Village to her apartment, we talked – in our minds

– about lots of things. It must have looked pretty weird, two people laughing without any conversation. Debra had been born in Cambodia, and her parents were brainiacs who taught graduate-level math at the local university. She became aware of her gift around the age of 14, but only discovered her ability to listen in to others with the gift much later. She had met a guy in college who was also like her, and they'd shared some kind of linking ability. Love at first thought, she called it. But he was killed in a motorcycle accident a year later, and she had never found anyone else she could link with, until she met me. I told her about my firm, and when I explained how Ewing Labs had become a client, her laugh played through my mind like Patron Silver. I also told her about being adopted, and how I had left after my adoptive dad had beaten the shit out me for being different.

Once inside her apartment, she immediately started tearing off my clothes. Debra had gotten me down to my pants and was doing a damn good job of teasing my hard-on. I had her down to her thong and bra and was licking the Hong Kong dragon. As I reached around to undo her bra, I noticed another dragon emblazoned across her lower back. It was larger and more sinuous than the Hong Kong one. I wanted to press up against it – and inside her. I started working her bra's hooks in earnest.

Debra grabbed my shoulders and shoved me onto her bed. *There's nothing more intimate than knowing what another person is thinking.* She straddled me and started slowly grinding on my crotch. *Combine that with intense sex and ...* She sat up and gestured, arms apart, palms up ... *Voilà!* Her bra was barely clinging to her beautiful breasts.

I had never experienced anything like this. It was as if our minds had become one. I could almost sense her every desire, and I knew she could feel the same with me.

She put both hands on my chest and leaned down. *I'm going to slip on something a little more sexy.*

You look great the way you are. I reached up for her bra, but she playfully swatted my hands away.

When I come back. She leaned in until the tips of our noses touched. *I want you to fuck me.* As she crawled off, she dragged her fingertips across my manhood.

Candlelight, especially during great sex, has a way of making any woman's butt look incredible. Debra Lao didn't need any help. Her ass was astonishing. I eyed it, and the dragon above it, as it disappeared into the bathroom. I fell back and watched the candlelight and shadows dance between the faux wood beams that latticed her bedroom's high ceiling. If there was a heaven for sex, I had arrived at its pearly gates.

"Is he the one?"

For a second, the man's voice didn't register because I hadn't heard a real voice in what seemed like hours. My first thought was that her clock radio alarm had gone off accidentally. The word one came across more like *vun*.

"Yes." Debra, now ensconced in a thick white robe, stood at her bathroom door passing a large brush through her dark hair.

I jerked up onto my elbows and saw two men, both wearing what looked like trim black Prada suits, just inside the threshold of Debra Lao's bedroom. Their eyes were locked onto me.

Jesus! I swung my attention between Debra and the Prada boys. "What the hell is going on?"

Debra continued to brush her hair, as if this were her normal bedtime routine. "What're his readings?" She addressed the men like assistants.

The one on the left checked what looked like a BlackBerry. Its glow highlighted well-groomed stubble trying in vain to hide old acne scars. "They're off the charts." His accent was more pronounced. Russian, if I had to guess. "Above twenty across the spectrum."

Debra acknowledged this with a slight nod. The sensuous woman I had been making out with a minute ago had morphed into an aloof uber-bitch.

The man on the left pocketed the BlackBerry, while the man on the right removed a small black case and some kind of metallic syringe-gun from his coat.

I felt more than exposed, lying on a strange woman's bed, half-naked and fully freaked. It felt like my dick had retreated into my abdomen.

All three began to approach the bed.

"Dillon, dear." Debra's smile looked manufactured.

My eyes searched hers as she walked toward me. All I could hear was static. Instinctively, I scrambled back but banged into the bed's leather headboard, which is when I realized the utter futility of my action. These men were big, thuggish, and grew even bigger as they approached. There was nowhere to run. I looked at Debra. "What the hell are you going to do?!" I might have screamed the words.

"These men are going to sedate you." Debra's tone was even, detached. "It will hurt a little."

One of them reached for my foot, and I kicked his hand away. That was not the right response. He grabbed my ankle and yanked me to the edge of the bed as if I were a sack of laundry.

"Don't fight, Dillon." Debra folded her arms across her chest. "It will only make the experience worse."

In the shadowy candlelight, the two men appeared to have merged into a four-armed, high-fashion Borg creature. Two of the hands pressed down on my knees, while another pinned my right arm to the bed. I'm not a small guy, but these two held me down like a 12-year-old girl. Debra put a hand to my left shoulder and pressed hard. The candlelight was now casting erratic shadows all over the bedroom. The effect pushed me to a new level of panic.

"Dillon, stop fighting. Dillon!" Debra took my jaw and yanked my head around. "If you keep fighting, it will only take the drug longer to enter your system. Now listen to me very carefully." Her French-tipped nails dug in. "You need to relax. We only want to make a small incision in your neck. It's like an IV."

What?! I tried again to squirm free, but that only resulted in excruciating pressure to my knees and arms. "Look, if you want a kidney, we can work this out—"

"I don't want one of your damn kidneys." Debra was past frustrated. "First you're going to feel a little prick. Then numbness will take over your body. Don't worry, it's nothing permanent."

She nodded to the guy holding my left arm, and I felt a sting in the meat of my shoulder. Almost instantly the frenetic shadows and light slowed.

She bent down until I could smell the faint scent of her arousal. "You'll wake up in a couple of hours, in your car, in your condo's parking garage. You'll think you've passed out from being too drunk. Kadin will ask how it went at the office, and you'll tell her you never made it down there. You'll have no memory of us meeting at Stage Left, or coming to my apartment, or of what we're about to do."

Debra relaxed her grip as the room went soft.

"Why me?" I barely croaked before my tongue went numb.

The all-business tightness drawn across Debra's face relaxed slightly. "I can't tell you."

The Prada Borg let go, and it felt like my body was merging with the bed's memory foam. I could barely sense my arms or legs. I tried to ask why again, but what came out sounded more like a baby gurgling.

Just before I succumbed to the fog, I heard Debra's voice at the margin of my conscious mind.

Forgive me, she said.

5. You don't look so good.

Something banged my head and jerked me out of a perfect dream. I was on a catamaran, the kind that you'd find floating in the Caribbean. I had a crew, fine exotic food, and an indecently hot girl in a white bikini who clung with one hand to one of the lines that rained down from the mast. The spray from the boat beaded on her tan skin. I couldn't make out her face. Something banged my head again. Carter, one of my condo's weekend guards, was rapping his hairy knuckles against the Merc's driver side window.

"Mr. Bradford?"

His voice was muffled.

I struggled with the button that lowered the window, my fingers fumbling across the armrest. The window moved, pulling the side of my face with it. I twitched back.

"Yes, Carter?"

The words came out more guttural than intelligible. I cleared my throat and tried again. "Is there something wrong?" Wrong? What the hell was I doing in the parking garage of my condo? I straightened and glanced at the dashboard clock.

6:03 a.m.

"Are you all right?" Carter, his fat face filling most of the window, rubbed at his salt and pepper moustache with the back of an equally hairy hand. "I've been watching."

I forced a smile. "I just got over-served last night. I was headed to my office, but I guess I never made it." The memory seemed distant. Still in my seatbelt, I unbuckled myself.

"Damn good thing, too." Carter straightened and backed away a few steps. He grabbed his belt and dug his thumbs into the space between his radio and gun. "You okay to walk?"

I opened the door and stepped out. I was a little wonky, but could manage. The Merc chirped as I locked it. "Yeah," I said, stretching. "I think I'm good to go."

Carter gave me the once-over, then put three fingers to his cap's brim. "You have a good day, Mr. Bradford."

"You too, Carter. I'll try not to make this a habit."

I found Kadin basically in the same position I'd left her, except she'd kicked off most of the sheets. In the dim light, she looked like an exquisite Ron Mueck sculpture mounted to a base of satin cloth. I thought about crawling back into bed, but frankly a shower sounded better.

I had designed the bathroom back in my wilder days, when I thought I would need a shower big enough to host a small party. It had three heads, each capable of filling a swimming pool. I stood there for I don't know how long, letting the water gush over me, when I felt Kadin's arms around my chest.

"Did you get a lot of work done?" She kissed the back of my neck.

"I never made it to the office. I fell asleep in my car." I tilted my head back. She leaned into it.

"You're kidding. You didn't seem that drunk last night."

"I didn't think so, either. Guess I was really tired. Remind me to call the office. My guys are probably wondering what the hell happened." I turned and gathered Kadin into my arms.

"Thank God you didn't drive." There was a puzzled look on Kadin's face, and her fingers began to explore something at the base of my neck. "What's this?"

"What?"

"Looks like you got bit here." Her thumb passed over a tender spot, and I winced.

"It's probably nothing."

"It looks sore." She began soaping it.

"These condos are old. Even though they've been renovated, there's no telling what's crawling around at night. Remind me to call the bug guy this weekend."

"He better bring traps. This is a big bite."

"Maybe I need garlic."

"Why?"

"Maybe we have vampires," I said, in my best Dracula voice. I leaned in and playfully nibbled her neck.

Kadin let out a soft moan and I changed my nibbles into light kisses. A distance runner in college, she still had the body of a disciplined athlete. With her wet hair slicked back, she looked like she could run the 100 in five seconds.

She tiltd her head, exposing the breadth of her neck, and as I kissed its glorious length, the rain of hot shower water washed the salt from her sweat into my mouth. She moved in sync with my motion until our mouths met in a dance of tongues and lips. My passion was turning into raw desire.

"Do you have to go in today?" Kadin raised a leg onto the bench that cantilevered from the tile wall.

"No," I said, and began to kiss her neck again.

She gently hooked her forefinger under my chin and guided me back to her face.

"Good," she said, now dragging her finger gently down my chest and headed south. "This weekend I want you all to myself."

■   ■   ■

Mondays were hard enough. Creative meetings. Status meetings. Meetings to decide when to have the next meeting. Sometimes I longed for the good old days, when I was a lowly designer and the only thing to worry about was my creative director's opinion. Over the weekend Tommy and Isato had kicked some major ass reworking the Eagle Energy identity, so I could backburner that crisis. Derek had made headway with a piece of new business that involved a mixed-use development in the Arts District, so maybe our third quarter wouldn't be the disaster our accountant predicted. And there was word in the media that a new club was going into Deep Ellum, which might signal a rebirth for the area (and our building's property value).

"Morning, Dillon."

I glanced up from my email. Cyndi was standing in my office's doorway. The cleavage meter was needling pretty low, and she was dressed conservatively in a pair of skinny jeans and a loose sweater. Without the stilettos and subculture makeup, she looked like she could have been 18.

"Hey there," I replied.

"Thanks for the drink Friday night."

"Yeah. That was fun, wasn't it?"

"We'll have to do that again, soon." She began leveling the bedroom eyes routine, although given the way she was dressed, the effect didn't work quite as well as it had at Piss Off.

"Are those Tommy's color chips for Eagle?" I asked, pointing to the manila folder she was holding.

Cyndi walked around my desk and placed the folder on my laptop. She took hold of the back of my chair and leaned over to review them with me. She was wearing the same perfume as before.

"Have you seen these yet?" I snuck a listen. She had seen them, along with the revised logos, strewn across Tommy's bed last night.

"No," she said.

Tommy had stayed corporate in his color selection for the new brand. PMS 5425 was a dusty dark blue that, coincidentally, was almost the same color as one of my favorite Armani suits. And PMS Cool Gray 10 could have been what the Navy painted its battleships. His secondary color palette was a little less conservative, straying into brighter colors and highlighted with a rich yellow any school bus would have loved.

"What do you think?" Cyndi asked.

"I think they're right on the money, especially this yellow. It's just the hit of color the brand needs. This brighter palette could be used to highlight different areas of the web site."

"That's exactly what I was thinking."

No it wasn't. Cyndi was still thinking of what she might do with me if given half the chance.

She cocked her head in my direction, and a lock of her hair fell across her face. I held her gaze for a long second.

"What are you doing tonight?" she asked, brushing it back into place. Her face was now inches from mine.

"Are you always this bold?"

A thin seductive smile spread across her face. "Only when I want something."

I let out an exasperated sigh, more from reflex than any conscious thought.

"Look, Cyndi I'm really flattered by your, um ... attention, but I never date an employee. Besides, I have someone in my life right now, and I don't want to jeopardize that." The words came out before I realized what I had said. Did Kadin really mean that much to me, or was I just using her to diffuse Cyndi's advance?

The flirtatious smile that had been playing at the corners of Cyndi's mouth faded.

"Can't blame a girl for trying," she said, solemnly.

For some dumb reason, I reached up and touched the side of her face. "Thanks."

The move clearly caught her off guard, but she didn't flinch.

"For what?" she asked.

"Making an old guy feel good about himself?"

Cyndi playfully rolled her eyes. "Please. You need help? With your ego?"

She had a point. "Yeah, well ... maybe you're right."

Cyndi moved in and gently kissed me. Her lips were softer than I had imagined, and I could taste the faint trace of nicotine on her breath.

"If you ever change your mind," she said, pulling away.

"Right," I said, and licked her saliva off my upper lip. "I know where to find you."

I pushed away from my computer, thinking the week was starting out to be a good one, and pulled my suit coat off the back of my chair. Cyndi's little show earlier this morning kept playing through my mind. I had had employees come on to me, but not with such intensity.

My cell phone vibrated on top of the desk. It was a text from Kadin.

Hey there. Thinking about u. :-)

Thinking about u 2, I texted back. **Wanna grab dinner?**

Can't. Working late. :-(

See you later this week?

If you play your cards right...

The sign-off emoji was a purple devil.

Kadin and I rarely saw each other during the week. She worked for a video game developer, coordinating their focus group testing and consumer research. No surprise, she was very good at it. Her company was headquartered in one of the northern suburbs, so she rarely ventured south during the week. I had been to her place exactly once. She lived in one of those trendy, master-planned communities that had sprung up all across Frisco. Her apartment was typical, with its lofted ceilings and neutral-colored granite countertops. The whole design exuded the sense that the developers were trying to cram as much faux luxury into 800 square feet as they could. Her rent matched my mortgage.

I slipped my cell phone into one of my coat's breast pockets and fished for my keys, but came away with a wadded up cocktail napkin. Its gold and black logo peeked out from the folds. Curious, I smoothed it out on my desk.

STAGE LEFT. THE CURTAIN IS UP ON DALLAS'S NEWEST STAR.

The logo – Tragedy and Comedy holding martini glasses – was as bad as the tag line. Please. I'd heard of the place, but how had one of its napkins ended up in my pocket? I inspected both sides, looking for a number or a website or some other clue. I tried to recall the different places I had been since I'd had that coat cleaned, but I couldn't think of anywhere I could have picked up this napkin. Weird.

The bite on my neck was sore, and I instinctively rubbed it. Kadin hadn't seemed too concerned about it and said not to worry. But I had an aunt discover the same kind of thing once, and she had died a month later from melanoma.

"Hey, Mr. Bradford, I've loaded Isato's creative onto the server," Jerry said from my office doorway. He was Isato's spring intern. Nice kid. A bit nerdy.

"Thanks. I'll check it out in the morning."

"Some of us are going to the Ginger Man after work. You want to go?"

I was all about bonding with my employees, but small talk with a bunch of 20-somethings was the last thing I wanted to do. "I'd like to, but I've got plans. Thanks, though."

"Cool." The kid started to leave.

"Hey, Jerry?"

He gripped the doorframe and pulled himself back. "Yes, sir?"

"Did one of you guys call me last Friday night, about 10:30?"

Jerry shook his head, and his mop of red hair flapped. "Not that I know of. Why?"

"I got a call that was blocked. I thought it might be someone from the team."

"Nah, we were too busy. Have you tried BackCall?"

"What's that?"

"It's an app that'll tell you the number of a blocked call. It's cheap. Like, five bucks. I got it when my old girlfriend was harassing me. Man, she'd call me every night at three—"

"Good night, Jerry."

Jerry saluted and vanished.

The bite was really smarting. I decided to call Marcus. It rang for a long time before he picked up.

"Hello, Dillon. What can I do you for?"

"Want to meet for a drink tonight?"

"A quick one, I have a dinner to go to. Where and when?"

"Come over to my condo, say thirty minutes?"

"Is everything okay?"

"Yeah. I just need your opinion on something."

.   .   .

Marcus removed his glasses and bit pensively at the frame. "This looks like a spider bite."

"But you're not sure?" I asked.

"Let me take another look." He slipped his glasses on again and poked around with his finger. He'd been a surgeon too long; his bedside manner was a little rough.

"Interesting," he said, straightening.

"What is?"

"It almost looks like two bites, one right next to the other."

Marcus helped me with my shirt collar. I turned and he eyed me. "What?" I asked.

"Are you into drugs?"

The look on my face must have been enough.

"Okay, okay," Marcus said, hands raised. He took his drink and leaned against the kitchen island.

"I don't do drugs, at least not any that involve needles." I buttoned my shirt and leaned against the other counter. I grabbed my Corona and took a swig.

"I saw a lot of those kind of bites in Nam. Nasty insects over there. Big as your fist."

"It hurts like a son-of-a-bitch."

Marcus, drink in hand, pointed. "It's looks infected. Better have that checked."

A shiver raced down my spine. I wasn't a fan of going to doctors. I set my beer down, having lost any interest in getting my drink on. "Know somebody good?"

Marcus finished his drink and placed the glass in the island sink. "I do. Call my office in the morning. Marilyn will give you Richard Tish's number. He's a friend and a damn good dermatologist. He'll fix you right up."

"What should I do in the meantime?"

Marcus looked over as he removed his coat from the back of the kitchen chair. "Do you feel bad?"

"No."

"And you haven't been abducted, have you?" He shrugged his coat on and pulled at its lapels.

"Very funny."

"Then it's probably nothing. A couple of unusual spider bites. Relax. Get a good night's sleep. Call an exterminator. And see Tish. He'll know what they are."

I started to walk Marcus out.

"That's okay, I know the way. I'm not senile."

"Thanks again, *old* man."

Marcus flipped me the bird over his shoulder and closed the front door.

I felt the lump at the base of my neck. It hadn't gone down much over the last two days. My car keys splayed on the counter caused me to think of the weekend security guard. Carter had said that he had been watching me. Watching? I removed my cell from its dock and thumbed my building's security number.

"Security. Billy. What can we do for you, Mr. Bradford?"

"You have cameras in the garage, don't you?"

"Yes, sir. Why? Did something happen?"

"No, nothing serious. I just wanted to see something. Do you use tapes or digital?"

"Tapes."

"How long do you keep them?"

"Two weeks."

"Mind if I come down and look at one from last Friday night, about

10:30ish?"

The guy hesitated. "Well, we don't usually do that–"

"Aw, come on. I just need to see something. It's personal, know what I mean?"

Another pause. "Okay, sure. Come on down. I'll have it cued up."

The Terrace's security office was a closet, and their equipment was about 20 years behind the curve. Billy was a sweaty, crew-cutted guard whose smile's nervous edge suggested he was pushing the boundaries of protocol. We crammed behind an old 13-inch CRT monitor, watching staticky black-and-white time-lapse video of my assigned parking area. The Merc was high in the left corner of the frame with only the back end visible. Last Friday I had pulled in at 8:23 p.m., gotten out of the car and walked out of frame. We fast-forwarded through the next three hours. At 10:51 p.m. I walked back into frame, got into the car, and pulled out.

What the hell? "Is this time code accurate?" I asked, not quite believing the footage I was watching.

Billy compared his current monitor to the office's wall clock. "Yes, sir."

We quickly scanned through the next several hours until my car reappeared and parked at 3:18 a.m.

"Slow it to real time," I said.

Billy did, but the time-lapse was still jerky. Sixteen minutes went by, and I didn't come out. Then a windowless white van pulled up and blocked our view of the Merc. It sat there for four minutes before it drove out of frame.

"What's that van?" I asked.

Billy shrugged, his interest waning.

"Don't you take down license plate numbers, stuff like that?"

Again he shrugged, this time even more apathetically. "There's no guard station at the garage entry gate," Billy said. "Could be a resident with a rental.

We get that all the time."

It was clear that I wasn't going to get Billy's full cooperation, so I put an ear to his mind. Billy was jonesing for a Big Mac meal with a large Diet Coke, and I was a major asshole for intruding on his break time. He was also telling the truth.

"Can you fast forward to six o'clock, please," I asked.

A few residents jumped through frame like an old Monty Python bit, then Carter the weekend guard stutter-walked up to my window.

"Pause this," I said.

The image froze, and two bands of static cut the screen in three sections. 6:03 a.m.

"Are you okay, Mr. Bradford?" I heard Billy ask. "You don't look so good."

6. Your kind of lady.

For a Monday night, West Village was jumping, which also meant parking was a bitch. I pulled the Merc into the last space on top of the garage and made my way to street level via the stairs. Echoes of West Village's energy wafted up through the stairwell. I passed a pair of fashion-forward West Villagers on the way up.

Stage Left was a single, non-descript door that looked like it had been force injected into the building. I entered on a shallow landing and had to descend a steep flight of stairs to access the bar. The Goth hostess, who looked like her previous night had been one for the ages, reluctantly pulled herself away from texting to greet me.

"I'm just going to the bar, thanks," I said.

She smiled half-heartedly and resumed leaning on her podium.

Four business types hugged the end of the bar; I parked myself as far away from them as I could. The bartender took about a minute to acknowledge me. He ambled over wiping out a highball glass.

"How ya doin'?" he asked, as if genuinely concerned for my well-being. His peroxided hair resembled the fur of a Rhodesian ridgeback, and his ears featured large chrome flesh tunnels. I hated those things, especially if I was out to dinner and the server had them. They were definitely an appetite killer.

"Good, thanks," I replied.

"What would you like?"

"What kind of Scotch do you have?"

The bartender gestured at the row of fine malts that were the base of a well-stocked bar.

"Give me an Oban. Lots of ice."

As he made my drink, I compared my wadded napkin with the ones at the bar. It was the same.

"Here you go." The bartender slid one of the napkins under my drink as he placed it on the bar. "Should I start a tab?"

"No."

"That'll be fifteen big ones."

"Did you work last Friday night?" I asked while I retrieved my wallet.

"Yeah, why? Did you leave something here?"

"No. I was just wondering if I looked familiar to you."

The question stopped the guy for a second. He scrutinized me as he took my money. "Maybe. It was busy. Need any change?"

I listened in. The guy thought I was hitting on him, and kicking my faggot ass crossed his mind. I shook my head at his question. "Look, I'm trying to re-trace my steps, but I can't remember much of it, if you get my drift. I would've been here just before midnight."

The bartender pulled a long stemmed wine glass out from a large dishwasher rack and started wiping it down. "You really can't remember?"

"No. Weird, right?"

"Not really. I've been shitfaced before."

"If you do recall, here's my card."

The bartender concluded I was gay and, without looking at it, stuffed my business card into his shirt pocket.

As I sipped my drink, I looked up the phone app Isato's intern had suggested. BackCall had three levels of service, each doubling in price. It offered the patented ability to trace and reveal blocked calls. I bought the entry-level app and waited as it downloaded to my cell. Another bartender appeared and ducked under the bar's counter. He popped up and acknowledged me with a tilt of the head, then, tying his apron behind him, hurried to the other end of the bar.

BackCall 2.0 required an extensive series of gyrations just to get the damn thing loaded and was littered with more techno-babble than my Denon receiver's manual. It would reroute all my incoming calls through its servers, which would ID any blocked calls and present the numbers. With old blocked numbers, all I had to do was select it out of the recent call log, and BackCall would do the rest.

I selected Friday's only blocked call and waited as a time bar slid across the screen.

"Excuse me."

I looked up into the acne blotched face of a new bartender. The kid, complete with a dark green Izod shirt and retro puka beads, was probably a grad student at SMU.

"Yeah?" I asked. The time bar was about halfway.

He thumbed at the other bartender. "Farris said you were asking if you were here last Friday night."

"Yes, I was."

"I remember you."

"Really?"

"Well, I remember the girl you were with more."

Something unfamiliar and cold arced through my nerves. "Why's that?"

"Dude, you two were going at it. And she was smoking hot."

The time bar finished its journey and a number popped up. I dialed it, making sure that my number went out as blocked. "What do you mean *going* at it?"

"That chick had her hands all over you. Dude, don't you remember?"

"No," I said, listening to the number ring through.

"Man, what are you, gay? She had the nicest rack I've ever seen. I'd sure as hell remember a chick handling my Johnson. She was my kind of lady."

The call clicked through. *The number you have reached is no longer in service. If you think—*

I ended the call and looked up at the SMU kid. "Why was she your kind of lady?"

The kid flashed the rock-on gesture with both hands. "Asian pussy, man. Sweeeeet."

7. One more thing.

The word *thanks* came out as a whisper, and I just stared at the blocked cell number. Who was the woman, and why did we meet? Had it been Debra Lao? She was the only Asian woman I had been around for probably the last year. And I didn't really know her well, at least not well enough to meet her at a bar in the middle of the night, much less grope her. Did I pick up some bar chic and get slipped Liquid G? Why didn't I remember any of it? And what the hell was wrong with my neck? I had always been able to maintain a sense of balance in my life, despite my ability, but now it felt like the foundation was showing cracks. I dialed Chris's number.

"Dillon, man, what's up?" Trance club music thrummed behind his voice.

"Nothing much. Hey, I wanted to get Debra's contact info, so I can add her to the group's email list." I tried to sound nonchalant. "Can you text that over to me?"

"Man, I'm right in the middle of some–"

"It would be a big help. I'm about to leave my office, and I want to get this done."

Chris said something away from his cell. There was laughter. "Okay. Give me a minute, and I'll send it over. What are you doing after work? You should join us at Tidal." There was another round of laughter and the background music shifted into an intense Latin beat.

"I'm going home to crash. It's been a long day."

"You work too hard, Dillon. You're going to wake up an old man one day. I'll catch ya later."

I finished my drink and waited for Chris's text. After five excruciating minutes, it chimed onto my cell's screen. I entered Debra's info into my Contacts, then looked it up through another one of Jerry's magic spy apps. This one claimed it could, with only a cell number, find anyone anywhere on Google Maps. After a few seconds of churn, it pinged up that she lived about two blocks from Stage Left, but didn't give a unit number or her home phone, if she even had one. It was almost seven o'clock. I dialed her cell, but it rang straight through to voicemail.

What the hell, I thought. I might as well go see her. Maybe she can shed some light on my missing night.

It took about 15 minutes to walk from Stage Left to Debra Lao's condo. She lived in an older complex called The Oaks. It was an upscale place, complete with doorman, numbered ID entry, and concierge service. The lobby was open to public traffic, although the concierge desk was menacing, as well as the guy behind it.

"May I help you, sir?" The concierge's head and neck appeared to be a single thick, steroid-fueled mass screwed to the top of a large dark suit. A small tire of flesh oozed over his shirt collar, and a film of sweat glistened under his nose.

"Yes. I'm a friend of a resident, Debra Lao, and I was wondering if she was in."

"We're not allowed to give out that information, sir."

Folks like hotel desk clerks and airline booking agents often thought of people by their stats. To them, people were just numbers. If I kept asking questions, the concierge would think of Debra the same way.

"I only have her cell, and she isn't answering." I leaned onto the counter. "Could you give me her home number?"

The guy looked down at a computer monitor tucked into the belly of the desk. Bingo.

"We aren't allowed to give out any information on our residents," he said, annoyed.

I drummed my fingertips on the counter. "Okay. Thanks anyway." I turned to leave.

"May I tell Ms. Lao that you were here?"

"Tell her Chris came by."

When the guy glanced at Debra's info on his monitor, his mind read the text automatically, which told me everything I needed. Debra lived in Apartment 1214. She usually came home around 7:30, and he'd wanted to hit on her for some time.

Now I had to get in, and not by way of the lobby. The Oaks had a keypad-secured side entrance. I had seen it when I walked up. All I had to do was wait by the sidewalk and listen in to a resident as they used their code. My OCD was kicking in, because I didn't care if there were cameras or whether a double entry with one resident's code would raise suspicions. I needed to talk to Debra, and I had to do it as soon as possible. I left the lobby and parked my ass on the bus bench. After about 15 minutes, a man in full Nike jogging gear dragging a very tired dog stepped up to the pad.

Surprisingly, the rest of The Oaks was not reflective of its lobby. The common areas were carpeted with a dated tight green pile knockoff bordered with a dirty gold vine spiral motif. That and the hallway's sloppy eggshell white paint made the place look more like a tired business-class hotel. Debra had a corner apartment and, judging by my location inside the building, probably a nice view of downtown. I pressed her doorbell and stepped back so she could get a clear view of me through the peephole. I could hear someone approach from inside. The lock unlatched, and the door slowly opened.

"Hello, Dillon." Debra, smartly dressed in a conservative black business suit, glanced at me with little surprise. Still holding her mail, she must have just come home. "How did you get up here?"

"You, of all people, should know that. Sorry to drop in like this, but I need to ask you a question." I handed her the crumpled Stage Left napkin. "Does this look familiar?"

Debra regarded it with detached concern. "Of course." Our eyes met. I didn't hear anything.

"Did you call me late Friday night?"

The corners of her eyelids tightened. "You know I did. You met me at Stage Left." She handed the napkin back. "Dillon, what's going on?" She started reviewing her mail indifferently.

"The bartender there said you were all over me that night." I didn't really want to say that, but it sort of just came out.

Debra looked up, bemused. "Well, we did sit close together, and I had a very nice time, but I would hardly say I was all over you. Don't you remember any of it?"

"No," I blurted.

"We talked business. The white papers?" She frowned. "The *website?*"

Shit. "Um … sorry. I'm not remembering anything."

"If you're going to do work with my department, you're going to need to get it together. Maybe your AE should call me."

"Right." This was going assways. "I'll have her do that." Debra's attention went back to her mail. "Did we talk about anything else?"

She glanced up, her look a little less harsh. "We talked about your childhood, and what it was like growing up with the gift. You also went on about Kadin and how you thought you were in love with her. You even told me what it was like to make love to someone you couldn't read, and how wonderful that was. You were pretty drunk. I had to walk you to your car."

I realized my mouth was open and closed it. Did I black out? Had I driven home, passed out, and now couldn't remember any of it? I didn't recall drinking that much.

"Are you all right?" Debra opened the door wider and motioned inside. "Why don't you come in and sit down for a second. I'll get you a water."

As I followed Debra into her apartment, I searched my mind for the slightest memory fragments of our encounter. Nothing. One moment I had been spooning Kadin, the next I was waking up in my car, thinking I had gone to my office when I had really had a late-night rendezvous with Debra. Was I getting Alzheimer's?

Debra retrieved a small bottle of Pellegrino from her refrigerator and handed it to me. I hadn't even realized I had sat down on one of her kitchen stools.

"Dillon, maybe you should see someone. It sounds like you had a blackout."

For the first time, I noticed Debra's apartment. It was painted in varying degrees of beige and sparsely furnished in a fusion of Crate & Barrel and Restoration Hardware. A toilet flushed from somewhere deep in the space.

"I thought I heard your voice," Chris said when he walked into the kitchen.

"I thought you were at Tidal." I tried to hide my surprise.

"Hello to you, too. And yes, I was. But now I'm here. So, Dillon, what brings you to Debra's on a Monday night?" There was a cut in Chris's tone that suggested I might have ventured across some male territorial boundary. His hand went to my shoulder and his fingers dug in.

"Dillon doesn't remember us meeting at Stage Left last Friday," Debra said.

Chris made a face. "What's the matter, buddy? Smoking too much wacky tobacky?" He mimed taking a hit off a joint.

"Were you there?" I asked, confused.

"Shit, no way. I was whipped. I told Debra to call you. I knew you'd be up. You're such a night owl."

The kitchen did a little vertigo dance, and I grabbed the counter.

"Easy there," Chris said, reaching again for my shoulder.

Debra came beside me. "Maybe you should lie down."

"No, I'm okay." I straightened and leaned on the stool.

"Are you sure?"

I nodded, but I wasn't remotely okay. Either I had blacked out and embarrassed myself that night, or these two were pulling an elaborate punk. The moment felt very awkward. "I think I've wasted too much of your time. Thanks for the water." I pushed away from the counter and walked toward the front door. "I'm sorry I came by without calling."

"It's not a problem, Dillon," Debra said. "I hope you're feeling better."

"Let me walk you out." Chris's hand went to my arm, and he guided more than helped me. In the hallway he spun me around. "Listen, man." He pulled me close enough to smell the gin on his breath. "I don't know what you're doing up here, but I don't like it."

"Look, Chris. I don't know what hap—" His grip cut me off.

"You broke a rule. We're never supposed to use our gift against another. What the hell are you doing up here? You're probably on some security tape."

Chris's drama was beginning to piss me off. I pulled out of his grasp. Anything I said now would only look like an excuse. I took in a breath. "Chris, I'm sorry about tonight. I overreacted. To be honest I got a little scared."

He stepped back. "You? Scared?"

"Yeah. I've never blacked out before."

"With as much partying as you've done? I don't believe that."

I didn't know what to say. I shrugged.

"When was the last time you took a vacation?"

Before CoolBrain had been formed. "A long time."

"You know what I would do if I were you? Take Kadin on a vacation and get some rest. I'll talk to Debra and smooth it out, although knowing her, she won't think anything of it." He glanced over his shoulder at the half-open door.

"We cool?" I asked.

Chris nodded. "No worries, man."

We shook hands, and I began to leave.

"Hey, Dillon, there is one thing."

I turned.

Chris dug his hands into his pockets, took a step forward, and turned slightly sideways. His eyes went to his Cole Haans.

"What's that?" I asked.

Chris looked up, his anger barely concealed. "Don't ever use my name again."

8. Just spit it out.

The offices of Dr. Benjamin Tish were a study in vulgar chic. Surely his wife had been his decorator; no self-respecting professional would have allowed this abomination. In the center of the lobby was a 3-dimensional, cubed cross-section of human skin about the size of an old 20-inch TV. It was right out of a medical textbook, complete with squirting sweat glands and hair – giant stalks of it – that kids could run their hands through. Infographics on the wall described, in detail, something called Mohs surgery. I hoped to God it was never done on me, and it definitely was the last thing anyone with a serious skin disorder would want to see.

"Mr. Bradford? Dr. Tish will see you now."

Gretchen, the nurse, was all business. I followed her into a maze of examining rooms. Tish had patients stacked up like planes at DFW. I had a bad feeling that I was about to join the holding pattern, but Gretchen led me past purgatory and ushered me into Tish's office. The man was waiting, hand extended.

"Come in, Mr. Bradford. Marcus said it was important." Tish was a gangly man with veneered teeth that looked like they were a half size too big. He gestured to an examining table against the far wall. "Hop up on the end, please."

He must have owed Marcus a big favor because I hadn't waited or filled out any forms yet. I thought about listening in to see if that were true, but dismissed the idea and climbed onto the table.

"Marcus told me what he'd examined and your discussion about his opinion."

"Yeah, it's weird," I replied. "I don't remember getting bit or poked or whatever these are."

"Have you had any high fever, headaches, hearing loss, that sort of thing?"

"No, just some soreness here." I rubbed at the area.

"Let's have a look."

I tilted my head to one side. Tish pulled down the medical loupes attached to his glasses and started probing the sore.

"Damn," I said, recoiling from the pain.

"Well," Tish said as he flipped the optics up, "these are insect bites, one right next to the other. One's become infected. I can give you something for that."

"You're sure they're just bites?" I asked.

"What else would they be?"

"I don't know."

Tish frowned. "Do you think these are needle marks?"

"Do you?"

"Mr. Bradford, insect bites and needle marks, for the most part, look practically the same. The discoloring of the skin suggests that an insect made these. Now if they were needle marks, then wouldn't you know if you were stuck with a needle?" He stared at me sourly.

"What?" I asked.

"Do you do drugs?"

"Jesus, that's what Markus said. And no, I don't do drugs." Then a weird concept hit me. "Could someone be taking something out?"

Tish pulled his head back in surprise, and his receding chin almost disappeared into his neck. "What would that be, Mr. Bradford? And who is this someone?" A raised eyebrow matched his sarcasm. He gestured to a curving rattan and wood chair in front of a desk that looked like it had come out of some Italian designer's wet dream. I sat and tried to get comfortable. Tish settled into the black mesh of his Aeron chair, leaned on his desk, and steepled his fingers into a nice little church. "I doubt seriously that anyone would steal tissue from you. Usually, it's harvested from cadavers or impoverished people. If someone were targeting you, specifically, that would mean you're special in some way. Are you special, Mr. Bradford?"

Part of me – the boy who woke up to this bizarre life so many years ago – wanted to say yes.

"No."

Tish spread his hands. "There, you see? Nothing to worry about. Insect bites. You don't need a dermatologist, Mr. Bradford." Cue the punch line. "You need an exterminator."

Tish stood and I could almost see the wall descend between us. I listened in: the man's mind had already shifted to the patient in exam room six. He despised her and her boils. And I had become an irritation, but I didn't need to listen in to know that. He walked to my side of the desk and gestured to the door. "Let's get you squared away with some sample hydrocortisone cream."

"Indulge me, doc. What if someone *had* taken tissue out?" I pressed. "What would I need to do?"

Tish thrust his hands into his lab coat's deep pockets and leveled a frustrated look. I listened in again. I had moved beyond being an irritation and was now pissing him off. He was considering calling Marcus and bitching him out. Expletives were abundant.

"Call the police, I suppose," he said. "Now, if you'll excuse me, I have other patients to see." He opened his office door and ushered me into the hallway. "I'll tell Jennifer at the front desk to get you some samples. Good day, Mr. Bradford."

We shook hands, and he quickly ducked into examining room six.

"Thanks," I said to the empty hallway.

As I drove back into the city down Central Expressway, I didn't know what to think. Had Marcus been right? Were these just insect bites, or was Tish blowing me off? He didn't have any reason not to tell me the truth. The more I thought about it, the more it made sense. Even though my ability was something straight out of science fiction, the chances of landing on some government radar and having experiments conducted on me were remote. I was an ad exec, for Christ's sake, and had kept pretty much to my business and myself. The only people who knew about my ability were the happy hour group. And they certainly weren't going to tell anyone.

Still, insect bites didn't explain away my blackouts. Something was wrong with me. I could feel it. Being adopted meant that I didn't have the luxury of knowing my family's medical history. My medical future was anybody's guess, and the blackouts could be some ailment all the men in my family had dealt with. Then again, maybe too much partying had finally caught up with me. I grabbed my cell out of the cup holder and speed dialed Marcus. It rang through to his voicemail.

"Hey, old man, I saw Tish. They're insect bites. But there's something else I need to talk with you about. I think I had a blackout. Call me."

A mosaic of brake lights built in front of me. Traffic on Central was coming to a halt. I quickly swerved onto the Knox Street exit ramp and pulled into a gas station. A cheesy commercial about some new apartments tried to entertain me as I pumped the Merc full of premium. The flat screen had a long crack and gang symbols adorning its metal frame. I watched the gallons tick past when a bolt of pain carved its way through my skull. I doubled over and cradled my head.

"Hey, you okay?" A rough looking blonde with blue eye makeup and an off-center ponytail poked her head around the pump.

"Ah, yeah. Just the start of a migraine." I straightened and leaned against the Merc.

"I used to get those. Back when I had my kids."

The pain struck again, and my stomach rolled. I stumbled to the waist container and retched.

"Oh, God, mister! Do you want me to call 911?"

I struggled to look at her. The container smelled horrendous, which brought on the urge to puke again. "No," I managed, "I'm okay—"

Whatever was torturing my brain swooped in for one last attack. It hit with an intensity that went beyond pain. I groaned and caved against the pump housing. The woman was over me in an instant, her cell phone at her ear. A man, even rougher than her, stepped up and peered down.

"Shit, baby." He snapped his gum and a tiny speck of spittle escaped through the angled gap between his two front teeth. He pushed his mesh cap back off his forehead. "He looks real fucked up."

■　　■　　■

"Mr. Bradford?"

My name emerged from a curtain of sound. There's a liminal point, just before I wake, when I can't block out all of the voices. It's like waking up in a crowded party — startling, if you're not used to it. The voices I was receiving now were a nightmarish blend of fear and agony filtered through English and Spanish both. I flinched, and the back of my hand hit something cold and metal. My eyes felt like they had been Crazy Glued.

"Can you hear me, Mr. Bradford?"

Shutting out the voices had become a reflex, and now this one, a husky baritone with a smoker's rasp, had joined the throbbing behind my right eye.

"Hey baby, it's me." Much sweeter. Kadin. I felt her hand at my cheek. "He's opening his eyes."

"Mr. Bradford, I'm Dr. Pierson. Can you understand me?"

"Yes," I heard myself say. The act of speaking felt distant and dreamlike, like my brain had been violently dislocated from my body. I lifted my hand and managed to unglue an eye just as the overhead lamp was clicked off.

"Is that better?" Pierson asked.

I nodded, but even that small movement took effort. Kadin's face was in partial shadow. The room beyond was a blur. I still couldn't see who was talking to me.

"Where am I?"

"You're at Baylor Emergency, Mr. Bradford. You were driven here by ambulance."

"When?"

"You were at the Shell station on Knox," Kadin said.

Right. I had gone to see Marcus's dermatologist friend, but it was all a bit fuzzy. Something pricked my arm. "What the—?"

"Easy," Pierson said, "we're just getting some fluids into you. You'll start to feel better in a few minutes. Do you feel like talking?"

"Sure."

"What was the last thing you remember?"

Good question. "I was pumping gas into my car. I don't remember much after that."

Pierson was in focus now. He was straight out of central casting, complete with hairy forearms and a pair of bright green Crocs. "How did you feel, just before you collapsed?"

"Normal, I guess."

"Do you have a history of fainting, seizures, or blackouts?" he asked.

"Not really," I lied.

"Any history in your family?"

"I don't know. I was adopted."

Pierson nodded. "Have you been under any unusual stress lately?"

"I'm in advertising."

The joke was lost on Pierson. "Well, your vitals are perfectly normal, and, with the exception of being a little dehydrated, you're in good shape. Let's have a look at your eyes."

The beam from Pierson's pocket flashlight felt as bright as one of the Merc's halogens.

Kadin leaned in with him. "What are you looking for?" There was deep concern scored in the lines of her forehead.

Pierson examined my eyes like he might find the cure for cancer there. He straightened and pocketed the light. "To see if the optic nerve is swollen. It's one way to check for a brain tumor, but yours looks fine."

I managed to sit up and swing my legs off the side of the bed. The IV fluids were doing their job. "So what do you think happened?"

Pierson folded his arms. "Well, without a full workup, it's hard to say." He emphasized this point with a shrug. "All of your vitals are normal. You probably got dehydrated." Another shrug. "Since I can't find anything, I don't really see the need for you to stay the night. I'd like you to rest here until you've gone through the IV bag. Do you have a family internist?"

"Yes."

"Then I'd make an appointment. You never know, and it's always good to be cautious, right?" Pierson's phone buzzed. "If you'll excuse me." His smile looked conditioned. "They'll be in with some forms to fill out. Take care, Mr. Bradford. You too, Mrs. Bradford."

Pierson pulled back the bay's curtains and walked away. A heavily tattooed orderly, jamming to his iPhone, was mopping up something in the bay next to us.

"*Mrs.* Bradford?" I asked.

Kadin grinned sheepishly.

●   ■   ■

Kadin pulled her Camry into one of my building's visitor spaces. As we walked to the elevator, I saw the Merc in its space.

"Who drove my car back?" I asked.

"I think one of your interns," Kadin said.

"Was it Jerry?"

"I don't know. I called Derek. He took care of it."

"Jesus," I groaned and rubbed my head.

Kadin put an arm around me. "What's the matter?"

"I don't know. I was feeling good after that IV, but now I feel pretty woozy."

"I want you to see Marcus as soon as possible."

I forced a grin. "Okay, Mom."

"It's Mrs. Mom to you."

"I hope they didn't scratch the Merc getting into my space."

"My God, Dillon. Quit worrying about that damn car. It's fine."

I thought about going down and checking, but the pain behind my eye was intensifying. We stepped into the elevator. "I need to lie down. I feel like shit." The elevator's movement was nauseating.

"I'll get you into bed, then I'm calling Marcus."

"No. I'll do it—" The throbbing behind my eye upshifted into a new gear. I leaned heavily onto Kadin's shoulder, and she took my weight like a champ. Maybe I should listen to her. The pain shifted again. I felt my legs give.

"Oh my God, Dillon." Kadin grabbed me just as I sank against the elevator panel. "You're turning white."

"Dillon?"

"Yeah?"

"How do you feel, son?"

I usually didn't care for Marcus's fatherly routine, but the old man's voice was a welcome sound. The bedroom was dark, and I was on top of the sheets in my underwear. The sheets felt wet, like I had been sweating heavily. Thank God the pain was gone.

"A lot better." I tried to sit up.

"Just take it easy." Marcus sat on the edge of the bed.

Kadin appeared at the doorway. "Is he awake?"

"Yes," Marcus said, "and looking much better."

"What happened?" I asked.

"You passed out ... again." Kadin approached the bed.

"More than that," Marcus said. "You may have had a mild seizure."

"What's going on with me?"

"That's why I'm here. Now tell me, what happened after you left the emergency room?"

"I felt pretty good. But when we got home, I got this sharp pain behind my right eye. Then it started again when we got on the elevator."

"Did you have any nausea or vision problems?"

"I threw up at the gas station, but not in the elevator. I just had the pain."

"Was it sharp or dull, throbbing or continuous?"

"Yes."

"On a scale from one to ten, how bad was it?"

"Fifty."

"What did Tish say?"

"He thinks they're insect bites."

Marcus scoffed.

I sat up and leaned against the headboard. "What? You disagree?"

"I don't like these episodes you're having." Marcus produced a prescription pill bottle from a pocket inside his coat. "I want you to take one of these tonight, then one as needed before bed."

"What is it?" I asked.

"Something that'll help you sleep. In the morning, I want you come by my office around nine, and we'll get you into radiology for an MRI."

"I have meetings all tomorrow–"

"Cancel them." Marcus's voice could go from fatherly to authoritarian in a millisecond.

"You didn't answer my question."

Marcus's sigh was not reassuring. "I did some research into those marks on your neck," he said, uncoiling his stethoscope from around his neck.

"What, you don't believe they're insect bites now?"

Marcus hesitated.

I was getting pissed. "Marcus?"

"I need to run some tests to be sure–"

"Just spit it out!"

"I think those marks are from an IV."

9. If I had to guess.

Marcus's office, with its leather wingbacks and dark paneling, was totally old school. I half expected a brandy set on the credenza behind his desk. Instead, it documented the photographic history of his marriage to Carol, his wife of 37 years. They seemed to have been everywhere. Devil's Rock. The pyramids. Machu Picchu.

"Here we go!" he said, charging into the room. A large manila envelope was tucked under his arm.

"What did you find?" I asked.

Marcus sat at his desk and slipped a CD into his computer. He spun the monitor to face me and knocked over a cheesy photo of him and Carol on a beach. They were both holding half-cut coconuts over their heads as if they were helmets. A little pang of envy moved through me. "Can I ask you something?" I said.

Marcus caught the direction of my look and righted the photo. "Absolutely."

"Is it hard?"

"What, being married to someone and know their thoughts?"

"Yeah."

"I don't listen."

"Ever?"

"That's right."

"You're a stronger man than me."

"You'd be surprised."

"How's that?"

"When you love someone as much as I love Carol, it's easy to do things that are hard."

"The old 'for better or for worse,' right?"

"You know, I envy you and Kadin. I won't lie to you. It's hard not to 'indulge,' as you call it. I would give anything not to be able to listen in to Carol's thoughts. Do you know how lucky you two are to have each other?"

The truth of Marcus's words cut through me like the prow of an icebreaker. Kadin was everything I wanted in a woman. I desperately wanted to love her, but there was a small part of me that furiously resisted. Maybe it was my abandonment issues? That's what Mr. Shepard, my eight-grade counselor, had said. An ex-girlfriend had blamed my "lack of intimacy" on the fact that I was, and I'm paraphrasing here, "a narcissistic, self-centered dick-head who wouldn't know a good relationship if it walked up and kicked me in the nuts." I had listened in once when we were making love, and found she was thinking more about a good friend of ours and that she had been sleeping with him for most of our relationship. Talk about a kick in the nuts. If only I could listen in to my own heart.

"Maybe you're right, Marcus." I turned my attention to the screen. "So, what have you found?"

Marcus searched through the rows of color images and brought two forward. "See this green area?" He pointed to one row that had a dozen axial cross-sections of my brain. They were progressive slices, and the area that Marcus was pointing at was behind my right eye. It changed shape and seemed larger as he scrolled through the images.

"I assume that's not how it's supposed to look," I said.

"This area is where I believe our ability comes from." Marcus docked all of the other images and removed a printout from the envelope. "This is the scan of you I did several years ago, remember?"

Shortly after joining our group, Marcus had run MRIs on all of us. He had been so excited discovering the green area, but I didn't recall it being so large. "I do."

"Here's the one we just did." He held the printout up to the image on the screen.

"The area is bigger," I said.

"Yes."

"Is that bad?"

"It's hard to say. Our gift is unique. I don't know what causes it or how it works. I have my theories, but that's all." Marcus removed his glasses and tossed them across the envelope. "I'm not a scientist, and I don't have the equipment or the knowledge."

"And we can't take this to anyone, can we?"

Marcus shook his head. "I'm afraid not. It's too risky."

"Marcus, what is happening to me? I'm blacking out. Having seizures. And now you're saying that this mark on my neck is ... what did you say?"

"I said it could be from an IV incision."

"Yeah, what the hell is up with that?" I sprung out of the chair and began pacing the room. "Not to mention the green shit in my head is getting bigger!" I turned and stared at the colored patchwork of MRI images and wondered.

"Dillon, calm down."

I exhaled an exasperated breath and leaned on Marcus's desk. "I'm sorry, Marcus. I've had a lot of weird shit thrown at me."

"It's going to be all right, Dillon. We just need to get to the bottom of what's happening. Now, is there anything that crosses over everything that's happened?"

"I don't know. Maybe."

"What is it?"

"Debra Lao."

"Chris's girlfriend? Why?"

I told Marcus about finding the Stage Left napkin, questioning the bartenders and using BackCall. And about confronting Debra.

"You went to her apartment?" Marcus seemed genuinely shocked.

"I know. Crazy, right? Supposedly we met at Stage Left. She said we had drinks, talked about business, and that I got shit-faced."

"That doesn't sound like you."

"I don't know, Marcus. I did wake up in my car in my parking garage with a ripping hangover."

"Oh," he said sarcastically, "maybe that's all it is. You got over-served."

I was in no mood for jokes, and his died somewhere on the table between us. "The next morning is when Kadin discovered the marks."

"That could be coincidence. What did you say Debra did again?"

"She may have told me, but that's just it...I don't remember! I know she works for Ewing Labs, but I don't know which division. I'll ask Chris."

"I wouldn't do that. Best to play this tight to the vest."

"You're making me paranoid."

"Just pragmatic." Marcus settled back into his chair. "You know, Dillon, those really could be insect bites, and your episodes might just be a heart issue."

"You don't sound too sure."

"First things first. We need to confirm that those marks are nothing more than insect bites, and it sounds like Debra might be the place to start. Maybe you should go to her office and listen in to her co-workers. Find out what they're working on."

"And how am I going to do that? I don't know which division she's with. Ewing has three campuses in Dallas and two in Ft. Worth."

"Look her up on LinkedIn and take her to lunch. Say you want to talk about bringing her into the group."

The thought of playing detective made my already high anxiety jump a notch. My attention moved to the image of the green blob, and I reflexively rubbed at the bite on my neck. "You really think these are injection points, don't you," I asked, breaking the awkward silence that had settled.

Marcus, looking like a kid who was hiding the fact that he'd broken the neighbor's window, started to say something.

"What's the matter?" I asked.

"There's something else I need to show you." He brought up another image onto the screen, but this one wasn't like the other MRIs. It was a detailed close-up of the blob, and in the center sat a fuzzy black mass.

"What's that?" I asked.

"I hesitated even showing you."

"Why?"

"Because I'm not sure what it is."

I sat on the edge of his desk and looked closer, but the image was too pixilated to make out any details.

"It could be nothing," Marcus said, leaning back in his chair. "A glitch in the software."

"But it could be something, right?"

"Possibly. This is a spectroscopic view of the area. I had it magnified. The technician did the best he could, but we're not set up for that kind of minute detail. This is the T2 image."

I pointed to the black mass. "And you think this was injected into me?"

"Not injected."

"How do you know?"

"I don't. I'm only guessing. But it isn't like anything I've ever seen."

"What do you mean?"

"The shape is too perfect. See the edges? It almost looks like a pentagon."

Now that he mentioned it, the mass did appear symmetrical. "Marcus, what are you saying?"

The old surgeon rubbed his forehead and looked at me with an expression I imagine he reserved for patients with a life-threatening condition. "It's not organic."

10. Sit down.

Dallas wasn't Paris or New York. We didn't have anything remotely close to the Eiffel Tower or the Empire State Building. What we did have were incredible thunderstorms, and from my balcony I could sip Scotch and see them roll in from the west. I called it watching the God Channel. It was about five o'clock, and the leading edge of a massive front was swallowing the skyline of Ft. Worth, which, on a clear day, I could barely see at the horizon with a pair of binoculars. The news said the thundercloud topped out at 70 thousand feet, and it packed golf-ball sized hail, torrential rain, and wind gusts up to 60 miles per hour. On the radar, half of its huge area was purple. In meteorological terms, purple represented the worst of the worst. I loved purple. It meant that there was going to be one hell of a show, and I had a front row seat.

After what Marcus had showed me, he went on to explain that if something was to be introduced into the brain, it could be done with a needle, yet you'd have to drill a hole first in the top of the head, and that it couldn't be done outside of an operating room. But if you inserted an IV into the carotid artery, you could angle a tiny catheter up the artery toward the brain and into the intracranial space behind the eye. This procedure, he said, could be done outside of an operating room. When I asked where you'd insert the IV, he reluctantly pointed to the mark on my neck.

I went on-line and researched anything related to bioware or nanotechnology. All of the articles were overstuffed with hyper-nerd technospeak, and most of what I read made it clear that, while the promise of microscopic machines was exciting, it was still future tech. If nanobots were a long way off, then what the hell was inside my head?

Kadin and I were supposed to have dinner, but all I wanted was to be alone. I couldn't share with her Marcus's theory that some kind of nanotechnology might be floating around in my brain. I just skirted her questions and assured her that there was nothing to worry about. That story hadn't gone over well, and I was beginning to learn there was a motherly side to Kadin that, given how sexy she looked, was an odd juxtaposition. I needed to regroup and figure out my next steps. It's not everyday that you learn you might have foreign technology in your head. Given the ramifications, I was pretty calm. Maybe I was just in shock. In any case, the Scotch was definitely helping.

An old girlfriend once told me I was too cocky. I liked to think of myself as self-assured, but she had a point. The truth was, when you had a gift like mine, you had to be cocky. Working in advertising just exacerbated the situation. Hell, clients almost expect you to treat them badly. But as I thought about my situation, I realized I wasn't feeling calm, or cocky, or self-assured. I was worried.

Marcus was right. Debra seemed the logical place to start. Since I couldn't listen in on her mind, I'd have to tap some of her co-workers to find anything. I had spent the better part of the afternoon trying to locate Debra online. The only Debra Lao on LinkedIn worked for Bank of America, and the three Debra Laos on Facebook were all under 17.

The wind began kicking at the trees in Turtle Creek, which meant the best part of the show was just moments away. I'd poured another finger of Scotch and settled in when I heard my cell ring in the kitchen. My mind tripped on the action of hitting "pause," like I could actually freeze the approaching thunderstorm. A friend of mine called this bizarre mental fart DVR Conditioning. Marimba music came through the screen door, and I went to the kitchen and read my cell's caller ID.

Debra Lao.

"Hello, Debra." I tried to sound nonchalant.

"Dillon!" Her voice was all sparkly. "How are you doing?"

"You don't want to know."

"Did you have another fainting spell?"

"Yeah. Marcus thinks it from dehydration."

"You have to be careful in this heat. I keep a big bottle of water by my desk just for that reason."

"Look, Debra. I wanted to apologize for the other night. Coming over unannounced and all. I acted like an ass."

"Think nothing of it. You were worried."

"I overreacted."

"Maybe a little. But it's in the past. You know, Dillon, you all have been very gracious to bring me into your group. Before I met Chris, I thought I was the only one with our condition. Living like that for so many years has made me overly cautious. And after hearing what's in people's minds, I don't trust many, know what I mean?"

"I do. That's why I formed the group: so we all could have some time to be normal and decompress."

"I'd like to show my appreciation," she said, still perky. "How about lunch? At my office?"

Here was my opportunity being dropped in my lap, but a ripple of apprehension shot through my nerves. Where was that cockiness when I needed it? "Sure. That would be nice."

"Why don't you come out to tomorrow? I'll show you around, and then I'll take you to this little hole-in-the-wall place I know. They serve the best comfort food in the world."

"I take off early on Fridays," I said, trying to sound light. "So why not the whole afternoon, right? I'd love to come out. What time?"

"How about eleven-ish?"

"Eleven's great."

"Fine. I'll email you our address. Bye."

I docked my cell, picked up my drink, and walked back to the balcony. The storm must have made a turn somewhere over the mid-cities; it was barely raining, and the wind wasn't blowing hard enough to bend a sapling. While the sky churned with heavy grey and green clouds, I leaned onto the railing and wondered what tomorrow's meeting would bring.

What was I heading into?

A crack of lightning hit the far side of the park and its shock wave reverberated across the face of my building.

■   ■   ■

The next morning Debra's email was the first to pop up. The address she gave was for TR Com-ISR – the intelligence, surveillance, and reconnaissance division of TR Com, a huge defense contractor based about an hour east of Dallas off of I-30. I didn't know of any Ewing Labs' divisions associated with

TR Com, so I asked "Jerry the Nerd" to do a little research on a Ms. Debra Lao for a case of Dos Equis. The kid was a computer savant. He needed about 10 minutes to track her down. It seemed Debra was a recent hire for a subsidiary of Ewing Labs called E.L.T., Inc. The ELT stood for Ewing Laboratory Testing, and it appeared they had recently entered into an agreement to share space with TR Com. But Jerry the Nerd couldn't find anything about what they tested.

"Am I interrupting?" Derek asked, standing halfway into my office.

Out of reflex, I folded my laptop down. "No, just answering some email. What's up?"

"Got the finals for the St. Pete's identity. Want to see them?"

"Sure."

St. Pete's Dancing Marlin was one of the few restaurants that was still thriving in Deep Ellum. Boasting "big, honest food" in a place "where the sun always shines," its owner was a charismatic native Texan whose family had been in the food business for generations. He had a particular look in mind for his restaurant's brand, and what Derek was about to show me was our second-round effort.

He handed me a stack of about 20 printouts, and I slowly paged through the different logo treatments.

"This one's nice." I separated it from the pack and spun it to Derek.

It had a retro look, utilizing an old engraving style reminiscent of something you'd see from the turn of the century. But its typography gave it a contemporary feel. The juxtaposition between the engraved marlin leaping beyond the ridged borders of the background frame and the condensed sans serif font was exactly what St. Pete's owner was looking for.

"What if the color broke the edges of the marlin engraving?" I suggested.

"Like torn paper?" Derek asked.

"Or loose brush stokes."

Derek nodded approvingly. "Could be cool. I'll tell Isato." He collected the layouts and stuffed them back into the account folder. "Want to go grab lunch?"

"Can't. Got plans."

Derek eyed me warily as he tapped the sides of the folder into clean symmetry.

"What?" I asked.

"Are you coming back this afternoon?"

"Maybe. Maybe not."

"Kadin?"

"Maybe. Maybe not."

Derek rolled his eyes disapprovingly. "Don't," he said, pointing.

"Don't what?"

"Don't fuck up what you have with Kadin. She's the best thing that happened to you in a long time."

I knew when Derek was past frustration. His voice dropped, and he looked at you like a father scolding a child. Now I knew what his son felt like.

"Look, it's not what you're thinking. I have to—" I stopped myself in midthought. What would I say that didn't sound crazy? And I sure as hell couldn't say the truth.

Derek stepped up to my desk. "Dillon, are you okay?"

My mind flashed on Kadin catching me in the elevator, of waking up to Marcus's grim stare, and the MRIs.

"You know, Derek," I said honestly. "I have no idea."

■   ■   ■

The highway patrol was out in force, so it took almost an hour and a half to get to the main road to TR's campus. The four-laner was about two miles long and dead-ended at a massive complex. Judging by the empty guardhouse and lack of gates, TR might have been a secure campus at one time, but all that protected it now was a perimeter of huge parking lots and video cameras. As

I drove down the main boulevard, a paunchy guard holding a Big Gulp and a clipboard stepped out of a black-glassed prefab building and waved me over.

"Can I help you?" His East Texas drawl was pronounced.

"My name is Dillon Bradford. I'm here to see Debra Lao. She's with the Ewing Laboratory Testing unit. She's expecting me."

"I'll need your driver's license, please." The guard took my license and retreated into the building. After a couple of minutes, he came out. "She's in building six. You go down here and take a right. It's the third building on your left. You can park in any open space." He handed back my license, and as I drove away, I glanced into my rear-view mirror and watched him pull a radio from his belt and start talking.

The TR campus was filled with row upon row of gigantic metal buildings, each probably big enough to house the world's largest airplanes. Jerry's rundown said that the ISR division retrofitted avionics and could turn any plane into a state-of-the-art spy platform. Debra Lao's building was about a quarter the size of the others. It had a nondescript black-glass door and a simple etched metal sign adjacent that said E.L.T., Inc. in Helvetica Light. Debra, wearing a white lab coat over a smart black business outfit, waited on the cement landing in front of the door. She waved.

"Hi there," I said, climbing out of the Merc. The sun was high, and the air was heating up.

"You found us," she beamed.

"I didn't realize you were so far off the grid." I stepped into her building's shadow, and the burning at my forehead abated.

Debra reached out for a demure corporate hug. "I know, right? I'd love to be in Dallas."

"Oh, I don't know." I stepped back and looked around. The tail sections of several large planes protruded from various buildings. "The country's not all that bad."

"This is not the country. Come on, let's get out of this heat."

ELT's lobby was stark and unoccupied. A simple, military-style metal desk sat in the center of a sterile white room. Two grey missmatched vinyl couches elbowed around an equally dull wooden coffee table. Dated industry magazines were spread out in a fan, but it appeared they hadn't been picked up for quite a while.

"No receptionist?" I asked.

"We don't get many visitors out here." Debra pointed to a tiny black half-bubble that was imbedded in one of the drop ceiling's water-stained panels. "The cameras do the job."

She pulled her I.D. card from its carabiner reel and held it up to a reader next to the only other door in the room. A tiny red light blinked green, and the door clicked open. We proceeded down a narrow corridor the same color as the lobby. Its walls were adorned with faded photos of old military planes. I peeked in a few open doors as we walked by. All of them were simple, nondescript, and unoccupied.

"These were TR's research offices before we took them over," Debra said, gesturing laconically.

"Kind of an interesting set-up." We came to an intersection with another black half-bubble and took a left. "Two companies sharing space. Do you rent from TR?"

"We have an arrangement that works well for both parties."

At yet another bubble-camera intersection, we made a right, but this time the hallway opened upon a large cubicle farm. Several offices, their doors closed and unmarked, ringed the area. The farm was an odd collision of Herman-Miller chic and '50s corporate utilitarianism. We passed through to another hallway with still more faded photos of obsolete aircraft. The fluorescents were giving me a headache.

"Are most of your projects for the military?" I asked.

"For the most part. A few consumer drugs bleed over, but that's rare."

"What's one of the more interesting things you're working on? ... That you can tell me, of course."

"One project I think shows great promise is a new drug that will help soldiers' resistance to certain types of chemical weapons."

"I remember a unit of Ewing Labs working on that at their Oak Brook offices a couple of years ago. We did a brochure on it."

"We took that over about six months ago."

The hallway ended at an imposing, eight-foot metal door. Its nameplate had the ELT logo lockup and the word LAB in the same Helvetica typeface. There was a sophisticated keypad mounted just below it.

Debra turned. "We usually don't allow non-employees in here, but since you and your firm are practically a subsidiary of Ewing Laboratories, I think we can make an exception."

I made a zipping motion across my mouth. "My lips are sealed."

A corner of Debra's mouth went up almost imperceptibly, and her former ebullience melded into a predatory stare. She turned and keyed in her code, all the while blocking my view with her body.

We stepped through the doorway and into a high-tech lab whose sheer size was soul-bruising, spanning at least two-hundred feet across and twice as deep. Glass-walled offices ringed the open workstation area, and toward the back I could see long rows of flat black supercomputers, their LEDs winking furiously. The fluorescent hum was gone, but in its place was the familiar drone of a HVAC system. I had photographed in rooms like this at Ewing Labs, and I remembered why I always brought a sweater to those shoots.

"Nice temperature," I said.

"You can't beat it when it's a hundred out." Debra motioned to the left. "My office is this way."

Several technicians looked up from their low-rise cubical workstations and gave me the once-over. An Indian guy actually smiled as we walked by.

"Ms. Lao?" A large man in a lab coat and casual business wear walked up. He was bald with a close-cropped beard, his skin lightly speckled with acne scars. His eyes went to me, and I had a weird sensation of déjà vu.

"Yes, Alex?"

The man whispered something into Debra's ear.

"Right," she said, "let me know when they're ready." She turned to me. "Alex Popprov, this is a friend, Dillon Bradford. His company does all the advertising for Ewing Laboratories."

Popprov barely revealed a smile. "Hello." His voice was deep and accented. He had cut off the "h," and it came out more like 'ello. He turned and walked into the workstation area.

"Brilliant researcher. A little shy," Debra said. "We stole him from the Russians."

Listening in was subject to proximity. The closer you were, the better the reception, so to speak. Popprov was walking quickly away, and I wanted to get a good listen. "I'd love to see what he's working on." Debra said something as I stepped away, but I didn't acknowledge her.

"Hi there," I said to his back. "What are you working on?"

Popprov stopped and turned. His expression went cold. I looked into his eyes, but his thoughts were in Russian. I couldn't make anything out, but the inflection of his thinking was definitely angry. A sharp pain twinged through my skull, but I didn't flinch.

"Dillon." Debra marched up, smiling but clearly annoyed. She was slipping something into a pocket. "Alex doesn't speak much English." He and Debra exchanged some Russian, and I couldn't help but think they were talking about me. The fact that Popprov's eyes darted between Debra and me might have been the giveaway, or maybe it was that whenever I was around people who spoke another language, I always assumed the worst. Debra's Russian sounded fluent. She turned to me. "My office is this way. Shall we?"

We rounded the outer edge of the lab area. It extended farther than I thought, almost half of it devoted to the array of supercomputers, which explained the cool room floor.

"Your Russian sounds perfect," I remarked.

"I minored in it."

We walked past several of the cubicles, and I snuck a listen with some of the technicians. All of them were engaged in their work, and most were thinking in their native language. I wasn't getting anything useful. "Why do you need so many Crays?" I recognized them from a photo shoot I had done a few years back.

"We do a lot of our testing in simulation," Debra said. One of the supercomputer's doors was open, and a technician, probably just out of school, had a large circuit board filleted on a brushed metal tool cart. "It's more cost effective to do it that way. You know Red. He likes to save his money."

"Do you ever get into nanotechnology?" I asked.

Debra threw me a surprised sideways glance. "You've done your research. How did you know about that?"

"Educated guess. Seems to be the new frontier, or so I've read."

"It shows great promise, but I'm afraid it's off in the future."

As we strolled past the Cray clusters, I could tell my comment about nanotechnology had unsettled Debra, because she kept looking around like we were being watched.

Debra's office was one of several that semi-circled the back workstation area. It had no windows and was smaller than I had expected. It continued the sterile white theme, but Debra had added a woman's touch. That is, if the woman's an anal-retentive neat freak. It was elegantly lit with a simple desk lamp and an up-light strategically placed behind a monolithic single-stalk cactus. Even Debra's PowerBook was perfectly positioned on her modern glass-and-chrome desk. Only the small bookcase, crammed with technical binders and reference books, gave any indication that a human actually worked there. But it was the Dirk Nowitzki bobblehead on top of the bookshelf that caught my eye.

"Are you a fan?" I asked, pointing.

"I love the Mavericks." This was the first time Debra had shown any real emotion.

"We'll have to go sometime. A friend of mine has season tickets."

"That's okay. Chris is a good friend of Mark Cuban."

Figured. Debra and I sat on the white leather Barcelona couch that dominated the wall across from her desk. Our knees bumped together, and I had that weird déjà vu feeling again.

"You're still upset about your blackout, aren't you?" she asked, settling in.

"I thought we couldn't listen in to each other's thoughts," I joked.

Debra smiled. "So, Dillon, did you ever go see a doctor?"

"Yes."

"What did he say?"

"I didn't talk to him about the blackout."

Debra's face went blank. "Really? Then what did you see him about?"

"Seems I've had some things done to me. Right here." I pulled my shirt collar away and exposed the marks.

Debra slowly rested her arm on the back of the couch. "What kind of things?"

"At first I thought they were insect bites." I studied Debra's face for any reaction. Her left eyebrow quivered and her posture stiffened. I wasn't kidding when I told Cyndi that I was attuned to reading body language. It came with the territory.

"How did you discover these?" she pressed.

"Kadin noticed them first. One was infected, so I had a doctor friend of mine look at it. You remember Marcus, from the happy hour you and Chris came to?"

Debra slowly nodded.

"He thinks they're made from a sophisticated IV." I was wagging it, hoping to spark a reaction.

Debra shifted and slid one leg under the other. "My God, Dillon, that's disturbing."

"I know. But the odd thing is, I didn't have these marks before I met with you Friday night. Then on Saturday morning, I had them."

Debra stared blankly. "Where did you go after you met with me?"

"Like I said back at your condo, I don't remember meeting you or any of it. I woke up the next morning in my garage."

"Maybe you got jumped walking to your car."

"I thought you said that you walked me to my car."

Debra's eyebrow quivered again. "I did? Right, yes. I remember now. You were pretty drunk."

"See, that's another part I don't understand. If I was so drunk, why'd you let me drive home?"

Debra, seemingly unruffled by my accusation, continued to stare. "What are you saying?"

"Well, I don't know, but if you were drunk enough to be on the verge of passing out, I would have called you a cab or driven you home. That's what friends do, right?"

Debra sat forward and tucked a lock of hair behind an ear. "Hmm," she said, nodding. "That's very interesting, Dillon." Her eyes shifted focus to something over my shoulder.

I twisted and glanced at the doorway. The smiling Indian guy walked by, pushing a cart loaded with racks of yellow-labeled vials. He walked with his left foot turned out almost 90 degrees. When I turned back, Debra was standing over me, her arms folded again.

"Dillon, Dillon," she said, shaking her head.

"Debra, *Debra?*"

Her attention went to the doorway again.

Turning, I found Popprov standing there. His shoulders took up almost the width of the frame. "They're ready," he said in clipped English.

Debra fixed her attention back on me. "Good."

I tried to listen in on Popprov, but now all I heard was hissing, like air escaping from a cut tire. The big Russian stepped into the office and clasped his hands behind his back. He looked down over his thin nose, and suddenly I had a weird phantom feeling, like my ankle had been grabbed.

"Come with me," he said.

My attention vacillated between Debra and Popprov. "What's going on?" I finally demanded.

"Dillon," Debra smiled politely, "let's not make this difficult."

Popprov made a casual "get up" gesture with one hand, but it was his other that worried me. It was clenched so tightly into a fist that it looked more like a weapon than an appendage.

I followed Debra out of her office. Popprov fell in behind, and we all marched past the Crays to a row of three glass-walled conference rooms that dominated the far side of the lab. The first two were unoccupied and dimly lit, but three men were waiting in the third. Two of them wore simple black business suits, complete with white button downs and solid ties. The other man was dressed like a lab technician and was older than anyone I had seen so far. His beard was ragged and dusted with grey. His skin was weathered like so many of the older tennis members at Toby's academy. Debra opened the door for me. This didn't look good. I reached up to hold the door. My hand was shaking.

"Is anybody going to tell me what's going on?" I asked, stepping in. Popprov stayed outside. Two technicians walked up and each took a position on one side of the door. Popprov spoke to them briefly, and then walked back into the sea of workstations.

The dark-suited men were sitting behind a large beech wood conference table. They stood as we entered. Their expressions were as austere as their fashion. A sharp, but fleeting, dagger of pain shot behind my right eye. Debra joined the older lab technician.

I stood alone on one side of the table, my back to the wall of glass and the expanse of the lab beyond. I rubbed my temple.

"Hello, Mr. Bradford," the technician said. "It's an honor to meet you."

An honor? The two suits sat almost in sync. The younger one opened a file folder, while the older one settled into his chair and unbuttoned his coat.

I grabbed the back of a conference chair with both hands and threw a hard stare at Debra. "What's going on here?"

"Mr. Bradford." The technician gestured. "Please sit down." It wasn't a request.

A dark shadow crossed the wall behind Debra and washed over everything. I turned and caught the last stretch of the glass wall as it turned an opaque grey. The overhead lights brightened slightly.

Suddenly I felt trapped. The panic that had been creeping into my system since Debra's office now became a torrent. Debra picked up on it; she leaned onto the table and offered a reassuring smile.

"Dillon, please," she said. "We have something very important to tell—"

"Sit down, Bradford," the suit reading the folder said sternly. He looked up and I saw the disdain settling behind his eyes. "Your life is about to be seriously bitch-slapped."

11. Can I ask you a question?

I sat, almost by reflex. Debra's expression was impassive. I glanced back at the suit who had given the order and tried to listen in, but the hissing was now static, like an old TV caught between channels. The pain struck again, and I winced. The younger suit smiled slightly as he studied the contents of his folder.

"I'm sorry," the technician said. "We're impeding your brain's cross-neuro synaptic protocol."

My confusion must have shown because the younger suit gave an affected sigh. "Your *gift*, Bradford," he said.

"You can do that?" I asked.

"Welcome to being human."

To lift a term from my old college roommate, I had just "crossed over." I looked at Debra. "What's going on? What do you people want?"

She met my gaze with trepidation. "I'll let Robert take the lead here."

"Mr. Bradford, let me introduce myself. My name is Dr. Robert Morgan. These gentlemen are Agent Harris," the suit reading the file folder nodded, "and Agent Stiles." The older suit flashed a clipped smile.

"So what are you two," I asked, "the Men in Black?"

"They're with a division of the National Security Agency," Morgan said.

"You run this operation, don't you?" I asked Harris.

"In a sense." Harris leaned back in his chair. "Look, Bradford, here's the lay of the land. We've known about—"

"Who's we? The whole government?"

"No, just us. Now, we've known about your kind for some time—"

"How long?"

"God, Bradford, I don't know. 10 years, tops." Harris was significantly younger than Stiles. Probably the protégé.

"Hey, it's my life that's about to be *bitch*-slapped. If I want to know something, I'm going to ask."

"And you should," Debra said.

This brought a stern glance from Harris.

"He deserves it," she said.

"Why do I deserve it?"

"Because we've been doing things to you without your knowledge." There was a slight hint of contrition in Morgan's voice.

"So you're the ones." Finally, some answers.

"Not completely." Harris went on to explain that a division of the NSA called the Special Activities Center had been "working" on civilians who had special powers of the mind, specifically telepathy. It was ironic, I thought, that of all of the wacky crap that had been depicted in movies, the only truly credible power that had ever come forward was our ability to listen in. He didn't elaborate on what "working" meant, but I had a bad feeling they were about to start on me.

"So you're more like Scully and Mulder," I said.

"I liked your other analogy better." Harris leaned onto the table. "We're with the Signals Intelligence Directorate, which is the unit devoted to foreign intelligence gathering. Over the last three years we've been tagging certain individuals who have exceptional power and range—"

"Am I one of them?"

Harris nodded. "ELT was formed to develop pharmaceutical enhancement technology. Because of Ewing's background with the military and their work in biomedical – plus the fact that Mr. Hampton is a decorated Marine and Washington insider – it was a natural fit. Dr. Lao is the lead researcher on the project. She was embedded into Ewing's biotech division—"

"That's not all she's been imbedded in." I loaded the statement with a heavy dose of contempt. Debra's eyes went to her folder.

"True." Harris turned to Debra. "With all due respect, doctor."

Debra barely acknowledged Harris's lame consideration.

"So tell me, Dr. Lao, what was the other night?" I didn't hide my scorn. "Were you just *doing* your job?"

"We call it softening, Bradford," Harris said. "I haven't read her report yet, but yes … she was doing her job. And when it comes to serving her country, I've found Dr. Lao to be one of the best." Harris started to pat Debra's hand, but she pulled it away and folded her arms.

"So then what *did* happen the other night?"

"Your first treatment," Harris said, matter-of-factly.

I had now moved beyond panic to reside somewhere between numb acceptance and resigned fate. "Did you know I had another blackout? I ended up in the hospital." I tried to sound tough, but it didn't come out that way.

"You didn't respond well to the treatment." Debra's eye contact was hesitant, at best.

"You had a seizure," Harris said. "After we got you stabilized—"

"What do you mean you got me stabilized?"

Harris motioned for me to look over my right shoulder. I turned and saw through the darkened glass two technicians standing and talking to each other. The guy on the right seemed vaguely familiar. He looked up from his clipboard and acknowledged me with a slight grin. The angled gap between his two front teeth sent a shiver through me.

I slowly turned back. "He's the guy with the white trash girlfriend ... from the gas station?"

Harris smiled. "I'll tell Monica you think she's attractive."

"I thought the EMTs took me to Baylor."

"They did, after we got you stabilized. Someone else had called them in—"

"So you let the paramedics dump me at the nearest emergency room?"

"Dump is a strong word. We were hoping you'd wake up and not recall anything. The drug we gave you inhibits short-term memory."

"What are you doing to me?"

"We're attempting to alter your insular cortex's ability with neuro-psychotropic enhancers," Morgan said.

"The green stuff?" I asked without thinking.

Morgan and Harris exchange puzzled looks.

"Marcus," Debra said, more to herself.

"Who's Marcus?" Morgan snapped.

"He's the brain surgeon with the ability," Harris said. "He's part of their happy hour group."

"He did an MRI on me the other day," I said. "He thinks we have the ability to intercept the neurotransmitters that leap between neurons. The area where our gift is shows up on an MRI as a green mass. Mine has enlarged from the last

MRI he took five years ago."

"Actually, we believe that you're listening in on the electrical waves that leap between the neurons," Morgan said. "It's similar to what an EEG does."

"Why didn't you just approach me, instead of all this spy crap?"

"Based on your psych profile," Morgan said, "we didn't think you'd be receptive to an official advance."

"So you sent Mata Hari here to, what did you call it?"

"Soften." Shame edged Debra's voice.

I turned my attention to Harris. "So what are you trying to do? Make me into some kind of superhero?"

The smirk on Harris's face wasn't because he got my joke. He slowly closed the folder he'd been studying. The curl of his upper lip exposed a rough scar just under his right eye. "Have you ever seen a man die from electro-shock torture?" he asked.

"No."

"I have. There are brave men and women all over this world who could use your gift to—"

I had had enough. I pushed back and stood, palms hard down on the table. "I'm done here." I looked at Morgan. "You can't keep me against my will, and you can't do the shit you're doing. I have rights, and I'm going to exercise one right now." I pulled out my cell and speed-dialed my lawyer. No goddamn service.

A cell phone slid across the table and stopped in front of me.

"Use mine." The suit named Stiles was leaning across the table, arm outstretched. He relaxed into his chair, a little amused by my declaration.

I began to reach for his cell, but he stopped me short.

"Go ahead," he said. "Call your lawyers. Explain what's happening. And don't forget to mention the mind reading part. I bet *that* will get them excited."

I sat back down and contemplated the striations in the table's beech veneer.

Who was I kidding? I couldn't go up against the nation's most powerful and secretive branch. What would I tell our lawyers? Hey boys, I'm being blackmailed by the NSA because they want to do secret experiments on me, since I can hear the thoughts of anyone within 40 feet. Jesus. This group had me by the cojones. They had just been waiting for me to realize it.

I looked up at Stiles. "I'm fucked, right?"

Stiles suppressed his grin. "I wouldn't say fucked, Dillon." He was the good cop. His salt and pepper hair reminded me of my adoptive dad's. "But we are in a situation that is uncomfortable for both parties. To answer your question, yes, we are trying to make you into a superhero. Hopefully, one of the most intuitive and powerful techlepath's ever."

"Tech-le-what?"

"Technologically enhanced telepathic human," Morgan said.

The '70s sci-fi movie Scanners popped into my head, but the cheesy images of people's heads exploding gave way to the detail of the tech from my MRI.

"Shit," I said to myself. "What you're doing ..." I looked at Morgan, then Stiles, "does it have anything to do with nanotechnology?"

The room grew oddly quiet; I thought I heard the hum from the overheads go up an octave.

Morgan leaned onto the table. "Why?"

"When Marcus did the MRI, he enlarged a section of it."

If the worry lines on Debra's forehead were any indication, her concern had just deepened. "And?" she asked.

"There was a dark spot in the middle of the green area. It was symmetrical."

Morgan slowly leaned back in his chair. The look on his face said it all.

Harris turned to Stiles. "They've beaten us."

Stiles seemed unfazed by this revelation.

"Would someone please tell me what's going on?" A tremor moved through my right hand.

"Well," Stiles said, "it appears that the game has changed."

"It hasn't changed, sir," Harris said, facing his mentor. "It's over."

"Don't be so dramatic, Bill. They haven't decoded his receptors yet."

"Let's hope not–"

"Hey guys, mind keeping me in the loop here?" All four heads turned in my direction. "I have a question."

"Yes?" Stiles asked.

"You said the other night was my first treatment. That can't be right."

Stiles's eyes went to Harris, then me.

"There's an another IV spot." I pointed to my neck. "Right next to yours."

"Right." For the first time, Stiles looked slightly uncomfortable. "We know about it." He flashed a casual smile and stood. "I need a break." He looked down at Debra. "Why don't you fill him in?"

Debra's eyes flared around her dark pupils. Before she could protest, Stiles and Harris were halfway to the door.

"I think I'll join you," Morgan said and fell in behind them.

I watched the three amigos march out, then turned to Debra and gave her my best *What the hell?* look.

Debra shook her head and let out a resigned sigh. She came around the table and sat in the chair next to me. I looked into her eyes. Still the static. The look on her face almost bordered on regret.

"What is Stiles saying? What's going on?"

"Dillon, let me put this in terms you can–"

"Can I ask you something?"

Her eyebrows arched. "Of course."

"I just have to know ... Why you?"

Debra's bottom lip quivered, and I thought she was going to lose it right then. But she tightened up and took a breath. "I joined the NSA to serve our country and save lives. My brother–" Her lip started quivering again.

I was having a hard time squelching this newfound sympathy for her. "What is it, Debra?"

"He was killed ... in Afghanistan."

"It's okay," I said. "For some dumb reason I'm not that pissed at you."

"Oh, Dillon, I'm so sorry."

"Look, what's done is—"

"No, hear me out. My brother was tortured to death." Debra swallowed back her emotion. "I saw the recon photos. When the Taliban had finished with him, they could only identify him through dental records. When Stiles approached me about joining his group, I was filled with hatred. I would've done anything to get back at whoever had killed Terry. What it did to my parents was more than I could bear." Debra had been staring off into a corner. She looked back. "I never wanted to hurt you, Dillon. Sometimes my job requires me to do things I'm not proud of. I thought we would be able to test at a distance."

"Debra, what's being done to me? I want to know everything."

"We've tagged nearly three hundred people in the U.S. who have what you call 'the gift.' But no one's come close to your strength level. Your stats are off the charts. Once we located you—"

"How did you do that?"

"Your cell phone."

"How?"

"We discovered that certain cellular bandwidths merged with our kind's NTP waves, and yours were well above the typical strength range."

I didn't even want to know what an NTP wave was. "You used GPS, didn't you?"

"Yes. It was pure luck that you lived so close to our labs, and even crazier that Ewing Laboratories was one of your clients. Once we had worked up a psych profile, it was concluded that the best way to 'get to you' was through your patterns with the women you dated. Since you were already in a relationship, I got to you through Chris."

"Through Chris?"

She nodded. "He was easy to approach."

"Probably a bar."

"Actually, his gym."

"How long did you all study me?"

"About three months."

A wave of unease washed over me with the realization I had been under surveillance for so long. "I hate to ask, but what's my 'pattern'?"

"You're a Type Six."

"And that is...?"

She grinned slightly. "Better than a Type Seven. Basically, you like flawed women you can rescue, but they have to engage you. Usually they're smart. Pretty in a mysterious way. And it's good if they're aggressive. You like to be led around, but not dominated...."

I put a hand up. "Okay, I get the picture. So you discovered me and knew that I liked mysterious women. So why secretly inject this stuff into me? I don't get it."

"During the time we were profiling you, my team was working on the last stages of development for the enhancers. We created one that we thought was ready for clinical trials, but Stiles didn't want to take the time to do animal testing. He wanted to go right into human testing. Specifically, you."

"Why didn't you just kidnap me or something? Why the whole seduction business?"

"Harris felt that by going 'quiet,' as he calls it, there would be less chance of leakage."

"What's that?"

"It's when a subject becomes aware of the project. That, according to Harris, opens up a whole host of legal issues and often compromises the outcome."

"And they chose you, right?"

"Chose isn't the word I would use."

I sensed that Debra hadn't been forced, but maybe strongly coerced into seducing me. The story behind that would have to wait for another conversation. Usually, my inner horn-dog would've been dying to know if we had had sex, but for some reason I wasn't that interested. "Well, it's pretty obvious why they chose you. I'm a sucker for smart and gorgeous."

Debra shied.

"So what are these enhancers?" I asked. "Are they dangerous?"

"Dillon, we're trying to enhance your insular cortex's ability to listen in with an experimental neuro-psychotropic drug and biomimetics."

"Is it dangerous?"

"We don't think so."

The word think put me on edge. I thought about asking what neuro-psychotropic meant, but there was a part of me that didn't want to know. Besides, it was too late anyway. "So what are the results from the testing? I don't think I can listen in any better than I could before."

"It's too early to tell, plus there are two more treatments."

"Yeah, what did Stiles mean when he said you knew about the other IV point? That's yours, right?"

Debra sat back and folded her arms. "When we learned that you had discovered our IV incision, we hoped that you would think it was an insect bite. But then you saw a doctor, and we had to change our strategy."

"Right, Kadin noticed it. But what I want to know is, what is this other one, next to yours. You can't see it unless you have on loupes—"

"Dillon, there's, um, another group."

A stab of icy fear shot through me. "There's another *group*?"

Debra offered a half-hearted nod.

This had now moved into all-out, batshit crazy. "What are you taking about?"

"It's complicated. For about six months, we've been aware of a 'rival group,' for lack of a better term. They're what Harris calls a sleeper cell, maybe based in one of the ex-Soviet states. He thinks it's Kazakhstan, but they haven't pin-pointed their location yet. They're basically a mirror of us, but they have several former Soviet scientists who have been ahead of the techlepathic curve for some time now. We suspected they had gotten to you, but we didn't know for sure, until now."

It all came together. "The nanotechnology."

"Yes," Debra said.

It was painfully apparent that my life – my former life – had come to an end. Whatever was in me, my situation was certainly going to get worse before it got better. "Who are they? How did they get to me?"

Debra looked off again, as if the answer rested somewhere in the corner of the conference room. "Can I ask you a question?" she finally said, looking back.

"Of course."

"How well do you know Kadin?"

12. Next step.

A memory of my first date with Kadin rushed across my mind. Her hair had been a little shorter, styled in adorable curls. They bounced slightly when she walked. (A month later, she had straightened it, saying she was bored with the retro look.) The dress she wore revealed just a hint of her athletic body. She had looked so innocent, so pretty. I had taken her to my favorite restaurant – a little French bistro tucked away on lower Greenville Avenue – where we talked and laughed and connected like I had never done with any other woman. I remembered thinking right then that Kadin might be the one. God, she had been so beautiful....

"Dillon, are you okay?"

I realized I had been staring at my reflection in the chrome water pitcher sitting on the credenza against the wall. "Please tell me you're kidding."

"I wish I were," Debra said.

"But she's the one who pointed out the incisions. This doesn't make sense."

"Maybe they decided to stop our work by exposing us to you?"

"Why would they do that?"

"Buy some time? Let us take the blame? It definitely deflects attention away from them and what they put into you. I don't know, Dillon. We hadn't factored this into our planning."

I found it hard to believe that Kadin was some kind of foreign agent who had suckered me in. As I thought about it, though, Debra's logic actually made sense. A surge of anger welled, because if all this were true, it meant that Kadin – and our relationship – had been a sham. "What is she?" I demanded.

"We don't know for sure. Harris thinks she's a paid operative. Trained for this one operation. Fluent in just enough English. Phony degree. Strategically planted. If we can profile you, others can."

Kadin rarely talked about her past, and her accent was thicker after she was drinking or mad. She said she had been born in Poland. Now that I thought about it, her family's story was a little idealistic. I remembered a CNN segment that profiled young European women who were kidnapped and sold into sexual slavery. I flashed on the rough scar across Kadin's thigh. "Think she's a prostitute?"

Debra shrugged. "Maybe earlier on. The former Eastern Bloc is littered with girls who would do anything to escape their situation. She could be one of the smarter ones. It's hard to say."

I didn't know what to think. It felt like someone had torn my guts out. "I-I don't believe this."

Debra reached across the table and pulled her file folder over. She opened it and leafed through its contents until she came to a paper-clipped collection of five-by-three photographs. She sifted through the stack, removed one, and slowly slid it toward me. Its time code labeled it five months ago. There were faded case and file numbers imprinted in the upper left corner of an image of Kadin on a crowded wintry street, definitely not Dallas. Shot through the windshield of a small car, much of the image was soft, but Kadin and the man she was talking to were in focus. He was older and handsome in a chiseled, military sort of way. It looked like his thick goatee has flecks of snow on it.

"What's this?" I dreaded the answer.

"These were taken by a team out of our Frankfurt bureau," Debra said, "in Warsaw, about five months ago. We believe Kadin reports to this man."

Kadin had said she'd gone home to see her parents. "Let me see those."

There were about a dozen prints, all documenting their sidewalk conversation. Kadin looked oddly rougher. Her clothes were drab and cheap. As I flipped through the stack it felt like each image was tearing off piece of my soul. The last file pic was of her hugging and kissing the man on the cheek.

"I'm so sorry, Dillon."

I slowly handed the photos back and felt like a part of me had died.

Debra returned them to the file, closed the folder, and pushed it away. I was at a loss for words. Kadin hadn't been like the other women that had flared in and out of my life. For one thing, she had the gift, which had meant a lot, or so I thought. When you know what your lover is thinking, there's no mystery to the relationship. I had mystery with Kadin and had come to love that about us. A lump swelled in my throat, but I swallowed it down. My old life was over, and I had better get on board with Debra and the NSA if I wanted to have any chance of making it through this nightmare. My chest felt tight, but only one question came to mind. "What's next?"

The door to the conference room opened, and Harris marched in. He came up behind Debra and grasped the back of her chair with both hands.

"Did you tell him?" His attention darted between the top of her head and me.

She didn't bother to look back. "Yes."

"How're you holding up?" he asked me.

I was barely keeping it together. "Okay, considering."

"Don't let it get to you. I know smarter men who've been duped. Nothing to be ashamed of. These girls know their stuff. They train for it. So ... what do you think?"

As if I had an option? "Sure," I said, bluntly, "I'll be your superhero."

For a split-second it seemed Harris didn't believe me, but then a feral grin spread across his face. "You surprise me, Bradford. I didn't think you had it in you."

"What's our next step?"

"Overachiever. I like that." He looked down at Debra. "You told him everything?"

"Yes," she said, frustrated.

"Well not everything, right?" Harris glanced at his watch. "No time like the present." His eyes locked onto mine. "Want to find out what they've done to you?"

"Do I have a choice?" I asked.

"Not in this lifetime."

Near the lab was a small medical facility. I followed Harris and Debra through a large common room with two operating bays and a workstation attached. We rounded a corner and entered what looked like an animal testing facility. Against one wall was a metal shelving unit that held litter-filled plastic containers, about half of which were occupied by white rats. Bright sticky notes labeled the containers Harriet, Tom-Tom, Jasper, etc. Next to the shelving unit was a large wire-framed cage. A lone chimp sat facing a corner, picking his toes. It looked over its shoulder as we passed.

"What's his name?" I asked Debra.

"Sir Michael J."

"That's cruel."

"I know. Someone's bad joke."

"Have you tested on him?"

"No." She gave me an eyebrow-raised sideways glance. "And I doubt we will."

"Right," I said. "You can call me Sir Dillon B from now on."

We walked into another brightly lit common area and entered a room with a smaller version of the MRI scanner from the other day. A technician whose lab coat embroidery labeled him *Sanjiv* was waiting. He smiled and gave a slight nod.

"I'm going to bow out here and catch up with you in imaging," Harris said and continued down the hallway.

"I'm glad he's gone," Debra remarked.

"He's the bad cop, right?" I asked.

"Asshole is more accurate."

"Mr. Bradford," Sanjiv motioned to a door across the room, "if you could step in there and remove your clothes, but not your underwear. There's a gown hanging on the back of the door. When you're ready, come out and we'll start."

"I might need some help tying my gown," I said to Debra.

She shook her head. "Maybe you are a Type 7."

.   .   .

The imaging room had a computer workstation with a large Samsung HD monitor. The low ceiling and dim lights created a somber scene. Sanjiv was seated in front of the monitor at a conspicuously simple console. The three amigos were semi-circled around him. Debra retreated to a corner, reviewing something on a small tablet. None of the guys took notice of me when I entered. Debra raised her attention from her work and gave me a *what's up?* tilt of the chin. On the screen, images that looked essentially the same as Marcus's

MRI images were flying out from a folder and arranging themselves in neat rows. Their resolution was amazing. The green area behind my right eye was now fully articulated, and after all the images were assembled, Sanjiv clicked through some dialogue boxes and merged them into a 3-D representation of my head. As he rotated it through different axes, we could see the green blob's complete mass from every angle.

"It hasn't tentacled," Morgan remarked.

"That's good." Harris tapped Sanjiv's shoulder. "Let's find the tech."

Sanjiv clicked through more dialogue boxes until the green blob became isolated.

"Zoom in," Morgan ordered.

The image enlarged, and we began moving into the center of it. Small dark brown and red masses move past us.

"This is an amazing application," I said.

"A little gift from our friends at Langley." Harris bent closer to the screen.

The imaging drilled deep into the green blob until a black spot grew in the center. At first it seemed like we were zooming in on the Pentagon, but as we closed, it was revealed as a cluster of individual Pentagons, connected by several branches.

"This thing is inside my brain?" I was stunned. The zooming stopped when the Pentagon cluster filled the screen. The surfaces were smooth for the most part, but there were several indentations on some of the larger sections. "How big is this?"

Sanjiv referenced something on the screen. "About 100 times the size of a cold virus."

Harris and Morgan were leaning on the counter, their faces inches from the image.

"Jesus Christ, this tech is complex," Harris said. "I've never seen anything like it."

Just when I thought my life couldn't get any stranger. "That's bad, right?"
I leaned in for a better view. Debra came beside me. Sanjiv rotated the image,
and we could see its true depth. It now looked like a dark grey space station
hanging in fresh guacamole, and I remembered an article that said you could
line up 20,000 nanobots across the head of a pin. I felt a twinge inside my skull
and winced.

Debra put a hand to my shoulder. "Are you all right?"

"I think so. Just a little spike."

"You saw what was in your brain, and your mind reacted," Sanjiv remarked.
"Very common response."

Common? Doubtful. I looked at Morgan. "Do you know what this thing is?"

Morgan's silence was not reassuring. He straightened, his eyes still fixed on
the screen. "That's the next step."

13. Tired of rules.

I hadn't been inside a Buster's restaurant since college, and it was a little disconcerting to find that not much had changed. According to Debra, it was the only game in town after 10 p.m.

"Come here often?" I asked as we settled into our red vinyl booth.

"Too often." Debra made a face.

"What?"

"I just sat in something wet."

"Don't look," I urged.

I waded through the extensive menu while Debra attacked the booth with her napkin. Buster's represented everything wrong with the American diet. Scanning the selections, I was amazed by the myriad permutations of bacon.

The menu even had a special insert highlighting, for a limited time only, Baconpalooza.

"So what's good here?" I asked.

"Breakfast." Debra hadn't even opened her menu.

"So tell me something."

"What?"

"Aren't you afraid that I might try and make a run for it?"

"Where would you go?"

"What do you mean?"

Debra removed what looked like a BlackBerry from her purse, held it up, and tapped the side of her head.

"Right. My own personal leash."

"Something like that." She stowed the tracking device.

A pasty, dark-haired, eyebrow-pierced waitress bounded over and flipped open a small spiral notepad. "Hi, folks. Know what you want?" She appeared all of 16. Her uniform was a size too big.

Debra ordered scrambled eggs, burnt bacon, and black coffee. I ordered the same, then watched our waitress disappear around a booth stuffed with a family of candidates for a reality weight-loss show.

"I'm going to have to yank that girl's Goth card." I took a sip of water and tasted all the rural goodness of East Texas.

"Why's that?"

"She's way too bubbly."

Debra shrugged disinterestedly. Quiet since the imaging room, she had offered only a few words of encouragement and hadn't said a thing on the ride to the restaurant. She seemed intimidated by Harris and Stiles, which aroused my curiosity.

"How long have you been working with the Men in Black?" I asked.

I hadn't noticed before, but when she smiled, her dark eyes creased into endearing slits, and faint dimples appeared in the center of her cheeks. "Two years," she said.

"I couldn't help but sense that you're, ah–" I stopped myself, realizing that what I was about to say could be taken wrongly.

"Frustrated with my situation?"

"Well, yeah."

"I shouldn't speak out of turn. Protocol, you know."

"And who am I going to blab to?"

Debra nodded. "Morgan's all right. A company man. It's Harris who's difficult."

"Why's that?"

"Nothing's ever good enough or fast enough, and he guards his agenda and enjoys keeping us in the dark."

"About everything?"

"No. But too often. He never mentions who their superior is. And we never know the budget, which is good and bad."

"Wouldn't you know? You work for the same organization."

"Technically, I'm what they call a permalancer. Permanent free-lance, whatever that means. When the NSA needs someone with a specialized skill, it fast-tracks them into the organization. Still, I'm on a need-to-know basis."

"So you aren't packing heat?"

"NSA agents don't carry a sidearm. We don't even have the power to arrest. Some field agents do, but those are special situations. I don't think Harris does. I don't know about Stiles. I hate guns, personally."

"So what's the deal with the budget?" I asked. "Doesn't the NSA have deep pockets?"

"Depends. Certain projects are more high-level than others."

"Where's this one rank?"

Debra sighed and turned her palms up. "Who knows? I can't get a handle on it. One day we have all the funding in the world, the next, zilch."

"Is this one even on the books?"

"It's on somebody's books."

"What about Stiles?"

"He's the decision maker. Harris won't do anything unless it goes through Stiles."

"I've worked on government projects before, and they can be very weird. Money is always an issue." Like a branding project even remotely compared to an NSA operation. "Maybe the thing with their boss has to do with the fact that this project is clandestine."

Debra, in the middle of taking a drink of water, swallowed a laugh. "Dillon, we're the NSA. Everything we do is clandestine."

The waitress appeared with our food. I had forgotten how Buster's compartmentalized their meals. Even the bacon, which had been burnt to perfection, rated its own separate dish. I gestured, "Ah, the carcinogenpalooza plate."

"I never liked bacon until I came to Texas." Debra began spreading strawberry jam across her limp toast. "All-organic was my mantra."

"Why the change?"

"Oh, I still eat healthy." She leaned forward and glanced around as if the patrons actually would care what she had to say. "But this stuff is really good, know what I mean?"

I wanted to ask about Chris's involvement, but she grew quiet while she ate methodically in order of color. Something was occupying her thoughts. I wondered what it might be. Then it struck me.

"Can I ask you a personal question?"

Debra looked up mid-chew. "Why do I eat by colors?"

"No, but that is something I was wondering about."

"I've done it since I was a kid. My mom thinks it's because I'm OCD."

"Are you?"

Debra polished off the last of her eggs. "Probably. So what did you want to ask me?"

"Are you embarrassed about what you had to do? With me, I mean."

Debra stopped cutting into her hash browns and stared.

"Listen, if the question makes you uncomfortable–"

"What do you remember?"

"When?"

"After happy hour at your condo."

I hadn't recovered any more memories from that night. "Not much, why?"

Debra set her fork aside and slowly wiped her mouth. "I won't lie to you. I was nervous. I'd read your file and spoke to the profiler at length about how to approach you. I even asked what kind of techniques to use when we were alone. There's a whole set of seduction tactics."

"Oldest trick in the book," I said to myself.

"Excuse me?"

"A honey pot."

She nodded. "But you know, after I met you, especially after we talked at Stage Left, I changed my mind. Somewhat."

"How's that?"

"I felt sorry for you."

Great, a pity fuck. "Really?"

"I think you use sex like some people use drugs. You're killing the pain of growing up an orphan. I read your background. Your adoptive dad sounds like a real jerk." She started eating again.

Her assessment was an understatement. The term was "functioning alcoholic," but it felt more like "raging drunk." He'd only beaten me once, but that was enough to realize that I'd be better off on my own. I don't know how many times he hit my adoptive mom. I left home when I was 16. Debra's answer brought it all back, but not because she had me pegged; it was more the tone in her voice: empathy instead of pity.

"The other night ... did we?..." I hesitated. "You know..."

Debra looked up again, her fork poised. "Have sex?"

"Yeah."

The smirk on her full lips seemed laced with satisfaction. She popped the last of her hash browns into her mouth. We finished our meals in silence. Frankly, I didn't want to know any more about how Debra had "softened me up." I had probably gone too far just asking the question. We tussled a little over the check, but Debra made it clear NSA was picking up the tab.

On the ride back to TR, Debra tried to make conversation, but the events of the day were weighing down on me. She went on about the fact that she had a small apartment set up just off the medical area, and sometimes Sir Michael J kept her awake banging on his cage at all hours of the night. Talking to comfort him had become a routine for her, one she had come to enjoy. I got the feeling that the only real man in her life might be the chimp, which made sense, given her line of work.

There were only a few cars in TR's vast parking lots. Debra said they ran a night shift in one of the buildings, but she didn't know which one. The parking lot around her building was empty, except for the Merc. Debra pulled up to its driver-side door and stopped.

"Thanks for dinner," I said. "Or should I say breakfast?"

She smiled, and the dimples reappeared. "Best grease in Texas."

"I assume I can go home, but you'll want me back tomorrow, right?"

"Bright and early. Eight-o'clock."

"And if I don't?"

Debra patted her purse.

"Right." I opened my door and put a foot out.

"Dillon?"

I glanced back. "Yeah?"

"When you asked me if we had had sex ..."

"Look, Debra ... it doesn't really matter now."

"We didn't."

The car's interior light highlighted only a few surfaces and set Debra's features in soft shadow. She opened her purse, removed the device, and clicked a few numbers. The interior did a little vertigo shift, like I had experienced in her kitchen. But before I could react, it was gone. Debra leaned onto the center console, and our eyes met. The static had dissipated.

This is what it was like the other night, she said into my mind. *We didn't speak a word. We just ... thought.*

No one had ever spoken directly to me before, except for that bum. Debra's voice sounded almost melodic, and her faint smile tugged at my emotions.

"How can you–?"

Debra pressed a finger to my lips. *Don't talk. Think.* She lightly dragged her finger down my lower lip.

How can you do that? My eyes went to her purse. *What is that thing?* I felt my lips moving.

A neurosynaptic impeder. It blocks our ability within a fifty-foot radius. It's a miniature version of what Stiles was using on us in the conference room. Her attention moved to her building's entrance. *I'm tired of rules.*

I had never noticed the bump in the bridge of her nose, the only imperfection in an otherwise flawless profile. Despite all that she had done to me, I couldn't help but like Debra. I had the sense that, like me, her life had been radically changed, and she still was struggling to make sense of it all. Just what her change had been, I didn't know. I meant to ask her at dinner where she had she grown up and how she handled being able to hear other people's thoughts. Maybe I had asked already at Stage Left. *God, I wish I could remember what happened that night!*

Debra leaned over the console between the seats. Her face was a few inches from mine. "You were a gentleman," she said.

14. Don't give up.

The distant sound of metal striking metal jarred me awake. My eyes opened to an unfamiliar ceiling. White acoustic tiles set in a wire framework hung above me like a giant industrial blanket. I remembered. Debra had brought me back to her apartment inside ELT. We sat on the bed and talked into the early morning hours. Supposedly, we had done this before, on the walk to her Dallas condo the night we met at Stage Left. She had been born in Cambodia, and her parents taught high-level mathematics at the Royal University of Phnom Penh. Like me, she became aware of her gift around puberty, but hadn't discovered her ability to communicate to others with the gift until college. She had met a guy who shared some kind of linking capacity with her. After he was killed in a motorcycle accident, she had never found anyone else with whom she could link – until me.

Apparently, I also looked a lot like her late brother. Not so much in the face. More my build and attitude. She used the word cocky, and for the first time in my life, it bothered me. Briefly, when she was answering my question about whether I was a good kisser, it seemed we might pick up where we had left off that fateful night. But Debra's professional guard was firmly in place, not to mention that I lacked my usual burning desire to jump a sexy woman's bones. Maybe it was all the shit I had been through. Maybe I was dead tired. Since going back to Dallas meant I'd only get about three hours sleep, Debra suggested I stay at her apartment. I offered to take one of the chairs, but she rolled her eyes at that. We would share the bed.

I was already drifting when the noise repeated. Debra stirred, then twisted toward me. I could barely make out her eyes in the darkness. I was in my jeans and t-shirt. She had opted for sweat pants and a Nowitzki jersey she kept on hand.

"Sir Michael J requests our presence," I whispered.

She grinned. *You're talking.*

Sorry. I'm not used to this.

A loud crash echoed outside the door. Debra's eyes widened. *He's pissed about something.*

Another crash.

He's going ape, I said.

Very punny. He'll have to deal with it alone tonight. She pulled the sheet over her shoulder. *Get some rest. You have a big day tomorrow.*

■   ■   ■

"Didn't you wear that shirt yesterday?" Harris asked.

I glanced at Debra, who was busy talking with a tech. "I don't think so," I said.

Harris made a face, like this didn't jibe with his recollection of what I had worn.

We were in one of the larger rooms in the medical area, which like the rest of the facility was filled with high-tech equipment and lab technicians. For some reason, the device where they placed me reminded me of the old TV show *The Incredible Hulk*, when Bruce Banner was injected with the stuff that made him go green. It was a chair that articulated out from a large armature, which itself was connected to an even larger machine. The technology here, however, was way beyond anything from the show or movies. The whole room was a labyrinth of brushed steel tubing, multi-colored wiring, matte-white housings and impossibly thin LED monitors. The fact that I was at the center of such an intricate array of technology made me question what was in store for me this morning.

"Are you going to strap me in like Bruce Banner?" I asked no one in particular.

Sanjiv looked up from the main workstation. "Who?"

"The Incredible Hulk." Harris was off to my right on the kind of cold aluminum stool you'd see in a doctor's office. He smiled, but all I could hear was static. What I would give to listen in on that guy's mind.

"Oh," Sanjiv said, "my kids loved that movie."

"Is that what you're hoping for?" I asked Harris.

"If only we could be so lucky," he said. "We have other plans for you, and they're not transforming."

"Too bad. I was kind of hoping to kick some ass."

"The kind of ass-kicking we do is under the radar," Harris said. "You won't be tossing around any tanks."

A gangly, scruffy lab technician holding a metal-and-glass syringe gun approached. Its needle seemed about the length of a framing nail. A memory of being held down by faceless men swept in and lodged itself behind my right eye. The fear and pain hit me with a vicious punch. I grabbed the technician's arm and pushed him away.

Harris came off the stool. "Lao, what's going on?"

Debra rushed to my side. "Dillon, what are you doing?"

"I don't know. I saw that thing." I pointed to the syringe gun. "And I had a memory about it ... a bad one." I rubbed my temple. "Damn, that hurt."

"What's happened?" Harris asked.

"He's experiencing synaptic discharge," Debra said, defensively.

"You said that wouldn't happen."

"Well, I was wrong." She helped me back into the Hulk chair. "I'm sorry, Dillon. That memory is from the other night at my apartment. You're a big guy, and you put up a fight." She began turning down the collar of my shirt. "Please forgive me," she whispered.

Harris stepped closer. "What are you two talking about?"

"She apologized for roughing me up the other night," I said.

"You got fight, Bradford. You'll need it." He sat back down.

The technician with the syringe gun cautiously approached again.

"It's okay," I said, "my eyes aren't going to turn green."

The guy grinned nervously.

"We're going to have to strap your head down," Debra said.

I didn't like the sound of that. The apparatus she unfolded from the large armature looked like something from an optometrist's office. Debra guided my head onto the chin rest and pulled a locking band around my head. It clicked into place with a faint servo hum as it tightened.

"How's that feel?" she asked.

My head was clamped down, and I had to strain my body to stay close enough to the machine so that it wouldn't pop my head off. "Fabulous." I could barely move my mouth. "Nudge me if I fall asleep."

"We're going to inject bionanos that will allow us to monitor the technol-

ogy already in your head." Although Debra tried to sound upbeat, I sensed
the procedure wasn't going to be a cakewalk. She rubbed my shoulder in what
I took as a sincere attempt to comfort me. "The next part is going to sting a
little."

The technician screwed onto the syringe gun's needle an impossibly thin
tube, the kind you'd see hanging from an IV bag. At the end of it was an even
tinier needle.

"Let me guess, that gets stuck into my carotid artery."

"It's just like an IV, and hurts about the same."

"But?"

"After we secure the central venous pressure line, we'll transverse the artery
with a catheter up into the brain. There we'll inject the bionanos—"

I cut her off with a raised hand. "I already know this part. Marcus filled me
in on the details. Let's just get on with it."

Debra nodded, and motioned to the technician.

The IV needle prick wasn't that bad. It was insertion of the catheter that was
the bitch. I gritted down a groan.

"Easy, Dillon," Debra urged, still rubbing. "Just another minute."

I let the groan out.

Harris was just out of my line of sight, but I could hear him suppress a
laugh.

"There." Debra came around to face me. "We're in."

It took a second to catch my breath. "What's next? Suck out my brains?" I
thought I could actually feel the catheter behind my eye. Maybe it was just a
phantom pain.

Debra pulled two spidery arms down, positioning one on either side of my
head. Out of the corner of my vision, I could see a small lens protruding from
the end of each arm. A single yellow cable snaked back up the armature and
disappeared out of my restrained view. The technician pressed two buttons on

the syringe gun's handle, and it began to hum.

"The nanos?" I managed through clenched teeth.

"Yes," Debra said.

"No skull cap with electrodes?"

"These monitor the brain/computer interface," Debra explained as she positioned an arm on the side of my head. "The nanobots we're injecting will attach themselves to the foreign technology. Then we'll be able to track their activity."

"What if they can't?"

"Can't what?"

"Attach."

"Then they'll get as close as they can."

"What if they disrupt the other tech, and something bad starts happening?"

"You ask a lot of questions for a guy in your position," Harris remarked.

The head restraint stopped me from giving him the evil eye. "When I turn into The Hulk, remind me to throw a tank at you."

The technician retracted the catheter back into the syringe gun's long needle, then tossed the gun into a red bio hazard waste can.

"Okay," Debra said, "just stay still while we monitor the nanos' travel."

"Like I'm going anywhere." My lower back was beginning to ache. I tried to inch forward just a bit.

"Dillon, please," Debra scolded. "Don't move."

A wall clock – the kind you might find in an old high school – was within view, and the next five minutes ticked away like I was in a slower reality. A bead of sweat made its way down the side of my face. After a few seconds, I felt another slide from my right armpit and down my ribs.

"I don't feel like I'm getting any–"

"Dillon, hush!"

Five more excruciating minutes passed before someone off to my left gasped. A flush of panic coursed through me.

"What is it?" I tried turning my head.

"Dillon, don't move!"

Before Debra could finish, a maelstrom of voices exploded across my mind. The sheer volume of them made me jerk violently, and I bit my tongue. A tremendous outward pressure caused my head to feel as if it was going to burst. The taste of blood spread through my mouth.

"Jesus Christ, get me out of this thing!" I yelled. "I'm in a billon minds. My head's exploding!"

My vision began to collapse, and the room went soft. Debra's distorted figure appeared in my view. The alarm on her face was frightening.

"Dillon, hold on!" She tried to sound professional, but failed miserably. "We're trying to disconnect you."

What?! Waves of languages and chatter crashed against my mind with convulsive repetition. With each surge, my body lurched and thrashed. Desperate, I tried to pry myself out of the restraint band, to no avail. Debra cradled my head in her hands through the apparatus and caught my eyes in hers.

"Hold on!" She looked away, then back. "We're almost there."

The voraciousness of the pain was overwhelming. Another wave crashed into my consciousness, and I screamed. Blood flecked Debra's face. She leaned forward in a futile attempt to hold me still.

"Come on," she whispered. "Fight!"

The voices became a roaring torrent, and my heart's frantic beating seemed somehow in sync with them. My vision collapsed around Debra's face, then my hearing suddenly vanished. The silence faded to black.

15. Beautiful.

There's something about the sun when it hits your face on a warm day. It's like its rays are your own personnel carrier wave that connects you with the universe. I walked along a trail that gently curved until it disappeared into a grove of tall trees. I kept to the narrow strip of dry dirt that cut a lazy, angular path through the field. It was the park near where I grew up. Suburban Chicago. I slipped into an unhurried cadence. A gentle breeze brushed the tall grass into rhythmic waves, causing the park to take on the appearance of a small lake. The stronger gusts flapped the collar of my plaid shirt against my cheek.

Off in the distance, a thin figure emerged from a grove of trees and jogged down the trail. A woman. Her long hair was sun-bleached gray and flowed with every stride. She wore khaki shorts and a blue work shirt tied into a knot just above her waist. Her skin was dark brown and weathered like the rich women at Toby's tennis academy, and as she approached I could see her athleticism despite her age. I stopped and waited. She slowed to a normal pace, then stopped about three feet away. Dust rose around her old work boots.

"Hello, Dillon." Her voice was light, welcoming, seemingly carried by the breeze.

"Hello," I replied.

Her blue eyes were set above Slavic cheekbones, and her soft crow's feet deepened as she took me in. "You're just as I imagined," she said finally.

"I am?"

She smiled. Strands of hair whipped across her face. She didn't bother to pull them aside.

"Who are you?" I asked.

Again the smile. "Your mother."

A shadow crossed my heart, and I knew it to be true. "What happened?" It was all I could think to ask.

Something in the distance, over my shoulder, caught her attention. The wind gusted. "I was young. Addicted to drugs. I didn't think I would be able to care for you the way a mother should." Her attention left whatever had caught it, and locked onto me. "I died giving birth to you."

I thought about listening in, but what would be the point? "Should I love you?"

She averted her gaze again, but this time it went to the ground. When she finally looked up, remorse had filled her face. "I don't deserve it," she said quietly. "But it would be nice."

"I forgive you." The words felt right, but I was filled with mixed emotions.

The smile she flashed seemed built from relief. She opened her arms and I stepped into her embrace. As we held each other, I could feel her heart beat against my chest. A lone bird squawked as it rode the warm thermals high above us. After a moment, she pulled away and stepped back. I tried to hold onto her hand.

"Is this real?" I asked.

"Only if you want it to be." Her eyes seemed to be swimming. The sun was now touching the tops of the trees; its rays washed the area around us in rich shades of yellow and orange. "I have to go now."

"Wait. What about my father? Is he alive?" I tried to step forward, but my shoes had become part of the dirt.

She nodded. "Yes." She held her stance for a moment, and her eyes drank me in. She forced a smile, turned and ran away.

I watched her figure first diminish, then disappear into the trees at the far end of the field. The sun was almost gone. A single word came rolling across the grass, borne by the wind.

Clear!

Searing white light filled my vision, and I gulped desperately for breath. My chest felt like it had been hit with a sledgehammer.

"Dillon, can you hear me?"

My vision returned, but everything was blurred and indistinguishable. A form entered my field of view.

"Hey, there." It was Debra. "We thought we lost you."

It took a moment to find my breath. "Not a chance," I croaked. My throat was dry and barely allowed the words to escape.

The form coalesced into her face. "How do you feel?"

"Like crap." I tried to sit up, but several hands put a stop to it. I settled back against crisp sheets and a pillow that cradled my head perfectly. The bed smelled of disinfectant. My breathing slowly became normal.

"Easy, tough guy." It was Harris. "You aren't going anywhere." He glanced across the bed at Debra. "I told you he's got fight."

Debra focused on me and smiled knowingly. Something pricked my arm. Harris waggled his fingers.

"Time to say bye-bye," he said.

"What's that?" I asked, giving a strained nod toward my arm.

"Something to help you sleep," Debra said. She patted my shoulder. "Now get some rest."

She turned to leave just as the room was getting fuzzy. Debra's form seemed to liquefy.

I pulled myself up onto one elbow and batted away a hand that was trying to stop me. "Debra ... wait."

What was left of her head turned back.

"What happened?" I managed.

What I took as a smile formed in the swirl of color that was Debra's face. "Something extraordinary."

.   .   .

Whatever Debra injected made me sleep for almost 12 hours. They parked me in a room adjacent to the animal testing area, but if Sir Michael J had raised a ruckus, I never heard it. Sanjiv brought me a simple breakfast of orange juice, milk, a cranberry muffin, and one of those small boxes of Cheerios. Probably direct from the gas station at the end of TR Com's feeder road and I-20.

Out of habit, I glanced at my cell and found my service no longer blocked. Maybe they had lowered the field while I had been sleeping. I quickly checked to see if Kadin had tried to contact me. She hadn't, which was odd. She usually sent a text or email if we hadn't spoken in a while. Considering what I now knew about her, however, the fact that she hadn't called didn't surprise me. One part of me never wanted to see her again, while another part, admittedly small, would always miss her. I ran through my emails. Things were slow at the office.

Typical for early summer, and couldn't have come at a better time.

It was Sunday, and I had been at ELT for two days. My clothes were rank, but fortunately someone had dropped a black Kenneth Cole bag in the corner of my room overnight. It held a change of clothes that must have cost a boatload. The shirt and jeans fit surprisingly well, but the shoes were a little tight. They were Cole knock-offs of Converse All-Stars, but in a combo of suede, rubber, and leather only a supermodel could appreciate. A small note from Debra rested on the black tissue paper.

Morning.
I took the liberty of buying you something different to wear.
Hope you like them. Come to the conference room at 10 and let's
see if Stiles notices, ha!
Debra.

I tried to text a thank you to Debra, but the No Service message was a cold reminder that the wall was back up, and it was business as usual.

There must have been an earlier meeting than ours in the conference room, because the lone bear claw left in the Granny's Donuts box had been torn in half. I was hungry enough to actually contemplate eating it when Debra and the three amigos entered. Everyone looked creepily like they had the first time I met them, except Debra. She was leading the pack and didn't seem intimidated anymore.

This time, I sat on the side of the table that faced the glass. Stiles and Harris took seats at one end, as if they just planned to observe. Debra and Morgan sat directly across from me. Behind them, the lab folks went about their day. Morgan flipped open a large matte-grey laptop. His coffee smelled heavenly.

"Can I get a cup of what you're drinking?" I asked Morgan.

"No stimulants for you, Bradford," Harris said.

"Why is the wall up?"

"The what?" Morgan asked.

"You're still blocking my ability, along with my cell service. Why?"

"It's a precaution."

"I don't think I like—"

"It's for your own good," Harris said. "We can't let anything interfere with the technology. It could destabilize you, and we sure as hell don't want to jump-start you again."

"Can I leave today?" It seemed a fair question, although it garnered a hesitant glance from Harris to his boss.

"Not today," Stiles said.

"Why?"

"Robert, tell Dillon why it would be best that he stay with us a few more days."

What the hell? I considered arguing the point, but the two technicians from the other day had taken root again on the other side of the conference room door.

"How are you feeling today?" Morgan asked.

"What?" I snapped back and met Morgan's stare.

"How are you feeling?"

"Ah ... a lot better than the last time I woke up?"

"Have you had any pain behind your right eye?"

"No. I'm hungry more than anything else."

"Have you had any stray voices or thoughts enter your mind?"

Odd question. "No."

"What do you remember about the other day?"

Just thinking about the cacophony of voices almost made me lose my Cheerios. "Well, it's hard to describe. One moment there was nothing in my mind, the next, it was like I had tapped into a higher consciousness or something. It seemed like I could hear the whole world ... at the same time. Billions of voices. It was overwhelming. The pressure inside my skull was intense, like my brain was going to explode."

"Can you describe what it was like just before you passed out?" Morgan asked.

I glanced at Stiles, who seemed interested for the first time. "The voices grew until I couldn't distinguish anything. It was like one painful crescendo, a chorus that just built and built like that Beethoven piece they play at Christmas."

"Ode to Joy," Debra offered.

"Yeah, that one. It built to a point that was ... I don't know ... beyond anything I could take. It was like I had reached the edge of my life and I was teetering. It was—" My heart suddenly began racing at the memory.

"Go on," Morgan urged.

I recalled standing at the precipice of my sanity, a billon souls in my mind. "Beautiful." I caught myself staring past Debra into the lab.

"Well, that's a word for it," Harris said. "Robert, why don't you show Bradford what he really tapped into."

Morgan spun his laptop around so everyone could see the screen. On it was a detailed animation of the earth with hundreds of white specks orbiting it. As Morgan rotated the image, many of the specks moved in synchronous relation to the earth. "This is a NASA model of the twenty-two hundred satellites that orbit the earth," he said. "Most of these are for communications."

"What's that have to do with me?" I asked.

"The technology in your brain has the ability to enhance your cross-neuro synaptic protocol, which in turn allows you to access certain global bandwidths."

"In English, please."

"Essentially." Morgan hesitated. "You're like a cellular receiver."

My attention bounced between Morgan and Harris until I finally let it rest on Debra. "A receiver?" I pointed at the NASA diagram and its orbiting satellites. "For all that?"

"Not all of it," Debra said. "Just the telecommunication satellites."

Morgan seemed genuinely excited. "You see, Dillon, the technology that was injected, as far as we can tell, makes it possible for you to interface with the global cellular net. As of now, you're like a telekinetic receiver that can be tuned to different communication frequencies. When we introduced our nanobots near the other tech, the two techs merged, and something caused the other tech to switch on and instantly connect you to every available cellular frequency. We didn't immediately realize what was happening, or we would have disconnected you sooner."

"We also didn't know what would happen if we disconnected you," Debra added. "We weren't sure you would survive such a jolt to your system."

"Obviously I didn't," I said, "since you needed to use the paddles on me, right?"

No one answered.

"Let me see if I understand this." I ran a hand through my hair. "The tech that Kadin's group stuck in my head somehow merged with your tech, and now I can connect with cell phones?"

"Not just cell phones," Morgan said. "Laptops, mainframes—"

Harris raised a hand. "Hold on. We don't know that for sure."

"So I'm essentially a hacker," I said.

"More than that," Debra said. "Remember when I said your NTP waves were strong, and we used them to find you through your cell phone?"

I nodded.

"We think that this merger of technologies somehow amplifies your waves to a point that allows an omnipresent interface."

Morgan leaned onto the table. "This may sound a little far-fetched—"

"Compared to what?" I said sarcastically.

He paused a moment before continuing. "We think it's possible for you to leverage your telepathic ability through the bionanotech's connection with your insular cortex."

"You mean I'll be able to listen in to a mind, using the cellular system?"

"Exactly. We don't know how just yet, but we think we can pinpoint a cell phone for you to connect with."

The ramifications were staggering. "But if I can connect into a cell site," I said, "then I can tap a Wi-Fi site, and that connects to the world, right?"

Morgan nodded excitedly. "Theoretically, you would be able to listen in on the thoughts of anyone who has a cell phone or computer."

"As long as it's on, and within a few feet of them," Harris added.

"And we know it's cell number or IP address," Debra said.

"And it's using TCP protocol," Morgan corrected.

I slammed my hands onto the table. "Hold on!" I surveyed the startled faces. "This is totally insane!"

"May I have a moment with Dillon?" Stiles asked.

The group exchanged troubled glances, then stood almost simultaneously. As they filed out, Debra turned back and mouthed, *It'll be okay*.

The room's imposing ten-foot oak door closed behind Morgan with a conspicuous clack. The two technicians resumed their posts outside. The distance between Stiles and me suddenly seemed large. I turned to the senior agent. "Look, I'm not the smartest guy on the planet, but are you trying to make me into some kind of paranormal spy?"

Stiles picked at a cuticle. "Yes," he said nonchalantly.

"Are you serious?"

The senior agent stood, buttoned his coat, and leaned onto the table. His detached air was gone, replaced by a predatory gleam in his eye. "As a *god*damn heart attack."

16. For God and country.

After Stiles went off, he informed me I was going to have another session and that I better get on board A-S-A-fucking-P. It had become abundantly clear that I was not going back to Dallas, at least not anytime soon. And after Morgan's revelations, how could I? I couldn't exactly skip back to my old life and pick up as if nothing had happened. In any case, Stiles would make sure of that. I had tech in my head that was Beyond Thunderdome; for better or worse, I was stuck with Harris and crew for the foreseeable future. At least I had Debra ... and another session in the Hulk chair for Dillon's torture.

"Tell me something, Sanj," I asked, settling back in the Hulk chair. "I thought nanobots were science fiction. Everything I've read says they're a long way off."

Sanjiv gave me a guileful look, his eyes a stark contrast to his dark skin. "There are a lot of things, Mr. Bradford, the public doesn't know about," he said, lacking his usual Indian sing-songish lilt. "Many consumer products had their inceptions in secret government projects. You'd be surprised what's happening behind closed doors."

"Yeah, but the stuff inside me is complex. It doesn't exactly seem like it was invented yesterday, you know? How is that possible?"

"The technology in your head is something quite extraordinary. I would love to see it firsthand."

"Which would mean opening up my head, right?"

Sanjiv rolled a metal cart laden with an array of medical looking devices to my side. A syringe-gun like the one from the previous day rested front-and-center. "Yes."

"Ready to connect?" Harris asked as soon as he entered the room. Debra followed behind him.

"What kind of rate plan am I on?" I asked.

"You don't want to know." He pointed. "Nice shirt. Ken Cole?"

"Yes."

Harris eyed Debra, who took a seat at the main workstation. "That's coming out of your budget, you know," he said. Seemingly irritated, he yanked a metal chair from a desk and sat against the wall behind the workstation.

"I hate to ask this question so late in the game," I said to the room, "but how do we know that what happened last time won't happen again?"

"We don't," Debra answered.

"The only way we can learn about this technology," Sanjiv said, "is to engage it."

Harris folded his arms. "There is another way, but it's a little more invasive."

"We've calibrated for the frequency issue," Sanjiv said. "The interference we experienced last time shouldn't happen again."

"Shouldn't, or won't?" I asked pointedly.

"Once we engage the technology, a connection should establish that will allow you to listen in, as you call it." Sanjiv wrapped the head restraint across my forehead. "The monitor over there will display the connection route. We should be able to pinpoint which network you can interface, and hopefully which cell phone."

"How can you do that?" I asked.

Sanjiv pressed a button under the armature that tightened the head restraint. He grinned. "Trade secret."

"So who are we calling?"

This question seemed to stump the room.

"It's supposedly a random number," Sanjiv said, finally.

I eyed Harris, who had tipped his chair casually against the white cinder block wall. "I know what you're trying to do." The restraint tightened again, and my chin pressed against the guard.

"What's that?" he asked.

"Create a virtual spy."

One side of Harris's mouth curled in faint acknowledgement. He glanced at Debra. "Let's get on with this."

"You going to use that again?" I asked Sanjiv, moving my eyes to the syringe-gun.

"Only if something goes wrong."

"Next time, can we leave off the strap?"

"If everything goes well with this test, we won't need it any more."

"Thanks, because this is really uncomfortable."

Harris grunted. "It's good to suffer for your country."

"Speak for yourself," I said.

"Dillon?" Debra leaned around her monitor and tried to look hopeful. "We're ready when you are."

"For God and country?" I asked Harris.

Harris dropped the chair's legs back to the ground, rested his forearms on his knees and stared at his wedding ring. He fiddled with it for a second, then looked up. "If this works." The seriousness in his voice suggested I had hit some unspoken nerve. "You're going to save a lot of lives." He gestured at Debra to begin.

"I'll count down from three, Dillon, and then engage the technology," she said. "I'm not sure what you'll feel, so prepare yourself."

"Oh, I almost forgot." Sanjiv held a clear plastic mouth guard in my line of sight. "Would you like to use this?"

"If I need that," I said, "then you'd probably better get those paddles ready again."

Sanjiv nodded knowingly and joined Debra at the main workstation.

"Ready?" she asked.

"Do like the man said," I answered.

Debra's head disappeared behind the monitor. All I could see was Harris, who was again propped against the wall, contemplating me like a work of art.

"Mark," Debra said. "Three, two, one."

For an eternal millisecond, there was nothing, then billions of voices exploded inside my mind. Unlike before, the volume was muffled somewhat, but the severity of the pressure was just as intense. Instinctively, I grabbed the two armatures on either side of the head restraint and screamed.

Sanjiv jumped out from behind his workstation. His eyes darted from Debra's monitor to me. "Steady!" His eyes darted again. "We're almost there!"

"Find another route!" Morgan said from somewhere off to my left.

"We're trying!" Debra said.

"Piggyback off of EchoStar 3," Sanjiv ordered. He grinned nervously and raised a finger. "One more minute, Dillon."

I closed my eyes and struggled against the pain crashing in waves through my mind. The voices merged into the resonating chorus and began rising.

"Hurry!" I yelled. "It's happening again!"

Suddenly, as if someone had opened a drain valve in the back of my head, the voices collapsed into one. I gasped and opened my eyes. The other technicians were still rooted to their chairs in fear, but Debra, Morgan, and Sanjiv had leapt to my side and were staring up at me like I was about to deliver the word of God. Harris was still leaning against the wall, his attention focused on something he held.

"Dillon?" Debra asked tentatively. "Are you okay?"

The voice in my head receded to indistinct static. The pain that seconds ago had nearly torn my head apart had completely vanished. "I think so."

"What do you hear?"

"I can't tell. It's ... digitized."

Debra hurried to the workstation. After some keyboard tapping she asked, "Is that better?"

The voice's tone modulated and eventually coalesced into a recognizable language. English.

Wa...t...go...ude, I barely heard in my mind.

The voice seemed familiar. I strained to identify it. Harris lifted his eyes and smiled at me.

Debra emerged from behind the workstation and joined the pack.

Wh...do I s...nd like? Harris's thought was still breaking up.

"Like the asshole you are," I said.

Debra's eyes went big, and she, along with everyone else, turned to look at Harris. He walked through them and stopped about three feet from the Hulk chair. In his hands was something that looked like a cell phone. He tapped across its screen and focused his attention on me.

Hey, Bradford. Can you hear me now?

17. Keeping the balance.

"Dude, where have you been?"

I had heard this tone in Derek's voice before – a subtle blend of anger and concern, often adopted after I had done something asinine, like the time I had spontaneously taken a girl I had met on Match.com to the south of France for 10 days. It was our first actual date.

"Look, Derek. Something serious has come up–"

"Is Kadin pregnant?"

"No, dick-head, I have cancer."

Silence. "Man, I'm sorry. What kind?"

"Testicular."

Another pause. "Like Lance Armstrong?"

"Yeah, kind of." I was praying that Derek would buy it. Harris had given me a cancer cover story. It was the only thing, he said, that would allow me to disappear for extended periods without anyone questioning it. After today's test, I figured I was going to be gone a long time.

"What are you going to do?" Derek asked. "How bad is it?"

"The doctors think they can stop it, so I'm heading down to MD Anderson in Houston. If they strike out, then I'm on to Plan B."

"And that is?"

"A special clinic in Germany that deals in alternative medicine. I might try them."

"Do you think it'll come to that?"

"I hope not. Just covering my bases."

"Can I do anything for you?"

"I'll have email, so keep me informed. Have Tommy take over my accounts. He's already involved, so the transition should be smooth. I'm sure the clients will understand. And don't worry if I don't respond to emails or calls right away."

"What should I tell the staff?"

"Tell them the truth, but I don't want to be contacted. No visits. No flowers or crap like that. The last thing I need is for people to go weird on me."

"Got it. What else?"

"If you talk to Kadin, don't say anything. I haven't decided how I'm going to break it to her."

"I understand." Derek sucked down an audible breath. "God, Dillon, good luck. You're about to head into some heavy shit. I know. My dad went through lung cancer."

If only he knew. The absolute seriousness of my situation grabbed hold, and I could feel my throat tighten. Even though I didn't have cancer, I did have potentially life-threatening foreign matter in my brain. I just didn't know the ramifications of that yet. "Thanks, Derek. I'll call when I can and let you know how things are going."

"Hey, Dillon?"

"Yeah?"

Another pause. "Love ya."

Derek could be a little high-drama sometimes, but he and I had been through a lot. The building of our business. His daughter's bike accident. He was about as close to a brother as I would ever have, and his sentiment was touching.

"Back at ya."

I sat on the bed and looked around Debra's small apartment, my unofficial home for the weekend. Actually, to call it an apartment was a bit of an exaggeration. It was more like one of those Ikea showrooms that displayed how easily a hip, young couple can live in 300 square feet.

I was feeling pretty wiped. Today's test had lasted barely five minutes, but in that short time, it seemed every scrap of vitality had been drained out of me. Sanjiv had wheelchaired me back to the apartment, where four more Kenneth Cole bags greeted me. Their neat little row on top of the blonde wood media cabinet reminded me that I was not going home. I thought about testing this theory, but there was something about Stiles that told me his ugly side was something I didn't want to challenge. If anything, I seemed in store for one hell of a wardrobe update. Debra, or whomever she had tasked, had an exquisite sense of style and seemed to have nailed my taste in clothes. Probably another byproduct of my profile. What I would give to glimpse that document! There was a soft knock at the door.

"It's open," I said, like I had any real privacy.

Debra, her hair pulled back in a simple ponytail, entered and closed the door. "How are you feeling?"

She was out of her clinic uniform and wearing jeans with a pullover sweater, her utilitarian lab shoes replaced with a pair of comfy sandals. Merrells, if I had to guess. Like most things I had seen her wear, this granola look fit her perfectly.

I took in a deep breath and slapped my thighs. "Like I could take on the world!" I coughed.

"Seriously."

I cleared my throat. "I'm tired, but okay. Thanks for the new clothes. You didn't have to do that."

"Actually, I did. Stiles wants to keep a tight leash on you until we can figure out your potential." She sat next to me. "Did you call Derek?"

"Yes."

"Did you use the cancer story?"

"Yes."

"And?"

"It worked." I was a little irritated.

"I'm sorry, Dillon, but this is the best way. Cancer is a great cover. Now," she patted my thigh, "you up for something to eat?"

"Please, not Buster's again."

She laughed. "No. There's a little Italian place that I–"

The door to the apartment flew open. Harris walked in.

"Whoa, sorry," he said. "I hope I'm not interrupting."

Debra stood. "You're not. We were just figuring out dinner."

Harris looked at his watch. "Maybe in a couple of hours. First we need to hook Bradford up again."

"Come on, I'm beat," I pleaded. "Can't we do it tomorrow?"

"Afraid not." Harris glanced at his watch again.

Debra's grin fell away. "What is it?"

"We have a situation."

•   •   •

I tried to keep pace with Harris and Debra, but their dash down the hallway was too much for me. My body ached and my head throbbed as if I had a bad sinus infection. The test had taken more out of me than I thought. "Hey guys, can we slow it down a little?"

Harris didn't even look back. "No can do, Dillon. Your country needs you."

"I thought this had been handled," Debra said.

Harris shrugged. "We did too, but apparently things have escalated. A Russian mob group is arranging to have the Minister of Energy assassinated."

Without slowing in the slightest, he turned his head and explained more to me.

"We need you to listen in. Try to find out when and where so we can stop it."

"Can't you all just ... I don't know ... eavesdrop on him with some high-tech satellite?" I asked.

Harris stabbed a thumb at me over his shoulder and looked at Debra. "Mr. 'I Watch Too Many Documentaries.' " He glanced at me again as we rounded a corner. "This group calls itself *Indeitsy*."

"What's that mean?" I asked.

"It's Russian for 'Indians,' as in the raiding parties of the old West. These guys control a city called *Novokuibyshevsk*. Big oil and gas area. They've been tapping into the state-controlled pipelines and trafficking the stolen crude. The Minister of Energy wants to shut them down."

We rounded another corner. "Yeah, but seriously, can't you tap their calls?"

"The Indeitsy never talks about this kind of stuff anywhere we can get close. They're tricky bastards. Very sophisticated. They know how we operate, and when we do manage to tap into a call, they're talking in code. Lots of disinformation. Screws with us all the time. Usually, we let Langley handle their crap, but the minister is a huge supporter of our agenda, so we have to stop this. It'll send a message, big time."

I rubbed my temples. "So you're tapping the call and hoping I can intercept his thoughts?"

"Yes."

"You know I don't speak Russian."

"Not a problem."

We marched into the testing room, and the tension practically slapped me in the face. A few new faces manned the workstations, but my attention immediately was drawn to the technician named Alex Popprov, who was standing next to the Hulk chair looking like my executioner. He had a pair of headphones wrapped around his neck.

"Hello, Dillon," Sanjiv said somberly. "Are you ready?"

It took me a second to peel my eyes away from the big Russian. "Not really. That last test session wiped me out."

"I have just the thing." Sanjiv reached for the syringe-gun.

"No way. I can't go through that again."

Sanjiv paused and picked up what looked like a pack of Listerine breath strips. He separated a tiny blue sheet from the pack and handed it to me. "Place this under your tongue and you will feel much better."

"Trade secret?" I asked, taking it.

He smiled. "Quickly, please."

I pressed the sheet under my tongue and climbed into the chair. The sheet cut across where I had bit my tongue, which caused me to wince. Sanjiv started to position the armature, but I reached up and stopped him.

"No restraints this time, okay?"

Sanjiv shot Harris a questioning look.

"It's okay," Harris said.

Sanjiv nodded and swung the armature out of the way. After positioning the two monitoring arms on either side of my head, he joined Debra at the main workstation. Without being locked into the headgear, I could finally take in the room. When my eyes met Debra's, a strange icy sensation crawled up my spine and splintered into my extremities. A surge of high-octane ass-kick hit the back of my head, and my face began to tingle. I rubbed the tip of my nose, but it didn't help.

Debra looked puzzled.

I may have smiled when I felt the top of my scalp lift off my head. I reached up and pressed my hair down.

"Does it feel like your head is growing?" Sanjiv asked.

"Yeah, it does. Nice stuff, Sanj."

He chuckled and focused on his screen.

Harris came up to inspect me.

"Will he be okay?" he asked the room.

"I'm great," I answered. "Amazing clarity."

"It's a simple neuroenhancer." Sanjiv glanced up. "He'll be fine."

Simple? Doubtful. Whatever Sanjiv had given me was not only expanding my mind, it was prepping my body. The tingling at my nose spread to the rest of my extremities, and I swear it felt like my muscles had increased in size. Maybe I was becoming Bruce Banner.

Harris stepped up onto the platform, took hold of the Hulk chair's armrests and leaned close. I had never really noticed the severity of the pockmarks on his face. He reminded me of a young Ray Liotta.

"This is how it's going to work," he said, his breath reeking of spearmint and stale smoke. "We're going to connect you with the guy we think is going to execute the hit. He's supposed to call the head of the Indeitsy ..." Harris glanced at the wall clock, "in six minutes."

"But I don't know any Russian," I said.

"You don't need to. Mr. Popprov is going to give you some key words to listen for. He'll be listening to the real conversation, as well, through conventional surveillance, so he'll cue you as soon as he hears what we believe are any code phrases for the hit. You'll be listening in on the assassin's thoughts, and with any luck, he'll think of the real location and time. Just repeat what he's thinking out loud, and we'll take it from there. Simple, right?"

The buzz from Sanjiv's speed blotter was settling down. "Yeah, but I can't speak this language. If it were French or Spanish I might be able to wing it."

"Just do your best. Mr. Popprov is great with languages, right, Alex?"

The big Russian flashed a curt half grin.

Harris slapped my shoulder and stepped back. "All right, Bradford. Let's see what you're made of."

Popprov replaced Harris in front of me; one of his hands went to my knee while the other grasped an armrest. He stared at me from under hooded eyes, and I could feel his index finger and thumb press the sides of my kneecap. He gave new meaning to the term Hulk chair.

"The code words are *butylka, papirosy,* and *gostinitsa.* They're Russian for bottle, cigarette, and hotel. If I hear them I will cue you. Now, repeat them." Popprov's fingers pressed against the edges of my knee.

"*Butylka, papirosy,* and *gosti...*" I stumbled on the last one.

"*Gostinitsa.* Again." Popprov's thumb and finger pinched a little harder. We did this dance three more times. On the third one – as I finished the last code word – Popprov dug his thumbnail under the side of my kneecap. A sharp pain shot through my knee.

"Damn it!" I grabbed his wrist and tried to pry off his hand, but it was like holding a cast iron pipe. I leaned close to his face, and we shared a momentary Cold War stare-down. "How do you say 'fuck off' in Russian?" I finally asked.

Popprov removed his hand and stepped back. The pain diminished. "Old KGB trick to make you remember. Sorry if it hurt." He donned the headphones and moved beside the Hulk chair.

"You two done bonding?" Harris asked.

"We're going to have drinks later," I said, rubbing my knee.

Harris turned to Sanjiv. "Let's get him connected."

"Without the head restraint," Sanjiv warned, "you will have to remain very still."

I gave him a thumbs-up and positioned my head between the two monitor arms.

"Ready?" Debra asked.

Popprov raised a hand and pulled aside the left earphone. "What are the words again?" he asked me out of the side of his mouth.

"*Butylka, papirosy, gostinitsa,*" I said.

"*Da.* Continue."

Harris held up two fingers. "Two minutes, people."

"Connecting on my mark," Debra said. "Three, two, one."

This time, there was no lag before the millions of voices shattered the relative quiet of my mind. Unlike the test, though, the unbearable pain and pressure lasted just a few seconds. I death-gripped the edges of the hulk chair's seat, fighting against the pain. Sections of noise dropped away like ticks on a clock until all that was left was a faint hiss.

"Guys," I said relaxing, "all I hear is dead air."

"He hasn't made the call yet," Debra said.

Harris checked his watch. "Believe me, these guys are into being on time."

Another minute passed before a woman's voice entered my mind. It was distant and in the background. Then the same woman's voice came in again, but a little louder. Typically the louder voice was what a person was thinking, and almost never overlapped the speaking voice. Speech, I was told by an English professor I had at U.T., is processed in the brain along two parallel pathways, each of which run from lower-to higher-functioning neural regions. This made it difficult to think one thing, and say another. If, for example, someone complemented me about my tie – all the while thinking it was ugly – the ugly thought lagged a fraction of a second later than the voiced complement.

"He's made the call," Debra announced.

"It's a woman's voice," I said.

Harris frowned. He pulled out his cell and left the room.

The woman's outward tone was light and conversational, as if she were ordering pizza. Her inner voice was occasionally blunt, however, like a Russian drill sergeant. What she said and what she thought seemed to match. I closed my eyes and tried to imagine how this woman assassin appeared. Maybe tall with severe Slavic features, long blond hair pulled back into a tight ponytail–

"*Butylka, papirosy, gostinitsa,*" Popprov whispered.

I kept my eyes closed and nodded. Then I heard the word *papirosy* in the underlying conversation. I focused on her inner voice. I felt my knee poked.

Sukin syn, zubnaya shyotka, she thought.

"Something *syn, zubnaya shyotka*!" I yelled and opened my eyes. Popprov was standing in front of me. He was bent over and keenly focused on my mouth. A faint smile sliced his lips and he nodded in approval.

I closed my eyes again and concentrated, which was hard, given that I was listening in on a language with which I was completely unfamiliar. I focused on the cell conversation, because that's where I'd hear the last two code words. The woman spoke under her breath, and it was hard to distinguish one word from another. Static crackled.

"There's some kind of interference," I said.

"Got it," Sanjiv replied.

After another burst of static, it cleared.

"*Butylka, gostinitsa,*" Popprov whispered.

I know, I mouthed. Eyes closed, I concentrated on visualizing the dual conversations as if the woman sat across a kitchen table from herself. I thought of a stage play with the table in a spotlight. The woman wore a simple black outfit. Maybe a uniform. It was all happening so quickly. Her inner voice was on the right; I focused on her lips.

Kuda poidyom? Gostinitsa Hilton? Da, she thought.

"It'll be at the Hilton!" I listened for another minute, and in my mind's eye the woman never moved. Her hands were clasped on the table, and I think there was a rug — similar to what you'd see in an old farmhouse — underneath her utilitarian shoes. There was a loud click, and the hissing returned. I opened my eyes. Popprov was still bent over and staring. Harris was behind him.

"We lost the connection," Debra said from the main workstation.

"Can we get it back?" Harris asked.

"By the time we do," Popprov said, pulling the headphones off, "the call will be over."

"Did you get anything?"

Popprov turned. "Enough."

"You make the call," Harris ordered. "I'll catch up."

Popprov quickly exited. Harris stepped up to the Hulk chair, holding a slide box of foiled gum. He pushed one out into his palm. "You did pretty well, Bradford. For an amateur."

I moved the monitor arms out of the way and rubbed my temples. I was wiped. "What the hell did I just do?"

Harris popped the gum into his mouth. "Kept the world in balance."

18. Go home Mom, you're drunk.

"Dillon?"

The sound of my name came to me like an echo. It seemed foreign, abstract. It skipped off my consciousness like a stone on water. A hand shook my arm.

"Dillon?"

I surfaced from a deep sleep to find Debra's face inches from mine. "Hey," I said, barely above a whisper. "What time is it?"

"About two in the morning."

"Something wrong?"

"No. I just ..."

"What's the matter?"

"I had a bad dream. Can I ... join you?"

All Debra was wearing was an oversized Mavericks Jersey. I was in nothing but my underwear. Sanjiv had failed to warn me about the aftereffects of his speed blotter. While its high was amazingly clear and had allowed me to hyperfocus, its crash was an ass-kicker. I had almost collapsed stepping out of the Hulk chair, and once again Sanjiv had to wheelchair me back to the apartment. Getting undressed and into bed was a blur.

The last time Debra and I had shared the bed was two days ago, and since then she had been sleeping in an empty room in the clinic. She said she wanted to maintain a semblance of professionalism. I pulled back the covers and slid to one side of the bed, but she snuggled against me until her butt was against my crotch. As a friend of mine used to say, spooning led to forking. She took my arm and pulled it across her stomach. My hand brushed across her breasts. Her butt fit nicely against me. I struggled not to grow hard, but failed miserably. I started to scoot away, but she reached back and pulled me closer.

I didn't know where to tuck my hand. "Um, is this okay?"

Just hold me, she said into my mind.

No neurosynaptic impeder? I asked.

It's down for maintenance. They do it while we sleep. I just needed to have you in my mind, that's all.

I grabbed her stomach and felt the taut results of her dedicated sit-up regime. This time, I pulled her close, and she went with it. I nuzzled up to the back of her head and breathed her in. My cock was now fully hard and had worked its way into the folds of my new briefs. Uncomfortable, I squirmed and tried to free it, to no avail. Debra reached around, deftly took the head of my cock and freed it, then gently patted my balls and withdrew her hand.

Better? she asked.

Much. Thanks. I was pressing against her lower back. *You, ah okay with ... you know?*

Debra shifted her position so that my cock was nestled firmly between the cheeks of her butt. I might have gotten harder, if that were possible.

Even though I was pressed up against this exquisite creature, I was dying to hear what had happened in Moscow. I knew it would kill the moment, but I had to know.

Did they stop her? I asked

Yeah, she replied. *Seems the intel was a little off. They weren't looking for a female assassin. The Indeitsy had set up the minister with a special lady for the night. A payoff, I guess.*

How was she going to kill him?

They were to meet at the Moscow Hilton. Something about putting poison in the minister's toothpaste. Harris says there'll be a report ready in the morning.

I don't know about you, I said, *but I'm sleeping in.*

Don't get your hopes up. Today's Monday, remember?

Shit, that's right.

You can try, but it'll probably be noisy.

When do you need to show up? I asked.

She yawned. *Nineish.*

Hey, do you think we could go into Dallas tomorrow? I really need take care of some business. I knew it was a long shot, but what the hell? Debra's breathing turned rhythmic. *Debra?*

Her grip on me had relaxed, but she wouldn't be dreaming for a few minutes. I thought about listening in, but my own fatigue dragged me down.

■   ■   ■

Debra was a bed hog. The next morning, I woke clinging to the edge of the mattress. It fascinated me how the smallest woman could dominate a bed, and Debra was no exception. She was already at work by the time I was dressed. On the media table, she had spread out her selections from the Kenneth Cole shopping spree, along with a note:

Hey, you—
Thanks for letting me stay. You "felt" so good. Maybe I could join you again tonight?
I picked out some things for you to wear. Hope you don't mind. Meet me in my office
at 9. Harris has okayed your request. We're going into town!
Debra
P.S. You did great yesterday. I'm proud of you.

I couldn't decide whether I liked her tone or not. And what was with that postscript? A little too intimate, maybe, although I'd certainly be down with some snuggling again. While Debra had apologized about her deception, a part of me still didn't trust her. She was, after all, an agent for one of the world's most powerful organizations, and I ranked barely above a lab rat. I half-expected to find a pink sticky note on the apartment door with the name Sir Dillon B scrawled on it. Maybe later this afternoon I'd spend some time with my homeys over in animal testing.

I swung my legs over the edge of the bed and eyed what Debra had laid out for me. All solids, fashionably dark. I always felt that Kenneth Cole was a kind of couture Garanimals for the fête set, but what Debra (or whoever) had bought was surprisingly elegant. I rummaged through each of the bags, inspecting my loot, and found at the bottom of the last one a dopp kit filled with men's toiletries. There was even a Braun electric razor and a sample bottle of Armani Attitude.

I cleaned up and found Debra in her office, her attention deep in her laptop. I gently knocked on the doorframe. She looked up and did a double take.

"Damn, I have good taste," she said, leaning back into her chair. "How did you sleep?"

"Well, thanks," I said. "And by the way..."

Debra cocked her head a little.

"You felt good, too."

Debra produced a little smirk, then came around her desk toward me. She undid the second button of my shirt. "There," she said as she adjusted my collar. Her fingers grazed my chest hair. She stepped back and admired her work. "You do wear clothes well."

Even though I had an ego the size of Cowboys Stadium, whenever a woman commented on my body, I usually blushed. "So, ah, are we going to Dallas?"

"Yes."

"How'd you manage that? I thought Stiles wanted a tight leash on me."

She raised an eyebrow and the smirk returned. "I have my ways."

■   ■   ■

It was a glorious day in North Texas. Debra's ride was a BMW Z4 convertible. I wondered how a public servant could afford such a nice ride. Maybe it had been some drug lord's weekend car she'd won in an NSA auction. Did they have that kind of thing?

I found a long-billed cap tucked in the passenger door's side compartment. It fit like I owned it. Debra was speeding a little too confidently, putting the Z4 through its paces. She slipped behind an eighteen-wheeler and began drafting its wake.

Don't you ever worry about the state troopers? Debra must have been running the impeder because she didn't react. "Don't you ever worry about the state troopers?" I asked, trying not to yell too loudly over the rush of wind. "I-20's usually crawling with them."

"We have a little arrangement with local law enforcement." She jerked the wheel and darted around the semi.

"A little NSA persuasion?"

"You could say that."

"But then you'd have to kill me, right?"

I couldn't tell if Debra's sideways glance was real or an attempt at humor, but her look reminded me what a serious and bizarre situation this was. And where I stood in the pecking order.

I turned my attention to the highway that stretched out before us. "Aren't you afraid I might try and make a run for it in Dallas?"

"What would be the point?" Debra passed a Church on the Rock van filled with remarkably clean-cut teenagers. "We can track you." She tapped the side of her purse on the console.

The impeder, I thought. Harris's leash.

We came over the crest of a small hill to find a state trooper strategically poised on the side of the road. His driver's side door was open, and he was crouched behind it with the radar gun propped on the doorframe and aimed. He stood and stared us down as we sped by. I glanced at the speedometer: *92 mph*.

"What do you need from your condo?" Debra asked, merging into the northbound lanes of Central Expressway. We were at the edge of downtown.

"I want to get some more stuff to wear," I said. "I'm guessing I'll be staying with you folks for a while. Plus I want to get my laptop."

"You don't need to pick up clothes. I enjoy buying them for you."

"I know, and I appreciate it. I just want some familiar things. You understand, don't you?"

Debra swerved onto the Lemmon Avenue exit ramp. "I do." She drove to the light and pulled into a gas station. "But I'm still going to keep buying you things."

I let out a laugh for the first time in days.

She angled up to a pump bay. "I have to get gas."

"Great, I need to use the little techlepath's room."

Go Mart's interior was an obnoxious riot of glass refrigerators filled with every bottled drink imaginable and wire shelving units overly stuffed with pre-packaged processed foods. Neon beer signs blinked and flashed above the row of refrigerators, and someone had sketched cartoon faces on the breasts of a Corona cardboard point-of-purchase Latina bikini girl that was propped in a corner. The tongue on the right breast slithered down to her belly button, and large spit drops semi-circled its flick marks.

The bathrooms were in the back, and I found the men's surprisingly clean. As I pissed, the graffiti entertained me. *Jesus is a Mexican mechanic. Trump is the only dope worth shooting. Bitches love the top hat ~ A. Lincoln.* But my favorite was: *Don't hate me because I'm beautiful. Hate me because I did your dad.* And right below it in thick black marker: *Go home mom, you're drunk.*

I finished washing my hands when the door to the men's opened and banged against the wall. I pulled some paper towels from the dispenser and began drying my hands. In the mirror, I saw the reflection of a large man. He was bald, dark, and wearing one of those wise-guy Adidas tracksuits. Beside him stood a dark-haired woman with large, thick-framed sunglasses.

"Hello, Dillon," she said, calmly removing the shades.

I almost dropped the paper. "Hello, Kadin."

19. The world's a crazy place.

Kadin – who usually wore trim Klein business outfits, often ones that I had bought her – was slumming in faded jeans and a bulky knit sweater. Knowing what I know now, the look made sense. Everything about her was very un-Kadin-like. And what was with the sweater? It was almost 90 degrees out.

"You need to come with us," she said, accent more pronounced.

Mr. Adidas stepped forward, right hand buried deep inside the front pocket of the warm-up. He shifted his hand, and a gun's barrel became obvious through the folds of the nylon.

I dried my hands slowly, hoping Debra would come looking. I methodically wadded up the paper and tossed it into the trash bin. I reached for more towels.

Kadin put a hand on my arm. "Don't."

"What about Debra?" I asked.

"Let's not make a scene."

I was ushered out the mini-mart's side entrance, sandwiched between Kadin and her Adidas heavy. They deposited me in the back seat of a tinted, black Lexus SUV. Kadin climbed into the driver's seat, and Mr. Adidas the passenger side. As we pulled onto the service road, I caught a glimpse of Debra cradling the nozzle back into the pump. I thought about texting her, but Mr. Adidas had a keen eye on me. I couldn't see his gun, but his posture suggested it was leveled at me. From this distance, he could easily shoot me through his seat.

"Where are we headed?" I reached for the seatbelt and saw that the cargo area was empty.

"Love Field," Kadin said, turning onto the northbound lane of Lemmon Avenue.

Why was I not surprised? Love Field was Dallas's inner-city airport, home to Southwest Airlines and a host of private aviation firms. Just six miles from downtown, it was known to most people outside Dallas as the place where Jackie Kennedy received that bouquet of red roses she held all the way to Dealey Plaza. I probably should have been freaking out by now, but the only emotion I could feel was resignation. I was no longer in control of anything, so what would panicking accomplish? The way I figured it, whatever I had in my head was more valuable if the surrounding brain was functioning. At least, that's what I kept telling myself.

The ride to the airport was excruciatingly quiet. My repeated questions went unanswered, and when I tried to listen in to Mr. Adidas, the guy's thoughts were stuck on some weird song in a language I couldn't place. Either he truly didn't know anything and was just passing the time, or this was some kind of intelligence technique designed to ramp up the fear factor. In any case, all it did was piss me off. Just when I was getting used to Harris's smarminess and becoming cozy with Debra, here I was being kidnapped to God knows where.

We pulled into one of the many private aviation firms that lined the main boulevard to Love Field. Kadin drove through a parking lot, past a large hangar on the right and onto the tarmac. A Gulfstream 550 was wedged between two Learjets. She pulled up to the magnificent plane and parked.

In high school, I had seriously entertained a career in aviation, but had neither the math skills nor the balls to become a commercial pilot. What I did have was a deep respect for the profession and a better-than-average knowledge of aircraft. The G550 could fly faster, higher, and more elegantly than any other private jet. Even used, it could set a person back a cool 30 million. It was also among just a handful of private jets that could fly transatlantic. Apparently, I was leaving the country; I just didn't know where. Fear was beginning to creep into my psyche.

"Here we are," Kadin said matter-of-factly.

Mr. Adidas stepped out and came around to my door.

Get out, he motioned with his free hand.

We ascended the plane's stairs as we had at the mini-mart: Kadin in front and Mr. Adidas bringing up the rear. Even though his hand remained in his pocket, I got the feeling that we had passed some unstated checkpoint, as if making it to Love without incident was a milestone. I thought about making a run for it, but Mr. Adidas's hidden right hand kept me in lock step.

The plane's interior – tricked out in cherry wood, gold leaf, and dark leather – smelled of money. I had photographed ads in luxury planes before, but nothing on this scale. Mr. Adidas hung back and blocked the exit as Kadin and I walked into the plane.

She gestured to the cabin. "Pick a seat." Her tone was friendlier now. "We take off in a few minutes."

I settled into a calfskin swivel seat that faced the front of the plane. Kadin took a similar seat across the aisle, but facing backward. The table in front of her was attached to the bulkhead and so heavily lacquered it looked wet.

"Welcome aboard," a familiar voice said from behind me.

I spun in my chair into the scrutiny of Christopher Banks. Standing in the galley next to an elegant wet bar at the rear of the cabin, he rolled the ice around in his drink, saluted me with the glass, and took a long sip. Like Kadin, he was casually dressed, sporting blue jeans and a black, V-neck t-shirt. He walked up and slouched into the calfskin seat in front of me. He propped his feet onto the lip of a thin cherry wood cabinet that seemed organically attached to the bulkhead. His shoes were off, and the bottom of his left sock was worn thin at the heel.

I was stunned. "Chris?"

He smirked. "Are you actually surprised?"

"I thought you were—"

"Debra's boyfriend?" He studied the inside of his glass. "That remains to be seen."

Mr. Adidas nodded to Chris and exited the plane. A uniformed Asian man with close-cropped black hair, presumably a pilot, stepped aside to let him pass. His short-sleeved shirt exposed sinuous, muscled arms.

"Mr. Banks?" the pilot asked. "We're ready to takeoff whenever you are."

"Great, Kin," Chris said without taking his eyes off his glass. "Let's hit it."

The pilot raised the stairs and locked the forward cabin door. The sound of the lock handle latching sent a chill through me. I started to say something, but it felt like someone had opened the trap to life's gallows, and I had fallen through.

Chris motioned with his drink. "What's the matter? Cat got your tongue?" He threw back the last of whatever he was having and tucked the glass into the armrest holder.

"Where are we going?"

"Overseas," he said, seemingly bored.

The G550 began to pull away from its parking spot between the Learjets. Its

Rolls-Royce engines whined up and down as it maneuvered onto the taxiway. We rolled over a bump, and I heard the muffled tinkling of crystal somewhere aft. I instinctively buckled my seatbelt.

"Hell, I never do that anymore." Chris hadn't moved from his lounging position. He adjusted his feet. "When's the last time you heard of one of these going down?"

He had a point. But something deep inside me – even though I knew how it all worked – still found it hard to fathom how a 30-ton object could defy gravity. Maybe it was an instinctual survival mechanism seeded in all humans; maybe it was just the fear of not knowing what was going to happen next. Whatever it was, I pulled the buckle tight across my hips.

The plane lifted off the runway with the grace of a Joffrey dancer, and as we ascended into the early afternoon sky, the identical, insidious quiet from the Lexus filled the cabin. I was ready to explode.

"So," I furiously pivoted between Kadin and Chris, "is anybody going to tell me what the hell is going on?"

Chris pulled his attention from the window and met my glare. Kadin was consumed with something on her laptop. Irritated, Chris said, "I thought you told him already."

"Traffic was too crazy," Kadin replied without looking up. "You explain it."

Chris shook his head, like cowing to Kadin's wishes was a regular issue. He took his feet off of the cabinet and leaned forward. "So," he said, gesturing with open hands. "What did Debra tell you about us?" The plane began banking to the right.

"That you're some kind of splinter cell based in Kazakhstan. That you have Russian scientists who are more advanced in the study of techlepathic ability, and the tech you put in my head is–" What was I doing?

"Are you listening to this?" Chris asked Kadin. "Go on."

"No! Who are you people? I want to see some ID."

Chris rolled his eyes and reached for his suit coat on the couch next to him. Removing the coat exposed a leather shoulder holster — with gun intact — on the seat. He dug through an inside pocket and removed an ID wallet. "Here." He flipped it into my lap and laid the coat back over the gun.

I opened the wallet and found the ID. *Central Intelligence Agency. United States of America.*

Disbelief must have been written on my face. Chris slid his index finger into the side of his mouth and pulled his cheek out. "Hooked ya, didn't they?"

My stomach lurched, but I couldn't tell if the cause was the plane banking or the confusion of the moment. The CIA badge looked official, but what did I know? I had never personally seen one, although I vaguely remembered hearing it had a large eagle emblem. The eagle on this badge was fairly large, along with the CIA crest. The accompanying ID had a bar code, height and weight details, and a picture of Chris that seemed a few years old. His hair was short, and he wore a scowl that looked almost comical.

"I thought Debra's group was the NSA," I said.

Chris wiggled his hands in front of his face. "Ooo. Welcome to Spookville."

"Then what are they?"

"Russian," Kadin said, still typing.

Chris pointed at me. "You, my friend, need a drink." He padded back to the galley. It felt like we were leveling off a bit.

I could use more than a drink. To say that my life had been twisted to shit was an understatement. What the hell was going on? Spy versus counter-spy versus ... who knows? I tried to listen in, but all I heard was the dead air that all people with the gift exude. I tried to focus on the pilots, but couldn't sense their minds.

"Didn't it seem just a bit odd," Chris said, opening an exquisitely hand-carved cabinet door, "that Debra and—" He snapped his fingers. "What's that guy's name?" The plane banked again, and Chris opened his stance and leaned into it.

"Alex Popprov," Kadin said.

"Right, Popprov. Anyway, didn't you find it odd that they spoke fluent Russian?" He removed two cut crystal glasses from the cabinet and plunked four ice cubes into each. After filling them with a generous amount of Scotch from a matching decanter, he walked back up the aisle. "Oh, and Dillon," he handed me my drink, "if you're thinking of calling or texting, don't bother. It'll be jammed. Don't bother listening in on the pilots, either. They don't know dick." He settled back into the chair across from me and regarded me with slight amusement. "You've had a pretty tough weekend, haven't you?"

"How would you know?"

"Little birdie told me."

"How do I know that you're really who you say you are?" I held up the ID wallet.

Chris's expression became stern. "In the last 48 hours, they did two tests on you. The first test stopped your heart for almost a minute. They defib'ed you and told you that you had tapped into the worldwide cellular system via communication satellites. Then they tested you again and connected you with Natalya Narykova, a high-end prostitute whose happy endings aren't so happy."

"The Indian gave you some kind of amphetamine. I can't read this chemical signature." Kadin looked up from her laptop. "By the way, did they stop Narykova from killing the Minister?"

She asked the question like it was one of a dozen things that she needed to check off. I wondered if this was really the same woman I had fallen in love with. "Yes."

She nodded like that was the expected answer and went back to her laptop.

"How did you know about that?" I asked.

"We have people everywhere," Chris said. "Plus, we're able to monitor the technology we put in your head."

"I don't understand."

Chris leaned forward and rested his elbows on his knees. He held his drink with both hands. "The tech we put in you is way advanced. Years in the making. About 40, in fact. I'm not going to get into its backstory, but let's just say you have the best of the best." He blew out a sigh. "Wish I could have it."

"You have tech, too?"

"Two-point-oh, unfortunately."

"Why unfortunately?"

Chris shrugged. "Stopped working for me. Something to do with my body's ability to interact with it. Hey," he motioned me close, "did Debra and you, you know."

I glanced at Kadin, who seemed engrossed in her laptop. I shook my head.

"Did she give you the story about her and her boyfriend in college having the ability to link up?"

I nodded.

"Yeah, she gave me that story, too. It's all bullshit, man. She's just playing you."

I gave a quick nod to Kadin and mouthed, *Does she have tech?*

Chris shook his head. *Nah,* he mouthed back. *She's all natural.*

Kadin closed her laptop and stretched her arms above her head. "I'll take a white wine, if there's any left."

"I'm here to protect and serve." Chris stood and headed aft again.

I turned and faced Kadin. "Can I ask you a question?"

The girl with whom I once had considered spending the rest of my life laconically lolled her head and arched her eyebrows in a way that asked, *Are you talking to me?*

"What hap—?" I couldn't formulate the rest of the question. The eyes that had once been full of love now seemingly considered me a nuisance. Maybe I had stumbled down hell's rabbit hole and this was Kadin's evil twin. I had convinced myself back at ELT that when I did face Kadin, I would rip into her with all the contempt I could muster. Now, however, sitting near her and re-membering the time we shared, I didn't know what to believe. She must have sensed my anguish; she reached across and put a hand to my cheek.

"Oh, Dillon," she said, "you think you're so hip and smart with your Prada suits and Hermes ties. Aren't you just sucking money from companies under the pretext that you're making a difference?"

Chris walked up the aisle and handed Kadin a long-stemmed wine glass. She took it like it was the Eucharist.

"You see," Chris said, sitting, "the world's a crazy place. The vast majority of folks don't have a clue about what's really going on. You should consider yourself lucky."

"Really?" I asked.

"Sure." Kadin took a drink and savored it. "You'll be able to make a real difference now. Won't that be better than kissing some client's ass?"

"Mr. Banks?" The voice of the Asian pilot filled the cabin.

"Yes?" Chris asked into the air.

"We're about to go around some major storms. I think you all should strap in."

Kadin set her wine aside and adjusted her seatbelt. Chris propped his feet back on the cabinet and clinked my glass with his.

"Come on, Dillon. Don't be so glum. Kadin's right. What are you going to do with the rest of your life? Sell your company? That's chump change."

I began to raise my glass but had lost my thirst. I set the Scotch in a drink holder and moved my attention to the darkening skies outside my window. The G550 shuddered as it rode the waves of turbulent air. The whole scene was sur-real, and the metaphor of the storm wasn't lost on me. I felt a hand at my knee.

"Hey, Dillon?" There was a seriousness to Chris's voice that suggested this was him speaking, not the spook.

"Yeah?"

"Remember, man, we're not like rest of the population." He made a circular motion between the three of us. "It's our time now."

It took a few moments for the initial shock to sink in. If Debra and the three amigos were some Russian black project squad, I was the biggest dupe on the planet. Chris and Kadin's version of events had impacted my reality with all the force of a head-on collision. I couldn't fathom the idea that Debra had been suckering me, but she had never showed me any ID. Was I that gullible? I had always considered myself a savvy guy, so how could I have missed something so obvious? And how had they secured space with a major defense contractor? My head was swimming.

"Don't beat yourself up, man," Chris interjected. "Drink your Scotch. It's Oban."

He must have sensed my angst, because I know he couldn't listen in. Or could he?

Kadin stood and stretched. On the way aft, she patted my shoulder in a condescending attempt to reassure me. The urge to follow after her and find out whether she'd ever had any true feelings pulled at me.

"You going to the spin room?" Chris asked.

"Yes," she said, from the galley.

"This plane has a gym?" I handed Chris his ID wallet, which he tossed onto his suit coat. He picked up his drink.

"No. A filthy rich Arab owns this jet. He had a special bed installed that rotates."

"Rotates?"

"Yeah, it continuously faces Mecca." He took a sip. "All right. I know you have questions. Ask away."

"Where are we going?"

"Next."

"Who are they?"

"Debra and her gang? Good question. Hell, you probably know as much as I do. Their back-story is out of my jurisdiction. DoD probably knows more, but they're only spooling out enough to tease us. Don't let all that homeland security camaraderie crap fool you. It's still business as usual. We think they're mob. Russian syndicate. They're into it for the money. Can you imagine what they could do with your ability? Listen in on a CEO's thoughts. Buy a lot of stock at the right time. Jackpot. And think of the power they could exert over rival mobs or the government. They'd reveal it all once they had their claws in you."

The session with the assassin kind of made sense now. "But how can they rent space from a big defense contractor?"

Chris smirked to himself. "Dillon, when you deal with anything high up in Russia, government or corporate, you're dealing with their mafia. It's just the way things are. And it wouldn't surprise me if the DoD was jacking their whole operation."

"What about you two?" I asked.

"Us?" Chris mock saluted. "For God and country."

"What did you say?" I flashed on Harris, just before our first test. I'd said the same thing to him.

"Easy, Dillon. It's a joke. Drink your Scotch, for Christ's sake, or I will."

Maybe I did need to take the edge off. If Kadin and Chris really were CIA, I guess I was in better hands than before. Or was I? I lifted the glass out of the drink holder's leather-lined cocoon and brought it to my lips. The Oban now smelled glorious. It burned down my throat with a sweet, educated delicacy.

"There you go." Chris clinked my glass again and knocked back what was left of his drink.

"I'm still a little confused," I said. "How can a group of Russian mobsters create a company like ELT?"

"Like I said, it's probably the DoD's program." Chris was holding his empty glass with both hands and eyeing me through its cut crystal. "They have the connection and the power over TR Com. They strongly suggest a joint venture between a Russian company – mob held, of course – and TR Com would be good for business. TR Com has no choice but to go along."

I made a face.

"Look, Dillon, the DoD doesn't give a shit so long as they get what they want. They'd get in bed with the devil if they thought it would advance their agenda. Once the mob's front company is embedded into TR Com's systems, it's a bitch to extract it. Who's the head honcho again?"

"That would be Stiles."

"Did he call the shots?"

I nodded, but the motion set my equilibrium spinning. Maybe the plane had moved at the same time I had. I'd felt this before, but usually the sensation went away. I looked at Chris, but it felt like the cabin and my movements were out of sync. There was a lag of reality. I noticed a faint halo forming around Chris's head. He was becoming 3-D, and I didn't have the special glasses.

"What's the matter, man?"

His voice seemed indistinct, and the halo was threatening to expand into a second Chris. My glass seemed heavier. I could feel my hand succumbing to its ever-growing weight. Now the rest of the cabin became as indistinct as Chris. Soft edges of blue, yellow, and orange began expanding in all directions. I sensed Kadin at my shoulder. I looked up. Her hair was pulled back, and she was wearing her glasses. The drone of the plane's engines, once virtually un-noticeable white noise, was now violently throbbing in my ears. I shifted my attention to Chris's two forms. They looked up at Kadin.

"He's about to drop it." Her words were thick syrup.

Chris's first form moved in slow motion to grab my glass. It's twin lagged a nanosecond behind. A wake of tracery after-images followed them.

I sensed, more than felt, the glass slip from my hand. Both Chrises made an "O" shape with their mouths and seemed to cover the distance between us in a split second. Their afterimages slammed into their forms and ricocheted in all directions. The light show hurt my eyes. The cabin exploded into a ballet of fissured color and sound. Kadin grasped my jaw with one hand and pried open one of my eyelids with the other. A spotlight mounted in the upper bulkhead hit my optic nerve like a knife. I tried to grab Kadin's hands, but my arms were dead appendages. She leaned down, and I could make out my reflection in her glasses.

"Damn it," she said. "You used too much."

When Kadin let go, my head fell back against the headrest and rolled toward the window. The dark skies outside beckoned, and I felt myself falling into the clouds. The last shred of my conscious self screamed for help, but it was too late.

Part 2. What's it going to be, cowboy?

20. What is this?

Waking up was like trying to swim to the surface of a deep and murky lake with chains wrapped around my legs. Every time I came up for air, the drug dragged me back down. I finally willed my eyes open and found myself in an old bed in an equally old room. The light was low, and I could feel a dampness I hadn't experienced since childhood, when I had played in my grandmother's storm cellar. The smell of wet, moldy corrugated boxes loitered in the air. I may have seen my breath. Sleep caked my eyelids, and something sharp from the mattress dug into my lower back. The tips of my ears were cold, and my chin rubbed against a wool blanket that smelled of sweat and mud and gasoline.

I managed to sit up and swing my feet over the side of the bed. It groaned in protest. The mattress felt like the old horsehair seats of a BMW 2002 I once owned. The bed was just a glorified cot. Cold cement seeped through the balls of my feet. My right foot nudged a pair of rubber deck sandals, which I quickly slipped on. I dug the sleep from my eyes and rubbed my arms briskly in a desperate attempt to create some warmth. The room came into focus. It was about 18 feet square with old packing boxes scattered about. Some were stacked up to the low ceiling. On the far wall, a basement window interrupted the symmetry. A black plastic garbage bag had been hastily duct taped over it, but one top corner was peeled back, which allowed me to make out the edge of the ground through dirty glass. It looked like it might be late afternoon. I glanced at my wrist, but my watch, along with my designer wardrobe, was gone. In its place was a black t-shirt and faded grey jeans with a small tear in the right knee. The clothes felt stiff, like they had been washed and left in a heap to dry.

The flare of a red dot in a corner of the room cut through the dimness. The dank began to smell of cigarette smoke. It invaded my lungs, and I reflexively coughed.

"Hello, Dillon." A man's voice came from behind the red glow. He sounded eastern European. "We didn't think you'd wake so soon."

"Where am I?" The sound of my own voice seemed distant and broken. I cleared my throat and hacked up a large phlegm ball.

"Use the floor," the man suggested.

I did. Twice.

"Better?"

"Yes," I said hoarsely and wiped spittle from my mouth with the blanket. "Answer my question."

"Poland."

I wrapped the blanket over my shoulders and tried to listen to the man's thoughts, but all I got was the same static I had heard at ELT. My mind didn't seem to want to focus on anything. I coughed again.

"After effect from the drug. Mucus builds in the bronchial tubes. It's also why we're keeping the room dark. Your eyes will be sensitive to light until the drug is flushed from your system. They brought you in earlier than expected. Your room isn't ready yet, so we had to stage you here. Sorry it's so cold. And for the clothes. We'll find you something more comfortable."

"Why was I drugged?"

"A precaution. The technology in your head might be ... unstable."

I tried to stand.

"I wouldn't do that. Wait for the drug to clear."

"When'll that be?"

The man's face lit up in green light when he looked at his watch. It was the same man in the pictures from Debra's case file on Kadin. Handsomely chiseled features framed a salt-and-pepper goatee. I glimpsed deep age lines at the corners of his eyes. His face winked out.

"A couple of hours." The glow from his cigarette reddened, and I could hear his exhale. I pulled the blanket tighter. My left leg was bouncing nervously.

"You're in no danger here, Dillon."

"Where's here exactly?"

"Szymany, Poland."

The name sounded familiar, but I couldn't place it. Then it hit me. "Are you the CIA?" I asked.

"Us? Heavens no."

"Isn't Szymany where they had a black prison base?" I couldn't believe I remembered this shit.

"Was. And cheap to buy." There was a hint of accomplishment in the man's tone.

"Did you work there?"

"We're scientists, Dillon. I could care less who's winning what war."

The man stood and stepped into the narrow shaft of light coming from the triangular flap of the garbage bag. He was tall and broad-shouldered. His leather jacket looked expensive, and his black boots were polished and clean. If we were in the middle of nowhere, he hadn't walked here. He dropped his cigarette and stamped it out. It must have hit some water because it hissed when he crushed it.

"Just lie back and get some sleep," he suggested.

I followed orders and eased my jet-lagged, drug-fatigued body back onto the cot. I sank into the horsehair, my eyes again heavy.

"That's it," the man said. "We'll have dinner tonight. There will be wine and good food. Everything will be explained." He walked to the only door in the room and opened it.

"Are you going to kill me?" It came out a little more melodramatic than I wanted, but I needed to know.

His form turned in the dark. "Quite the contrary." He closed the door quietly behind him.

This declaration didn't make me feel any better. I curled onto my side and faced the crack-filled wall, tucked into the tightest ball I could comfortably make.

I opened my eyes to a water-stained, industrial drop ceiling. The fluorescents were off, the room dimly lit in yellow light. A hospital bed in half-reclined position had replaced the horsehair cot. An IV ran from a bag on a rusty metal armature into the top of my left wrist. Something the color of weak orange juice flowed into my veins.

A deep breath told me that my lungs had cleared. As my eyes adjusted, I saw that this room was about the size of the previous one, if not a little larger. It had no windows but was warm and clean and filled with monitoring equipment. The lettering on many of the stacks was Cyrillic, which applied to everything I could see on the flat LED screens, as well. A single lamp sat on a military-style metal table in the far corner. The lampshade, with its cheap flower pattern, probably came out of some old woman's living room. I sat up. The crisp white sheets fell away to reveal a pale blue hospital gown with a pattern of gray sponge-print triangles. It was nauseating.

After I extracted myself from the sheets, I swung my legs off the side of the bed, which unfortunately sent the room into motion, and I flashed on my last distorted memories from the plane. My stomach rolled, and I swallowed back a swell of bile. The rubber deck sandals had followed me. I slipped my feet into them and eased myself upright. Part of my gown fell open, and the room's air wafted across my butt. Draped on the top of one of the monitors was a white lab coat. I took a step toward it, and the room shifted again. Steadying myself against the monitor, I removed the IV bag from its hook and wormed it through the coat's sleeve. I eased my other arm through and buttoned up. The silver nameplate was in English letters: *Irina Tarasova*.

Two double doors dominated one side of the room, their circular windows covered with more poorly taped trash bags. Something inside me wanted to run, but with my body attached to an IV and my limbs feeling like lead, all I could manage was a decrepit shuffle. I tried one of the doors, surprisingly it pulled open. The dimness I had woken up to became overwhelmed by the caustic glare of fluorescent lighting. Squinting, I futilely held up my hand to block the nearest bank of lights. I seemed to be at the intersection of three clinically white hallways. The one to my right dead-ended after about 15 feet into two more double doors. The hallway to my left ran for about 90 feet and terminated in a grimy glass door with a red fire alarm box attached to it. Above it, an exit sign hung from the ceiling, but it said, *Zjazd*. Probably Polish. An innate urge to run welled in me again, but I was in no condition to escape. The hallway in front of me stretched about 150 feet until it reached another T intersection. And directly catty-corner from me was a lab-coated guy sleeping in a chair. Probably my "guard," but he looked deep into REM. There was also a strange aroma in the air that, curiously, reminded me of the lunch buffet at Kebab N' Kurry in Dallas.

I quietly shuffled past the sleeping guard and down the bleak hallway in front of me, dragging the IV stand like a dead appendage. The smell of curry grew stronger, and I couldn't remember the last time I had eaten. A lone desk and a metal shelving unit were parked on one side of the hallway. Even though I was up and functioning, I was still fighting a fog of jet lag, drugs, and hunger. Yet with each step, I could feel my body coming back online. All of the doors along the hallway were closed. I didn't bother trying them because one door at the far end was open and beckoning me. As I approached, I heard the murmur of voices, but the languages were foreign. It sounded like a party. As I got closer I could separate the distinct aromas of my favorite Indian dishes. God, was I starving.

Just as I rounded the open door, the IV stand caught on the threshold. The antiseptic whiteness of the hallway gave way to dark wood paneling and dirty green shag carpet. Red leather wingbacks ringed a large, claw-legged dining table. There were foil trays of Indian food, and people in lab coats eating and talking. Everyone turned simultaneously, and the hum of conversation dissipated like a cold breath. The cigarette smoker, now clad in a black turtleneck and dark blue jeans, emerged from the small crowd. Judging from his face, he was shocked to see me. Kadin, wearing skinny tan corduroys, a rust brown crew neck sweater, and a thin down vest, stood behind him. Her expression mirrored his. Someone gasped, and a few people pointed and whispered.

The man feigned a small grin. "Dillon." He glanced at his watch. "We, ah, didn't expect you to wake so soon."

My fog had returned with a vengeance. A movement off to my right caught my eye. A guy — full beard, grey collared shirt — parted the crowd. He was calm, yet seemingly coiled to strike. A second man, shorter, moved into my left periphery. The smoker exchanged a quick glance with each and motioned for them to stand down.

"Everyone," he said, raising the pitch on the one, "this is Dillon Bradford.

Please make him feel welcome." Trepidation vibrated in his voice.

Someone started to clap, and everyone joined the polite applause. For a fleeting moment, the energy was welcoming, but my rational self quickly reminded me that these were the same people who had, at gunpoint, drugged and flown me halfway around the world. The two heavies had disappeared into the crowd.

The man approached and reached for my free arm.

"Please, Dillon. You shouldn't be up."

I thrust out a defiant hand. "Stop!"

He did. His arms dropped to his sides.

"Who are you? What is all this?" I made a sweeping gesture. The fog from the drug was lifting.

"My name is Dr. Peter Wardinski. I run this facility."

Kadin, who hadn't moved a muscle, remained about five feet behind him. The concern on her face seemed more academic than emotional. Behind her, the crowd stood stiffly transfixed on me as if I were a curious artifact that had escaped its diorama. Staring at Wardinski, I demanded, "Answer me!"

"Dillon!" It was Kadin. She had stepped closely behind Wardinski, hands clasped in an awkwardly pleading gesture. Wardinski looked back at her and stepped aside.

"We're not here to hurt you," she said. She spread her hands, palms up. "Come on, let me take you back to your room. You shouldn't be up." She took another step toward me.

Not hurt me? What kind of fucked up cult nightmare had I been dragged into? I looked over the gathering of technicians. An Asian man grinned and gave a slight nod, eyes never leaving me. A petite black woman with a close-cropped Afro produced a gummy smile, her head tilted as if admiring a cute little baby. Two Indian women clasped their hands, mouthed *Welcome*, then bowed deeply. As I took in each face, it dawned on me that they weren't curious; they were in awe.

The whole scene assaulted my fragile reality. My heart started racing as panic invaded every cell. Breathing, which only moments before had been innate, now became a conscious struggle. The attack was consuming me. I desperately needed an emotional anchor. I glanced back at Kadin, who had moved within 10 feet. Wardinski had stepped closer, too. Unexpectedly, Kadin smiled that smile that I had fallen in love with, and something inside me gave way. The last of my emotional strength broke off like a huge column of ice on a dying glacier and slid into the darkest part of my soul. I had always felt distant from the world. The gift had ensured that. Now, though, looking at Kadin and remembering our time together, everything came crashing down. The cold reality of my situation plowed through my heart. I felt like a child again. Isolated, exposed, scared. The words of my adoptive father echoed in my mind. *You're nothing but a goddamn freak.* His fist, under the influence of a bottle of gin, crashed into my jaw, and the memory hit with all the fury of the original event. I tried to fight the swell of emotion, but it leaked out in convulsive gasps.

Deep concern pressed into the corners of Wardinski's face, and he cautiously inched toward me. "Dillon, please calm down. We aren't here to—"

I raised a fist and glared, barely supporting myself with the IV stand. "Get … away … from … me!" I punched out the words in a venomous rage. The room was swimming.

Shocked acolytes, some with hands pressed to their mouths, began to step back. I turned to Kadin and unleashed my wrath. "You!" I said, pointing.

Kadin, mouth agape, started to speak.

I pointed again. "You bitch. Fuck you!" I swept my finger like a loaded gun across the whole room. "Fuck all of you!" The motion sent me stumbling. I banged into the IV stand and caught myself.

Wardinski surged forward, arms poised like he was going to tackle me. The two heavies swooped in behind him, one actually pushing up the sleeves of his coat.

A surge of adrenaline hit. I yanked the IV line out of my wrist, grabbed the stand, and swung for the fences. Wardinski jumped back and slammed into his two heavies. As the three of them stumbled against each other, I swung the stand in a sweeping 360. Two women behind me screamed and dove for cover. I caught a guy wearing a turban on the side of the face. He let out a guttural yell and crumpled to his knees. I swung again, almost clipping Wardinski's chin. He batted at the stand, which sent it flying out of my hands. I followed in its wake, pushing and shoving. I shouldered a stocky woman into a short technician and sprinted toward the door. The woman shrieked as her plate of tandoori chicken splashed across her face and lab coat.

"Dillon, wait!" Wardinski yelled, tripping over the fallen IV stand.

I stumbled in my deck sandals and tripped into the doorframe. I pushed off and headed back down the hallway. I staggered into the desk, the metal shelving unit, and then skidded to the T intersection in front of the room where I had awoken. To my right was the glass door. The guard was sleepily rising from his chair and eyeing me with shock.

Run, goddamn it!

I did, as fast as I could, toward the door. Over my shoulder, I caught sight of Wardinski rounding the hallway corner, the guard at his side. As I kicked at the door's emergency exit arm, he called for me to stop. On my second try, the door swung open. An alarm sounded at the far end of the hall.

Cold night air stung my eyes as I ran into the middle of a dirt parking lot. A herd of small cars stood off to my right. Deep muddy ruts crisscrossed the area. A tall, chain link fence enclosed the grounds. I could see farmland in the distance, and beyond that what looked like the green pulse of beacon at a municipal airport control tower. Dark tree masses framed the farm plots on either side of me. My breath was coming out in quick gusts of condensation. Boot steps crunched through the muddy gravel behind me. I spun around. Wardinski and Kadin approached, but stopped at about 20 feet.

"Please, Dillon, listen to me." If Wardinski was angry, there was no trace of it in his voice. He was also huffing out quick breaths, his hand rubbing his side.

Several of the people from the dinner spilled out after them, their figures silhouetted by the light from the doorway. The guard and the two heavies began to approach me.

"Leave me alone," I growled between breaths.

"Stop!" Wardinski barked. The three men did, then stepped back behind Wardinski.

Kadin stepped forward. "Dillon, you have to—"

"Shut up!"

Kadin stopped herself and backed away to Wardinski's side. Only then did I notice the similarities: the closely set eyes, the curly, unruly hair. Even the man's stature was echoed in Kadin's athletic build.

"Are you her father?" A bitingly cold wind whipped around me.

Wardinski put a hand to Kadin's shoulder. "I am."

My scorn dropped to new depths.

"Did he put you up to this?" I lashed out at Kadin. "Did your father pimp you out? Or was it Chris?"

Murmurs rose from the crowd as someone pushed through. Chris sidestepped two lab technicians and trotted into the parking lot. He cautiously came alongside Wardinski.

"What the hell?" he said. The sleeves of his white dress shirt were rolled tightly above his elbows. His loosened yellow tie flapped in the night air. He turned to Wardinski and Kadin. "What did you two say to him?"

"We didn't say anything," Kadin spat back.

Chris threw his hands up. "Jesus *H*. Christ!" he yelled, exasperated. "I told you not to do the party!" He motioned for me to join them. "Man, it's freezing out here. Come in and get something to eat. Have a drink, at least."

A light duty truck — one of those narrow European ones — lumbered past about 300 feet from the parking lot's entrance. I turned and found that Wardinski and the heavies had inched closer. I took a few steps back.

"Dillon, where would you go?" Wardinski pointed. "You're barefoot."

The paleness of my feet was a stark contrast to the dark frozen mud. Blood was splattered against the side of my right foot, and I now noticed a sharp stinging across my arch. I forced the pain down and shouted, "Away from this!" I waved an arm to indicate the industrial building we had just exited. Its single story elbowed around half the parking lot.

"You don't even know what *this* is," Chris pointed out.

"Really?" My furtive eyes had noted a damaged part of the fence that had been pulled away from the top bar. With a little luck, I could scale it and be at the road beyond in seconds. "Then tell me. What is *this*?"

Kadin stepped forward, arms spread. "Your future."

21. Tired.

Another gust of cold air cut across the parking lot. It kicked at the lab coat and rushed up my legs to my butt. I swallowed a gasp. "You're not CIA, are you?"

Wardinski shot a harsh sideways glance at Chris.

"It's complicated," Chris said.

"Great," I said, shivering. "Just great! I'm in the middle of Poland, at a black CIA prison, held hostage by some ... some *cult*!" Another part of me seemed ready to separate and fall away. I sucked in a breath. The air bit into the corners of my lungs. "If you're not exactly the CIA, then what are you?"

"We're not a cult," Wardinski said.

"Look ..." Chris rubbed the back of his neck. "... it's complicated. Just come in and we'll–"

"Fuck you."

"Right. I know we should have been straight up. But if we'd told you everything, you might not have come."

I folded my arms across my chest and tried to hold in my warmth. I couldn't feel my fingertips, and with each breath, my teeth chattered.

"Dude, come inside," Chris urged. "You're going to freeze to death out here."

A technician emerged from the crowd holding the same kind of thick wool blanket that had been on the cot. He handed it to Kadin, all the while staring at me.

"What is with you all?" I asked. "You look at me like I'm a ... I don't know ... freak or something."

Wardinski shouted to the crowd: "Go in! All of you! Now!"

While they shuffled back indoors, Kadin offered the blanket at arm's length.

"Dillon, please." Her voice broke on the word please. "I swear to you – on my mother's grave – no one forced me to do anything." She came toward me, arms outstretched.

The wind gusted, and my whole body began to go numb. I couldn't remember the last time I had eaten. My right calf was cramping.

Kadin was now close enough to speak privately. "Dillon, you have to believe me. It was my–"

"Is your name really Bolek?"

"That's my middle name. It's my mother's maiden name."

"Why did you do it?"

"I–" She looked away.

"You what?"

When she looked back, the moonlight caught a glimmer of tears welling in her eyes. What a fucking show.

"You are so full of shit," I said.

I summoned every last ounce of strength I possessed and ran for the fence. It was about 12 feet high and had a cross rail halfway up. An eight foot wide swath of the chain link was torn away from the top rail and drooping over the cross rail. Above the top rail four taunt rows of barbwire had been strung at an inward slant.

I jumped and grabbed the cross rail with both hands. The galvanized metal was ice cold, and I fought the primal need to yell. Stabs of pain shot up through my ruined foot as my toes clawed the chain link.

"Dillon, stop!" Chris screamed.

I hooked my right knee onto the cross rail and put all of my weight against the loose flap of damaged chain link. I rode it on hands and knees as it sagged like the petal of an enormous industrial plant. It stopped about four feet from the ground and I pitched myself over. My forearm scraped across an exposed edge of chain-link. My feet hit the ground and a new wave of intense pain rocketed up from my feet.

"Get someone to unlock this fucking gate!" Chris yelled as he ran to the fence. He slammed into the chain link, arms spread wide.

I staggered upright and started hobbling to the road.

"Dillon!" Chris shook the fence in frustration. "What the hell are you doing?"

"Getting the fuck away from you and your fucked up cult!" I yelled over my shoulder.

"Dude, you're wearing a hospital gown and a lab coat in the middle of bumfuck Poland. Get your ass back here." His last statement was punctuated by another shake of the fence.

Chris's plead seemed to give me new strength and my hobble turned into a trot.

"Where are the fucking keys to this goddamn gate?" he yelled behind me.

I ran across the compound's dirt driveway and into thick brush.

"Dillon? Come on, man. Get back here." Chris's voice, along with the clinking of the fence, echoed through the trees. "Look, I'm sorry. Let me make it up to you."

I stepped on something sharp and went to my knees. I bit down a scream and desperately rubbed at my arch. I looked back over my shoulder expecting to see the two heavies behind me. Nothing. Odd. Why didn't they scale the fence and tackle me?

I got up and limped through the bushes. After several of minutes of snaking my way, I emerged into the blinding glare of headlights. A truck's air horn blared, and I stumbled back. It trumpeted again and dopplered away as the rig rushed by. In its wake, a torrent of cold air swirled around me and ripped open the lab coat. I folded the coat closed and clutched it to my body.

In the dim moonlight I could barely make out the striping of a narrow two-lane road that curved away on both sides. I was standing in the middle of its gravel shoulder. Across the road I could see through the thin shrubs a tall chain link fence, and beyond that open fields. In the distance, the green beacon of a private airport's control tower pulsed.

Off to my left, the beams from another truck were bathing the tree line in harsh cool light. Its headlights exploded around the corner, and I turned and desperately raised a thumb.

This truck didn't sound its contempt, but its windstorm battered me again with dust and bone chilling air.

"Fucker!"

The word detonated from my throat and was framed by upraised middle fingers. I hunched forward, hands on knees, and watched the truck's taillights disappear around the other corner.

"Come on, Dillon," I urged myself. "You have to keep moving."

I trotted along the road's shoulder, raising my thumb to every passing vehicle. Finally one slowed and pulled onto the gravel. It was one of those small Euro pickups, but this one was very used. Its front cab was a patchwork of rust and faded yellow, and its bed had been fashioned together from thick planks of weathered grey wood. Its backend was an exposed chassis and might have been from another vehicle that had once been painted blue. As I approached, the blackened out passenger window cracked open and a hand, cigarette dangling from its fingers, emerged and motioned to the truck's bed. It retreated back into the cab and the window went silently up.

Climbing into the bed took the last of my strength. I rolled onto my back and my shoulder slammed into what sounded like a stack of 2 x 4s. The truck lurched forward, and something big and metal shifted behind me. It slid into the stack, and then we all slid to one side as the truck took the curve. A canvas tarp blew across my face, and I breathed in bits of sawdust and dirt. I yanked it over me and tried to fend off the backdraft of wind. A passing truck's headlights flooded the bed, and I saw that the stack was a pile of pre-stained flooring, and the metal object that had slid into the stack was their portable circular saw. Its jagged blade glinted menacingly as the truck passed.

As the pickup drove through the forest, I caught glimpses of the Polish night sky. Patches of stars peeked through the low-level clouds, and raindrops sporadically dappled my face. After what seemed like many miles, the truck slowed and pulled into an old gas station. The hand emerged again, banged on the cab's roof and pointed to it.

I grudgingly unwrapped myself from the tarp and crawled out of the truck's bed.

"Thanks!" I yelled as the truck pulled away.

Its horn tooted what was either you're welcome or good luck asshole. Probably the latter.

I was back where I had been earlier, just farther down the road. But now my body was shaking uncontrollably, and I feared I was minutes away from a full-blow hyperthermic collapse.

In the semidarkness the gas station looked like it had been abandoned for decades. Its pumps were gone, its roof was half-collapsed, and it was the only structure for miles. I needed warmth and water, and I needed it all fast.

I limped to its front door and peered in. Through the gloom all I could see were the ghostly structural remains of a forgotten business. A dilapidated wooden armchair, its rattan seat shredded, was tilted back against a wall covered in faded graffiti. A counter display case, its glass front and shelves broken into shards, stood sentinel by the front window. But on the floor were an old mattress and a tattered blanket, and in the grey glow of moonlight they beckoned like gifts from heaven.

I threw open the door and literally crawled to the mattress. I wrapped the blanket over me and tucked into the fetal position. The history of the station had been captured in the fabric, and the fetid odor of ancient mold and dirt and gasoline enveloped me. But I didn't care. The blanket was my shield, and I was determined to cocoon myself against the cold night air.

My breathing had become ragged and shallow. The uncontrolled shivering, which moments before had gripped my body, had subsided. Then, out of nowhere, a deep and peaceful apathy moved through me like a warm current. It was as if I just didn't care anymore about my condition or even my life. If I was going to die on the floor of some antique burned-out Polish gas station, then I was good with that.

"I never thought it would end like this." I rasped out a laugh. "Derek is going to be so pissed."

The angled fingers of dust filled moonlight that played through the room, suddenly faded out.

"I'm tired, God," I whispered into the darkness. "I am really ... fucking ... tired."

22. Faith.

Dillon?

I opened my eyes from a dreamless sleep to the muddy toe of a hardcore climbing boot. Its embossed Nike swoosh was accentuated in the soft pre-dawn light.

"Dillon?" a female voice asked, as a hand a brushed hair out of my eye.

I strained to lift my head off of the mattress and looked up. Kadin was on one knee, leaning over me and gently stroking my forehead. Her hair hung down and framed her angular face like an expensive fur collar. The grin she wore was fragile.

Chris stood in silhouette behind her, arms folded. He removed his aviator sunglasses and extended a hand down to me.

"Come vith me if you vant to live," he said.

Chris's lame Schwarzenegger riff from *Terminator 2* brought reality crashing back, and I dropped my head back onto the mattress. I tried to pull the blanket over my head, but something thwacked my face. I looked at the IV line stuck into the top of my hand and followed it up to Wardinski's face. He was holding the fluid bag and regarding me like a father might a gravely sick child. He acknowledged me with a curt nod.

My throat felt like I had swallowed a bucket of sand, and my lungs didn't feel much better.

"Tell me I'm dead," I croaked.

"Your dead," Chris answered.

Kadin shot him an angry look. She continued to stroke my forehead.

"Heaven sucks," I said, trying to lift myself upright.

Kadin grabbed under my armpits and helped me sit up against the wall. Its pitted surface was cool against the back of my head. This simple movement sent the room spinning a little. I nodded thanks to Kadin, and that set the room into chaos.

I brought a hand to my mouth. "Whoa, shit," I said through my fingers.

"Dillon, what's the –?"

Before Kadin could finish the question, I jerked onto one arm and wretched across the mattress. The force of the action tore at my guts.

Chris squatted down. "Guess you won't be sleeping here again."

"You always this funny?" I asked, and wiped my mouth with the blanket.

Chris patted my thigh. "Only when I'm with friends."

"Here," Kadin said handing me a bottled water.

I swirled a mouthful around and spit out what was left of the vomit, then took three long slow gulps. The water tasted like life.

"Easy, Dillon," Kadin urged. "Just take small sips."

After another gulp, I cradled the bottle in my lap and leaned back against the wall.

"Feeling better?" Chris asked.

"A little." I could feel my body building strength. "What's in the bag?"

"Just simple fluids," Wardinski said. "You were severely dehydrated."

I lifted my right foot and the blanket fell away. "I really screwed my foot up." Dried blood caked one side of it and the joint of my big toe throbbed.

"We'll get Tarasova to look at it," Chris said.

"So." I took another swig. "How'd you find me?"

"Since the tech interfaces with the cellular grid," Chris said. "It isn't hard to track you."

"My own personal GPS?"

He nodded. "You could say that. Reception is crappy out here, that's why it took so long to get a fix on you."

"Maybe you should change carriers."

"You always this funny?"

Chris delivered the touché void of his usual snarky inflection, and there seemed to be genuine concern in the way his hand went to my shoulder.

"Listen, man," he said. "I'm really really sorry for the way this all came down. It's just that ..." He struggled to find the next words.

"You aren't going to go all touchy-feely on me, are you?" I asked.

Something solemn settled behind Chris's eyes. "Too many good men and women have died because we didn't have the right intel," he said. "Ever since 9/11, we've just been guessing. I'm tired of guessing." His attention shifted to the ground. "With you, we can get the right intel and make a difference."

I sensed that this was the real Chris talking. No pretense. No hidden agenda. No bullshit. This was the CIA soldier who had lost too many close friends in the War on Terror. The label on my bottled water was peeling away from the plastic. I picked at it with my thumb.

"What do you want from me?" I asked.

"Your faith, man. That's all."

"Faith? In what?"

"In what we're doing." His voice became earnest. "You're the only one, man, don't you get that? We've tested a lot of our kind, and nobody comes close to your strength." He tapped my forehead with his index finger. "That brain of yours is special, and it would be a colossal mistake to waste it in advertising."

"Dillon?"

Kadin took my hand into hers, and a part of me wanted to pull away.

"Yes?" I asked.

"We never intended to hurt you," she said rubbing her thumb across my knuckles.

"Could have fooled me."

Kadin let go and picked at a bottle cap half buried in the dirt. "I know. You're right," she said nodding with acceptance. "We screwed this up beyond all repair." She looked up again, her anguish molded in upturned eyebrows and wrinkled forehead. "But if you could just give us a second chance, I know you'll come to believe in our work—"

"Kadie?" Wardinski interjected.

"Yes, Papa?"

"We have to get him back." Wardinski was squeezing the last of the fluids out of the IV bag.

"You up for traveling?" Chris asked.

"Sure," I said with a shrug. "It's not like I have a choice."

"Dillon, I'll make you a promise."

"What's that?"

"If we can't prove to you that what we're doing is the right thing, then I'll fly you back to Dallas. Hell, I'll personally drive to your condo and tuck you in bed." As Chris said this, an impish grin played at the corners of his mouth.

"Promise?" I asked.

Chris raised his right hand and mimicked the Scout's sign. "Scout's honor."

Then he stood and offered the same hand. "Come on, tough guy. Give me a chance."

I grabbed Chris's hand with both of mine and struggled to my feet. Kadin steadied me as I stood.

"You okay to walk?" she asked.

"Yeah, but slowly. I don't want to puke again."

"Let me remove this." Wardinski pulled the IV line from my wrist, and then pressed a bandage over the wound. He wrapped the IV line around the bag and tossed it all into a rusted barrel in the corner of the room.

I slowly shuffled out of the station, Kadin holding my right arm, Chris my left. The morning sun was beginning to fill the sky with beautiful striations of mauve and crimson. A bird chittered melodically somewhere near the edge of the forest.

A large black rakish Mercedes sedan sat idly on the other side of what would have been the pump island. It chirped twice as we approached.

■   ■   ■

The ride back to the compound was a blur. I must have fallen asleep or maybe there had been something in the IV bag, because the trip seemed a lot shorter than the night before. They put me back in the same hospital room. It looked just the way it had even down to the sheets, which were still wadded up at the end of the bed. I settle onto its 10 inches of memory foam and as Wardinski hooked another IV bag up to me, Kadin told me again how sorry they all were for what they had put me through. Chris, leaning against a counter and engrossed in his cell, had obviously disengaged from the whole affair.

The tension that hung between Wardinski and Chris was almost visible, yet neither man had said a word to each other since the gas station. Kadin seemed oblivious, and tucked me in with all the care of a doting mother.

"There," she said, folding the sheet neatly over the edge of the blanket. She reached across me and patted the blanket up to the sides of my body.

"Get some rest, Dillon," Wardinski said in a low tone. He glanced at Chris. "May I have a word?"

A millisecond ticked by before Chris pulled himself away from his email. "Sure," he said, and followed Wardinski out.

Kadin watched them leave. Before I could ask her what was up, she turned.

"Need anything?" The sincerity in her tone seemed genuine.

"No. Thanks." The words were coated in the station's dust.

"Try and get some sleep. We'll have dinner tonight with papa."

Kadin clicked the lights out as she left and pitched me into a thick darkness. As my eyes adjusted, the glow from the equipment's readouts cast the room into harsh contrast. After several minutes, their hum washed away my futile attempt to stay awake.

.   .   .

A loud bang detonated at the edges of my sleep. Light from the hallway cut into the room, and a tall blonde girl walked in pushing a bent IV stand in front of her. She looked all of 25 and, like Kadin, had an athletic grace about her. She was the first person, besides Chris, Wardinski and Kadin, not wearing a lab coat. She wore a simple white collared shirt, faded jeans, and black Converse high-tops. She stepped into the shaft of light and grabbed the coat I had been wearing off of the chair. I couldn't recall how it got there.

"You forgot something in dining room last night," she said putting it on. Her Russian accent was thick.

"Irina Tarasova, I presume?" I had to squint to make her out. She noticed this and back-kicked the door shut.

She had one of those girlish faces that hinted what she looked like as a child.

It was a stark contrast to her resonant voice. She smiled, and her modestly made-up eyes disappeared into slits. "*Da*, that's me." She nodded, causing her ponytail to bounce.

"Hope you didn't mind me borrowing your coat."

"No problem." She rolled the IV stand to the bed, then fished a new bag from a drawer.

"What's in those bags?" I asked as she inspected the empty one.

Irina shot a glance, but her tough-girl look wasn't convincing. "Magic formula. It will make you strong, like bull."

I started to comment on her bad cliché when one of the double doors opened and sliced the room with light again. Kadin entered with a clear plastic dry cleaning bag. I assumed the writing on it was Polish, and a cartoonish dress shirt with spindly legs and arms danced across it. Kadin's other hand held a plastic grocery bag with more Polish. I could see the heels of my shoes peeking out from a tear.

"I see you've met Irina," Kadin remarked, hanging the bag on a hook in the wall.

"Yes," I said. "She's been very nice."

Irina lifted the blankets off my feet and inspected my right foot. "You cut yourself bad. I fix." She removed a pair of thick black glasses from a pocket and put them on. Instantly professional.

"Will it need stitches?" I asked.

"No." She retrieved antiseptic and gauze from another drawer.

"Does that bag have my phone in it?" I asked.

Kadin shook her head.

"I didn't think so."

"I have to go talk with Papa. When Irina's done, get dressed. I'll be back to help you to dinner."

There was a nervous edge to Kadin's manner. I started to ask her what was wrong, but she spun and left too quickly. Irina started humming while she dressed my foot.

I leaned forward as best I could in my thermal cocoon. "Old Russian folk song?"

She looked up, puzzled. "No. Maroon 5."

Irina left after she bandaged my foot and shin. I didn't bother mentioning my forearm. I washed it in the small sink that barely clung to the only wall not filled with equipment. My clothes smelled of over-processed dry cleaning, and the trees in my Kenneth Coles were cedar and looked extremely used. At least my shoes had been buffed and polished. I suppose Wardinski wanted to make a good impression, but anything short of a plane ticket home was going to fall short. Just as I reached to push open one of the double doors, Kadin stepped in.

"Dillon!" she exclaimed. "You're looking better."

Beyond her surprise at nearly running into me, the nervousness seemed gone. I didn't feel much better, though. My stomach was feeding on itself, and my foot was throbbing. Cramming it into the Cole boot reached the frontier of my tolerance for pain. I tried not to damage Irina's wrap job, but nevertheless made a mess of it.

"Let me help you." Kadin reached for my waist.

"I can manage." I took a cautious step, then tried my full weight. Pain shot up from my foot, and I yelped. "Shit, that hurts."

She reached again.

"No. Please. I don't think I want your help right now."

She folded her arms tightly against her body. "Dillon, I'm—"

"What. Sorry?"

She shied, then nodded.

"Really? I find that hard to believe. In fact, I find all of this hard to believe." I leaned against the bed. "What have you dragged me into, Kadin?"

"I didn't mean for it to go this way."

"Why didn't you just approach me? I have a life, for Christ's sake. And a company, with employees who depend on me. What gives you the right to do what you've done?"

My anger was fueled by hunger, stress, and fatigue.

"When we discovered what Debra's group was doing – that they had begun implanting – we had to get you out of there. Chris insisted it had to be this way."

"Is there something wrong with the technology?"

"We don't know."

Great. I shook my head. "This keeps getting shittier and shittier." I shifted my weight off of my bandaged foot. "Can I ask you a question?"

Kadin cautiously nodded.

"Why the whole seduction thing?"

"Chris felt you–"

"Fuck Chris. I'm talking about you. Why you did it."

A steely air of resolution descended through Kadin. The ice queen from the plane was back.

"There are things in this world that are more important than you." Her tone was now cool, tactical. "Hopefully, you'll understand that soon. I'll let Papa explain the details." Then, as if she'd suddenly realized she had slipped too far into bitch mode, she summoned a weak smile. "Come on. You must be starving."

She offered her arm, and I reluctantly let her wrap it around my waist. I had no choice. My foot was killing me, and there weren't any crutches in sight. I draped my arm over her shoulder and was surprised at how natural she felt next to me. Even after all that she had done, I guess a small part of me still wanted to love her. Maybe I just needed someone familiar to hang onto. That, and the fact that I was ravenous.

"Are you with the CIA?" I tried to shuffle in step with her, but I couldn't seem to match her cadence.

"No," she said, still all business. "Just Chris."

"Why can't I listen in on your dad's mind?"

"We're blocking Debra's group from tracking you. But in doing so, we're also blocking our ability." We neared the dining room door. Kadin let go and steadied me. "You okay to walk the rest of the way?"

"Yeah, I'm fine."

I limped into the room and found that three place settings were arranged at the near end of the table. A pitcher of orange juice and three bottled waters sat in the center, and full plates of food already waited. No worshipers, though. Thank God, so to speak. Wardinski unceremoniously entered.

"Please, have a seat," he said. "I took the liberty of making us plates. I hope you like breakfast."

I sat at the head of the table and grabbed a bottled water. The smells emanating from my plate were heavenly. I scooped out what looked like homemade strawberry preserves and spread a wide swath across a slice of thick toast. The scrambled eggs had a wonderful cheese cooked into them that tasted like cheddar, but with distinctly sharp bite. Wardinski and Kadin flanked me, and we ate in silence. I could feel my strength returning. Kadin attempted a few caring glances between forkfuls. I tried not to acknowledge her. Wardinski poured generous portions of the orange juice into each of our glasses. He took a large drink, then leaned into the silence.

"I have to apologize, Dillon. Our handling of this whole affair was very, very sloppy."

He shook his head with each *very*.

Kadin looked up from her plate. "Papa, maybe I should explain—"

Wardinski raised a hand to stop her. Beyond the weariness in his eyes, I could sense a deep frustration simmering.

"I gave Chris and Kadin too much latitude. Chris, especially, can be so–" He pondered the right word.

"Reckless," Kadin suggested, her eyes on her food.

"More like impetuous."

"There's only one way with him," she said.

"And not with you?" Wardinski cupped his glass and studied it contents. "I don't know why you think he–"

"Papa, all Chris wanted–"

Wardinski glared. "Kadie, why did you go along with his CIA charade? How do you expect Dillon to trust us if you two never stop lying?"

"Chris thought Dillon wouldn't come if he knew we were–" She cut herself off this time. "What did you expect?" she said, softly.

Wardinski slammed his fist onto the table. "Professionalism!"

Chris had the gift, technology, and had been a spy? What a perfect combination. I said, "You're clearly not a CIA operation."

Wardinski shook head. "No. Chris was an operative for many years. Now he's ... independent."

Jesus. "So, if you're not CIA, what are you?"

"We're a loose collection of concerned scientists. Each of us has been affected by your kind in one way or another."

"You know, I don't even care anymore. I just want to know what's inside my head."

Wardinski's eyes moved between Kadin and me before he nodded to himself like this was the moment he'd been dreading. He set his orange juice aside and laced his fingers together.

"The technology that was injected into your brain has been in development since the Cold War–"

"Both yours and Debra's?"

Wardinski nodded. "Russian scientists, working inside a special unit of the

KGB, developed a rudimentary form of nanotech. They'd worked with techlepaths for years, long before your kind became known in the West. After the
Soviet Union broke apart, many of these scientists found their way into the U.S.
intelligence system."

"Like Alex Popprov?" I asked.

"Yes. He was very high up in the group. Some of them remained in Russia,
while others scattered to the breakaway republics. I was a chemist working for
the Russian government. We were in the early stages of developing nanotechnology. After Kadin was born, her gift, as you call it, became apparent, and
I sought the help of some old friends who knew many of these scientists. I
thought maybe the nanotechnology we had been developing might help Kadin.
But as the research advanced, it became apparent that it could only work on
those whose techlepathic strength was of a certain level. Only a few people have
the physiology to accept the technology. Kadin's body rejected it. Eventually, we
realized there were only a handful of candidates. You're at the top of the list."

"Great."

"Papa," Kadin said, "maybe I should explain."

Wardinski acquiesced and settled into the chair.

Kadin put her fork down and faced me. "Chris didn't think approaching you
directly would work. He thought you might contact the police or the FBI. I had
only planned to befriend you, but one thing led to another."

"You became more than a friend?" I asked.

She shrugged.

"But you still went ahead and injected me."

Kadin's eyes went to her plate. She nodded.

"What I don't understand is why was Chris with Debra? She told me that
they had gotten to me through Chris."

"Chris knew about their operation through some old contacts he still had
within the CIA. He was trying to learn more by getting close to Debra."

Some of it was beginning to make sense. If Debra were NSA, then they would have known Chris and never let him get close.

I said, "She thinks that you pointed out the incision marks to deflect attention from what you were doing."

"Chris didn't know exactly what Debra's group was up to," Kadin said. "The intelligence from his CIA source was sketchy. We didn't know how advanced they might be. To be honest, when we discovered their needle mark, we panicked. We had no idea how the two technologies would interact. Their incision had become infected, so I decided to make you think they were insect bites, so you wouldn't fuss too much. But in true Dillon fashion, you began to connect the dots."

"That's when I went out to ELT, right?" I asked.

"Yes," Kadin said. "And after Marcus did the MRI, Chris and I contacted Papa. We waited until the right time to approach you."

"You mean take me."

"I told them to bring you here," Wardinski said. "For your safety."

"Am I in danger?"

Wardinski and Kadin exchanged glances.

"What?"

Kadin hesitated. "We were only going to inject enough of the technology to see if you would reject it or not. But Chris insisted we implant all of it."

"What does that mean?"

She hesitated. "We're not sure."

I exhaled an exacerbated sigh.

"We need to run some tests," Wardinski said. "To see how our technology is interacting with the other."

"One of Debra's researchers," I offered, "thinks that the nanos they injected into me triggered a reaction from your technology."

"Possibly." Wardinski tugged at his goatee. "It's experimental bioware."

"Back up a second. How did you develop this experimental bioware? I mean, is this some kind of Russian black program?"

"I performed work for the Russian government for many years. In weapons research. I headed up a team of nanotechnologists, biotech engineers, and neuroscientists. But we're not a black program, Dillon. When I learned what was being done with techlepaths, I became very interested—"

"Obsessed," Kadin interjected.

Wardinski raised an eyebrow.

"Because of Kadin, I became *interested* in the technology. It mirrored much of the weapons research I was already doing. I began working at night with some of the scientists from the original Soviet program. Our research grew, and we decided to create this facility."

"So you're Russian?" I asked.

"No. I am Polish."

"How is this place funded? You can't exactly go to a bank."

Wardinski paused.

"Oh, wait ... It's Chris, right? He's the money."

It all made sense now. Wardinski nodded.

"And he's ex-CIA?"

"Yes."

"I've heard there's no such thing as an ex agent," I said. "Where's the money come from?"

"Private investment. There are some Middle Eastern investors, but I believe it's mostly companies with ties to the U.S. intelligence community. They think we're working on a new data monitoring platform."

"Are you?"

Wardinski pursed his lips and nodded. "Yes, in a sense we are. But they don't know about how it's achieved."

"You mean using our kind, right?"

"Yes."

I could have pressed further, but who knows what kind of bullshit Wardinski would spin.

"Why did Chris leave the CIA?" I asked.

"He has a health issue," Wardinski said.

"What's the matter with him?"

"He has MS," Kadin said.

"Is it advanced?" I asked.

"He has his good and bad days. Mostly good, though."

I didn't know what to believe. Was Debra actually mixed up with Russian mobsters? Had Cold War scientists created the ultimate voodoo technology? And who was really backing Chris's little venture? The CIA?

I said, "This isn't the whole story, is it?"

Wardinski exchanged another look with Kadin.

"No, Dillon," he said, his voice low.

Shit, I thought. Here it comes.

"When we developed the nanotech and discovered its ability to connect with the communications grid, we stumbled onto something else."

"Like Debra's group?" I asked.

"Well, yes. Chris told me how they integrated you."

"And that's given you some new ideas?" My patience was wearing thin. "Wire me up so you can listen in on the other side of the world?"

"Not the world, Dillon."

"Well, where then?" I took a sip of orange juice.

Wardinski's eyes narrowed. "The galaxy."

23. The bullshit quotient.

I almost did a spit-take. Judging by the look on Wardinski's face, though, his conviction level was at full strength. Whatever sense of ease I had built through breakfast quickly vanished. Maybe I *had* been abducted by a cult.

"Are you serious?"

Wardinski's nod was all business.

I needed a second just to process the concept. On the other hand, maybe the drugs were still affecting me. I turned to Kadin. "What about you? Do you think I can phone home to ET?"

"Kadin has reservations about my theory." A pained spirit in Wardinski's voice suggested he'd been on the losing end of this argument more often than not.

"Papa, please." Kadin took her father's hand. "It's not that I don't believe your theory. It's just that we've already spoken to the people at SETI."

"That's the place where they listen in for ET, right?" I asked.

"Yes."

"Did you tell them about our gift?"

"No," Kadin said. "Just the theory."

"I told them I was an author researching a novel," Wardinski said. "They were very helpful."

"But doesn't it take hundreds of years for stuff like that to reach our planet?" I couldn't believe I was actually having this conversation.

"Well, not hundreds. Some signals could be as short as twenty years," Wardinski said. "But there's—"

"So even if you could extend my ability and listen in to ET's mind, he's probably dead. End of story."

"You're correct that ordinary signals like TV, radio, and the like travel too slowly to be useful in real time. But what if abilities like yours and Kadin's have been developed somewhere else in the universe? Developed in such a way that transcends time and space? What you can do with your minds is beyond anything we've ever seen. But out there," Wardinski gestured toward the bank of windows on the far side of the room, "it could be commonplace." He leaned onto the table. "It could be how they communicate."

Kadin, hands folded in her lap and staring at her plate, was clearly uncomfortable with her father's theories. An awkward silence settled between us.

I cleared my throat. "Look, Peter," I edged my glass up to my plate. "I don't think—"

Kadin's gaze lifted to her father. She smiled that smile. "Papa, could you give us a moment?"

Wardinski's eyes tightened, but she patted the top of his hand, and his anger melted.

"My theory is not the only reason you're here." Wardinski's voice was softer and more reflective. He wiped his mouth with his napkin and pushed back from the table. "I'm sure you two have much to discuss." He began to leave, but stepped back. "Dillon?"

"Yes?"

"Try and have an open mind."

Kadin watched her father's exit. Her attention lingered on the doorway. "He's really a brilliant man."

"Is he serious about all that ET stuff?" I asked.

"Somewhat. He usually doesn't get so verbose on the subject. He knows how I feel."

"And that is?"

"As a theory, it's plausible, but I doubt seriously that there's a giant alien thought network waiting to be hacked. My father's pragmatic. He's worked hard all his life to help me. If he wants to believe his pet theory, I think he's entitled."

"Look, Kadin, if you want me to have faith in what you all are doing, I need to know why was I brought here. No more bullshit."

"Papa and Chris want to monitor the nanotech. We're not sure what it's going to do."

"What do you mean *going* to do?"

Kadin hesitated. "It's adaptive."

"Like, it could affect my mind?"

"No. We think it has to do more with how it will interface with other technology."

"The cellular thing?"

"Yes. It has the capacity to expand, but not to the point of becoming life threatening."

Life threatening? "This monitoring ... will it hurt?"

"It shouldn't."

Shit. I reached for the pot of coffee, but Kadin stopped me.

"Better not. We'll need you free from any chemical influences this morning."

"Right." I said. "You can call me Sir Dillon B."

"What?"

"Never mind. Bad joke. So, not to change the subject, but your dad said I was going to get a room upgrade. Tell me that hospital room isn't it."

Kadin smiled. "No, it's not. Your new room isn't five-star, but it's better than where they stuck you at first." She stood. "Come on, I'll take you to it."

.   ■   ■

Kadin offered her arm, but my foot was feeling better. As we walked in silence through the maze of hallways, it seemed she was holding back. When I finally asked about Chris's involvement, Kadin was vague. I sensed that Chris had a completely separate thing going on, but what it was and how it involved me remained a mystery. A few times, Kadin and I bumped shoulders, and I could swear there were sparks. Not the kind ignited by sexual tension, though. Real sparks. Maybe the place was full of static.

"Does it meet your standards?" Kadin asked, stepping across the threshold.

My new digs weren't even two-star, but at least the room was heated. The bed looked like a queen and sported a mound of pillows, brown sheets, and a thick, dark green comforter. I also had a separate bathroom that, surprisingly, was large and updated. I guess the finish-out was about par for an ex-CIA installation. But hell, what did I know?

I came out of the bathroom and leaned against the doorjamb. "Is there free Wi-Fi?"

Kadin eyed me quizzically, but a smile crept onto her face. "In a few days, you won't need Wi-Fi."

What the hell did that mean? I was too tired to ask, and besides, I was already far too deep into what Derek called the "bullshit quotient." It was a term he used when an account had gone so far off the rails that it was beyond saving. "I can hardly wait."

"Sleep tight," Kadin said, her look softer, more like the girl I had fallen in love with.

I flashed on her saying the same thing, about a billion weekends ago, after we had made love for the first time. Thinking back, Kadin had been a little detached. I probably should have picked up on her energy that night, but I had been too taken with her to notice.

"You too."

 She studied me for a second, but the street-tough Kadin reappeared, and she left. I stared at the closed door and wondered how she could turn it on and off like that, one minute caring, the next minute treating me like I was just a vehicle for their agenda. I also wondered how many other guys she had seduced to get what she wanted.

Whatever Wardinski and Chris had planned for me, it was becoming painfully obvious that I had no choice in the matter. The muffled sound of Kadin securing a bolt and lock hammered home the stark truth: this wasn't my room. It was my cell.

23. Let's get party started.

Sometime during the night, my bathroom had been provisioned with a bag of disposable razors, a tube of shaving cream called Pollena Linder, towels, and a robe. I didn't know what was more disturbing: the fact that someone had snuck into my room in the middle of the night without waking me, or that the robe had been lifted from the Warsaw Westin.

The shower felt good, although I had to hold my foot outside the curtain so as not to ruin what was left of my bandage. I had just splashed the excess shaving cream off my face when someone knocked at my door.

I figured it was Kadin, so I answered it wrapped in a towel. What the hell? It's not like she's never seen me half naked before. I tried the doorknob, forgetting it had been locked from the outside.

"Mr. Bradford?" a female voice asked from the other side.

"Just a sec—"

Before I could finish, the lock and the bolt unlatched. The young Russian nurse who had bandaged my foot poked her head in. Behind her thick-framed glasses, her eyes grew wide and traveled from my face to somewhere just below my waist.

"Morning, Irina." I cinched the towel tighter.

"You're not ready." Her eyes searched the room. "Dammit," she said to herself.

"What's the matter?"

"They didn't leave you gown."

"It's okay. I'll wear what I had—"

"No. This is a special one. I will come back with it." Her head disappeared, and I heard the bolt.

Back in the bathroom, I continued cleaning up. In a weird way, it was refreshing to have my brain quiet for a change, rather than having the world constantly buzzing at my mind's doorstep. I called the buzzing black noise, because unlike white noise, it could become distracting. There was another knock.

"Room service?" I called out, toweling the last of the Pollena Linder off my face.

Irina marched to the bathroom door carrying a dry cleaning bag similar to the one Kadin brought me. Inside was what resembled a white jumpsuit. She thrust it toward me. "Put on."

.　　.　　.

The jumpsuit had a hood and booties and was made of Tyvek. Every step made a crinkly noise, and as Irina led me through the empty hallways, I felt like a reject from a microchip plant.

"Why do I have to wear this?" I asked. The lab coat she wore today was at least a size too large, and I wondered if she had one of those hot Russian bodies hidden underneath.

"Static," she said.

"Why's that bad?"

"I think the term is short-circuit."

We entered the main hallway. At the end were the double-doors of the hospital room. To my right was the cafeteria where my little meltdown had taken place. It was closed. Other doors were open, and I could see lab technicians busy at stations like those at ELT. A few glanced up. One older woman jumped from her stool, rushed to the door, and stared as I walked by.

"There's the man!" Chris caught us from behind and put a hand on my back.

Irina, who was several steps ahead, looked sternly over her shoulder. "Don't touch him."

Chris removed his hand and saluted her backside. "Protocol Nazi," he whispered into the side of my hood.

"So what're we doing today?" I asked.

"Routine crap," he said. "We've got to get a handle on what the tech is doing before we can move forward."

"Kadin told me what you did ... with the full injection and all."

Chris dug his hands into his front pockets and shrugged. "Yeah, I've been a bad boy."

Asshole. "For God and country, right?"

"Country, at least." He gave me a sideways glance. "Man up. It's not every day you redefine evolution."

Irina led us past the hospital room and down a hall to another set of double doors that opened onto an area that looked like an operating room for a supercomputer. The technicians here were dressed liked me. They all looked up.

"I go change now." Irina disappeared through a side door.

Chris pointed to a large bank of glass windows on the far side of the room.

"I go watch now," he said, mimicking her rough English. "Seriously, man, just relax. You're in good hands."

"The best the Iron Curtain could offer?"

Chris half smiled. "Look," he said, lowering his voice, "I know what I did wasn't cool – bringing you here drugged up and shit." He leaned closer. "It's like I said before, you're the next step. Your brain has evolved. Hell, I have the shit in my head, and I can't do a tenth of what you can." His eyes narrowed. "You're the first of our kind to have this much power. Don't screw it up." He stepped back, grinned slightly, and jerked his head to the operating table. "Now get up there and kick some ass."

While Chris walked away, I recalled Harris saying the same thing just before they discovered a CPU growing in my head. I surveyed the room. About a dozen jump-suited technicians were situated at various workstations. Four of them with surgical masks surrounded an operating table that looked like it could have come out of the execution chamber at Huntsville. Because of the jumpsuits, I could only see their eyes. They were all trained on me. I gave a sheepish wave and one actually waved back.

I pointed to the table. "You want me here, right?"

A tall technician to the left of the death table nodded and waved me over. As I walked, another technician stepped up. She, too, was wearing a jumpsuit and a surgical mask. I tried to listen in on her mind, but all I got was static.

"Are you ready?" It was Irina.

"As ready as I'll ever be."

She took my arm and led me over. One of the technicians looked up from a laptop on a medical cart. "The team is ready, doctor," he said from behind his surgical mask. His accent was also Russian.

I looked at Irina. "Doctor?"

Her eyes suggested a big grin under the mask. "Don't be nervous," she said. "I just got my degree."

Actually, I was plenty nervous. At Debra's, the equipment was state of the art with recognizable names like GE, Philips, and Siemens. Here, though, it looked like the middle of a Cold War-era medical garage sale, and some machines were even dented and in need of a fresh electrocoating. But it was the leather straps dangling from the table's armatures that were freaking me out.

Irina caught me staring and pulled her mask down. "I know what you're thinking, but don't worry. Outside looks bad. Inside, all custom-made."

"Can I ask you a question?"

"*Da.*"

"How old are you?"

"Thirty-one." There was a hint of pride in her voice. "And that was a joke before."

She pulled up her mask and motioned to one of the technicians. "Let's get party started!"

From somewhere behind me, Marilyn Manson's "The Dope Show" rose up. One of the technicians helped me settle back against the tabletop and guided my head into a padded brace with a cutout for my neck. The two other technicians maneuvered a halo ring netted with brightly colored wires onto my head. It fit snugly but wasn't painful.

Irina looked down. "Comfortable?"

I gave a thumbs-up. "Living the dream."

The technician tightened the halo down, stopping after each crank to ask if I felt any pain. I could feel about a dozen tiny pinpricks across my scalp, but nothing unbearable.

"So what are you, Irina?" I asked. "Some kind of child prodigy?"

"Good luck getting her to admit that," the technician offered as he fiddled with the halo.

"Earned her doctorate at sixteen," said another.

Irina's eyes remained impassive as she studied the laptop.

I looked up at her. "Is it true?" On the ceiling above her, they had stuck posters of mountains and dolphins in an absurd attempt to calm me.

"What we're doing today is diagnostic," Irina said. "You won't feel pain. Maybe a little tingling at the contact points. All you have to do is relax and not think. That shouldn't be hard for big-time ad exec."

Why did the world think that all we did in advertising was drink Scotch and waste clients' money?

"When I get through all this," I said, "I'm going to take you back to Texas and show you what I do. Contrary to what you might think, I work my ass off."

One of Irina's eyebrows arched. "I doubt you will be going back to your old job."

I was motionless as the team scurried around me. Someone mentioned an hour had passed, but it seemed more like five. Irina was right; there was no pain, although for about 10 minutes the halo seemed to be vibrating. Most of the technicians spoke Russian and seemed to revere Irina like a rock star. I heard a few ma'ams in English, but the rest was incomprehensible. She led her team like a seasoned professional, first barking orders, then turning on the charm when someone became a little testy about a slight equipment malfunction. I couldn't believe she was 31. She looked even younger. When the battery of tests was completed, Irina assisted one of the technicians and lifted my head out of the neck brace like a prized possession. She even helped me swing my legs off the table.

"How do you feel?" she asked.

I stood and rubbed my neck. "A little stiff, but okay."

"Any headache, dizziness, nausea?"

"No. What's the matter, doctor?"

"Nothing. Just making sure." She removed a penlight from her coat. "Watch the light, please."

She studied me as if she could see straight through my retinas and into my brain. Something was up, but the good doctor wasn't going to let me in on it. Maybe something bad turned up during the tests.

"You must be hungry," Irina said in the soothing voice she had used with the frustrated technician. "We could not have you eat before testing. Come, let's go to dining hall."

The wall clock said it was almost noon. "If you don't mind, can I have something brought to my room?" I didn't feel like being around the worshipers.

"*Da*. What do you want?"

"Some eggs, toast, fruit. You know, breakfast stuff."

"Okay," Irina said, "I'll make it happen."

"Thanks." I started for the double doors.

"Dillon?"

I turned back.

Irina pointed to her head. "Forget something?"

I suddenly became aware of the mesh skullcap they slipped on my head before they attached the halo.

"I was thinking of wearing this the rest of the day," I said in my best gay voice.

Irina wasn't amused. The tall technician reached over and peeled the cap off my head. Behind him, the two rough-looking heavies from the party, wearing too much black and looking far too Eastern European, pushed through the room's double doors.

"Really?" I remarked.

"Protocol," Irina said flatly. "Your food will be there in an hour."

I met the stare of the leather-jacketed one. He produced a nicotine-stained smile.

"After lunch, you should rest." Irina said.

"Why's that?"

"This afternoon." She folded her arms. "We do big test."

.   .   .

Shortly after the Euro heavies ushered me back to my room, my brunch arrived. It consisted of nothing I had requested. Instead, I was served a lean steak, spinach salad, and a fruit cup. The fruit cup must have been old because its foil lid shredded as I peeled it. The girl who brought my tray was new – and anything but talkative.

After devouring everything in sight, I decided to heed Irina's suggestion and catch a few Z's. Without a clock or wristwatch or cell, however, it was hard to judge time. I was just about to slip under when a knock snapped me back.

"You got the key."

The lock unlatched, and Kadin poked her head around the door.

"May I come in?"

"If I said no, would it matter?"

I scooted up against the headboard. She sat tentatively on the edge of the bed.

"How are you feeling?"

"Why does everyone keep asking that?"

When Kadin wanted to avoid a subject, she often bit the corner of her bottom lip – like she was doing right now. "They're just concerned."

Yeah, right. "How did the test results come out?"

"Inconclusive. This afternoon's test should tell us more."

"So why the locked door and the muscle escorts?"

"After you tried to escape, Chris thought it was necessary."

"Where were you this morning?"

"I had some things to do ... with Papa."

"You going to be there this afternoon?"

Kadin nodded. "I'll have to watch from another room."

"Is it going to be bad?"

Kadin patted my thigh. "Get some rest. I'll be back in an hour." She stood and went to the door.

"Are these Chris's or your dad's tests today?"

"What do you mean?"

"Am I searching for ET or becoming a spy?"

24. A couch. An ottoman. A love seat.

The tall technician who had removed the mesh cap met me and the Euro heavies at the lab's double doors. Gone was the hooded jumpsuit, and on his nameplate was the name Ivan. "How was lunch?" he asked in fairly good English.

I shrugged. "Meh."

The kid nodded with a solidarity I hadn't experienced yet with either Debra's or Chris's group. He pushed open one of the double doors, and as he ushered me to the death table, I sensed the somberness in the room had cranked up a bit. Gone was the high-energy music and upbeat attitude, and as I glanced into the other technician's faces, I sensed the importance they placed on this afternoon's test.

There was also some new equipment: shiny racks of what looked like servers, but I didn't recognize the logos. Asian markings ran down the side of one tower. Little green LEDs winked furiously. Irina was waiting next to the table; she forced a half-smile.

"What happened to the jumpsuits?" I asked.

"Don't need them," she replied.

"So what are we doing this afternoon? Listening in on the Ayatollah?"

I've had a joke die before, but not to this extent. The room became deathly silent, and Irina's brow furrowed.

"That comes later," Chris said, walking up from behind. He leaned close. "I got your joke," he whispered.

I looked about the room. "So why's everyone so uptight?"

"It's me," Chris said. "I spook them."

"Very punny."

The grin Chris flashed resonated deep in that part of my brain that housed our ancestral, predatory reactions. Something about the curl of his lip, the exposed canine, and the slight lift of his eyebrow. The grin disappeared, and Chris casually gestured toward the table. I wasn't sure if that was a signal for the crew to get going or if he was telling me to get the hell up there and take it like a man.

Irina glanced at her wristwatch. "We have a tight window."

Ivan struggled a moment placing the mesh skullcap onto my head.

"I'll do it." I tucked my hair under it as best I could, then climbed onto the table and eased into the neck brace. Ivan slid the halo onto my head and tightened it down. No eye contact.

Irina barked out some Russian, and the technicians scurried to their tasks. She glanced down, but I couldn't read her look.

"This will be similar to what they did at ELT," she said, almost monotone.

"You connecting me to the grid?"

"Yes. There will be an initial linkup, but it won't last. We'll focus the stream and wait for you to engage. Tell us immediately when you create connection. We'll take it from there."

That sounded simple enough.

Irina marked down three, two, one in Russian. For a second nothing happened, but then a billion voices exploded across my mind. I involuntarily lurched out of the neck brace. Hands went to my shoulders and pressed me down.

Behind the voices, I could barely make out a heated Russian exchange between Irina and one of the technicians. The volume in my head jumped dramatically. I yelled.

Irina took my chin and met my eyes. "You fight now!"

I grabbed Irina's wrist like a lifeline. She stared down with strange intensity, and I felt like a lab rat back at ELT. Suddenly the voices collapsed into one, and I gasped.

"Are you in one mind?" Irina asked.

I could hear a lone voice. Female. A bit garbled. She sounded young. Maybe early twenties. She was jabbering on about the color of a sofa, or something like that. I think I said all this out loud. Maybe. God, my head was throbbing.

"Good," I heard Chris remark off to my left. "Keep telling us what you're hearing."

"She's thinking," I said, "about a couch, an ottoman, and a love seat. They're on sale at a Target in Colorado Springs. She can't believe how cheap they are. Wait a minute, she's talking to someone now."

… this is Sergeant Espinoza …. Roger that. I'm getting reports from my TRACON that inbound American 1245 heavy is too tight to the grid. … Roger. 367 knots and descending to 12,000. No, no affected air space. … Okay, thanks LAX. No need to file …

I tried to repeat everything the girl had said, but it came out more like gibberish. "What the hell am I listening to?"

Chris walked up. "If I had to guess...Sergeant Espinoza?"

"No, *who* is she?"

Chris glanced over to Irina, then back. The same ugly grin crept back onto his face. "Sounds like NORAD."

23. It's not just a job.

To say I couldn't wrap my head around this was an understatement. I had just penetrated one of the most secure air defense facility on the planet. I hadn't exactly hacked into its mainframe, but damn close. Now, I was wading into some deep and potentially dangerous waters.

I sat up and elbowed aside a technician who had moved to push me back down. I gave Chris my best death stare. "Are you kidding me?"

Chris half sat on the table and looked at me like I had five minutes to live.

"This is how the world works, Dillon," he said tightly. "Ever since our little Jihadi wakeup call, the DoD has been in a full-tilt spending mode."

"But–"

"Where do you think the next war is going to take place?"

"I don't know. Iran?"

"Wrong. It's going to take place everywhere." Chris let that little bomb penetrate before he walked over to Irina's laptop and pointed to its screen. "Right now, all over this big, bad world, terrorist cells, rogue nations – China for God's sake – are trying to hack our most sensitive grids."

Every technician's attention was locked onto Chris. I crossed my legs Indian style, leaned on my knees and listened.

"What if they took down our power grid or air traffic control systems?" He looked around the room. "What if they hacked our nuclear launch codes?" Chris paused for dramatic effect. It worked. "No one wants to think about it, but that's how it will go down." He returned to the table, his expression a little less fierce.

"How did you get me into that NORAD officer's head?" I asked.

"Radar is basically an open computer door. It's open so it can receive the electronic signals it has sent out to look for objects in the sky. Tap into that radio frequency–" Chris gestured to a young guy – a kid, really. I hadn't noticed him before, but I could barely see his mop of dark dreadlocks peeking over his monitor. He was stationed near one of the new computer stacks. Our eyes met, and he hunkered down like someone might throw something at him. "–and just like that," Chris continued, "you're in." He once again propped his ass on the table. "You see, Dillon, it's very unlikely that we'll use our arsenal of 40-year-old nukes in the next big war. Even if a terrorist group used a small one – and eventually they will – it'll be nearly impossible for us to retaliate. Who would we bomb? Hell, where would we bomb? Now, I'm not one of those guys who thinks we should make half the Middle East a glass parking lot, but I do think this stupid nation-building is getting us nowhere."

"Look, Chris," I said, "I'm on the same page with you about these wars. But why use techlepaths? Why not just hack into their computers?"

"Because that's a game of one-upmanship. We hack into their system; they build a better firewall. We bust in again, and they build it bigger and better. It's a pain in the goddamn ass. But with our kind, we can slip in totally stealth. They'll never know you're in their minds. They'll never know we're learning *everything*."

"Yeah, but can't they just block me out, like you're doing right now?" I caught Irina's attention. She shifted it to her laptop.

"The chances of them developing this technology are remote. Besides, as far as 99.99 percent of the world's population is concerned, we don't exist." He leaned closer. "We know the truth, but to the rest of the world, we're an urban myth."

"What if someone defects, like a Debra Lao? What then?"

"First of all, it would have to be someone with complete knowledge of the technology. On top of that, they'd still need a ton of funding. It's the new Manhattan Project. He who gets there first wins. And I plan on being first."

"Chris, I'm not sure if I'm cut out for—"

"Come on, man. It's not like the bad guys can stop thinking. And don't forget, there are thousands and thousands of them out there. One defector can't work for all of them. Don't sweat it. It's the perfect gig. We'll set you up for life. Big money, believe me. All you have to do is do your thing. Sneak in, tell us who's buying the enriched plutonium or whatever, and get the hell out. Shit, you could phone it in from the Caymans. I don't care."

The lure of Chris's rationale was its simplicity, and for once I didn't have a snappy comeback. The idea of helping rid the world of terrorist scumbags sounded pretty appealing, and if being a spy meant doing it from the comfort of my living room, I could buy into his little scheme.

"So," I said, "how did you hack into NORAD's radar?"

"I wouldn't be a good spy if I told you that." He rubbed his chin. "All I can say is that we used LPIs."

"What are those?"

"Low-Probability-of-Intercept. They're takeover packets. Trojan horse."

The intensity on Chris's face said this was the real thing, with deadly consequences.

He folded his arms and let his stare linger.

"What are you going to do, Dillon?" he asked finally.

Good question. "Tell me the truth. Are you CIA or not?"

"Let's just say I'm a patriot and leave it at that." He shrugged. "Does it really matter who signs my check?"

"Maybe. I don't know."

"Dillon, yes, I've done bad things, but I've saved a lot of lives, and you can, too and that's what matters." Chris leaned toward me again. "Look, I'm not asking you to pick up a weapon and step into harm's way. I'm just asking you to consider the concept that you can make a difference. The intel you can get with your mind in a couple of minutes would take a dozen agents months, maybe years, to collect. Dillon, China hacks us everyday, and they're getting better and better at it. It's only a matter of time before they do something really bad. I don't want to come off corny, but you're the only man for the job, soldier."

Even though Chris made it sound like I had a choice in the matter, I knew the score. The only good news was, at least I'd be doing something that mattered and getting paid handsomely for it. I had done well in advertising, but not well enough to really retire. If all Chris wanted was for me to dictate the inner thoughts of our country's most wanted, who was I to look a gift horse in the mouth? Maybe Kadin was right ... maybe it was time for me to do something meaningful. Besides, the probability of going back to my old life was pretty slim.

I sat up and gave a mock salute. "It's not just a job. It's an adventure."

"That's my man!" Chris slapped my knee. "Now kick back and let us do the driving."

Over the next two hours, I was inserted (or, as Chris preferred, "embedded") into four different minds. The NORAD sergeant was an ID Tech named Selina

Espinoza. A single mom, she had been in the Air Force for seven years. The next person was a Syrian national. His name was sounded like someone hacking up a loogie. I couldn't tell anything he was thinking because it was all in Arabic. The third person was on the aircraft carrier Ronald Reagan, somewhere in the Indian Ocean. Officer Dwain Thomas was also a radar specialist, and he thought about gay sex way too much.

The last mind was the scariest – and the most intriguing. It was the President's Chief of Staff, Alicia Hughes. Either she was severely ADD, or she could multi-task like nobody's business. Presumably in the middle of a meeting, her thoughts ricocheted all over the place. After a minute of trying to repeat them verbatim, I gave up.

With the exception of Hughes, I was never embedded longer than a few minutes, and with each insertion the connections became clearer. I thought about asking how they had gotten me in, but knowing Chris, the answer would be finely spun bullshit. Obviously, these were some sort of dry runs to test how far in we could penetrate secure facilities. I was amazed that Chris was able to infiltrate the White House.

Irina had appeared more reserved through the testing. Her orders came out more like strong suggestions rather than her previous hard commands. Chris was running the show this afternoon. Irina was just his assistant.

Ivan helped remove the halo. I stretched my neck.

"Feel like a hero?" Chris asked.

"Do you really think this is the right approach to national security?"

"You weren't far off with that Ayatollah crack," Chris said. "Just think if we could listen in on that guy's mind. Shit, those ragheads wouldn't know what hit 'em. Every time they made a move, we'd be waiting. We might even change a regime without losing a single life. That, alone, is worth the price of admission."

If the "price of admission" was a product as risk-free as Chris was selling, I could get behind his little project. The only real wild card in the equation was Chris's leash. How tight would it be? How long? As for myself, once I went to the dark side, I presumed "Dillon Bradford" would be departing this earth. Some CIA apparatus would arrange a boating accident or a plane crash. A fake, yet tragic, media push would seal the deal. Maybe I could attend my own funeral?

"I think I know why you embedded me into Alicia Hughes," I said. "But isn't that a little too close to home?"

"She was the ultimate test. People at her level use secured smartphones. If we can access her through one of those, we can get to anybody. So, what do you think?"

"Well ... I don't know—"

"Just think about it. Now, come on. Let's go get a drink." The expression on Chris's face was all friend.

"Really?"

"Absolutely. Let's get the hell of this shit-hole and see what the town has to offer."

"Aren't I a flight risk?" I gestured quotations.

Chris stepped back and stretched. "A risk I'm willing to take. You tried that once and it didn't go so well. Besides, you don't have a passport, or even a motive, now that you know the master plan." He pointed to Irina, who was powering down her laptop. "You in, doc?"

Irina impassively looked up. "*Nyet.* I have to review data logs."

Chris swung his pointed finger around to me. "We, my friend, are going to get our drink on." He glanced at his watch. "Meet me outside of here in the hallway. Thirty minutes." Chris spun on his heels and exuberantly pushed through the double doors with both hands.

I slid off the table and steadied myself against the counter. The tests had been fairly easy, but jumping in and out of that many minds had thrown off my equilibrium. Irina took my arm. There was strength in her grip that didn't quite match her stature.

"Are you okay to walk?" she asked.

"Yeah … I'm fine."

Irina started back to her laptop, but turned. "Don't let Chris snow on you."

"I think the term is snow job," I said. "But thanks for the warning."

.   .   .

When I left the operating room, the two muscle boys weren't waiting. I suppose I could have walked out of the building. But Chris was right, where would I go? And how would I get there? I wasn't a spy. I couldn't hotwire a car or steal a plane. And my attempt to escape before had almost gotten me killed.

When I entered my room, a sack of new clothes was waiting, but nothing inside was remotely close to Debra's Kenneth Cole swag. Inside it were a couple of cheap dress shirts from what was probably a Polish label, two sets of skinny Gap jeans (which would have been great if I were in high school), and a pair of black Puma cross trainers. I half-expected to find a note from Chris with some catchy male-bonding language. *Dude, lets get our drink on* or *Come on, bro, be my wingman.*

I showered, dressed in a matching selection from the bag, tied up the Pumas, and almost ran back to the meeting spot. Not that I was that eager to go drinking with Chris. I just had a lot of questions. What would I be paid? How much freedom would I have? Would I keep my old life, or have to assume a new identity? I was also excited to get out, even if it was just for a couple of hours. Or was I beginning to get into my new role as virtual spy?

Kadin waited in the hallway, a leather jacket draped over her arm.

"Joining the boys in our quest for the perfect Polish martini?" I asked.

She flashed a polite, though slightly condescending, smile. "I've been requested to accompany you. Here." She handed me the jacket.

"Thanks. I wondered how I was going to keep warm." The jacket fit a little snug, but its leather was remarkably soft. "So is this what you wanted?" I asked while adjusting my cuffs.

Kadin reached over and straightened my collar. "What do you mean?"

"You know ... to make me the ultimate spy?"

She hesitated. "Sort of."

"You don't sound so sure."

Kadin pulled my jacket tight and patted me on the chest, and for a fleeting second I thought about taking her hand and pulling her close. God, I had loved her.

She nervously brushed some hair off her face.

"Am I going to have to separate you two?" Chris asked, walking up.

Kadin, when pushed, could produce a glare that could cut any guy to his knees. She leveled it at Chris. "Fuck you."

"Ooo," he said, rubbing his gloved hands together. "I *love* when you talk dirty." He fingered the leather of my lapel. "Nice material."

"Thanks for the bag of clothes," I said.

"No problem. Did it all fit?"

I looked down at myself. "For the most part."

"Good. I can't have my star player looking shabby. We'll go shopping in a couple of days."

Kadin sighed and started toward the door that I had kicked open the other night. Someone had affixed a hinge armature and padlock to its frame.

The air felt colder than the other night, and a misty rain was falling. I turned the collar of the leather coat up against the back of my neck and followed Kadin to the big black Mercedes sedan. Its lights blinked and horn chirped. Kadin climbed into the front passenger seat and slammed the door. I stopped at the rear passenger door.

"She always this touchy?" I asked Chris across the sedan's roof.

He glanced back and cocked his head. "You, of all people, should know that asnwer."

As we pulled out of the gated parking lot, I looked back at the compound. The torn part of the fence I had escaped through had been repaired, and through the open gate I caught a glimpse of the building. It was long and seemed more of a turn-of-the-century barn than a CIA black site. Three small satellite dishes dominated one side of its roof, while a cluster of radio antennas loomed over the other side.

The gravel driveway was long and winding and lined with the same thick undergrowth I had crawled through the other night. We came to the road, and off in the distance the airport beacon winked. Chris turned in the opposite direction I had gone.

"The closest town is called *Szcytno*," he said. "It's a little shithole of a place."

"No it's not." Kadin's glower matched her tone. "It's quaint."

As they argued the merits of *Szcytno*, I settled back against the worn leather of my seat and watched the thick dark forest blur by. At one point, around a tight turn, we almost hit a cow standing halfway in the road.

"Welcome to Hicksville." Chris had oversteered to miss the cow, and the car's backend fishtailed slightly on the rain-slickened road.

"Wardinski said the place used to be the CIA's," I remarked.

"Sort of," Chris said over his shoulder. "More of an extension campus. The main site was part of a Polish intelligence school. It's a couple of miles from here. We had use of it, back in the heyday. It was part of our extraordinary renditions network."

"Isn't that where they waterboarded that guy who planned 9/11?"

"Khalid Shiekh Mohammed."

Kadin shot him another dirty look.

"What?" Chris glanced at her while he piloted the car through another tight turn. "Let me tell you," he continued. "If that asshole kidnapped your dad, you wouldn't hesitate one second to waterboard him, right?"

Kadin's pursed lips said it all. Her silent routine could get under your skin, and I didn't have to read Chris's mind to know that she was getting to him. I could hear it in his voice when he went on about the 9/11 guy. He definitely had a gung-ho side to him. He also had a cynical edge, though. Maybe something happened that caused him to be drummed out of the CIA. On the other hand, maybe it was just the MS. That would piss anyone off, especially a guy as fit as Chris. I tried to listen in on his mind, and something vibrated in the front seat.

Chris shot me an amused glance in the rearview mirror. "You not going to hear much." His eyes returned to the road.

"Let me guess. A neuro dampener?"

Kadin twisted around and produced a small device that looked just like the one Debra had used. She shrugged apologetically and faced forward.

"Can't let ya in, buddy." Chris eyed me again. "Company policy."

"Can't blame a guy for trying," I said.

Chris smirked and steered into another turn.

The town of Szcytno wasn't jumping tonight, but it wasn't a shithole, either. Picturesque tile-roofed buildings rimmed a town square that could have served as a backdrop for a Rick Steves travel doc. According to the car's clock, it was a little after seven, but the town had already rolled up the sidewalks. Chris said the only option was the bar at the Hotel Krystyna.

We angled through some narrow streets and found the hotel nestled just west of town. From the road, it might have been the residence of a wealthy family back in the 1800s. Two large, three-story homes ringed a walled-in courtyard. Inside the shag-carpeted lobby, the lady at the front desk directed us to the hotel's "club." We grabbed a four-top near the pool table.

"You play?" Chris asked, jerking a thumb toward it.

"Only when I'm drunk," I said.

"Chris is a shark," Kadin cautioned. "Watch your wallet."

"I would if I had one. And speaking of which, now that I'm a team player, can I have my cell and passport back?"

"Love to, Dillon, but you learn a lot about people in my business. How they react under stress. What motivates them. Things like that. I just gave you a reprieve from Hans and Franz. Let's take it one step at a time."

"I call them the Euro-Muscle Boys."

Chris grunted a laugh. "That's funny."

"You know this team player is going to have to check in with his company pretty soon."

"Did Debra have you use a cancer cover?"

"How'd you know that?"

"SOP."

"Yes."

"What kind?"

"Excuse me?"

"What kind of cancer?"

"Testicular."

Chris nodded approvingly.

"So what about my stuff?" I asked.

He looked around. "Where's our waiter?"

The club was either decorated to look retro or hadn't been updated since the '70s. Its mirror ball wobbled above an empty dance floor. The three of us and a bored gaggle of business types were the only customers.

Our waiter stepped out of a third-world barbershop quartet. His black bow-tie was clipped on, and his white short-sleeved shirt sported a stain across the breast pocket. He lumbered up and, I assume, asked what we wanted to drink in mumbled Polish. Kadin did all the talking. When the waiter returned, he presented three martinis on a tarnished silver tray.

"The vodka here is made out of potatoes," Chris said and took a large drink from his martini. He smacked his lips. "Smooth, like glass."

It did taste great. I could have downed the whole thing in one gulp. I pulled off an olive and popped it my mouth.

"Let's see what kind of munchies the club has to offer." Chris grabbed the menu from between the salt and pepper shakers.

Kadin leaned onto the table and picked at something on the rim of her glass. "Their nachos really aren't that bad...."

Dillon...c_n you he_r m_...?

A sharp pain ripped through my head. I coughed a little of my drink back into the glass.

"Easy there. Don't drink that all at once." Chris lightly patted my back. "I need you clear for the next round of testing."

Can you h__r me? Dillon?

The pain ripped again, and I winced. Like a faint dream, the garbled voice was demanding my attention. It seemed to be coming from somewhere near the edge of my consciousness. I started to think something, then clamped the thought down.

"Dillon?" Kadin put a hand to my forearm. "Are you all right?"

"Yeah." I rubbed a temple. "Just a little headache."

"I told you this would happen," Kadin said to Chris. "You should have listened to Irina."

Chris, taking a sip, waved her off. "You want to leave, Dillon?"

Another bolt of pain wedged itself into my sinuses.

Hello? Am I co__ng throu__?

I stood and almost knocked over my chair. "I, uh, need to use the bathroom."

The waiter appeared. "May I help you?" he asked, in broken English.

"Bathroom?"

He pointed to the lobby. "Take right at desk."

Before Kadin or Chris could help, I quickly walked into the lobby and found the men's.

Dillon. If you can hear—

I pushed open one of the stall's heavy wooden doors and collapsed onto the commode.

If you can hear me, think, don't talk.

Who the hell—?

Dillon. There was a pause and another carving of pain. *It's Debra.*

26. Keep the eyes forward.

Listen to me, Debra said. *We don't have much connection time.*

How can you do this? I asked.

It was our next step with you.

But—

The door to the men's opened. "Dillon?" The tips of Chris's shoes appeared below the stall door. He knocked. "You okay, man?"

"Yeah. I am. Must have been that wonderful brunch. It's talking back, if you know what I mean."

"How's your head?"

"Better, thanks. Can you give me a minute?"

"Sure." His shoes disappeared, and the bathroom door slammed shut.

Where are you? Debra asked.

I'm in Poland—

We know that. Where are you right now?

In a hotel bathroom. Whatever you're doing hurts like hell.

Sorry. It's still experimental. We've been trying for days to connect. Their damping is too strong, but we managed to hack and link through the handheld dampener. Where are you, exactly?

I have no idea. Do you know I'm with Chris and Kadin?

Yes. Listen to me—

I don't think so.

Dillon, please. Whatever they're saying about us is not true—

Yeah, right. Tell that to your Russian handlers.

Dillon—

Don't even go there. I don't care what you really are. I get these people. I mean, I didn't at first, but now I see what they're trying to do. There's a future here. And — I bit off the thought.

It's Kadin, right?

No … I don't know. But there's more. And it's good.

The bathroom door opened again and banged against the tile wall.

"Chop-chop, man," Chris called out.

I have to go. As I hurried out of the bathroom, Debra continued telling me that Chris, Kadin, and Wardinski were just war profiteers. That whatever they were saying about her was a lie. I tried to keep my mind clear and entered the lobby. Chris and Kadin were waiting.

…Dillon, are you listening?

"We better get you back," Chris said, scrutinizing me. "Just to make sure."

"You sure you're okay?" Kadin asked.

You can't trust these people, Debra said. *They've got an agenda, and it's not—*

"I'm okay," I said. "It's just a headache."

Do you know why he was fired from the CIA? Debra asked.

Fired? We hurriedly walked to the hotel's parking lot.

Dillon, we're losing you. Are you moving?

Yes. We're heading back. I climbed into the back of the Mercedes.

I might lose the feed. You have to get out of the compound and get to a computer. Even a payphone might work. We'll keep this feed open.

I don't think this town has a cyber café, I said sarcastically. Chris wheeled the car onto the main road and pulled into traffic. *So why was he fired?*

Because he ____ without the ____–

Debra?

Dill–

I felt Kadin's stare and shifted my attention away from the window. "What?"

"You look lost in thought," she said.

"Maybe. Is that a crime?"

"What's on your mind?" Chris asked.

"How's this going to work?" I asked him. The Mercedes angled into a corner. A light rain dappled the windshield.

"Simply." He clicked the wiper blades on.

"How simply?"

Chris explained that his backing came from various defense contractors who thought they were funding a new cyber evasion program. It had an acronym that stood for some techno-babble. At least his story and Wardinski's matched.

"How will I get paid?" I asked.

"Out of the operating budget."

"How much?"

"TBD, but don't worry."

It figured. "Will I keep my name?"

Chris did a double take over the front seat console. "Of course. You're not some Mafia squealer. Leverage the cancer story."

"Will I be able to keep—?"

"Jesus!" Chris yelled, standing on the brakes.

I caught a blurred glimpse of a cow in the rain-streaked headlights, cud spittle hanging in one long tether from its mouth. It was clueless to its imminent death.

The Mercedes swerved violently, its rear tires desperately grabbing for traction on the wet gravel shoulder. The backend fishtailed to the left, then jerked violently to the right. I tried to hold onto the back of Kadin's headrest, my shoulder pressed against the passenger door.

"Hang on!" Chris's hands flicked the steering wheel to the left. "Fuck. Shit!"

We were spinning. Out of control. The trees were streaks of black and green. A flash of cow passed by the windshield. Branches scraped across the hood. Suddenly it all ended in a sickening convulsion of metal on metal as we slammed against the guardrail.

The sound of my own breath flexed in my ears. The cabin was dark. No instrumentation lights. The engine, vibrating the chassis, droned like an angry bull. There was smoke.

Kadin's form was slumped against the passenger window. I saw my hand move to her head.

"Kadin?" I asked.

She stirred, but only briefly. My palm came away wet. Too dark. Smelled like blood. Oh God, no. I thought the worst.

"Everyone okay?" Chris struggled to get the words out.

"Kadin's hurt." I tried my door, but the handle was jammed, so I slid across the back seat and felt for the door handle.

I exited the driver's side and ran around to the front passenger window. We had come to rest against the guardrail. Kadin's door had impacted a support post and was partially crushed. Her face, streaked with dark blood, was pressed against the glass. I tried the door, but it was jammed against the beam. I could see Chris struggling with his seatbelt. I ran to his door and opened it.

The belt clicked open. "Is Kadin hurt?" he asked.

"Yeah. She's bleeding. See if you can pull forward so I can open her door."

Chris shifted the car into drive and managed to inch away from the guardrail. There was a noise of metal and plastic tearing, then Kadin's door broke free. As it swung open, her body slumped and caught in the shoulder belt. *Shit.*

Chris put the car in park. I began to unbuckle her.

"I'll do it," he said, appearing at my side. The rain had tapered and was beading on his forehead. Blood seeped from a small cut above his eye and mingled with the rain, creating a red rivulet that traversed his eyebrow and down the side of his face.

Chris extracted Kadin from the seatbelt and laid her gently next to the car. His motions were frantic, yet controlled. He ripped his gloves off, flung them to the road, and began examining her body like a field doctor. He listened for her breath.

"Come *on*," he said, almost pleading. "Wake up."

Then I saw it. What she meant to him. His love was carved in the worry lines of his face, in the way he cradled her head and stroked her hair. There was even a slight edge of panic in the way he said *Wake up,* as if the thought of her dying in his arms on a bleak stretch of Polish road was more than he could bear.

I knelt next to them. She was coming to. A wave of relief moved through me.

"Hey, there. You're back." Chris wiped blood from her cheek with his thumb.

"What happened?" Kadin's voice was raspy, but strong.

Chris smiled. "Goddamn Polish cows."

"I think my right hand's asleep," she said, eyelids heavy.

"We're going to take you back," Chris said. "Try and stay awake." He looked at me, his face now lined with tributaries of blood and rain. "Help me with her."

We eased Kadin into the back seat. She yelped as I moved her right arm to shut the door.

I crawled over the stick shift and settled into the front passenger seat. The door needed a few yanks before it would latch. "Is it drivable?" I wiped at the blood on the window with my forearm, but the leather just smeared it.

"This thing's a tank," Chris said, slamming the Mercedes into drive. He moved onto the road, did a U-turn, pulled to the far shoulder, and slowed to a stop. The front right passenger tire wobbled in the turn.

"What are you doing?" I asked.

Chris ignored me as he leaned across the center console and tried to crank my window down. The lower part of the door was pushed in, and the window stuck halfway. Over the top of the tinted glass, I could see the cow had wandered into the field next to the road. It was about 30 feet away, and its white form stood starkly against the dark trees.

"Hey cow!" Chris yelled out the window.

The animal didn't respond.

Chris dug inside his coat and removed a military-style handgun and silencer mount.

"Dude, what the fuck are—?"

Chris shot me a steely sideways look as he methodically screwed the two components together. He stretched across the console and rested the barrel on the top of my window. He reached back and honked the horn. The cow looked up. I pushed back into the seat as far as I could and instinctively covered my ears. Chris aimed, let out a shallow exhale, and fired. The left side of the cow's head exploded in a fine pink mist, which the light rain washed out of the air. Half of its ear went spinning off out of view. The poor animal staggered, its legs buckled, and it collapsed into the tall grass. Even with the silencer, my ears were ringing.

Chris set the gun onto the driver's side floorboard, put the Mercedes into gear, and peeled away from the shoulder.

"Jesus," I said, rubbing my left ear. "Why the hell did you do that?!"

Chris gripped the wheel so tightly his knuckles were white. He didn't answer. As we drove away, I avoided looking over as much as possible. *Keep the eyes forward,* I thought.

"Goddamn Polish cows," he said finally, and gunned it.

27. Do terrorists play poker?

"Hold still," Irina said. "This will hurt."

Kadin shrieked into Chris's chest as Irina moved her right shoulder back into place. We were in the same operating room where I had woken up after escaping. Wardinski was standing in the corner, arms folded tightly across his barrel chest.

"See?" Chris said, stroking her head. "That wasn't so bad."

Anger pushed through the blood and mascara that streaked Kadin's face. "Speak for yourself," she said.

Irina positioned Kadin's arm onto her lap. "Lucky you don't have concussion." She grabbed some antiseptic and cotton balls and wiped at the cut on Kadin's forehead. "Even little head wounds bleed a lot." She pressed a fresh wad to the cut, took Kadin's good hand, and put it over the dressing. "Hold this," she said and turned to me. "Now I have a look at your head."

My head? Before I could protest, Irina's gloved fingers were at my temple. They came away bloody. I pulled back, startled. "What the–?"

"Don't be baby." Irina tipped the antiseptic into more cotton balls and dabbed at my cut.

"Didn't know you were hurt, did you?" Chris said, inspecting the bloodied cotton ball from his own cut.

"Maybe–"

"I've seen guys run for miles before they realized they'd been shot." He tapped the side of his head. "The mind is a powerful thing. You should know that."

"Chris," Wardinski said gravely, "can I have a word with you ... in the hallway?"

"Sure."

Wardinski opened one of the double doors for Chris and followed him out.

Irina placed a wad of cotton balls to my temple, took my hand, and made me hold it there.

"I have to get some bandages and a sling," she said. "Apply pressure."

I leaned against the counter and watched Irina leave. The room fell quiet.

"Crazy night," Kadin said, staring blankly. She was sitting on the edge of the bed wearing nothing from the waist up but her black bra. She'd never been bashful about her body, but Irina had removed her coat and sweater so quickly, we hadn't had time to walk out. I guess it didn't really matter. All of us loved her ... or at least had.

"Don't you want to wash up?" I asked. The side of her face was still streaked with dried blood.

She shrugged. "I will back in my room."

"You cold?"

Kadin looked over mournfully. "A little."

The word "little" trailed off into raspy whisper. I took her coat off the cart behind the bed and wrapped it around her shoulders.

"Thanks," she said.

I went back to leaning against the counter. The hum from the fluorescents filled the small room.

After a shared silence, Kadin asked, "How's your head?"

It was my turn to shrug. "I'll be—"

"Here we go," Irina said, pushing open one of the double doors. She tore into a nondescript white box and pulled out a blue sling. "Take a deep breath as I pull this over your head." Kadin did, but gasped as Irina guided her arm into the sling's cradle.

"Hurt a lot?" Irina cinched one of the Velcro straps.

"Yes."

"I know. I did this once, playing soccer. Hurts like son of bitch." Irina peeled open a pouch and removed a square bandage. "You'll have to wear sling for about a week. Then we see how your shoulder is doing. Try and sleep on one side." She applied the bandage to Kadin's forehead and turned to me. "Your turn."

Irina pressed another bandage against my temple and smoothed its edges with her forefinger. "Try not to get this wet." She looked us over. "You're both good to go." She wadded up the used bandage pouches, tossed them into a silver, dented trashcan, and left.

"You need help back to your room?" I asked, gathering Kadin's sweater.

She nodded and pulled her coat tightly around her. I opened the double doors expecting to see Wardinski reaming Chris out, but the hallway was empty.

"Wonder where Chris and your dad are?"

"Probably in the lab."

Kadin was clearly irritated. She was favoring her right knee.

"You okay there?" I asked, pointing.

"I'll ice it when I get to my room."

Walking wounded, we shuffled to the end of the hallway and stopped at the T intersection. My room was to the right, hers the left. Kadin began to walk away.

"Don't you have to lock me in?" I asked to her back.

Kadin stopped, and her shoulders dropped a little. "Typical," she muttered.

"What is?"

"Chris," she said, like he was the bane of her existence. "I'm the one who gets banged up, and he's nowhere to be found." She turned and shuffled back. "Come on, I'll lock you in."

I put a hand to her good shoulder. "You don't have to." I rubbed gently. "I'm not going anywhere."

Kadin glanced up. Her stare lingered.

"What?" I asked.

She hesitated. "I know how you must feel."

"Kadin, I'm past all that—"

"Please. You need to know." She looked away.

"What?"

Kadin shook her head, like there was some conflict going on inside her. She slipped out of my grip.

"Forget it," she said over her shoulder.

I started to ask "forget what," but as I watched her walk away, I thought this might be how she'll look when she's old. Shuffling. A little hunched. Still beautiful, but weary and damaged by life. I had never told her how I felt. Classic of me. Guess it didn't matter now. I followed Kadin through the maze of halls back to my room. She didn't say anything as I collapsed onto the bed. My head was throbbing, but I couldn't tell if it was from slamming against the car door window or Debra's invasion. How had she done that? Sanjiv's team must have figured out a way of using the technology. This sure blew a hole in Chris's national defense reasoning to use techlepaths. If Debra's group could do it, I'm sure others could, too.

Kadin began to close the door.

"Good night," I said.

She looked back and forced a weak grin, then closed the door and locked it.

I was still holding her sweater. It was the one I had bought for her one weekend in Austin. The 6th Street clothing store had been empty, and I had joined her in the dressing room. After modeling the sweater, she slipped it over her head and asked if I wanted to have some fun. We did, until a salesperson shushed us. I brought the sweater to my face and savored her smell. I recognized the perfume, along with the faint air of Chris's Marlboros. Now it felt like I was clutching a bad memory, and I tossed it into the corner. I started to get up, but my eyes were too heavy.

"Fuck it," I said, and let exhaustion take over.

■　　■　　■

"Tell me something," I said to Chris while Ivan adjusted the halo. "You realize I can only listen in on people's thoughts. I can't read their memories, unless they happen to be thinking of one."

Chris glanced up from his tablet. "So?"

"So when you embed me into the minds of America's Most Wanted, you might not get the info you want. I mean, they might not be thinking, right then, of how they're going to blow something up."

"It may take a few tries."

"Yeah, but—"

"Man, we're not embedding you randomly." Chris leaned back into his chair, but then the exasperation stitched across his face unlaced and fell away. "Look,

Dillon, the trials we've run may seem a bit arbitrary, but we're just testing the system. When we embed you in a real target, we'll have a pretty good handle on whether or not the person will be thinking the right thoughts."

"How would you know?"

"Know what?"

"That a target will be thinking the intel you want, at a particular time."

The exasperation flash for a brief second, but then was gone. Chris pointed to the room. "See all these people?"

I cast my gaze across the dozen or so technicians hunched at their consoles, diligently focused on whatever was on their computer screens. "Yes."

"They're here for you, my friend." He gestured to a dark-skinned Indian in the last row. The guy was probably 30 and looked like he hadn't slept for days. "Ram is tapped in the NSA's DNI."

"What's that?"

"Digital Network Intelligence. You might know it by the name X-Keyscore. It searches and analyzes Internet data from foreign nationals. Email, Internet activity, browser history. You name it, it finds it." He pointed to another technician, a woman in her late 40s. She was in the second row and four people down from the Indian technician. "Cassy is jacked into MAINWAY, the NSA's metadata records. This database has over 2 trillion call details. So, yeah." He looked about the room. "I think we'll have it narrowed down a little before you go in."

"Alright, I get all that, but there's something I don't get. If you have these guys' cell numbers and metadata and God knows what else, then you know where they are. Why not just send in a SEAL team, like they did for bin Laden?"

"Sometimes, that's not an option. Those operations can foster bad PR, especially if the target is in a high-density situation with a risk of collateral damage. With you, we're stealth."

Chris took a sip of coffee from a large black mug. It smelled delicious. He set the tablet down next to a laptop and pointed with the mug.

"Here's the rundown for this morning's test. We're only embedding you into one mind. You might be in there a while."

"Who is it?"

"An Afghan national named Abdollah Hassani. He's nobody special. A low-life enforcer in one of the tribal gangs. I want to verify that we can piggyback off of U.S. ground forces. We're linking off of MTN."

"Who's that?"

"They're a South African multinational putting cell towers up all over the place. AT&T was going to buy them out, I think."

"I don't know the language." I eased my head into the neck brace and folded my hands across my stomach. "Do you want me to listen for code words?"

Wardinski and Kadin waited impatiently near the table, to the left of Irina. Kadin looked a lot better this morning, but her dad seemed to have aged overnight.

"Code words?" Chris asked.

"Yeah. Debra's team had me listen for some code words an assassin was going to use in a cell call she made. Something the Russian mob does so they can communicate. When I heard them, I repeated what I heard. I guess it worked."

Chris approached and took another swig. "We won't be doing that today. In the future, we will, but for right now, all you have to do is lay there."

That's kind of weird. "How'd you get the cell number of this Hassani guy?"

"Friends in the DoD. Terrorists use disposables all the time. When Operations captures one of them, we get their cell. Then we UFED it—"

"What's that?"

"Universal Forensic Extraction Device. Lifts the data clean off. Images, names, other cell numbers. Depending how many minutes are left on their cards, we can extract everything. The higher-ups usually don't use disposables. If we can get their numbers, we're golden. This douche-bag, Hassani, even has a Facebook page. Go figure."

Irina came alongside Chris. "Okay, Dillon, this is going to work just like it did yesterday, but first we're going to see if hitting the window did any damage to the tech. How's the cut feel?"

I gave her a thumbs-up.

"*Da*. Now relax. You won't feel a thing."

After a few minutes of literally twiddling my thumbs, I grew restless. "When are y'all going to change these posters?" I pointed to the ceiling.

"You don't like dolphins?" Irina was somewhere off my right shoulder.

"They're okay, if I was getting my teeth cleaned."

A technician snickered behind me.

"What would you prefer?" It was Kadin.

"A centerfold?" I suggested.

"We'll work on that," Chris said from out of view.

I closed my eyes and tried to relax, but Chris's comment about not needing to listen in had me puzzled. Why was I going into this tribal thug's mind and not dictating what I heard?

"Okay," Irina announced, coming into my peripheral vision. "The tests are good. We're ready to start." She patted my shoulder. "Now, like last time, keep your mind blank."

"Can I sleep?"

"No. We need your brain awake. This should take about ten minutes."

"Maybe longer," Chris interjected.

"So why aren't I dictating?" I asked.

Chris sighed. "We're just testing today."

"You might hear a lot of voices," Irina said.

"Why's that?" I asked.

"We're going through an AWACS platform," Chris said. "They're all linked up onboard. Shouldn't last long."

"What's an a-whacks?"

"Airborne Warning and Control System. A big plane with long-range radar.

Military use them to detect hostiles. It can also coordinate ground troops and aircraft. Our eyes in the skies."

"On my mark," Irina said. "Three, two, one."

About a dozen male and female voices burst into my mind. It was like being dropped into the middle of a loud cocktail party, except many of the conversations were full of acronyms and technical military speak. My head started to ache.

"One more minute," Irina said.

Compared to the millions of voice I had experienced before, this was a cake-walk. "No problem."

The voices condensed into one male voice. It was soft in timbre with a light southern drawl. Deep South, if I had to guess. I waited to hear a name.

"I'm listening into a guy named Glantz," I said to the room. "Anyone familiar?"

"Yes!" Chris said, with a resounding clap of his hands. "It worked."

Mr. Bradford? Glantz said into my mind.

Whoa! "Hey guys, he knows I'm in his head."

"That's good," Chris said. "He's in on the test."

I know we can't communicate, Glantz said. But if you're listening, it will take a minute to downlink you. Please standby.

"He's telling me to standby."

"Then hold tight." Chris walked into my field of view and handed me a cell phone. "Want to talk to him?"

"Absolutely!" I put it to my ear. The halo made it a little hard to hear.

"Mr. Bradford?" Glantz's voice was distant and full of static.

"Yes?"

"Com Specialist Richard Glantz, sir! It's an honor to have you, um … aboard."

I felt like saluting. I could hear his voice in my ear, then half a second later I could hear his same words in my mind … along with him thinking that this was totally awesome.

"Pardon me, sir?" Glantz asked. "Can you tell me what am I thinking right now?" *Big chicken fried steak from Mardy's.*

"About a big chicken fried steak from a place called Mardy's," I answered.

Glantz laughed. "Gawddamn! This is outstanding! Ah, excuse my language, sir."

"Don't worry. Just don't go thinking anything naughty, soldier."

"No sir. Only clean thoughts. May I speak to Mr. Banks, please?"

I handed the cell back to Chris.

"Freaky, eh?" he said, taking it.

"My tax dollars at work," I replied.

Chris walked away, talking to Glantz. After a few seconds of conversation, he said, "Showtime, people!"

I tried to relax, but if we were hooking up with the Air Force, this was probably an important test. It had to be classified. If this was any indication of what I would be doing for the "big" money Chris had promised, I could get used to this gig.

"On my mark," Irina called out. "Three, two, one."

At first there was nothing. Then a lone male voice rose from the ether. It was guttural and raspy like a smoker's. I had no clue what he was thinking. For all I knew, he could have been asleep, although the volume of his thoughts didn't suggest it.

After a few minutes of listening to a language of fur balls, I asked the room, "How's it going?"

"Be quiet, Dillon," Irina scolded.

"Sorry." I went back to staring at the ceiling. The tagline for the jumping dolphin poster was "CELEBRATE. YOUR TIME IS NOW!"

After a few more minutes, Hassani's inflection became agitated. His words seemed to be panicky, even scared. He repeatedly called out to Allah.

"Guys?" I said. "Hassani is freaking out for some reason."

"Don't worry," Chris replied. "These guys scream for Allah all the time. He probably just lost a hand of Texas Hold 'Em."

I seriously doubted terrorists played poker. Hassani went on calling out to his God when his voice vanished. The lab grew quiet.

"I don't hear him anymore," I said. "Are we still connected?"

Chris strolled to my side. He looked pleased. "All done."

"That's it?"

"Chill out, will you." He took a sip from the big black mug. "You just did your country a huge favor."

28. Still here.

I had developed a pretty good headache during Chris's piggyback test, which must have concerned Irina because she kept me after to run a "cerebral diagnostic." I'd asked Chris repeatedly what the huge favor had been, but he skirted the question. I figured a squad of SEALS had busted down Hassani's door and taken him out. Probably why he was freaking out so bad.

All of the other technicians had left, so I put the halo back on myself and perched on the edge of the death table. It was hard to tighten down, but I managed. Irina was busy on her laptop.

"So how'd you get involved with Wardinski and Chris?" I asked, tightening the last knob.

Making small talk with Irina was like trying to chat up a guard at

Buckingham Palace. You got a sense that you were getting through, but good luck on any reaction. I tried again. "Are you techlepathic?"

This got her attention.

"No."

"You didn't answer my first question."

Irina sighed. "If you must know," she said, resuming her typing, "they seeked me out."

"It's—"

"I know, it's sought. Seek, sought. Who cares? English is stupid." Her typing became more vigorous.

"Right. Who am I to correct?" I sat there and tried to keep my mind blank.

"My sister's techlepath," she said finally.

"Really. Is she here?"

More vigorous typing. "She's dead."

"Oh, I'm sorry." My attention went to one of the computer stacks. I tried to discern the pattern in its blinking LEDs, but none could be found.

"She hated it," Irina said. "Especially the voices."

"I know how she felt. It's hard, sometimes, to block it all out. How'd she die, if you don't mind me asking?"

Irina slowly closed her laptop, removed her glasses, and stared into the lab. Finally, she looked at me. "She killed herself."

■   ■   ■

Instead of having dinner sequestered in my room, Kadin invited me to join her in the dining area. There weren't many people, just a few lab-coated technicians at a six-top. One of the dining tables was set up with three foil-serving platters and two cafeteria-sized drink dispensers. One was filled with tea, the other lemonade. An ice-filled bucket of water bottles completed the buffet.

I found Kadin alone at one of the smaller tables in a corner. She was reading a newspaper, her glasses perched at the edge of her nose.

"This seat taken?" I asked, leaning on one of the metal-framed chairs.

She coolly looked up over the tortoise rims. "Sit down."

"What are you reading?" I asked, setting down my tea. I hadn't seen a TV or newspaper in days.

"The usual." She placed the paper on the table. It was the front section of the New York Times. "Death and destruction. Is the Middle East ever going to change?"

"They've been fighting for thousands of years. Why should they stop now?" I glanced at the front page. "Mind if I have a look?"

"Sure."

After a few moments, a small Asian woman with straight, sharply cut bangs approached with two plates that consisted of a lightly peppered chicken breast, mixed vegetables, and what resembled cornbread, although the color was too pale to actually be cornbread.

"Thanks, Lu," Kadin said.

Lu bowed slightly and placed the plates in front of us. Her eyes were repeatedly drawn to me.

Odd that I didn't get to choose my food. "Hi, Lu." I extended my hand. "My name is Dillon."

Lu giggled and backed away. She bowed and scurried off.

"What did I say?"

Kadin folded over her section and scrutinized me. "She thinks she's not worthy, or something like that. I don't get it, really."

I watched Lu move between two tables and dart through a door. "You're kidding."

"You're a god, Dillon. Get over it." Kadin set her paper aside and started into her chicken. I watched her stoically struggle to cut it with her slinged arm.

"You need help with that?" I said finally.

Kadin stopped in midcut and pinned me with a stare. "I can manage."

"*Okay*. Just trying to help."

I turned my attention to the front page. Kadin was right. Death and de-struction were the order of the day. Seems I hadn't missed much during my captivity. I continued reading through the national highlights. One caught my attention.

PRESIDENT'S CHIEF OF STAFF STILL IN COMA.

I turned the paper toward Kadin and pointed. "Did you see this?"

She took a bite and glanced over. "Uh huh," she said, chewing. "Terrible."

"I was inside her mind, right?"

Kadin nodded and stabbed some sliced carrots with her fork.

"How's dinner?" Chris asked, walking up.

I presented the front page and pointed to the headline.

"Do you know about this?"

He took the paper and read.

"It says she might not recover," I said.

His eyes went to Kadin, who didn't look up.

"That's really a shame." He folded the paper and tucked it under his arm. "Eat up, man, you're going to need your strength."

Chris abruptly headed for the buffet. I saluted his back and cut into my chicken. It was dry, but not unpleasant. It had a hint of rosemary that reminded me of my stepmother's cooking. She had a bush in the backyard that always supplied fresh sprigs for her chicken dishes.

"Guess Chris doesn't want me keeping up with the outside world," I said.

"He always takes the front section." Kadin reached down and grabbed the rest of the paper from the floor. "Here." She slid several sections across the table.

We both ate in silence: she skimming the entertainment section, me sports. Chris hadn't made it to the buffet. He'd been stopped by one of the lab techni-cians and had taken a seat at their table.

"What did you mean last night?" I asked, finally.

"About what?" Kadin folded the entertainment section across the middle and laid it on the table.

"You said I needed to know something."

She removed her glasses and tossed them onto the paper. Her eyes went to Chris, who was still chatting with the technician.

I followed her gaze. "Is it about you and Chris?"

"Yes."

"He loves you, you know."

Still watching Chris, Kadin raised her dark eyebrows and blinked.

"I saw the way he handled you at the accident."

Another blink.

"Do you love him?"

"I think so," she said softly.

"Did I ever know the real you?"

Kadin looked back, expression blank. "No."

"Tell me something."

Silence.

"Who did I fall in love with?"

I'm not sure what kind of reaction I was expecting, but the look that spread across her face bordered on pity.

"I'm really sorry that it had to happen that way," she said.

The old Dillon would have had a snappy comeback, like *At least I got some good sex out of the deal.* Something along those lines. But that reaction seemed foreign now. I thought about pushing away and heading back to my room, but I didn't want to seem petulant. That would give her too much satisfaction.

"I'm over it," I said, and resumed eating.

Kadin gathered her glasses and stood. "Good." She pushed her chair in. "I did what I had to do. We're on the verge of changing a lot of what's bad in the world." She began to walk away, but stepped back. "You're the center of it, Dillon. I know you won't believe this, but I'm proud of you. You've changed."

"Thanks, I think."

"You'll see," she said.

I finished my dinner alone and left the dining room. As I walked down the hallway, it occurred to me that the compound – with its chipped white paint and stained ceiling tiles – was like a run-down version of ELT. It could have been a school at one time, with what looked like poorly patched drill holes in the walls where lockers had been bolted.

Wardinski rounded the corner at the far end of the hall styled in his signature black turtleneck, jeans, and ass-kicking boots. He smiled.

"How are you feeling today, Dillon?" He extended his hand.

"Not bad," I replied, shaking it.

"Come with me, will you?"

"Sure. What else do I have to do?"

I followed Wardinski into the middle of the parking lot, where he proceeded to light up a foul cigarette. The air was cool, and the moon hadn't risen yet. It felt good to be outside. Car lights sliced the darkness on the road beyond the gate, and my attention went to the repaired part of the chain link. The stars, sprinkled across the inky black dome of the cosmos, stood guard above us.

"Nice night," I said, trying to make small talk.

Wardinski took a long, deliberate drag and let the smoke linger around his lips.

"What do you think about Chris?" he asked, exhaling.

"What's there to say, Peter? He's a spook."

"I meant about what he's trying to accomplish." Another drag.

"Ridding the world of scum with a super stealth infiltrator?"

Wardinski gave me a second glance. He nodded.

I shrugged. "Sounds worth it to me."

"Really?"

"Well, sure. What's not to like? I go in, retrieve information no one else can, and get out." Unless they have the same technology as Debra, I thought. "What are you getting at?"

"Chris can be … unpredictable."

"Ya think?" I said sarcastically.

Something swooped low over our heads. I ducked.

"Bats." Wardinski looked around. "They're attracted to the radio waves we produce. They're prevalent in this region of Poland." He sucked in a couple more drags, then stamped the butt out in the muddy gravel. "If Chris ever makes you uncomfortable, you let me know."

I considered telling him about Chris's anger management issues with cows, but decided against it. "Will do." It was getting cold.

Wardinski took in a deep breath and exhaled. "The air feels good, yes?"

"Yeah. It's cold, too. Can we—"

"May I ask you something else?" A serious tone limned Wardinski's words, his breath equally visible.

"Sure."

"Do you think Kadin and Chris are in love?"

Oh, God. "Look, Peter. Given all that's gone down, I'm probably not the best person to—"

"Indulge me."

"I know one of them is."

"Chris?"

I nodded.

By the expression on Wardinski's face, this didn't sit well. He stood there with his hands behind his back and contemplated the stars. He vigorously kneaded the knuckles of his right hand into the palm of his left.

"I know what Kadin did to you," he said, clearly uncomfortable broaching the subject.

"It's okay, Peter. She's passionate about Chris's work. Besides, she's not the first girl who's jerked me around."

"If you fell in love, I'm sorry." There was a trace of sincerity in Wardinski's voice.

I found the Big Dipper. "Yeah, well. The price of fame, right?" I blew warmth into my cupped hands.

Wardinski nodded. "You see, Kadin is my only child and I–"

Dillon? A flash of pain accompanied Debra's voice.

I flinched. *Hang tight, will you?*

"Am I boring you?" Wardinski asked.

"Not at all. Please, tell me about Kadin as a little girl."

Wardinski's expression relaxed. "All right. She was a frail child. Her mother and I–"

Dillon?!

Okay, I can think now.

How are you? Debra asked.

Managing. How are you getting through their system?

Sanjiv's a genius. Something about modulation. Where are you? Your thoughts are coming through clearly.

Outside, in the parking lot. What do you want?

We're working on a way to get you out of there.

What if I don't want to leave?

Dillon, haven't you ever heard of the Stockholm Syndrome? You're sympathizing with your captors. Believing what they're doing is for a just cause.

It is.

They're using you.

And you weren't? I asked.

Silence.

Debra?

Okay, she said. *We* didn't *go about bringing you in the right way. I'll admit that—*

Another bat flew low over my head, the beat of its wings snapping against the cold air like thin plastic. *Shit!*

What's the matter?

Bats.

Gross.

Tell me about it. Another flew by, and I swatted at it.

Dillon, Banks is nothing more than a war merchant. Who do you think he works for?

DoD?

Wrong. He's working for a man named Sadiki. He's a Saudi national with British dual citizenship. He brokers weapons to the highest bidder. Guess what his new weapon of choice is?

Enlighten me.

You.

I'm not a weapon. I just retrieve information.

Is that what they're telling you?

Yes.

How many minds have you been in?

I don't know. Half a dozen. Why?

Who were they?

Why should I tell you?

Were any of them important?

I don't think so.

You don't think, or don't know?

Okay, one was.

Who was it?

Alicia Hughes.

The president's Chief of Staff?!

When a person yelled a thought, their volume went up, which I felt as a slight increase in pressure at the temples. Some people's scream/thoughts could hurt a little, like Debra's did right now.

Yeah, so? More silence. Debra?

When were you in her mind?

A few days ago. Two, I think. Why?

What did they have you do?

Nothing. It was a test. I was in her mind for a minute, that's all. What's the matter?

This time I could almost feel Debra's angst through the silence.

Do you know what happened to her? she asked.

Wardinski's cell phone rang, cutting off his monologue about Kadin's childhood. He glanced at its screen. "Excuse, Dillon. I have to take this."

I motion for him to go right ahead. He walked away, talking rather sternly in Polish.

Yes, I continued. *She's in a coma.*

And you don't find that just a little coincidental? Debra asked.

Debra, I can't magically put something into her brain. "It's a coincidence, that's all."

Yes, but—

"Who you talking to, Dillon?"

As Debra began to explain how Hughes's coma was the result of an aneurysm, I spun around to see Chris's puzzled face. I had been so engrossed I hadn't even heard him step up.

"H-hey, Chris." *Shut up, Debra. Chris is here.*

Wardinski turned, but only acknowledged Chris with a nod. He then went back to bitching the caller out.

"Thought I'd join you two." Chris pulled out a pack of Marlboro Reds from somewhere under his coat and tapped one out. "It's good to breath some fresh air for a change, right?" He bit down, drew it free, and lit it with a battered Zippo.

I was desperate to distance myself from my outburst. I turned to Chris and said, "Isn't that Wardinski's? It's a classic."

Chris looked the lighter over as if he'd just stumbled onto it in a drawer. "No, it's mine. He bums it all the time." He glanced at Wardinski, who was now about 40 feet away and gesturing angrily with his free hand. "Guy smokes like a chimney." He rolled the lighter over in his fingers, and I glimpsed a faded Army Ranger emblem.

"I noticed that."

Dillon?

Hold on, I snapped.

Chris stood beside me and looked skyward. "Beautiful night."

I followed his gaze. "Yep. It is."

After a moment of awkward stargazing, I could feel Chris's attention settle on me.

"So what's 'a coincidence?'" he asked.

Fuck.

What? Debra asked.

Shhh!

"I was just talking to myself," I said, still looking up. "Bad habit. My parents died. A while back." This was going completely assways. "Sometimes I talk to them ... out loud." Shit.

Chris took a long drag and let it out slowly. "I thought you were adopted."

I looked at him. "Yeah. Weird, isn't it?"

He shrugged. "Whatever works." He sucked in another drag and resumed stargazing. "I hated my folks. They were druggies."

I let my eyes follow the handle of the Little Dipper and looked for Polaris. It was getting colder.

Dillon, Debra said. *Is he gone?*

No, Debra. Chris's thought cut into my mind with acrid clarity. *I'm still here.*

29. Go with the flow.

Fear passed through me like a bolt of glass lightning. Chris was still gazing skyward. How could he listen in?

"There's Polaris, Dillon." He pointed and took a fierce drag.

What's going on? Debra's thought bordered on panic. *How are you able to hear my thoughts? Dillon, can you hear Chris?*

You've been outed, Debra, Chris said. *Nice work, too. Sanjiv's?*

How are you-?

Brilliant. I'd love to see the programming for that app. Did you tell Dillon yet?

Tell me what? I said. *And yes, I can hear him.*

That Alicia Hughes has died, Debra said. She was pissed, and it came through in her voice. *They're using you to kill people.*

What are you—?

Chris pressed the gun barrel against my temple and cut off my thought. He had grabbed my arm in the same movement, his fingers digging deep into my bicep.

Oh, Debra? Chris said.

Yes?

I have our boy here, and you're not going to like the position he's in.

Debra, he has a gun to my goddamn head! I said.

Please, Chris. Listen to me—

No, you listen, bitch, Chris said. *If you don't back off right now, I'll end this party line.*

You wouldn't.

Chris pointed the gun down and fired.

"Jesus Christ!" I yelled. *He just shot the ground!* I tried to pull away from Chris's grip, but he held me firm. The barrel was hot against my temple.

Wardinski spun on his heals, eyes wide with shock. "Banks?!" he bellowed.

Okay, Chris. Calm down. Debra's voice was even, and had a distinct undercurrent of authority. *We won't break in again. I'm disconnecting now.*

You better not. Chris shoved me away and leveled the gun.

Wardinski charged up, eyes slitted in rage.

I backed away, hands raised like they could actually stop a bullet. "Hey, hey, wait a minute!"

"Were you ever going to tell me?" Chris pulled out what looked large like a Blackberry, thumbed it a couple of times, and shoved it back into his pocket. A flash of pain cut through my head.

I lowered my hands. "Look, Chris—"

"How long has she been in your head?"

"Just since the other night ... when we went into to town. Chris, believe me, I don't want to go with them."

"What the hell is going on?!" Wardinski demanded. The pace of his gait suggested he was going to slam Chris into the dirt and beat the living hell out of him.

Chris pivoted the gun at Wardinski and hit him with a *Don't fuck with me* look. "Hold up, old man."

Wardinski did. "How *dare* you," he said, incredulously.

Chris's gaze swung back to me. "You talk about trust, and you're doing this bullshit." Chris lowered the gun and shook his head. "Come on, Dillon. For this to work, you and I need to be simpatico."

"Simpatico? You just put that fucking gun to my head—"

Behind Chris, Kadin, accompanied by the two Euro-muscle boys, rushed from the compound.

Chris turned, hands raised palms out. The gun dangled from his forefinger. "Everything's cool," he yelled. "Just taking care of a little business with Dillon."

Kadin trotted to a stop about 15 feet from us. Her eyes went to the gun. The muscle followed in her wake and flanked her.

The look on Kadin's face was filled with an odd mix of shock and fear. "We saw that something had penetrated the dampening field."

"And we heard a shot," the taller muscle said.

Chris relaxed and returned the gun where the Marlboros had come from. He stepped up to Wardinski. "Peter, this is what happens when protocol gets sloppy."

"What are you talking about?" he growled.

"Guess who's been visiting Dillon's mind?"

"Lao," Kadin said, more to herself.

Chris wagged his finger. "I told you, Peter, we should have hired that Indian." He pulled out the pack of Reds again and casually fed himself one.

Wardinski moved his anger onto me. "Is this true?"

"Yes," I said with a reluctant nod.

"She's been in his head since the other night." Chris flicked open the Zippo and lit up. "When we went into town." He blew out a large cloud of smoke.

"What was the shot for?" Kadin asked.

"He put a gun to my head." My anger spilled out with the words. "He threatened to kill me if Debra didn't back off."

Chris spun around, arms spread in a mock gesture of solidarity. "Dillon, come on. I would never blow a hole in that beautiful brain of yours." He snapped the lighter shut. "It's worth too much."

"Then why did you fire the gun?" Kadin asked.

"I shot the ground. Theatrics. I needed Dillon genuinely scared to buy some time with Debra. You can't fake something like that. It's hard to lie in a thought." He patted the side of his coat. "Nothing like a Glock to bring out the fear."

I shook my head in disgust.

"What?"

"Do you know about Alicia Hughes?" I asked Wardinski.

"No," he said. "What happened?"

"She died."

Wardinski turned to Chris. "What?!"

Chris shrugged. "Oopsy."

"Did I do that?" I asked.

"No," Chris said. "You didn't do anything."

"How did this happen?" Wardinski asked.

"The quarry wave test. Remember?" Chris didn't hide his impatience. "You signed off on it."

"I never did anything of the sort!" Wardinski said.

Chris took an angry drag and pointed with the two fingers holding the cigarette. "Don't act all surprised, old man. You knew the risks."

"You said you were testing the wave."

"Okay, so we overdid the levels a bit. Sue me. We're still analyzing the data. We may have had nothing to do with her aneurysm."

"My God, Chris! Do you know what the repercussions of this will be?" Wardinski looked like he was about to kill Chris right there with his bare hands.

Chris savored a long drag, flicked the cigarette, and met Wardinski's glare. "Fully." He exhaled.

Wardinski stepped back and made a slight gesture with his hand. The muscle with the fashion stubble reached into his coat, but Chris drew the Glock out and shot him with frightening grace. I barely saw the gun appear. Kadin's scream pierced the air as the man staggered and collapsed. His partner went for his gun, but the Glock was in his face before he could arm himself.

"Don't." Chris motioned with the barrel. "Pull it out slowly, then throw it at my feet."

He did. The gun bounced twice and landed near Chris's right foot. He grabbed it off the ground and pocketed it. His aim never wavered.

The wounded man, tucked tightly in a ball and holding his left thigh, groaned in agony on the rutted mud.

"Have you lost your mind?!" Wardinski screamed.

"You're the one who told him to pull out his gun," Chris said indignantly. "Besides, I didn't hit the artery."

The wounded man spit angry Polish that pierced the air, then went back to clutching his thigh. Blood oozed between his fingers.

Chris moved his aim onto him. "Don't tempt me." He swung the gun toward Wardinski. "Let's get some perspective here. *I* run this show. *I* supply the money. *I'm* taking the risk."

The look in Chris's eyes reminded me of a documentary I had seen about Mexican dog fighting. The fevered disregard for life, fueled by money and blood lust in the spectators' eyes, had stuck with me. I could see it in Chris as he waved his Glock in Wardinski's direction.

Kadin wrapped her hand around the barrel. "Chris, please." She eased the gun down. "That's my father."

Chris tilted a glance toward her, and his face went blank with uncertainty. It was a fleeting look, and I wondered just how close he'd come to completely losing it. He flashed a reassuring smile, pulled back his coat, and tucked the Glock away.

"Sorry, baby. My bad." He pulled at his lapels and stepped up to Wardinski. "Alicia Hughes was a liberal pit bull," he said, as if this were simply a heated political conversation. "She led a bullshit agenda that sent good soldiers to their deaths." He let out a defeated sigh. "Look, if we find out that the test caused her aneurysm I'm sorry. Really."

Two lab technicians emerged from the compound, each with a hand in their coats. I vaguely remembered one of them from the operating room.

"Took you long enough," Chris said to them.

"Sorry," the shorter one said, trotting up. His reply betrayed a German accent.

"All right, Chris." Wardinski, clearly shaken, was trying to diffuse the situation as best he could. "We'll discuss this later. Now let's get Marko some help."

Chris nodded to his men. "Take him to Tarasova."

The two technicians, along with the remaining muscle, carried Marko back into the compound. The guy moaned all the way. Chris watched them until the door closed. He turned and surveyed the three of us like naughty children.

"I'm surprised at you all," he said. "We've had a major security breech, and you're looking at me like I'm the crazy one? Believe me, this isn't a game. The stakes are very real." He faced Wardinski. "Peter, what did I say when I first approached you?"

Wardinski thought for a second. "You had an idea that could change the war on terror."

"Right. And what else?"

"That it might get dangerous," Kadin said.

"That's right. And now Lao knows where we are, and she'll be up our asses within 24 hours. Mark my words. Their extraction team will be coming in hot."

"What's a quarry wave test?" I asked.

Chris twisted around and regarded me like an interloper.

"It's a penetration test. To see how deep we can go inside a tight organization. The White House is as tight as they come," he said, then started toward the compound.

I exchanged confused glances with Wardinski and Kadin. Between them, I could see that Chris was almost to the door. He stopped and turned back.

"Well, come on, people." He clapped his hands. "No time to waste. We've got to pack up and get the hell out of here." He entered the compound and slammed the door.

Kadin wrapped her good arm around her father's waist, and they started toward the compound. From the way they were holding onto each other, the Wardinski family was having trouble processing what had just happened.

"Excuse me?" I caught up to Kadin's slinged side.

They both stopped and looked at me blankly.

"Can either one of you explain how Chris got into both mine and Debra's minds?"

"I know he's been working on a way to cross-platform the frequencies," Wardinski said. "It's only good within a small radius of a secondary source. I didn't think he had perfected it yet."

"Guess he has."

"He told me he wanted to be able to participate."

"Well if he can do that, then what does he need me for? Why doesn't he just do it himself?"

"Dillon ... No one else has ever come close to being as powerful as you.

[

Chris is augmented, but something about your brain allows you to integrate over the whole grid. We don't know why." Wardinski shook his head.

"What?"

"I'm worried about Chris."

"He's a little … you know." I did the crazy gesture by the side of my head.

"I think he comes by it legally," Kadin said. "He was in Afghanistan and saw a lot of action. He lost several close friends."

"Yeah, but he just hauled off and shot that guy," I said. "Either he's truly close to the edge, or there's something else. Who's Sadiki?"

Wardinski's brow furrowed. "How do you know about him?"

"A little voice told me."

"What did Ms. Lao say?"

"He's a Saudi arms dealer and, if I had to guess, our real benefactor."

Wardinski walked out of Kadin's grip and began pacing.

"Papa, what is it?"

Wardinski stopped, looked up, and sighed. His breath came out like hot steam against the sky's blackness. "I knew this was wrong."

"Aligning with Chris?" I asked.

He nodded.

"Look, I can get behind the idea of taking out the bad guys. But this Alicia Hughes thing is way out of line."

"He wasn't like this before," Kadin said.

"So what's flipping him out?"

"I believe there are money issues," Wardinski said.

"How do you know?"

"I've heard Chris say things … in passing. He's never mentioned Sadiki until recently. I think he's getting pressure to show results."

"That's probably why he jumped the gun on Alicia Hughes," Kadin said.

Wardinski puffed out his cheeks and rubbed the back of his neck. "I don't like the way Chris is changing."

While we stood there and contemplated how deep in the shit we were buried, a cow mooed somewhere in the distance. The image of Chris blowing the bovine's head off passed through my thoughts, and a shiver went through me. I hugged myself.

"Cold?" Kadin asked.

I nodded.

"Kadie?" Wardinski asked. "Can you talk with Chris? Find out why he's so on edge?"

"I can try."

"Look, I wasn't going to tell you guys this, but the night we had the accident – after Chris and I got Kadin into the car – he stopped and shot the cow that caused it."

Kadin's face flushed with shock. "What?!"

"I'm surprised you didn't hear it. Blew its head right off."

Wardinski started doing the kneading thing again. "This is definitely not good."

"Let me talk with him, Papa." Kadin grasped her father's hands. "Maybe I can calm him down."

"Not to dash your hopes," I said, "but I don't think a guy like Chris can be easily swayed. He's not wired that way. He's driven by money and power. I work with his type all the time. When money gets tight, these guys can get very weird."

Wardinski nodded. "He's right, Kadie."

"But it can't be just the money," she said. "It must be the..." Her voice trailed off.

"What is it, Kadie?" her father asked.

"His MS."

"Why's that?" I asked

"It's how it interfaces with his tech," she said. "I've been seeing glimpses of its effect. Little outbursts. For no reason."

Wardinski listened intently.

"Look," I said, "the best thing to do right now is just go with the flow."

"What do you mean?" Kadin asked.

"Don't stir things up. Don't get in his face about what he's doing or his MS. Just be the understanding girlfriend. Is there anyone you trust? Someone who's working directly on the project?"

Wardinski shook his head. "Chris purged my original staff and brought in all new people."

"What about that girl who brought us dinner?" I asked. "She seems innocent enough."

Kadin shook her head. "No. Lu's typical of Chris's staff. She's a surgical nurse, but she can't get a decent job in her country. Chris waved a ton of cash in her face. Most of these people send the better part of their salaries back home. Chris has them in his pocket."

A bat darted over us. Kadin tried to retreat into her coat. The creature circled the far end of the parking lot, then fluttered up and disappeared into the inky void.

"You know," I said, "there might be one person who Chris doesn't influence."

"Who's that?" Wardinski asked. "Maybe I can talk with them."

"No." I blew into my cupped hands and tried to warm them. "I think this is someone I should approach."

30. A little secret.

I hung out at the back of the operating lab and watched Chris snap orders to his staff. Part Patton, part Dr. Phil. It was equally intriguing to see how they could pack a dozen rooms of equipment into 30 cases, each the size of a refrigerator. Near midnight, a large, nondescript semi backed into the parking lot. Not long after, the worker bees began loading it. Kadin had disappeared shortly after we returned to the compound. She probably went to pack. I considered doing the same, but my belongings would fit in a small duffle bag. I had asked Wardinski if there was anything I could do to help, but he assured me there wasn't. And nobody could, or would, give me a straight answer about where we were going.

I found Irina in the parking lot, leaning against the wall next to the door. An unlit cigarette dangled from her full lips. She was tapping away on a smart phone.

"Sexting again?" I joked.

A faint grin spread into the corners of her mouth.

"Ah-ha," I said. "You do smile."

"Only when I'm tired." She was still focused on her texting.

I stood there, watching the worker bees load the mother truck, and waited for her to finish.

"So, how long's it been?" I asked after a minute.

Irina, her blond eyebrows arched questioningly, glanced over the top of her dark-framed glasses.

"Since you quit," I said.

Again the smile. "Fourteen months." She tucked the cigarette behind an ear and continued texting.

"Boyfriend?" I feigned taking a peek over her shoulder.

"Hardly." She hit send. "My mother." She pocketed the phone into her jeans.

"Wish I had my phone." I joined her against the wall and folded my arms.

Irina dug the phone out and handed it to me. "Knock yourself up."

I laughed.

"What?"

"It's out."

She frowned.

"Never mind."

I took it like a precious gift and tapped in the number to retrieve my voice-mail.

"Our secret, *da*?" She looked around.

"Don't worry. Thanks."

Oddly, I had just 10 messages. Six computer-generated political ads from my district's representative. Two from Derek. One from my condo association and one informing me that the Merc's 30,000-mile service was due. Surprisingly,

Derek didn't even ask how I was doing. He just updated me on a couple of account issues. For a second, I was disappointed. I did have cancer, after all. Then again, it hadn't been that long since we had spoken. It only seemed a lifetime ago. I handed back her phone.

"Bad news?" Irina asked.

"No one's looking for me."

"Unsettling, isn't it?"

"What is?"

"To find you might not be missed after all."

One of the worker bees jammed the wheels of her dolly into the loading ramp, and the case she was moving toppled over.

Irina shook her head. "Great," she said disgustedly. "Probably the neuro monitors."

"Can't get good help these days."

"You always this funny?" She removed her glasses and hung them in the "V" of her sweater.

The light above us was cracked, and its frame caked with the carcasses of dead bugs. It top-lit Irina harshly and highlighted the edges of her blond hair. I noticed for the first time the way she tucked her chin after asking a question. It was a charming idiosyncrasy, probably something she'd done since she was kid.

"Only when I'm tired," I replied.

She nodded as if to say, *Touché*.

"Can I ask you a question?" I leaned closer.

She shifted her stance to meet me halfway. "Yes?"

"What's the quarry wave test about?"

"Chris finally tell you, eh?"

"Kind of."

"It's become the main focus of the operation."

"It wasn't before?"

"No. In the beginning, we were to develop a way to get you into the target's mind. But we discovered a way to embed a cataleptic waveform that could impair brain function. When Chris's benefactors learned about that, our funding tripled."

"What's it do?"

"It's hard to describe. Think of it as the mother of all seizures. Depending on the level used it can induce anything from fainting to coma."

"Can it kill someone?"

"Yes."

"What do you think about it?"

"If it rids the world of terrorist bastards, I'm good with it."

"What if it's used on the wrong people?"

"Not my problem."

I had a friend who worked for a defense contractor in Dallas. They built components for the cruise missile. I asked him once how he managed his feelings about building something that could cause so many deaths. He said he got paid a ton of money, and that if he didn't do it, someone else would. Besides, it wasn't his problem. The guy retired at 42. I changed the subject.

"So what do you think about Chris?"

Irina's eyes lit upon the worker bees over my shoulder, then came back. "Who wants to know?"

"Just me."

She shrugged slightly and frowned. "I've had worse employers."

"I meant ... as a person."

Irina edged closer until the side of her body was against mine. She scrutinized the parking lot, and some of her hair brushed against my cheek. "He's teetering," she whispered out of the side of her mouth.

"Between what and what?" I whispered back.

"Weird and weirder."

"Well, he is intense."

"It's more than that." Irina faced me. "Before, I could manage him."

"What do you mean?"

"You know, work with him. Discuss things. We had mutual respect. But the last few weeks, he's become short. Too demanding." She glanced around again. "He's more like–" She seemed to be searching for the right words.

"Like what?"

"My grandfather."

"How so?"

"He was KGB."

Jesus. "How did you get involved in all this? I know your sister was like me. Did Chris know about her and approach you?"

"Yes. At the time I was struggling to understand why she killed herself. Early on, I had gotten interested in the science. Then I joined–" She cut herself off.

It was clear this line of questioning was pushing Irina's emotional buttons. She wasn't about to cry or anything, but I could tell that her late sister was an uncomfortable subject.

"I was doing a research fellowship in bionanotechnology at Moscow Medical Academy," she continued.

"Are you the inventor of the tech in my head?"

"No. That's Dr. Rechenko. He's the real genius. I'm just a smart girl who worked for him."

"How did you meet Chris?"

"He approached me at a coffee shop. He showed me his CIA credentials and suggested we chat. He mentioned Tanya–"

"Your sister?"

Irina nodded. "He said he could relate to my pain. He had also lost someone close. At first I blew him off, but he was persistent."

"Why'd you change your mind?"

"Something in what he said. I couldn't tell you the exact words anymore. He made the work sound noble, like we were going to end terrorism for good. Change the world. Make Tanya's death meaningful, in twisted sort of way. I don't know. It made sense at the time."

"Just like Debra," I said, catching myself staring at the ground.

"Your girlfriend?"

"What? No. Just someone I know."

We stood there, leaning against one another and staring at nothing.

"Why don't you leave?" I finally asked.

"You making joke, right?"

"No, really. You can leave anytime. Can't you?"

"Chris would make life miserable. Besides," she glanced at the worker bees again, "he pays more than I would ever make ... anywhere." She kicked the dried mud. "I need the money."

"For your mother?"

She nodded. "She's in early stages of Parkinson's. The facility she's in is horrible. I want to—"

The door opened, and a lab technician with a thick beard and shaved head stepped out. He asked Irina something in Russian and glanced at me.

"*Da*," she said.

They spoke more Russian before he hurried back inside.

"What's up?" I asked.

"We leave in an hour."

"Where're we going?"

Irina pulled the cigarette from behind her ear and flicked it away.

"Looks like Peter is getting his wish." She yanked the door open.

I grabbed its frame and held it. "*Where* are we going?"

Irina bored her clear blue eyes into me. "Russia."

Part 3: To Russia, without love.

31. Welcome to Oz.

We took off from the municipal airport around three in the morning. Chris, Wardinski, Kadin, Irina, and I flew through the Polish night in a very old, very used private jet. Chris knew about my love of planes and informed me it was a 1972 Yak-40: a three engine, ex-Aeroflot short hauler that would cover the distance to our destination in about four hours. Most private jets could easily cruise at 400 mph, so that meant wherever we were going was roughly 1600 miles away. The Yak's pilots looked like they were coming off an all-night bender.

When we had pulled up to the plane, I thought about making a break for it, but the memory of Chris holding the gun to my head made me reconsider. On the way to the airport, Chris had been in full-twitch mode, like a guy who had too many Red Bulls. He wouldn't shut up about how the work we were doing was vital to stabilizing the world order, and that it was important was for me to be a "team player." I assured him I was, so long as we stuck to killing terrorists. He acted like nothing had happened the other night, as if shooting Wardinski's security man was just business as usual. Maybe it was for a guy like him.

In truth, I was longing for my old life. I had rationalized being an instrument of death as patriotic, but the Alicia Hughes situation had really rattled me. I hoped to God Chris had unintentionally screwed up the quarry wave test. Then there was Hassani. I couldn't get his screams out of my mind. Even though he was probably scum, something about being inside a mind reinforces that person's humanity. Derek, who had been a Marine, would probably call me a pussy. Hell, there was a part of me calling me a pussy. Whether I liked it or not, I had become the ultimate weapon. Derek once told me about a buddy of his who had been a Special Forces sniper, and that the military had a rifle that could take someone out from two miles away. Neat. Clean. Impersonal. What I did to Hassani was more like hand-to-hand combat. The only saving grace was that I didn't have to look into his eyes as he died. Just his soul.

"Dillon?"

I looked up from skimming a two-year-old Time Europe that had been shoved deep into the seat pocket in front of me and found Irina regarding me quizzically over the top of her seat. "Yeah?"

"Where were you?"

"I was just thinking."

She nodded and ducked back down.

I reached forward between the seats and tapped her shoulder. "Tell me about where we're going," I whispered.

She reclined her seat and faced me. "We're landing at Mineralnye Vody. It's the closest airport to the radio telescope."

"Radio telescope?"

"They didn't tell you?"

I shook my head.

"We're going to the RATAN-600. It's the world's largest, next to the one in Puerto Rico. It's run by the Russian Academy of Science. My old employer. I don't know if we're staying there. Chris said there was a facility on the grounds, but who knows what he's got set up." Irina stared for a second. "You know why, yes?"

I shook my head again.

"Wardinski. He knows people there. Worked a deal out. I think Chris wants to appease him a little. Keep him happy."

Oh, shit. "ET?" I asked.

Irina smirked and nodded.

"It's not funny."

"Yes, it is."

"It's not your head they're screwing with."

She reached between the seats and patted my knee. "No worry. I take good care of you."

I scooted forward. "What if Wardinski's right?"

Irina peered over her seat to the back of the plane, and I followed her gaze. Wardinski and Chris were passed out in their seats. Kadin was a row in front of them, busy on her laptop.

"I'm not much of a believer," she said.

"Yeah, but what if he is?"

"Then you'll be the most famous person in the world."

"I don't want to be."

Irina frowned. "Don't be pussy."

The Mineralnye Vody airport was a study in bizarre juxtaposition. Most of it looked new, but some looked like nobody had been informed that the Soviet

Union was kaput. Two hammer-and-sickle emblems, along with giant Cyrillic letterforms that spelled out the airport's name, adorned the top of what I assumed was the old main terminal. A large map of the Soviet Union dominated the departure lounge. And while I desperately searched for a men's room, I stumbled across a guy selling antique swords and knives. On the wall behind him was a computer printout. I asked the vendor what it was, and he actually understood me. The printout, he answered in rather good English, was a list of local criminals wanted for murder.

As we stowed our gear in the back of two old Chevy Suburbans, I saw three MIG-23s lined up at the end of the runway. Some of the buildings looked like they could have been built during World War II. They – along with the MIGS, the hammer and sickle, and the cloudy sunrise – lent the whole scene a dystopian, Cold War feel. I half-expected Soviet soldiers to goose-step past.

Kadin and her father got into the white Suburban. Chris, Irina, and I piled into the black one. On the way to the radio telescope, Irina briefed me about the area. We were in Southern Russia in the mountainous region of Caucasus, and the telescope was nestled in a remote place called the Bolshoi Zelenchuk Valley. The Black Sea, Chris interjected, was about 100 miles southwest. He was driving and fielding calls, literally one after another. Two were in German and one was in what sounded like Spanish (Portuguese, maybe?). He handled the different languages like he'd been born into them. A particularly long conversation, in English, was with someone named Bouazizi. This person must have had some authority over Chris; instead of giving orders, he mostly listened. Occasionally he would grunt "yes" or "uh-huh." When he finally hung up, we drove on in silence.

∎   ∎   ∎

I had never visited Russia. A friend of mine had gone to Moscow before the wall came down and said it was like stepping into the 1930s. We were in the countryside, and in a way, I could understand. Instead of huge, tricked-out combines lumbering across expansive fields, ancient tractors and old-world collective farms seemed to dominate the landscape.

The RATAN-600 was situated in a large, flat valley; the foothills of the Caucasus range gently rose on either side of us. When we arrived, I was a little surprised; instead of an array of giant satellite dishes, there was a huge, four-story wall of reflector panels that ringed an area the size of six football fields. Each panel looked like it could be tilted to various angles. The area inside the ring was mostly open grass, but in the center stood several large metal blockhouses mounted on railroad tracks. A platform spanned almost the length of the field. It, too, was on tracks, and probably could rotate on its axis. On top of it ran still more tracks, and mounted to those was piece of equipment that resembled an upside-down Apollo capsule. Topping it all off was some sort of pilothouse. The whole place looked like it hadn't been used in years. Rust streaked most of the equipment, and the weeds reached my waist. I asked Irina if the overturned Apollo capsule was the radar dish, and she informed me that everything was the dish. The capsule was just the collector. She claimed the facility had been updated, but considering that everything looked like it could have come off the deck of a mothballed Soviet battleship, not to mention the retro airport, I wondered if "perestroika" had ever been heard around these parts.

"He was born here," Irina said as she slung her backpack over a shoulder.

She had lent me a duffle bag. I pulled it from the back of the Suburban and shut its cargo door. "Who was?"

She looked at me like I was a dumbass. "Gorbachev."

"Forgive me."

Two plainclothes guards wielding Kalashnikovs and magnetometers approached. I dropped my bag and raised my arms.

"Russian history isn't my strong suit," I said.

The fat guard ran his mag wand across my outstretched arms.

Irina likewise raised her arms. "What's this 'strong suit'?"

"It's a term that comes from playing cards. It means to excel at something."

The fat guard ran his mag wand up my inner thigh and jammed it into my crotch. I rose onto my toes and fought back my natural reaction.

Irina said something in Russian out of the side of her mouth. The fat guard chuckled.

We picked up our bags and started down the cracked cement road that ringed the inside of the array. Each massive panel was comprised of three individual aluminum panels. The bottom and top panel were about six feet tall, while the center had to be at least 50 feet tall. Each array had its own hydraulic armature system that, I assumed, could tilt the whole thing to any angle. There must have been hundreds of them. When we passed near one of the blockhouses, I noticed what looked like bullet holes pockmarking one side. The position of the sun suggested it was nearly noon, and with each step, the heat was building. I wiped my brow with the back of my sleeve and regretted not grabbing a sausage biscuit from the vending machine at the airport. At least, that's what I assumed it to be, nestled in its little carousel glass cubby.

"What did you say back there?" I asked, stepping around a huge dandelion. A bee was hovering above it.

Irina didn't answer, and we walked on. Chris was about 400 feet ahead of us, on his phone. No one had searched him, but the guards didn't seem concerned enough to chase after him.

"It's unfair, you know," I said as we approached the opening on the far side.

"What is?" she asked.

"I'm a stranger in a strange land."

"You have no idea."

"Come on ... what did you say back there?"

"I told the guard that you'd set off the magnetometer."

"You did? Why?"

Her eyes went to my crotch and a small grin creased her lips. "Balls of steel."

Just outside the reflector wall was a collection of one-story buildings made of the same metal and cement as everything else. The shrubbery hadn't been watered in years. Wardinski's white Suburban was parked in front of the closest building. Kadin was unloading her bags.

"Why'd they get to drive over here?" I asked.

"Wardinski probably had some equipment to unload."

Chris, still on his phone, approached Kadin and ran a hand affectionately across her shoulder before he continued into main building. She didn't acknowledge him.

"I love what you've done with the place," I said, walking up. "Beautiful shade of dreary."

Kadin ignored my barb and slung her computer bag over her shoulder.

Inside, the main building was similar to the compound back in Poland. Half-glass doors, the kind from an old lab or college, lined a dimly lit hallway that bisected the front of the structure. Chris was already at the far end, talking with a short bearded man in a white lab coat.

"Wait here," Kadin said. She joined Chris and the man. They exchanged handshakes, and Kadin pointed back at us. The bearded man jerked a look. He left Chris and Kadin and walked briskly toward us.

"Dillon Bradford!" the man exclaimed, hand outstretched.

Irina shied away and leaned against a wall. The man grabbed my hand and shook it vigorously.

"My God," he said, pocketing wire-framed glasses. "I've wanted to meet you for a long, long time." With the lab coat, receding hairline, and closely cropped salt and pepper beard, he could have played Freud in a B movie.

"Thanks. Mr....?"

"Forgive me. Victor Rechenko."

Irina pulled her sunglasses down. "Dr. Rechenko."

Rechenko acknowledged her with a cool sideways glance. "Irina."

I began to say something, but bit it off. The tension between the two was palpable.

"We're going to set you up in Building 3 next to the lab." Rechenko's English was only slightly accented. "After you've settled in, we'll have lunch." He looked at his wristwatch. "Let's say, one?"

"Sure," I said.

"Excellent!" Rechenko abruptly turned and hurried back down the hall. As I watched him disappear around a corner, I noticed Chris and Kadin were gone.

Weird. I picked up my duffle bag. "Okay ... I guess we have to find Building 3 on our own?"

Irina, still leaning against the wall, shook her head in disgust. She grabbed her roller case handle and charged down the hallway.

I caught up and matched her pace. "What's up with you and Rechenko?"

"What's the term?" she asked. "Douche box?"

"Douche bag," I corrected.

"Whatever. He's it."

"How do you know him?"

"I tell you sometime."

We rounded the same corner as Rechenko, only to find ourselves at the far end of another long, empty, door-lined hallway.

"Where did–" Suddenly, a faint Russian female voice entered my mind. "Whoa!"

"What is it?" Irina asked.

"Do you think in Russian or English?"

"Depends."

"Think my name ... in English."

Irina blinked, and I clearly heard her say Dillon Bradford in my mind.

"The impeder must be off. I can hear your thoughts."

Just then, more voices flooded in. I had been denied my gift for so long, it was a little startling. I quickly suppressed them.

"You're kidding." Irina let go of her roller case and dug through her backpack. She pulled out a pocket flashlight. "Let me have a look." She pried open each of my eyelids and studied my eyes with the flashlight.

The voices, as if a switch had been thrown, vanished from my head.

"Are there a lot of voices?" she asked.

"No. They're gone now. What do you think that was?"

"I don't know. Maybe the dampening field has been turned off." Irina clicked off the flashlight and returned it to her backpack. She was clearly worried. "The voices still gone, yes?"

I nodded. "Maybe they had a—"

Paging Mr. Dillon Bradford!

"Hello?" I asked.

Irina looked at me. "Who you talking to?"

I pointed at my head and shushed her.

Get over to Building 3, Chris said. *Your country needs you on the double.*

Where's Building 3? And why can I hear you?

Something resembling a holographic diagram of an industrial area abruptly appeared an arm's length in front of me. It took me a second to realize I was looking at a schematic of the RATAN-600 complex. Additional dialogue boxes with Russian text materialized and lingered to the right of its frame. The whole thing hovered and moved with my head.

"Jesus!" I pointed. "Do you see that?"

"See what?" Irina asked.

"The graphic!"

So, Bradford, Chris said. *What do you think?*

Amazing! The image was almost nauseating. I reached for it, but my hand passed through. I stumbled forward, and Irina caught me.

Something our Russian friends have been working on, Chris said. *Now get over here and I'll tell you all about it.*

The Russian text shifted to English, and a small section of Building 1's floor plan changed color and began flashing. A dotted line moved away from it and snaked through Building 2 before it zigzagged outside, moved through Building 3, and stopped near its center. An area around the arrowhead labeled The Lab began blinking a dull yellow.

You get that? Chris asked.

Yeah. I was in awe. *We'll be right there.*

Chris laughed and disappeared.

The infographic shrank, slid into the upper left corner of my vision, and dimmed. I imagined it enlarging again, and hell if it didn't respond exactly to my thought.

"That is so cool," I said to myself.

Irina yanked me around, and the infographic swung between us. I could barely see her face through it. I thought about it shrinking into the corner, and it did. I flinched.

She tugged my sleeve. "You going to let me in on the fun?"

I focused on her. "You wouldn't believe it."

"Try me."

"There's a map graphic … in my field of vision. I can see it. It's interactive."

"Shit," Irina said under her breath, as if this revelation were something she had been dreading.

"The cool part is, when I think, it responds. Come on." I picked up my bag and started walking. A bright yellow dashed line appeared under my feet. Instinctively, I jumped off it. It zoomed down the hallway and turned left. A left-pointing arrow faded in at the intersection like a road sign, after which a

Russian text box dissolved up. Both hung four feet in the air.

"Okay," I said, gesturing to the dashed line only I could see. "That's brilliant!" I started down the hall, and with each step the trailing part of the line disappeared. Irina rushed up to my side, almost tipping her roller case.

"What do you see now?"

I turned my head, and the map slid to the other side of my vision, no longer blocking my view of her.

"The yellow brick road," I said and swatted at the arrow.

32. Let it out.

We found the "lab" buried deep in Building 3. Buildings 1 and 2 were practically identical in layout and neglect. The people in the many offices didn't even look up as we walked past. The infographic was still guiding the way, but what it didn't reveal was the junk that littered the hallways. In some areas, Irina and I had to inch our way around refrigerator-sized boxes and Stalin-era furniture. At one point, in Building 2, we had to sidestep a mound of used takeout boxes from Pizza Hut. Globalization. *Good Lord.* The flies were disgusting.

"Do you still see the path?" Irina asked.

The dashed line ran over anything in its path, conforming to hard or smooth edges. The heads-up display had shrunk even farther into the upper-right of my field of vision.

"Yeah," I said, angling around an old metal file cabinet whose leather inset top was pockmarked by years of use. "We take a left here."

We reached a surprisingly clean hallway that dead-ended into a door with a Russian word in chipped gold leaf painted on frosted glass.

"The Lab?" I asked.

Irina shook her head. "Cafeteria."

Stepping into the "cafeteria" was like passing through a wormhole. I shut the door on old Russia, and entered into a large space similar to the lab at ELT. All of the equipment looked ultra-high-tech and new. Chris was in the center of it all at a computer console, leaning over the dreadlocked kid. Both were eyeing a large flat-screen. I gave a listen to a few of the technicians, but their thoughts were all foreign. Chris looked up as the door clicked shut.

"You found us!" He straightened.

"How could I not?" The infographic disappeared, which caused me to stumble a bit. Static faded in as the dampening field returned. "Man, could you warn me before you do that?"

Chris slapped the kid's shoulder. "Build that into the CMS." He walked up, arms spread like a proud father. "What do you think of our new location?"

Irina's awe morphed into a scowl. "Why didn't we come here in the first place?"

"I didn't own it." Chris looked around proudly. "Now I do." He thrust his hands into his jean pockets and stepped closer. "It's amazing what a little venture capital can buy." He leaned in, keeping an eye on the lab. "It's always been in the works," he whispered out of the side of his mouth. "These guys were desperate for cash. Debra just accelerated the move-in date."

"Who's VC-ing it for you?" I asked.

A grin stitched across Chris's face. "That's what I like about you, Bradford. Always the businessman." He rose up on his toes and sucked in a breath. "Since you're practically family, I guess it wouldn't hurt to tell you."

I put my hands up. "On second thought, I don't want to know."

"It's a holding company, of sorts. They have interests in several vertical markets."

"Like arms trade?" Irina said.

The twitch at the corner of Chris's right eye was barely perceptible. I had seen this plenty of times from clients pushed too far by one of my creatives. Usually, I would interject some witty remark to dial down the tension. I started to again, but quickly discarded the idea.

"Maybe," Chris said. "In a prior life."

Irina let out a disdainful sigh.

Chris inched closer to her, and an innate protectiveness caught me by surprise. I almost grabbed his arm.

"You need to get on board with this," he said, steely.

Irina held her ground. "*Da*, I am."

Chris eyed her harshly. "You better mean that."

It's hard to judge when someone is thinking the truth, especially if their pathology runs deep. But after many years in advertising, I had become adept at recognizing the signs. It's a tonal thing. A way a person talks in his or her mind. Too bad I couldn't hear them now. I wondered if Irina really meant it.

"So, what's with the interactive graphic?" I asked, trying to deflect Chris.

He peeled his attention off of Irina and considered my question. "All part of the master plan," he said, the tension erased from his voice. "Come on, check it out."

I followed him back to the kid, who was busy with something on the screen. Chris gestured at it. "We call it TIGI."

On the screen was the RATAN-600 infographic that had been in my vision. In the upper right corner, next to an info-banner filled with Russian text, was a rotating, exploded 3-D MRI image of a brain. Mine, I assumed.

"Techlepathic Informational Graphic Interface," Chris said proudly. "But you haven't seen the best part." He nudged the kid's shoulder. "Bring up the grid."

The RATAN-600 infographic shrunk into the dock and was replaced by a beautifully rendered earth. It rotated against a detailed star field. Half of the globe was blanketed in shadow. The lights of major cities created a complex organic pattern against the darkness. Unlike typical Internet maps, the rendering was flawless. A complex patchwork of yellow network lines appeared across the globe's surface, and small info boxes framed the image. Each had a headshot, along with an ID and stats. When the kid passed his cursor over an ID box, it enlarged, and a connecting line projected to a point on the grid. Simultaneously, that part of the grid glowed.

I pointed to a pasty young girl with curly blonde hair and thick black glasses that looked like Irina's. She wore a blank expression. "Click on her."

The kid enlarged her ID box. Irina and I leaned in. It was in Russian.

"You hacked the Motor Vehicle Department?" Irina asked.

"Among other places," Chris replied.

As I studied her driver's license photo, I sensed something powerful behind her dull expression, pacing like a caged animal. And I couldn't help but sense a connection, as if I had known her previously. A kind of techlepathic déjà vu. I leaned closer and studied her eyes, their half-closed lids disguising her true nature. Then it became clear.

"Agents," I said, almost under my breath.

Chris smirked. "A whole damn army of 'em."

"And the grid?" Irina straightened and tucked her chin. "Like an AT&T for techlepaths?"

"More like TT&T," I said.

Irina folded her arms. "The technology only works fully in Dillon."

"Right now," Chris corrected. "But in a year, maybe less, we'll make it work in anyone with the ability. In the meantime, we're tagging every known techlepath on the planet." Chris gave me a sideways glance. "Thank God there aren't that many of us."

I leaned against the edge of the desk. "So after you inject this new special souped-up tech into, what ... 1,000 ... 10,000 ... you're going to link us all up? To what end?"

Irina, still staring at the grid, put a hand over her mouth and sucked in a breath.

"The good doctor seems to have figured it out," Chris said.

"*Chekisty.*"

Irina uttered the word under her breath. Whatever it meant, it had completely dismantled her tough-girl persona.

"That's a bit melodramatic," Chris said. "I like to think of them as a future special operations force."

I looked from Irina to Chris. "Someone going to fill me in here?"

"After the revolution," Irina said, still studying the infographic. "They were called the *Cheka*. It's an acronym. An old term, but still used ... informally." The tone in her voice suggested a visceral reaction to this word.

"Who uses it?"

Irina glanced over the rims of her glasses. "Secret police."

I let that sink in, then knifed a look at Chris. "You can't be serious."

He sternly pointed at my forehead.

"Get this into that beautiful brain of yours. We're in a war with a bunch of fanatical martyrs who wouldn't think twice about slitting your mother's throat just to get your attention. We can't win this conventionally. It's going to have to be stealth. And I can't clone you." He gave an approving glance to the room. "Although, if I gave these guys enough money, they might figure that out, too." He tilted a glance at Irina. "And they're not going to be like the *Cheka*."

"The technology has never been stable in any other brain," Irina said, pocketing her glasses. "We've tried everything."

Chris let out a tense sigh and put a hand to her shoulder. "I know," he said. "I was going to talk to you later, but now's a good a time as any."

Irina jerked out of his grip. "What are you saying?"

Chris thrust his hands deeply into his pockets and stiffened. "Doctor, it's time for some new blood."

"Rechenko?"

Chris hesitantly nodded.

"Fuck!" The word came out more like fauk. She gave her roller case a frustrated kick. It skidded to an empty computer station. A couple of the technicians looked up from their workstations.

"Easy, girl. I'm not firing you."

"You might as well," she snapped.

I turned to her. "What is with you and—"

A door squeaked open on the opposite side of the room. Rechenko entered and weaved his way around two large computer stacks and hurried over.

"There you all are!" he said.

Irina muttered something in Russian and headed to her roller case.

"So, Dillon," Rechenko said, companionably, "how do you like our improvement to your technology?"

"Um, impressive?"

Rechenko picked up on the lingering tension. His scrutiny cut from Chris and me to Irina, then back. He raised an interrogatory eyebrow. Chris gave a nod to Irina.

"She's a little touchy about you being her new boss," he whispered.

One of Irina's roller case's outer compartments had popped open, and she was gathering some white socks.

"Well," Rechenko removed his glasses and picked at something on the right lens, "I guess that's to be expected."

"Care to explain why?" I asked.

Chris shushed me and did a tight head shake. Irina joined us, case in tow. Rechenko slipped on his glasses and looked down his nose.

"So, you're not pleased with the fact that you'll be working for me again."

Irina pulled her case to her side and slowly collapsed its handle. She moved deliberately, like she was fighting the urge to punch him.

"I've done it before," she said.

"Really, my dear. You shouldn't be upset. So far, you've done an admirable job. No one is faulting you for a lack of progress. I feel – and I know I'm not alone in this – that considering the conditions you dealt with in Poland, your work has been exceptional." Rechenko turned to me, hand raised like he was showing off a new car. "Look at all you've achieved. The first stable neural techlepathic implants."

"Victor." Chris cleared his throat. "We didn't implant the primary tech."

"We only modified it," Irina said.

"What are you talking about?" A glint of anger flared behind Rechenko's eyes. "Who did the initial implementation?"

"Popprov," Chris answered.

Rechenko nodded to himself, although I had my doubts about his lack of surprise.

"Is that a problem?" I asked.

"Not at all," Rechenko said. "Alex is very good at what he does. It's just–"

"What?"

"It would have been *cleaner* if it was all our technology."

■　　■　　■

Chris dumped us in front of our rooms and handed us keys. When I openly questioned why I wasn't being locked in, he called me family again, clapped me on the back and hurried off. Our rooms were more like closets; the one back in Poland seemed like a Ritz-Carlton in comparison. Irina had a compact re-frigerator tucked next to the bed. A cheap office desk lamp sat on top of it and cast the bottom half of the room in a harsh shade of digitized green. It flickered when we entered.

"Look," I pointed, "a mini-bar."

Irina sat on her bed and sank halfway into it. She muttered something in Russian as she tried to climb free.

"Here, let me help you." I offered my hand.

Irina took it, and I yanked her up. Her left foot caught in the blanket, which caused her to slam into my chest. We stumbled back a few steps, holding each other from falling. I straightened and began to pull away, but Irina held me, her fingers pressed into my back. I went with it. Through her light coat she felt more muscular than I had imagined. She looked up. The anger towards Rechenko – incised across her face since we had left the lab – had coalesced into a tight knot between her eyebrows. Her glasses were askew.

"Nice trip?" I said, trying to dodge the awkwardness.

A slight smile pushed through, but instantly disappeared. Irina stepped back and straightened her glasses. She glanced at her watch.

"It's almost one," she said flatly.

The doctor was back in. "Right," I said. "Lunch."

Irina heaved her roller case onto the bed and unzipped it. She began attacking its contents.

"I'll just go, ah ... put my things away, okay?"

Irina nodded, still focused on unpacking.

I tried to unlock the door to my room, but now the key didn't want to turn. "Shit." I walked back to Irina's door and started to knock, but the muffled sound of three sharp breaths stopped me. Her door was ajar. I put an eye to the opening. She was hunched over her roller case, arms folded tightly against her body in a desperate attempt at self-comfort. Her glasses dangled from two fingers. She was trying to fight back tears. She sucked in another breath.

"Hey." I opened the door the rest of the way. "What's the matter?"

Irina raised a defiant hand, and I held my ground in the threshold. Several tears fell from her face and disappeared into her suitcase. It was awkward catching her without her Russian tough-girl armor. I wanted to say something to comfort her, but I couldn't think of anything helpful. After a moment spent staring into her roller case, she shook her head.

"I'm sorry," she mumbled around a sniffle.

"You don't need to be with me."

She wiped her eyes with a coat sleeve and tried to compose herself.

"Is it Rechenko?" I asked.

She slipped her glasses on, but didn't look up. "Yes," she said with a hesitant nod.

"Why, if you don't mind me asking?"

Irina began to speak, but stopped.

"It's okay," I reassured.

She finally looked over, eyes rimmed with tears. "Rechenko killed my father."

33. How long do you need?

The word "killed" hit me like a slow gut punch. Maybe Irina had her terms mixed up. One of her Russian-to-English manglings.

"He murdered your father?"

"Not exactly."

"What do you mean?"

Irina sniffed, picked a white t-shirt out of the case, and blew her nose into it.

"It happened a long time ago," she said, wiping.

"Why isn't he in jail?"

"It's not like that."

She blinked away some tears, then dabbed at the corners of her eyes with a clean edge of the t-shirt.

"You can't prove what he did," she said.

"Sorry, I'm a little lost here. You say he killed your father, but you can't prove it?"

Irina pushed her roller case into the pillows and sat on the edge of the bed.

"Rechenko was in charge of overseeing my sister's development. I joined his group in the last year of her life. After she killed herself, my father slipped into depression. He started drinking a lot...."

I could tell Irina was right there, remembering. "Did he kill himself?"

She forced a nod.

"I'm really sorry."

"Thanks."

"Irina?"

She looked up, her eyes red.

"You're not blaming yourself, are you?"

She looked away and shrugged. The Russian tough-girl armor was sliding back on. I couldn't imagine the loss of a sibling, yet alone a father. And both by suicide? I guess if she wanted to blame Rechenko, who was I to question it? But to blame herself for her sister's suicide was wrong.

"It's not your fault, you know."

"We pushed her too hard. The technology wasn't ready."

"And now you're trying to give her death some meaning by working with Chris, right?"

She pulled her shoulders back, inspected her glasses, and put them on. The armor was complete once again.

"Come on," she said. "I'm starving."

She glanced over, and a weird feeling moved through me. I realized I was looking at myself a few years from now. Sucked into Chris's world, resigned to my new existence. I tried to imagine what Irina might have been like a few years ago. Vibrant? Happy?

Irina caught my stare. "What are you thinking, Dillon?"

Thinking I had been a fool, tricked into believing I was doing something noble. And thinking I'd had enough of Chris and his seedy underground arms deals, his techlepathic army, and enough of playing pseudo-patriot and being lied to. I shook my head in disgust.

"I'm sick of all this shit," I said.

Irina coughed out a small laugh. "Too late for that."

"Is it?"

She sat on the bed, then looked down. "It is for me."

I sat beside her, and the bed sank in. Our bodies pressed together, but Irina didn't scoot away.

"Why?" I asked.

"No options."

"Bullshit."

Irina pulled back and looked skeptical. "Dillon, we've passed the point of no retire."

"It's return," I said, with a small chuckle. "Point of no return, and I don't think so."

"Even if you could get away, where would you go? How would you get there? You don't have passport or ID. Besides, Chris would know what you were thinking. He'd come after you."

"Yeah, what's going there? Techlepaths aren't supposed to be able to listen in on each other."

"I know he's been working on trying to achieve this. It has to do with the temporal platforms and their frequencies. I used to work on it, but he moved me off of it a month ago. Why?"

"He was in my head the other night."

"When Debra contacted you?"

"Yes."

"Hmm."

"Is the 'hmm' good or 'hmm' bad?"

"Depends on your objective. I know that when I was working on it, we thought it would only work within close proximity to the other techlepath."

"Take it from me, it works very well. I heard him loud and fucking clear."

"It's only a matter of time before he perfects it at a greater range."

"You said he has trouble listening in sometimes."

Irina nodded. "His MS."

"That screws with his ability?"

"It attacks certain nerves associated with your ability. We have not figured out why."

"Is there anyone else who can listen in to other techlepaths, besides Chris? I mean, another techlepath, that is?"

"*Nyet.*"

"Are you sure?"

"I helped create this technology. I think I would know whose head it's in."

"Okay. I just need to make sure no one else can listen in on me."

"Why?"

"If I could get connected with Debra again – let her know where we are – she could spring us."

"Us?"

"Sure. You could come with. Back to the U.S. I'm sure you could find work." *With Debra.*

Irina slowly shook her head. "I can't."

"Why not?"

"It's complicated. Chris would –" She cut herself off.

Irina was afraid of Chris, but now wasn't the time to question why.

"Well, just think about it, okay? Now, how can we stop them from blocking me?"

"I've never been here before. I don't know where the base impeder is. It could be anywhere in the complex."

"Then we'll have to find it on our own. In the meantime, let's act like good little team players."

As we sat there, I noticed how Irina's glasses made her eyes look smaller and closer together. She was actually kind of cute, in a Russian swimmer sort of way.

"I think Chris is getting unbalanced," she said, finally looking up at me.

"Getting?"

"He might hurt us if he finds out what we're doing."

"Kill."

"What?"

I feigned a meager smile. "I think the word you want is kill."

■   ■   ■

Lunch consisted of cold sandwiches, stale chips, and a mix of Russian and American sodas. I grabbed one called Leninade. Its silk-screened label said there was a party in every bottle, and if I drank enough of them, I would get "hammered and sickled." It was surprisingly refreshing. If it had any alcohol, I couldn't taste it. I spun the bottle around. Made in California.

The RATAN's other "cafeteria" looked like it might have been a classroom at one time and, like the rest of the complex, had seen better days. Irina and I sat near the back by a bank of old casement windows angled open. The sun was pouring in and heating the metal chairs and chipped Formica tabletop.

"Yum," I said. "Salami and Swiss on dry."

Irina looked up, puzzled. "You mean rye?"

"Not really."

"I'm so hungry I could eat anything," she said. She sat across from me and studied her meal.

"Watch what you wish for."

I was about to take a bite when I caught Wardinski approaching out of the corner of my eye. "We're about to have company."

Irina had her back to the room. "Chris?"

I shook my head and said, "Hello, Peter."

"May I join you?" Wardinski asked.

"Nice place you have here."

My sarcasm elicited a half smile. I motioned, and he took the chair next to Irina. We ate in silence for a few minutes. I stole a few glances at Irina, but she was keeping to her sandwich. After a few more slurps of his soup, Wardinski wiped his mouth and moved his attention to the windows. The chatter of birds drifted in with the sunlight.

"Do you ever wonder?" he asked, staring.

"About what?" I had a pretty good idea of what was coming.

"If there's life."

Here we go. "To be honest, Peter, I do."

"Wonder?"

"Believe." This got Irina's attention.

Wardinski looked back, eyebrows raised.

"Why so surprised?" I asked.

"I thought you'd be a skeptic."

"You'd be surprised what I believe in."

Wardinski canted his head slightly, then nodded.

"So when am I going to talk with ET?" Might as well get to the point.

"I have to fit you into Chris's schedule."

"Screw him," I said casually. "Let's do it today."

"Timing's not good. Maybe tomorrow morning, if you're up for it."

"Compared to what I'm doing now, chatting with ET shouldn't be too hard. What am I in for?"

"It isn't unlike what we put you through for Chris's work. We'll set you up just the same, except instead of channeling you through the world cellular network, we'll connect you directly with the array."

"So you're broadcasting my ability out into space?"

"No, Dillon. The array collects radio signals. Since you'll be connected directly into the system, the theory is that you'll be able to pick up any telepathic transmissions. Essentially, listen in to whatever ET is thinking."

"If he is," Irina interjected.

"How will I know when I've connected to ET?" I asked. "It's not like they speak English."

"Think of it as a radio dial," Wardinski said. "The static is background noise. Space noise, if you will. As you turn the dial, you happen upon a radio station. Intelligent life! SETI listens in for an alien radio station."

"Right, I get all that. But what will I *hear*?"

Wardinski's jaw flexed as he struggled to produce an answer. "I don't know," he said finally.

"Well, at least you're honest. What time tomorrow?"

Wardinski's face brightened. "I'll have to check. Probably very early."

"What about Chris?"

"He should be gone most of the day."

"And the staff?" Irina asked.

"It's Sunday. Most of them will have the day off. There's just a skeleton crew."

Wardinski seemed a little too confident about this fact.

"Okay," I said, "but I have one condition."

"And that is?"

"You turn off the base impeder."

Wardinski leaned back and folded his arms across his barrel chest. For a second, I thought he'd bring up Debra.

"Tired of being normal?"

"Maybe."

I passed my thumb across the Leninade's raised hammer and sickle logo and caught a drip sliding down the bottle's neck.

"Well, you're in luck. In order for us to conduct the experiment, we have to turn it off."

"Really? For how long?"

Wardinski considered my question with reasoned graveness. After a long second, the half-smile emerged again.

"How long do you need?"

34. Falling.

The mattress in my room must have been Styrofoam. My fitful sleep was brutally ended by two deliberate knocks.

"Dillon? Are you awake?"

Wardinski's voice, even through the door, had a commanding presence probably cultivated from a military past. I'd have to ask him sometime if that were true.

My room was warm, and I had kicked off most of the sheets. It was still fairly dark out, but given that we were in southern Russia, the famous "White Nights" probably didn't apply here. The door creaked open, and Wardinski's imposing form filled the frame. I recalled the first time we had met, back in Poland, in the lab's basement closet. I groped for the edge of the bed sheet to pull over me, but found only air.

"Sleep well?" he asked.

I fought my body's plead for more sleep and swung my legs over the edge of the metal bed frame. As I pushed off to stand, my fingers grazed the frame's pitted metal frame.

"Like a baby." I said through a yawn and stretched.

The only light clicked on. Wardinski was a bit too eager to get the day going.

"Good," he said. "You'll need to be rested."

"Can I shower?"

"Yes."

"Breakfast?"

Wardinski hesitated. "We don't want you throwing up."

Jesus. "How 'bout coffee?"

"No stimulants either."

Crap.

Irina appeared behind Wardinski. The hall's safety light backlit her cotton nightshirt and revealed a hint of her toned figure.

"Everything okay?" She passed a hand through her tousled hair.

I grinned. "Just an early start before breakfast with ET."

.   ■   ■

"So Chris actually lets his staff have time off?" I asked as we walked the same hall that had been mapped in my head.

"Surprising, isn't it?" Wardinski answered, eyes forward.

"We negotiated it," Irina said.

"Why so early?" I asked.

"Best time for the telescope," Wardinski said.

"Not a good time for humans." I forced back another yawn. "When do you turn off the impeder?"

Wardinski glanced at his watch. "In a few minutes."

We entered the main lab and marched through its maze of workstations and super computers to two unassuming swinging doors near the back. One had a Russian word stenciled just below its circular glass window. I pointed as Wardinski ushered us in.

"Kitchen," Irina translated.

The "kitchen" didn't have any of its former equipment and was also devoid of any impressive tech. In the center stood a 1940s metal desk, and on top of that a nondescript laptop and a gooseneck desk lamp straight from a bargain bin at the Russian equivalent of Office Depot. In contrast, next to the desk was a tricked out, waist-high computer stack. A bundle of brightly colored, zip-tied cables snaked from the stack and out another door across the room. The desk lamp was the lone light source, and as we neared I could see that another set of low computer stacks semi-circled a conventional hospital bed. Kadin's head popped up from behind one of the small stacks. Her hair was pulled back in a ponytail, and she wore a UT sweatshirt and skinny jeans. She wasn't wearing the sling.

"Everything set?" Wardinski asked.

"Yes." Kadin was clearly tired and favoring her hurt shoulder. She wiped some hair out of her face on the way to the desk and began to review something on the laptop.

I looked around. "Where's all the big-time equipment?"

"We're tapping off of Chris's." Wardinski pointed to the multi-colored wire python.

There was another closed laptop. I had missed it because it blended into the desk. Kadin opened it and spun it toward Irina. "You'll be monitoring his vitals," she said.

Irina sat in the only chair and assessed the application's interface. "Why aren't you wearing the sling I gave you?"

"I will later," Kadin said. The lock of hair had gone astray again, and she blew it out of the way.

"You'll be here, Dillon." Wardinski gestured to the bed.

"Shirt on or off?" I asked.

"Off."

I tossed my shirt across a computer stack and climbed onto the bed. Its mattress felt a lot better than the one back in my room. I settled back and fought the urge to close my eyes. Suddenly, a mix of soft voices entered my mind, and I pushed them down. The impeder was off.

"I can hear you all now." I looked at Kadin. "Well, almost all of you."

"Good." Wardinski glanced at his watch. "Right on time."

I yawned and leaned back against the pillows.

Wardinski poked me. "Sit up, please."

"Right. Sorry." I scooted forward. "Who else knows we're chatting with ET?"

"Trace."

"Who?"

"The kid showing us Chris's army," Irina said.

"Did he turn off the impeder?"

"Yes," Wardinski said.

Kadin began applying sticky electrodes to my head, chest, and stomach. She pulled at my scalp with little regard for my comfort and pressed three smaller electrodes into place.

"There," she said, clipping something to my right earlobe. "All wired up."

"What if I have to use the bathroom?"

Kadin looked around and fetched an empty plastic water bottle that had been sitting next to a trashcan in a far corner. She plunked it into my lap.

"Here."

I unscrewed its cap and eyeballed the inside. "The opening's not big enough."

"You wish," Kadin said, taking it from me.

Irina suppressed a laugh somewhere off to my right. I tried to twist around, but the wires stopped me. "Laugh it up, girlfriend."

"Give ET my regards," she said.

"Let's get started." Wardinski stepped up to the bed. "Dillon, I want you to relax and empty your mind."

"Tell me again, what am I listening for?"

"You'll probably hear some static, along with some blips and pops."

"No, I mean ET. What will it sound like?"

"As I mentioned, I've never done this before ... I don't know what you'll hear."

"Comforting," I remarked.

"Try to be calm, Dillon," Irina said. "Your heart rate is up."

Wardinski patted my shoulder. "Don't be nervous. It won't be painful.

"I've heard that before, too," I said.

Wardinski, who had been glancing across the bed at Kadin's laptop every other second, regarded me like an insect he had just pinned down to dissect.

"Something wrong?" I asked.

"I wish I had your gift," he said reflectively.

"I wish I could give it to you."

Wardinski's attention settled into a stare. "Are you listening to us right now?"

The idea had crossed my mind. "No."

"Why not?"

"Peter, when you have this ability, you learn not to look behind the curtain too much. Know what I mean?"

My answer seemed to resonate with Wardinski. He tapped the bed's arm rail. "Let's begin."

For about two minutes, all I could hear was the buzz from the fluorescent desk lamp. Then faint Russian voices wafted up and hovered near the rim of my consciousness.

"I'm hearing some Russian voices."

"We're getting bleed-through," Wardinski said. "Kadie, can you fix that?"

The voices abruptly disappeared. "How's that?" she asked.

"They're gone," I replied.

"Relax, Dillon," Irina said.

I realized I had been clutching a wad of the bed's top sheet in my right hand. I unclenched my fist and spread my fingers. I didn't feel nervous. Maybe it was something subconscious.

More minutes passed, then a hiss faded up. This wasn't like static from an old radio or something. It sounded distant, as if the wave had barely made the vast trip and was limping into the radio telescope.

"I'm hearing some static now," I said.

"That's just background noise," Wardinski assured. "It's normal."

"Space noise?"

"Essentially."

"Where are you looking?"

"Pardon?"

"What part of the universe are you targeting?"

"Gliese 581g," Wardinski answered, like it was obvious.

"Right, that's what I thought," I said sarcastically.

"It's a planet about twenty light-years from earth," Kadin offered. "It orbits a red dwarf in the constellation of Libra. It's typical of a planet that resides in a star's habitable zone."

"Habitable zone?"

"The perfect distance for life to evolve."

"Like Earth," I said.

"Exactly," Wardinski said.

My crappy night of sleep was catching up to me. After a few more minutes of listening to tired static, the pillows I was against demanded that I close my eyes. Their cases had been washed in some flowery detergent, and the whole cushy setup was doing a serious number on my need for Z's. I felt my eyelids closing. I blinked them open.

"Stay awake!" Irina snapped.

"Sorry."

The static, which had increased in intensity, had become a hypnotic white noise. I tried to ignore the pull of circadian rhythm, but my eyelids were growing way too heavy, and my mind was drifting....

I opened my eyes to a thick darkness with no sense of space or form. I was floating. Weightless. There was no up. There was no down. I was suspended in an ocean of warm, black gas. I was breathing, but not in any recognizable sense. Where panic should have flooded me, peace reigned. I drew my hands close to my face, yet couldn't see them. I tried to touch my nose, but couldn't sense where it was. None of my body was visible, yet I knew it was there....

Dillon?

Debra!

You're barely coming in. Where are you now? Where have they moved you?

Russia. South. The Caucasus Mountains, I think. They have me wired up to a radio telescope.

A what?

A radio telescope. It's the second biggest one.

You're breaking up. Where?

Russia! The southern part. Near the Black Sea ... Debra? Nothing. *Debra? Are you there?* More silence. *If you can still hear me, we're at the RATAN 600 radio telescope ... hello?*

Something moved past me. I couldn't see it, but I knew the soup around me had been disturbed, like I had floated through a colder current of whatever this was, and a sharp chill carved up my spine. Something, a hand maybe, brushed against my right arm. It felt delicate and bony. There were fingers—

"Jesus!" I said, jerking awake.

Wardinski was shaking my right arm. "What did I say about dozing off?" He let go. "Did you fall?"

"What?"

"You know, you're falling, then before you hit you wake up." Wardinski grinned. "Happens to me just before I go to sleep."

"How long was I out?"

Wardinski gave me a puzzled look. "Well, you weren't technically out. You just closed your eyes, then—"

"How long?"

"A second. Why?"

▪   ▪   ▪

If I stared long enough, the disrepair of my room's ceiling created a kind of faux map. The bigger cracks were major rivers, and the peeling paint, which ran from one wall to the other, was a mountain range – similar to the Rockies – that split my imaginary country into two equal halves. I imagined myself on the porch of a cabin, in the mountains. Maybe at the base of the large flap of paint that formed the tallest peak in this inverted world. I had a Scotch, lots of ice, and an Arturo Fuente. A Corona Imperial. It went well with Macallan 25 Year—

"You okay?"

I blinked out of my fantasy and found Irina standing near the edge of my bed. She wasn't wearing her glasses, and I noticed for the first time that her eyes weren't really blue but a dusty cool gray with flecks of cerulean. Without the glasses, they appeared larger, and at the moment they were regarding me with a good deal of worry.

"Feeling better." I scooted up against the headboard and noticed the connecting door between our rooms was open. "Hey, how'd you unlock that?"

Irina canted her head slightly and regarded me down her slim nose. "You learn things in the army."

It didn't surprise me that Irina had been in the Russian military. "Credit card?"

"Pocket knife. You didn't come down for lunch."

Wardinski's ET test had ignited a pisser headache. After my odd one-second dream, I listened to another hour of space noise. ET never made an appearance, and I could tell Wardinski was more than a little disappointed. After they uncoupled me from the cosmos, I went back to my room to lie down before lunch. Without my watch or cell phone, I was living in a time limbo, which made it hard to gauge when to wake up.

"I must have slept through it," I said.

"That's what I thought."

"What time is it?"

"About three o'clock."

I rubbed my face and stretched. Irina's demeanor didn't change. She was actually pretty, even through her scowl and lack of make-up. And after living in Dallas for so long, the no make-up thing had a certain appeal.

"Why don't you have a boyfriend?" I asked after a moment.

"Don't change subject."

"I didn't know there was one."

"You were different after Wardinski woke you."

"How so?"

"You seemed ... scared."

"Really?"

"What happened?"

"When?"

"After you dozed off."

I had a vague sense of the dream, of hearing Debra's voice, and of floating in a strange black void. The only thing that really stayed with me was the phantom sensation of a hand touching me.

"I know Wardinski said I was out for just a second—"

"You were." Irina's glower deepened. "What happened?"

"I had the weirdest dream. It felt like it went on much longer than a second."

"I'm not expert, but if you dream doing something for five minutes, the dream itself will take about five minutes. They've done studies."

"Then how could I dream something that took so long in just a second?"

"Tell me what you dreamed."

I told Irina what I could remember about floating in the murk and hearing Debra. I didn't tell her about feeling the hand, though. All the while she listened as if I was revealing the meaning of life.

After I finished, she pondered what I had said for a long time.

"Do you think it was really her?" she asked finally.

Wardinski said he'd keep the impeder offline until noon. I hadn't heard anything else from Debra, but I had been asleep. "I don't know. I hope so."

"Did you dream anything else?"

I nodded hesitantly. "This is going to sound really silly. But I felt a hand come out of the blackness. It touched my arm ... here." I mimicked what I had remembered by brushing my upper right arm.

"Not surprising," she said. "Wardinski was shaking you there. To wake you up."

"It didn't feel like his hand. It was thin and bony, like an old woman's. And ice cold, like my skin might stick to it ... you know, like cold metal." More was coming back.

Irina considered my last statement. "Why didn't you tell Wardinski?"

"I didn't remember much of it at the time."

"And now you do?"

"Yes." We stared at each other for a second. "What do you think?"

"I'm not big believer in ET. I'm sure what you felt was just your brain processing Wardinski's grip."

"No!"

The clarity of my declaration surprised even me. Irina's expression became defensive.

"Look, I'm sorry," I said. "I know all this is sounding a bit freaky, but I'm pretty sure it wasn't Wardinski."

"How do you know?"

"Because ... I only felt three fingers."

The door to my room suddenly banged open. Chris was standing in the threshold, his Glock leveled, silencer attached.

A shitload of adrenaline surged into every corner of my body, and I practically jumped off the bed. "Hey, what the hell are you doing?"

Chris skinned a tight smile across his teeth. "Nice try," he said with cool professionalism.

"What are you talking–?"

"Don't. I'm not a dumbass." The man standing before us was different. His tone carried vehement intensity, his anger hinged like a spring trap. Even the way he was holding the Glock said, *Jack with me, and I'll kill you.* He jerked the tip of the silencer twice to the right. "Let's go."

"Can I get my shoes–?"

"Now," he snarled through gritted teeth.

"Look, Chris," I said. "We were just helping out Wardinski."

"I thought I could trust you. I thought we were friends."

The look in Chris's eyes suggested the guy might snap right there in front of us. I tried to will the fear that had risen up in me back to wherever it came from.

"We are," I said trying to sound reassuring. "And you can trust me. Really. I just wanted to appease the old man. You know how the guy is. He thinks I can listen in to some kind of alien thought network."

Irina stood, her hands raised in a pleading gesture. "Chris, please. It wasn't his—"

Chris moved his aim imperceptibly toward her. A distorted flash exploded from the silencer's muzzle. Irina's name emerged from my throat, but all I could hear was the gun's crack and her scream as it ricocheted off the cinderblock walls.

35. You know what I hate?

"Irina!"

I rushed toward her, thinking, absurdly, that I could push her out of harm's way. She was doubled over from the recoil, her arms pulled tightly against her stomach.

"Oh my God!" I put an arm around her. She was shaking.

Irina slowly pulled her hands away from her stomach and stared at her palms. No blood. She pinned Chris with a glare that went beyond hatred and was hyperventilating through clenched teeth. She unfolded from her position and lunged toward him. It took most of my strength to hold her back.

Chris didn't flinch.

Irina convulsed a string of Russian expletives, and with each she tried to jerk from my grip.

"Irina!" I said, struggling against her vehemence. "Stop it!"

She twisted around, the whites of her eyes flaring around her pupils. Her attention went behind me. I turned and saw a small crater-like hole about a foot above the bed. Flecks of beige cinderblock had left a loose triangular spray pattern across the dark green blanket. I pulled her close.

Don't, I mouthed.

Irina's rage reluctantly ebbed. She stepped out of my grasp and brushed the hair off her face.

Chris jerked the Glock again. "Come on."

Irina and I silently exited. Chris followed behind us. I had never been into hunting or shooting, and I certainly had never been marched at gunpoint. I did shoot once at a friend's hunting lease in West Texas. He was into guns, and when he handed me his pistol, its density seemed to suggest that death itself might reside somewhere in its matte black housing.

I kept my eyes forward, so I had no sense of where Chris was. The Glock, however, felt an inch away from my back. He was marching us to the main lab, and it felt as if it were taking forever. When we entered, I could see his two enforcers from Poland posted in the center of the room, near the largest workstation. They weren't wearing lab coats, and their guns were identical to Chris's, complete with silencers. They didn't bother to look over. Chris prodded us toward them.

We edged ourselves between a desk and one of the supercomputers. The taller enforcer casually took account of us as we stepped into the large open space that ringed the main workstation. Except for a few fluorescent desk lamps, most of the lab was dark. There was a row of four chairs, and Kadin and her father occupied the two on the right, their backs against the workstation's large cabinets and their heads hung, staring at the floor.

Chris motioned with the Glock to the two empty chairs. "Sit."

I took the outer chair. Irina sat beside Kadin. Neither she nor Wardinski acknowledged us. The enforcers fanned out on either side of the chairs, guns loosely leveled. Chris leaned against a desk across from us, his face partially lit by a task lamp. He folded his arms and regarded us like a frustrated coach might his losing team.

After excruciatingly long consideration, Chris finally spoke. "Am I the only one who gets it?" He was still holding his gun, but it was tucked under his left arm. "*Well?!*" He spread his arms to emphasize his question, and I instinctively shied away as the Glock swung past.

Wardinski looked up. "I thought we had an agreement."

"That's my line," Chris said.

"You told me I could conduct my experiments during off hours."

"Not when I'm *gone*." Chris looked away and shook his head.

Kadin lifted her eyes. "What does it matter—?"

Chris cut her off with a raised hand. He focused his frustration on Wardinski. "Why'd you turn the impeder off?"

"It interferes with the radio telescope's ability to process transmissions."

"What's our first rule?" Chris's smarm factor was on full display.

Wardinski sighed. "Don't turn off the impeder."

"Correct. And what does that mean?"

"We have a conflict."

Chris rushed Wardinski, his gun aimed. "You're god*damn* right!"

Wardinski didn't balk as Chris pressed the silencer against his forehead.

"Chris!" Kadin exclaimed, standing. "Put that gun—"

Chris pointed a finger into Kadin's face as if it were another Glock. "Shut ... up."

Kadin, her mouth still caught between words, slowly sat.

Chris cocked his attention back to Wardinski. "Peter," he said, leaning into Wardinski's obstinacy, "what am I going to do with you? You're my link to this facility. But if you keep testing me, I'm going to get pissed."

He straightened, walked back to the desk, and sat on the edge of it, one foot on the floor. He leaned his forearm on his thigh, the Glock still vaguely pointed at Wardinski.

"You know, Peter, you and I are a lot alike."

As he spoke, his gun hand gestured slightly, and all I could see was the mouth of that black silencer.

"We aren't anything alike," Wardinski replied.

"You want to do good. *I* want to do good. It's just our methods that are different."

"You're out of control."

"And you're out of line."

"I'm through working with you!"

Chris, exasperated, looked down and shook his head. In the second it took to take a breath, he raised the Glock and fired. Irina had leaned forward and blocked my view of Wardinski. In stunned silence, I waited for his body to fall, but a guttural inhuman moan lacerated the air.

"No!" Wardinski screamed.

As if in a fractured dream, Kadin's lifeless body slumped from the chair and collapsed to the floor. Wardinski followed it, falling to his hands and knees. His wails were a mix of English and Polish.

I was shit-scared frozen, teetering on the edge of my chair. Irina whimpered into her hands. A small pool of blood spread below Kadin's head. Bits of flesh and brain moved with the flow. She had fallen with her face turned away, but when Wardinski gathered her into his arms, her head lolled toward me. The bullet hole was surprisingly small, and in the dead center of her forehead. I averted my eyes, but the image had done its damage. The exit wound was lost in her hair. Wardinski cupped the back of her head and pressed her face to his cheek. Blood seeped through his fingers. The pain in his sobs was visceral.

"You know what I hate more than arrogance, Peter?" Chris asked.

Wardinski didn't acknowledge the question. He continued to rock Kadin's limp body in his arms, his moans now reduced to muffled whimpers.

"Defiance."

Chris approached me, the Glock loose at his side. "Did Debra try to contact you when the impeder was off line?"

"No."

"Don't lie to me now, or you might end up like your ex-girlfriend." He flicked the Glock in Kadin's direction.

"I'm not lying."

"Good. Now," he glanced at his watch, "be back down here at six. We have some business to do, and no fucking around. This one's important. We have guests tonight, and your performance has to be stellar." He nodded toward the enforcers. "Hans and Franz here will be with you three from now on." He turned to the taller enforcer. "Take these two back to their rooms." He pointed to the shorter guy. "You watch Dr. Wardinski."

Clearly unnerved, the taller enforcer gestured toward Kadin. "Vhat about her?"

It was obvious Chris didn't have an exit plan for the mess he had created. He sighed and bit his lower lip. "Peter, what would you like done with her body?"

Chris asked the question as if getting rid of Kadin was another chore, like taking out the trash. Maybe it was for men like him.

Wardinski, his cheek smeared with Kadin's blood, looked as if he had been shot, too. I guess in a sense he had been. We all had.

"I want to take her home," he barely managed.

"I'm sorry, Peter. You can't do that yet. Maybe in a few days." There was something new in Chris's voice now. Pity? Maybe his conscience was working on him, although I seriously doubted he had one.

"You." Chris shot a look at the shorter enforcer. "Put her in there." He jerked his head towards a large meat locker door on the back wall. "That refrigerator is still working." He looked down at Wardinski, who still clutched Kadin to his chest. "Is that okay, Peter?"

The shorter enforcer took a step toward Kadin.

"No!" Wardinski shouted. "I'll do it!"

The guy looked questioningly at Chris.

"It's okay," Chris assured him. "When he's done, escort him to his room and stay outside his door." He spun on his heels and left.

Wardinski reverently surrendered Kadin's body back to the floor. Then he stood and lunged at Chris. He was able to grab one of Chris's arms and whip him around before the enforcers had their guns to either side of his head. His other hand, clenched in a tight fist and covered with Kadin's blood and brain matter, was drawn back and poised to strike Chris square in the jaw.

Chris looked surprised, but not fearful. "Stand down," he ordered.

The enforcers withdrew their weapons. Wardinski held his ground.

"Peter." Chris's eyes went to Wardinski's hand at his shoulder. "Don't make me break your arm."

Wardinski grabbed him by his jacket lapels and yanked him to his face. The guns returned to his head. "I'll kill you," he growled.

Chris regarded the threat casually. "Don't bet on it."

36. Release the hounds.

My ceiling was now just a ceiling. No mountains. No coastlines. No fantasy. As I stared up, its peeling paint and cracks provided a convenient metaphor for my life. Irina and I had offered to help Wardinski with Kadin's body. Irina actually wanted to close Kadin's head wounds, but Wardinski wouldn't hear of it.

"Please," he had said, stifling a sob, "let her rest."

Watching him carry the body of his only child into the refrigerator was the hardest thing I had ever witnessed.

As the taller enforcer escorted Irina and me back to our rooms, my mind kept returning to the images of Kadin's pooling blood and the wound to her forehead. The horror of it was too much to process. About halfway, I bumped Irina's shoulder, and the enforcer scolded me with a hard jab of his gun into my back. And now I was lying on my bed, wondering what the hell had become of my life.

There was a soft knock at the connecting door. The enforcer didn't know our rooms were joined. Before I could get up, the door cracked opened and Irina's head appeared.

"Hey," she said, barely above a whisper.

"Hey."

Irina opened the door and leaned against the doorjamb. She hunched slightly and folded her arms across her chest, glasses dangling from her fingers. She started to speak but stopped when she spied the bullet hole in the wall.

"How're you feeling?" I asked.

"Numb." She was still staring at the tiny crater.

"Me too."

Still hugging herself, Irina approached the bed.

"Come here," I said and scooted over.

She tossed her glasses onto the side table and tucked in next to me. Her head felt warm and comforting as it rested on my chest. Both of us knew that our lives hung precariously in Chris's crosshairs. I hesitated putting my arm around her.

"Just hold me, Dillon."

I did. We lay there for a few moments, bounded by collective fear.

She said, "You have a murmur."

"You have a good ear, doctor."

"Have you had it checked?"

"Only a thousand times. It's nothing."

She patted my chest. "Good."

I gently stroked the top of her head. Her hair smelled of the same citrus as the sheets on Wardinski's lab bed. I remembered Kadin when she stood from behind the computer stack, and I realized that was probably the last image I had of her alive. She had looked exhausted. I fought back an overwhelming urge to cry. Irina must have sensed it.

"It's okay," she said.

"I can't." My voice cracked. "Not now."

Irina nodded against my chest. "Tell me something?"

"What?"

"When did you first realize you were different?"

"Middle school. I was playing dodge ball in the gym."

"What's this dodge ball?"

"It's a game you play with a big rubber ball. You try to hit the players of the opposing team. If they catch it, you're out. If they drop it, they're out."

"In Russia we call it Sniper." Irina snuggled closer, and I pulled her tightly to my body. "So how did you first know?"

"I dropped the ball, and a kid called me a faggot," I said. "Thing was, his lips didn't move. I heard him plain as day, though. He was looking right at me."

"How did you know you were the only one?"

"I'd go up to kids and think mean things. See if they'd react. They never did."

"Must have been weird, knowing what people thought at such a young age."

"It was at first, but I got used to it. If you're not careful, it can really mess with you, but I guess you know all about that."

"How did your parents take it?"

"They were corporate types. Climbing the ladder. When I first told them, they brushed it off. A kid's fantasies. I tried to talk with my dad a second time, but that didn't go well."

"What happened?"

"He slapped the snot out of me and told me to straighten up, or there'd be hell to pay."

"Was there?"

"Oh, yeah. When I was sixteen, I made the mistake of getting in the middle of one of their gin-fueled arguments. Mom demanded to know what he was thinking. Dad wanted to know what she really thought. You can guess how that went."

"You sided with your mother?"

"Yeah. I don't remember him actually hitting me. I came to in what was left of the glass coffee table I fell onto after he punched. I left a week later."

"I'm sorry."

"Don't be. It's the best thing I ever—"

The door to my room swung open. The taller enforcer's eyes went to the connecting door, then to us, and narrowed.

"Time to go," he said, gun leveled.

As we walked back to the lab, I glanced at one of the windows. It was summer in Russia, and I had no idea when the sun went down. It could have been 10 in the evening, for all I knew.

The lab again was partially lit, except for the center, which was completely dark. I wondered if Kadin's blood had been mopped up. God, I hoped it wasn't still congealing on the tile floor.

We angled around one of the larger computer stacks, and I noticed Chris and some technicians near the back of the lab. I strained to see if the blood was gone, and the enforcer prodded us in Chris's direction with a jab of his gun. Rechenko was hunched over a laptop, intently studying its screen. Two other men – a young guy in his 30s, and an older man in his early 60s – were chatting with Chris next to a tech chair similar to the one Debra had strapped me into at ELT. They were dressed in stylish black suits, and with their close-cropped beards and dark complexions, I assumed they were Middle Eastern.

Rechenko looked up. The tall enforcer had pocketed his gun and was now walking alongside us like we were all best friends.

Rechenko removed his glasses and smiled. "Dillon. Irina."

Chris glanced over, his smile equally convincing. Business as usual. "Ah, the star of the show." He beckoned us over. "Come meet your benefactors."

The two Middle Eastern men eyed me impassively.

Chris put a hand to my back and guided me toward them. "Dillon Bradford, I want you to meet Mr. Haidar Sadiki and his associate, Mr. Namir Bouazizi."

Both men's handshakes were loose, and I recalled an article I had read once that said handshakes in the Arab world were long and limp. Sadiki's stare was creepy.

"And this is Dr. Irina Tarasova," Chris continued.

Sadiki let Bouazizi shake her hand.

"Too bad about Kadin and her father," Rechenko remarked.

"Yeah," Chris said, trying to avoid any awkward questions, "tell your cook to watch what he serves." He put his hand to his stomach and made a face to the Arabs. "Nasty stuff, that food poisoning."

Chris's lie and charm were flawless.

"Mr. Bradford," Sadiki's voice was deep and sounded British, "how do you feel?"

The question caught me by surprise. I shrugged.

Sadiki stepped up. "I understand you have quite an extraordinary talent."

I stared at Chris and said, "I can kill better than most, I guess."

Sadiki's face went blank. Chris spit out a laugh and came alongside me.

"Dillon was in advertising. You know those guys. Always dripping with sarcasm."

He squeezed the blood out of my upper arm. Bouazizi nodded uncomfortably.

I pulled out of Chris's grip. "My talent is God-given." *Fucker.*

Sadiki flashed a highly bleached smile. "Praise Allah," he said and looked to the heavens.

Chris glanced at his watch. "Gentlemen, we're under a deadline. Please." He gestured for them to stand about six feet from the chair, after which he walked around it and leaned onto one of its arms. An operating lamp down-lit his face, casting his eyes into deep shadow. He paused and ran his gaze across us.

"What if I said I could neutralize a high-value target across the globe without risk or potential of any blowback? Neat. Clean. Simple." Chris paused for effect. "What would that be worth? How could you assign a value to such an offering?"

"I'm sure you have," Sadiki said. He exchanged a chuckle with Bouazizi.

Chris flashed his boyish grin. "That's why you're a good businessman, Haidar. Straight to the point." He placed his hand on my shoulder. I wanted to throw up. "Dillon Bradford is the most powerful techlepath on the planet. He has been enhanced with the latest in biomedical telepathic technology. His gift can interface with the world's cellular–"

"We've read your brief." Sadiki didn't hide his impatience. "I'd like to see what Mr. Bradford can do."

"All right, then." Chris clasped his hands. "Showtime."

Rechenko's tech chair was far more refined than Debra's. Its head restraint wasn't as menacing, and its padding appeared to be real leather. Two technicians approached. One held a chrome-mesh skullcap that looked straight out of a Nike swim catalogue. It had about a dozen electrodes woven into it, and while they fitted it to my head, they took great care to tuck my hair completely under it. I waited for Irina to throw me a worried look, but she had her game face on.

"Irina," Rechenko said, "if you could monitor Dillon's vitals."

He pulled out a chair from the main workstation. Irina sat and spun the laptop around.

"Tonight, you'll witness something quite extraordinary." Chris emphasized his last statement with a sideshow flourish to the skullcap. He turned to Rechenko. "Doctor, please begin."

"Dillon, I'm sure this will be quite similar to what you did in Poland." Rechenko's tone was coolly professional.

"No head restraint?" I asked.

"No. Just relax and let us know when you've connected."

I sat back and crossed my legs. "What high-value target am I connecting with tonight?"

Rechenko looked questioningly at Chris.

Chris's boyish grin appeared. "It's a surprise."

The two technicians rolled in a large flat screen and parked it so everyone could see the show. It had the same global map as previously, but rather than info boxes of future techlepathic warriors orbiting it, there was just space and stars.

"We're here." Chris pointed to an area in southern Russia, near the Black Sea. "The target is here." The globe rotated as he slid his finger to London. "Once we link Dillon to the world communication grid and acquire the target's land line, it's simply a matter of downloading the virus."

"Virus?" Sadiki asked.

"Think of it as a disrupter for the brain's electrical impulses."

"What you call ... short circuiting?" Bouazizi asked.

Chris nodded. "Yes, but a powerful short circuiting."

Sadiki frowned. "How is this possible?"

"The process involves multiple wave forms," Rechenko explained, "each with a digital signature that–"

"How it's achieved is unimportant." Chris swept his hand over his head. "The technology is over my head, so I know it's over yours." He walked up to Sadiki. "Haidar, the truly important thing is that it works." Chris put a hand to his shoulder. "You have roadblocks to your goals, right?"

Sadiki nodded.

Chris winked. "I'm your bulldozer."

The analogy was lost on the Arab. Bouazizi whispered something into his boss's ear, and Sadiki smiled and nodded.

Chris glanced at his watch again. "It's almost time."

Rechenko rolled a chair over to the workstation and sat in front of a large computer monitor. "The pipeline is clear," he said after reviewing the screen.

I tried to free my mind of any thoughts or distractions. Given the present situation, it was difficult. For a few seconds, all I heard was the fizz of dead air as a yellow line spidered outward from southern Russia on the global map. It webbed its way to London, which is when two male voices came through the static-chewed incoherence. Both had British accents, but one was more pronounced than the other.

"I have two voices," I announced flatly.

"We're in," a technician proclaimed from behind me.

"Good." Rechenko turned to Irina. "How are Dillon's vitals?"

"Stable," she replied.

The phone conversation I was listening in on resembled a bad BBC drama. I could tell one of the men deferred to the other, probably a CEO or something. The names they kept dropping were a political who's-who list. The web of network lines on the global map kept shifting patterns. Probably adjusting for optimal bandwidth, but more likely redirecting to avoid detection. The whole thing was beginning to feel wrong.

"We're ready," Rechenko announced.

Nigel, this new speaker is a horse's ass. There's no way to tell what he'll do.

Nigel? Speaker?

Barry, if I had a euro for every time I heard that—

"Release the hounds," Chris said.

"Wait a minute!" I jerked around in the chair and faced Chris. "Are we taking down Nigel Gale or this Barry guy?"

Chris turned from Sadiki and casually regarded me. "Gale. Why?"

"He's the goddamn Prime Minister of England!"

37. I will.

"Screw this." I turned started to peel the skullcap off, but the cool metal of the Glock's silencer digging into my temple stopped me.

Chris leaned into my ear. "Not a good move."

I met his anger out of the corner of my eye. The Glock stayed in place.

"Mr. Banks!" Bouazizi demanded. "What is going on?!" He had stepped in front of his boss, although Sadiki seemed the kind of man who could easily handle a situation like this. He motioned for Bouazizi to step aside.

"Chris, have you lost control of your dog?" Sadiki asked, half amused.

"I'm not a dog, asshole," I blurted and instantly regretted it. Irina and I traded glances.

Sadiki's displeasure manifested as a quiver under his left eye. He removed a pair of Porsche sunglasses from a jacket pocket and slipped them on.

"We are done here," he said matter-of-factly.

He and Bouazizi began to leave.

Chris brought the Glock around and took dead aim. "No, we're not."

Both men turned. Bouazizi, his expression locked down into serious badass, reached under his jacket. Chris shot him without hesitation. The side of Bouazizi's head exploded across the face and chest of a female technician standing to his left. She screamed, and her eyes, wide with shock, followed Bouazizi as he crumpled at her feet. The taller enforcer drew his weapon but clearly had no idea where to point it.

Rechenko sprung to his feet. "My God!" he yelled. "Are you out of your mind?!"

Chris swung the Glock in his direction. "Sit."

Rechenko raised his hands and cautiously sat.

Sadiki removed the sunglasses and impassively regarded his slain associate. He pocketed the glasses, removed a white handkerchief, and dabbed at a bit of brain matter clinging to his lapel. He looked over. "All right, Chris." Another wipe. "You have my attention."

The Glock returned to my temple. Chris said, "Finish this and you'll get a bonus." He jabbed my head with the barrel. He looked at the enforcer and gave a nod to me. The guy leveled his weapon.

I was now balancing on Chris's unraveling tightrope of sanity. The looks on the technician's faces ranged from panic to dismay to all-out terror. My hands shook as I adjusted the skullcap. I kept my position forward in the chair.

Chris, the Glock hanging at his side, approached Sadiki. He glanced down at Bouazizi's contorted heap and shook his head. The blood-smeared technician, hands covering her mouth, was still shaking. Blood pooled at her feet.

"Your associate left me no choice, really." Chris's forehead was slick with sweat.

Sadiki shrugged. "Occupational hazard, yes?"

Chris put an arm around Sadiki's shoulder, but it wasn't a friendly gesture. He lifted the Glock and scratched the side of his cheek with the tip of the muzzle. "Haidar, how long have we known each other?"

Another shrug.

"A long time. Been through a lot. So you know I'm a man of my word." Chris looked at Rechenko. "Are they still talking?"

Rechenko studied the monitor. "Yes. It's a scheduled conference. They should be on for another five minutes."

"All right, then," Chris said. "Let's try this again." The blood-splattered technician audibly whimpered. He regarded her harshly. "Would someone please help her?"

Another technician, an older woman, guided her away by the shoulders.

Chris stepped up to the chair, faced the room, and folded his arms. The Glock was tucked under his left bicep and pointed in my direction. "People," he announced, "let's get this right."

Rechenko slowly swiveled and studied something on his monitor. "We're clear to go," he said somberly.

The conversation between Gale and Barry faded up. They seemed to be having an argument.

On the far side of the lab, the main door opened slightly and Wardinski sidestepped inside. All heads turned.

"What the hell?" Chris said, under his breath.

Seemingly oblivious to us, Wardinski hurried to one of the secondary workstations and clicked on the lamp. The small island of light stood in stark contrast to the darkened expanse of the lab. He had his back to us and was hunched over the console.

"Peter?" Chris called out, trying to sound nonchalant. "What are you doing?"

Wardinski ignored the question and began furiously tapping on the keyboard.

"Get him back to his room," Chris said to the taller enforcer. "And find out where the hell Armando is."

The enforcer started edging through the maze of equipment, his gun poised.

Chris motioned to Rechenko with the Glock. "Keep going."

"We're in," he said.

The enforcer was about halfway when Wardinski turned, aimed a gun, and fired two shots. The echo bounced around the lab's hard surfaces. Many of the technicians cowered. The enforcer ducked behind a computer stack and held his ground. He looked back at Chris and made a gesture that asked, *You want me to shoot him?*

Chris was clearly losing it. "For the love of God!" he exclaimed.

He aimed at Wardinski and fired. The top of the console burst into white bits. A warning shot. Wardinski flinched violently, but continued tapping away at the keyboard.

"Peter, you're hopelessly outgunned here." Chris looked at Rechenko. "What is he doing?"

Rechenko shook his head nervously. "I-I don't know."

"Are we still connected–?" Chris grabbed his head with both hands and stumbled backwards. "Goddamn it! What the hell?" He groaned and doubled over.

I saw my shock mirrored in Irina's face. She swiveled to see what Wardinski was doing. Without warning, the thoughts of everyone around me came flooding in. The jolt was almost nauseating. I heard Irina's distinct huskiness in the cacophony of voices. I focused on the back of her head.

He's trying to disrupt Chris's tech! She turned back, her eyes bright with disbelief.

"Boss, vhat's the matter?" the enforcer yelled.

Chris pointed frantically with the Glock. "Ki–!" He groaned again.

"Vhat?"

"Kill him!" He grabbed his head, screamed, and dropped to one knee.

When the enforcer turned to take aim, Irina vaulted over the top of the workstation.

The word "No!" came out of my mouth as the enforcer fired. The left shoulder area of Wardinski's shirt puffed, and blood sprayed against the LED screens of his workstation. He cried out and collapsed behind the console.

The enforcer pivoted, gun aimed, but was body-slammed by Irina. She drove him into the computer stack, and they both toppled and disappeared from view.

Chris staggered to his feet, the effects of Wardinski's sabotage ebbing. His eyes were feral. He jerked his attention from where the enforcer had been to the island of light on the far side of the lab.

"Did he kill him?" he asked, breathless. Blood dripped from his nose.

Wardinski's imposing figure rose unsteadily from behind the console. He started tapping again.

"Fuck!" Chris yelled. He raised the Glock and took aim.

I leapt from the chair and tackled him, jamming my right shoulder into his stomach. The Glock fired into the air, and we landed on the hard tile. Chris broke part of my fall, but my left shoulder caught the edge of a countertop and popped with a sickening crack. Pain shot up through my teeth. The back of Chris's head whiplashed against the floor, and his eyes swam with confusion.

I had managed to pin down the arm with the Glock, but it was with my damaged left arm. My shoulder was screaming. Then, as if some demon entity had entered his body, Chris focused on me with a deadly loathing. I reared back and punched him as hard as I could with my right hand. One of my knuckles went out of joint. His eyes didn't waver. I reared back and swung again, but he caught my punch with the meat of his forearm. His free hand flew to my throat and dug in. He pulled me to his face. I gasped for air.

"You're out of your league," he said through bloodstained teeth. His fingers tightened.

I tried to hold him down, but the guy was as strong as a bull. Even through my struggle, he managed to twist me onto my side. White tracers shot through my vision, and black edges formed at my periphery. I grabbed his wrist with both hands, but his fingers were like a vice grip. He straddled my waist, slammed my head to the floor, and held me by my throat. My tunnel vision was tightening. The Glock came into view.

"We would have made a great team." Chris leaned down and pressed the muzzle of the silencer to my forehead. "You could've had it all."

I clenched my eyes and waited for death. Time slowed to an infinite crawl. My mind fled to my condo's balcony, where I saw storms rolling in from the west. I stood there, the wind whipping around me. There was a loud crack of thunder and rain hit my face. I tasted something wet and bitter on my lips.

"Dillon?"

I opened my eyes to find Chris still on top of me, the Glock loose at my head. There was a gaping hole just below his right eye, and the bridge of his nose was missing. Blood pumped from the wound. He tried to spit out some words, but the blood drowned them. His grip at my throat slackened, and he slumped off to one side. Irina, aiming the enforcer's gun with both hands, stood behind him.

"You okay?" she asked.

Her tone was rough. Hurt. My eyes went to the spreading bloodstain just below her right breast. She collapsed to her knees. The gun clattered out of her hands. She glanced down at the ever-growing stain, then back. A mix of shock, fear, and surprise filled her face. "I–" A thin trail of blood leaked over her bottom lip, and she slowly sank backward, her legs tucked underneath her.

I moved so fast I didn't even feel my shoulder. I gathered her in my arms and cradled her head. The technicians began emerging from under desks. Sadiki was nowhere in sight. Irina's eyes narrowed into pain filled slits.

"Come on now, stay awake," I said. "You're going to be okay." I tried to sound reassuring, but I wasn't. The bloodstain on her shirt had doubled in size. I pressed my hand to it.

She sucked in a ragged breath and coughed. Blood splattered the front of my shirt. Rechenko knelt next to her. The geek with the dreads loomed above him, shock etched across his face. I lost it.

"Do something!" I pleaded. "Get a med kit!"

Rechenko barked some Russian to the geek, and the kid bolted away.

Irina coughed again. Her skin was becoming pale.

"You need to wash your face," she mumbled. She raised a feeble hand and wiped my cheek. Her fingers came away with what looked like red bits of shredded fat.

"I will." My voice cracked. I lifted my hand from her wound. It was awash with blood. Her life. Tears welled in my eyes. She whispered something, but the blood in her mouth garbled her words.

I leaned down. "Don't speak. Just think it."

Irina's eyes searched mine. Her spirit had almost departed.

I want to see Texas...

Part 4: The stars tonight, are big and bright.

38. Company man.

The pilot opened the forward door, and the Texas summer heat mercilessly introduced itself. I stepped off the Hawker/Beechcraft stairway, dropped my duffle bag, went to my hands and knees, and kissed the ground.

"Is this a Texas custom?" Irina asked over the whine-down of the jet's engines.

I stood and brushed my jeans. "Just mine."

She looked around. "So this is Dallas?"

"No, this is Addison. A suburb of Dallas."

Half of the sky was clear, but to the west, a dark, angry storm front was carving a path through the Mid-Cities. A searing gust blew across the tarmac.

"Is it always this hot?" She brushed her hair back.

I smiled. "Just wait till August."

Irina fanned herself with the *Stern* she had picked up at our Berlin stopover. "Do all American suburbs have private airports?"

I picked up my bag and met her sarcasm. "Just in Texas."

The screech of tires on hot asphalt seized both our attentions. A black Cadillac Escalade with darkly tinted windows, closely followed by a silver Honda Civic with equally dark tint, weaved through the Learjets and Citations. The Escalade squealed to a halt near the tail of our plane, the Civic just behind it. An Asian man – 20-something and wearing a white lab coat – climbed out of the Escalade. He had a narrow port wine stain down one side of his face, and a stature that, though small, suggested he could probably go Krav Maga on somebody twice his size. His wrap-around shades only added to the tough-guy aesthetic. He stepped briskly to the back of the SUV and stood, hands clasped behind his back.

In the Civic, the driver was finishing a cell call while the passenger waited. After a minute, Debra Lao and the passenger emerged. The passenger didn't register at first. Then she removed her sunglasses.

"I'll be Goddamned," I said to myself.

Dressed in a simple, black business suit and carrying two manila envelopes, Debra approached and spread her arms like the real estate agent who sold me the office building in Deep Ellum: wide enough to say hello, but no hug.

"Welcome back," she said.

"Thanks."

She gestured. "You remember Cynthia Hampton."

Seeing Cyndi standing there in practically the beige version of Debra's suit, it all clicked into place. She was, after all, a military brat. Probably top of her class at the Naval or Air Force Academy, and majored in computer science and foreign languages. Fast-tracked by her dad or some such bullshit. More than likely they had sent her in first, to infiltrate CoolBrain. She got in tight with Tommy, then came after me. When that hadn't worked, they sent in Debra. Or maybe they had both been working me at the same time. God, I had been such an idiot. "I do."

"Good to see you again, Dillon," Cyndi said with detached professionalism.

I motioned to Irina. "Everyone, this is Dr. Irina Tarasova."

Debra extended a hand. "Doctor, so good to meet you. How are you feeling?"

Irina shook it reticently. "I am better, thank you."

"I read your paper on the genetics of the techlepathic condition. It was very enlightening."

Irina frowned. "That was classified."

Debra's attention swung back to me. "How was your flight?" she asked around a hollow smile.

Something was different. Her taut comportment, reflected in the distance she kept between us?

I nodded to the jet. "Not as nice as a G5, but beggars can't be choosers, right?"

Debra grew suddenly solemn. "I want to say how sorry we are—"

"We?"

"The NSA. For what you've been through."

"Look, Debra. It wasn't your fault. What's done is done...."

She put a hand up. "No. This was bad. Very bad. It shouldn't have happened. We had no indications that Chris had become so unstable...."

Debra's pause was telling.

She continued, "Former intelligence operatives will sometimes freelance after service. But we wouldn't have dealt with Chris had we been fully apprised of all the intel." She drew in a hesitant breath. "That said, we want to make things right."

"The technology was experimental," Irina offered. "You had no way of knowing how it would affect Chris. Especially with his medical condition."

Irina's statement hit a nerve. "Yes, we did," Debra said, sharply, "but we turned a blind eye. The reward outweighed the risk. Or so I was told."

"What do you mean *dealt* with Chris?" I asked.

Debra's pursed lips suggested that what she was about to say was difficult, even for her. "We knew about Chris's affiliation with Rechenko."

"You did?"

"Yes. It's not uncommon for us to partner on an ad hoc basis with groups that under normal circumstances we would consider a threat to the United States."

"Playing both sides of the fence?"

"In a manner of speaking. Rechenko's work is legendary. Popprov was close, but his tech wasn't giving us the same results."

"So you allowed Chris's group to inject their tech into me?"

The corners of Debra's eyes tightened. "We didn't know they had injected the full tech. We thought they'd done a rejection test."

"Did you know who Chris was?"

Her eyes shifted to something over my shoulder. She was clearly caught between embarrassment and frustration.

"No," she said flatly.

"It was Stiles, wasn't it?"

Her eyes came back. "Yes."

Learning that the NSA had played fast and loose with my life should have pissed me off. Honestly, though, I was just glad to be alive. Part of me wanted to know more, but I sensed Debra was through letting us peek behind the curtain.

"So what happened to the Men in Black?" I asked.

"Agents Stiles and Harris have been ... reassigned."

"So you're in charge?"

"For the moment."

"Cleaning house?"

"Something like that." She handed us the envelopes. "We've replaced many of the items that you lost or that were taken from you." She faced Irina. "Doctor, we have you at one of Ewing Laboratories' corporate suites here in Addison. My assistant unfortunately reserved the room next to Dr. Rechenko for you. Given your history with him, I wasn't sure if that would be acceptable."

Irina dug through her envelope and produced a hotel swipe-key packet. "He saved my life," she said, inspecting it. "I have no issue with him."

"A Crowne Plaza." I eyed the key, then Debra. "*Nice.*"

"Doctor," Debra said, "we've set an appointment for you with a specialist at Baylor Medical at nine tomorrow." Debra gestured to the SUV driver, who hadn't moved a muscle. "Phat will pick you up at eight-thirty."

"God, Debra, I don't think you have to worry about Irina suing."

Exasperation flashed across Debra's face. "This has *nothing* to do with any legalities."

"I had good treatment in Russia," Irina said. "I am fine."

"With all due respect, doctor," Debra's professionalism clicked back in like a gun cocking, "you didn't, and you're not." She turned to me. "As for you, I took the liberty of restocking your condo's refrigerator. I know how you like to cook."

"I didn't know you liked to cook," Irina said.

I leaned into her ear. "Agent Lao is being facetious," I whispered. She looked at me quizzically. "I'll explain later."

Debra impatiently resumed her spiel. "You'll also find in your packet, Dillon, a new iPhone, passport, wallet, and security key for your condo." Debra pointed to both our packages. "There are debriefing files in here. We'd like to do a postmortem as soon as possible. The forms will help you organize your thoughts." She tapped the top of my envelope. "I want to know everything about Chris's little techlepathic army."

"So," I said, peering into my envelope, "guess I'm a Company Man now."

Debra raised a mocking eyebrow. "Do you want to be?"

The implications of the question hit me with a surprising weight. I didn't like the prospect of being Debra's bitch. And after all that I had been through, I certainly didn't want to be the NSA's virtual spy.

"I've done some thinking." I folded the flap of my envelope closed and bent the tabs of its clasp down. Debra watched intently. "I don't think I want to be a Company Man," I said, handing it back.

Slowly and deliberately, Debra took the envelope and inspected the edge of its flap. "Are you sure you want to play it like this?" She flicked the clasp with the nail of her forefinger.

"Yes."

For a moment, I thought she would protest, but then a hint of a half smile edged into one corner of her mouth. "Guess you're not a Type 6 anymore."

She pulled from her coat pocket some high-piss sunglasses, the kind that made women look like insects. Cyndi did the same. Both started toward the Civic, but Debra turned and gestured with the envelope. Cyndi continued toward the car.

"I forgot to ask you," Debra said. "How is Dr. Wardinski doing?"

"He will recover from his wound," Irina said, "but I don't know about his mental state. Only time will tell."

Debra looked away and shook her head slightly. "Tragic," she said. She gave us a curt nod, then walked up to Phat and said something. His attention was on us as he listened. A distant clap of thunder reverberated across the airport.

"Do you know what you're doing?" Irina asked.

"Hell no."

By the way Debra peeled out, she wasn't pleased by my defiance.

"What's a Type 6?" Irina asked, watching the Civic disappear around a hangar.

I heaved my duffle bag and slung it over a shoulder. "The old me." I grabbed the handle of Irina's suitcase and rolled it forward. "Come on," I said. "Let's see what Phat here has been ordered to do."

A cool wind swirled and kicked up some dust.

"The pressure's dropping," Irina remarked. "The storm will be here soon."

"You know about this kind of stuff?"

"We have weather in Russia, Dillon."

Phat greeted us, "Hello, Mr. Bradford. Dr. Tarasova." His grin was a stark contrast to the mental backstory I had created for him. It was also infectious. He raised the Escalade's cargo door and stowed our bags.

More thunder rumbled through the area.

"I will be taking you to your hotel first, Dr. Tarasova." Phat's English was perfect. "Is there any place you need to stop on the way?"

"I don't know." The question caught Irina off guard. I could tell she was tired.

"You need to get a good night's sleep," I said, helping Phat close the cargo door. "Although on the way to my condo, I want to stop at Whole Foods."

Irina regarded me oddly. "Is there a Half Foods?"

Phat and I exchanged a stifled chuckle.

"What?"

"It's a grocery store," I said, but she clearly didn't get it. "Never mind. I'll take you there tomorrow. You'll love it."

Irina affected an eager smile, but it faded quickly. She grabbed her side and sought support against the SUV.

I stepped closer. "Are you okay?"

She steadied herself and nodded. "Just a long flight. You're right. I need rest."

I felt where the wound had been. The bandage seemed dry through her thin blouse. Her eyes went to my hand, then to me. The smile was genuine this time. A shadow passed across us as the cloud front moved in.

"Ever watch a storm roll in from a swanky condo in Dallas?" I asked.

"Of course not."

I guided some stray hair off of her face and gently tucked it behind her ear.

"Would you like to?"

Irina leaned into my touch and searched my eyes.

"Yes," she said softly. "Very much."

I turned to Phat, who was waiting by the open passenger door.

"We're not going to the Crowne Plaza," I announced.

"Half Foods?" He was doing a poor job of restraining his grin.

Raindrops started patting the ground around us.

"Yes. I'm in the mood to cook."

39. Puppet.

Everything in my life seemed slightly out of place, skewed, like I had gone through a wormhole and was living an alternate reality. My condo seemed foreign, Dallas unfamiliar. Even the act of driving the Merc felt pretentious. It wasn't that things had changed. I had changed.

"What do you think?" Derek asked. He leaned against the door of my office and pointed to the stack of new Eagle Energy logos in my hands. I had skimmed them earlier, and the old me would have pulled the best one and tossed the others in the recycle bin. Now, they were just abstract symbols. Meaningless. I studied the top one.

"That's Isato's fave," he said, stepping in.

"It's really good." I gestured. "Bet it gets into *Graphis*."

Derek's attention settled into a stare.

"What?" I asked.

"I can't get used to you with short hair."

Neither could I. Irina had insisted that I shave my head to prop up the cancer story. I argued against it, and we finally settled on a military style, close-cropped buzz. Now, according to Irina, I was "very sexy" and looking "more Russian," whatever that meant. In reality, as long as she was happy, I was happy. Or as happy as I could be, I guess.

"I'm getting used to it."

Derek nodded. An awkward second ticked between us.

"I'm going to have to go back down to Houston for follow-ups, you know," I said.

Although I had decided not to join Debra's crew, I knew I'd hear from her again. It was only a matter of time. The NSA would never let me just walk away, so I might as well start planting the seeds to explain my sudden disappearances.

Another awkward nod. Derek turned to leave but stopped at the threshold. He turned slightly to regard me over his shoulder.

"You know you've changed, don't you?"

If only he knew. "I'm sure I have. Cancer changes everyone."

I placed the logo treatments back into the file folder.

"Anyway, it's good to have you back, man." Derek smiled and walked out. "Hey," he called from the hallway. His head reappeared around the doorjamb. "I like your new Russian friend." He laughed.

"What's so funny?"

"You haven't changed completely. Only you would have the balls to start dating your radiologist."

"That's me," I said, waving my hands on either side of my head, "still crazy when it comes to women."

"Hey, whatever happened to Kadin? I thought she might be the one."

His question lodged itself in the pit of my stomach. My thoughts went to

Wardinski cradling Kadin's head, his hand cupping the exit wound, and her blood flowing through his fingers.

"Dillon? You okay?"

"She, uh ... she kind of freaked out and split." I caught myself wanting to succumb to the love that I once felt, but I swallowed the emotion down.

"Really? Man, that's so chicken-shit. I guess some people just weird out when it comes to life-threatening illnesses." Derek waved her off like just another used girlfriend. "Screw her, right?"

"Yeah." Another hard swallow. "Screw her."

■   ■   ■

I stayed late and plowed through what must have been a thousand emails. Everyone at the office had kept an awkward distance. A few folks said it was good to have me back, but for the most part, my employees treated me like nothing had happened. But their nonchalant attitudes didn't wash. I could see their minds working in the passing glances. Is the boss going to die? I guess in a sense, the old Dillon had.

I always considered the fact that I could listen in on the thoughts of others the biggest thing that ever happened to me. Now, however, even that seemed trivial compared to my recent ordeal. The old Dillon would have masked the events of the last few weeks with a steady regimen of Monopolova martinis and vacuous sex. That, too, seemed foreign: something that someone else would do. An old friend maybe; one I hadn't seen in years.

The Merc chimed that it was low on gas. There were only a handful of stations between the office and eatZi's – a New York Italian deli wannabe where I told Irina I would grab some dinner. The closest station was off of Turtle Creek Boulevard, so I turned onto it and headed into Lee Park. The Merc chimed again–

Hey, douche bag!

The stray words cut through my mind like a chainsaw. I recognized the voice as the homeless man I had encountered weeks ago, just before my life had been turned upside down. I gripped the wheel and winced.

Fucking rich bastard.

"Jesus!" The guy's tone cut a nerve, and I spun the Merc through a hard U-turn. *I'm coming for you, asshole.*

Bring it on, tough guy.

I don't know why I was so angry. Maybe everything – all the shit I'd seen and suffered – finally boiled over. Maybe the new Dillon was pissed off at his new life. Maybe I was just tired of being jerked around.

I drove the Merc over the curb and into the grass. I probably tore the undercarriage all to hell. I didn't care. I *was* a rich bastard.

Oh, too bad. You went and tore up your pretty car.

I jammed the Merc into park and flung the door open. Its halogen projector beams cut two perfect swaths across the creek and illuminated a grove of trees on the far bank. I stepped in front of the headlights and yelled, "Show yourself, asshole!"

The guy from weeks before emerged from the dark, his form appearing over a small knoll like some urban apparition. He still looked like he had before, although the windbreaker had been swapped for what might have been a really nice dress coat once, the kind you'd find at a Korshak's or Neiman's half-off sale. He walked into the Merc's beams and stood.

"You want a piece of me?!" I screamed.

This started him laughing. I charged him and took him by the lapels. Unlike before, he didn't smell like he'd spent most of his life in a dumpster. His teeth, oddly, were damn near perfect. And being so close he didn't seem so decrepit.

"Who are you? Why do you keep fucking with me?"

His eyes were a brilliant blue. The longer he stared at me, the more it felt like he saw right into my soul. I tried to listen in, but there was nothing.

"Quit ... fucking ... laughing!" I shook him with each word, but he was as limp as a rag doll in my hands. His face slackened, but the laughing continued in his mind. Something in me snapped. I grabbed his throat with my left hand and reared back, right fist tightly wound to strike. "Get out of my head!"

The laughing vanished. A grave visage spread across his angular features like a brittle canvas. He grabbed my shirt, and there was a fresh strength in his grip and stance, like the bum routine had just been an act.

"Tired of being a puppet?" His words came out with an intelligent earnestness.

The sudden reversal had pulled me off balance, but I managed to right myself. Sharp pain knifed through my left shoulder. My attack on Chris flashed through my mind, particularly the rage I felt when I punched his face. I dug my fingers into the guy's throat and drew my fist back even farther.

"Shut up!" I screamed.

He forced a wicked grin through my chokehold. *Tell me, Dillon.* His words, along with his eyes, drilled deeply. *How did you like working for Rechenko?*

40. No turning back.

Rechenko's name lingered in my prefrontal cortex like the last drunk at a party.

"How do you know him?" I asked.

His eyes went to my hands, and I relaxed my grip.

The guy shoved me away and rubbed at his neck. He removed a pack of Gitanes from an interior coat pocket and tapped one out. The blue box was unmistakable.

"Everybody knows Rechenko," he said, lighting the end with a simple wood match with the flick of his thumbnail. The smoke lingered around his face. His gaze never left me.

The moment fell into oblivion. I reflexively took a step back and tried to make sense of it all. I focused on his thoughts again, but still there was nothing.

Not even static.

The guy must have picked up on it, because a grin formed around the slim white shaft of the Gitane. He sucked in the mother of all drags.

"I'm not going to let you in," he said exhaling.

"How can you do that?"

The grin widened. *A little trick I developed. Comes in handy at parties.*

His invasion sent a ripple of pressure through my head. I rubbed at my left temple.

"So tell me, Dillon," he said. "Are you tired of playing in the minors?"

I didn't give him the satisfaction of an answer. This seemed to resonate with him.

"They said you'd be difficult. Said it'd be a bitch to convince you."

"Convince me of what?" I asked. "And who are you?"

"My name is Stellan. Come on, let's go for a ride."

Jesus.

"He's not going to help you." Another fierce drag.

"What if I said no?"

"You won't." Stellan stepped closer. "Debra fed you a line of bullshit I would have given my right hand to have crafted, and then teased your nut sack into a tight little knot. You bought into her 'my brother was killed by the Taliban' shit." He did a little jig and saluted. "You swallowed it hook, line, and fucking sinker. Then the girl you loved kidnapped you, ripped your heart out, and basically ate it in front of you." He rolled his eyes with dramatic flair. "No wonder Chris blew her away."

Rage swelled like lava. I felt my lip curl.

Stellan's eyes narrowed. "Save that anger, Dillon. Kadin and Chris played you, and you know it. Now embrace it. Revel in it. Take that hate and channel it."

"Into what?" I growled.

The grin returned and filled the corners of his mouth like Oban into cut crystal. "Come on," he said flicking what was left of the Gitane. "I'll show you."

.   .   .

I turned off Oak Lawn Avenue and onto the northbound I-35 entrance ramp. It's the main highway everyone takes to Oklahoma or south to Austin. It cuts through Dallas like a bad scar, bisecting the main part of the inner city from the warehouse farms that stretch all the way to the suburbs that linked Dallas with Ft. Worth. And if you really wanted to, you could take it north all the way to Canada.

The Merc didn't ride like its belly had been torn apart, and Stellan hadn't said a word about where we were headed or who he worked for. He just grunted out directions and for me to watch for cops, because he'd just come down I-35, and they were "all over the place like fucking cockroaches."

I tried to engage Stellan, asking him how he knew Rechenko and Chris and Kadin, but he was tight-lipped. After telling me to get on I-35, he went back to staring out the window. The southbound lanes were packed. Probably folks going to a Mavs game at the American Airlines Center.

"Fascinating," he said finally, more to himself.

"Ah, he speaks."

A string of six ninja bikes flew past us riding the divider line like it was their own personal lane. They cut scarily between two semis and raced into open traffic. The high-pitch whine of their liquid cooled engines Dopplered away.

"What's so fascinating?" I asked.

"Dallas."

"How's that?"

Stellan moved his attention to the 12 lanes in front of us. A straggler ninja bike ripped past and barely made it between the same two trucks. "It's been over fifty years," he said, almost remorsefully. "And to most people, we're still the city that killed Kennedy."

"Maybe we'll know someday."

"Know what?"

"Who killed him."

This got half a smirk. "Trafficante. Hands down."

"I think it was Oswald."

The smirk completed. "Suit yourself." He pointed to the 183 split. "Take 183 to 114. Get off at the Royal Lane intersection."

Highway 114 took us toward the north entry of DFW airport, and Royal Lane was a creepy two-laner that fed into Dallas's industrial warehouse district. This was the area of town where local real estate tycoons like Trammel Crow and John Carpenter had made their billions decades before. The last time I had been down Royal was for Derek's bachelor party. We had ended the night at a club called Cougars. Its I-35 billboard touted a semi-naked girl in a Cirque du Soleil pose, body painted like a cougar. In reality, the club had very few girls as gorgeous as the one on the billboard, but it did have over a dozen "private" booths where you could engage Dallas's skankiest in almost anything money could buy. I think this is where Derek got his case of chlamydia.

"Take a left," Stellan said.

The unnamed street was lined with monstrous one- and two-story ware-houses. Each one looked like it had been built just yesterday, and each had rows of semi-trailers parked at the loading docks. There were only a few streetlights. After about a mile, I started having some serious doubts about playing this all out.

"Where the hell are we—"

"Take it easy, Dillon. You're not in any danger." Stellan pointed to a massive nondescript warehouse on our right. It was easily 100,000 square feet. "Turn in here."

There were no loading docks, at least that I could see, and a lone mercury vapor lamp loomed over a single metal door in the center of the structure.

"Pull up in front of the door," he said. "Turn off your engine and kill your lights."

I did as instructed. The interior lights came on as the Merc powered down. We quietly sat as the dome and door lights slowly faded out. The guy just stared at the door.

"What now?" I asked turning to him.

"Don't move."

A cold unease spiked along my nerves. "Why?" I whispered.

"We're being scanned."

I froze in position, hands gripping the wheel. After an agonizingly long minute, I slowly twisted my head in Stellan's direction. "Can I breath now–"

The front door of the building jerked forward like it had been pushed from the inside. It shifted toward the car about a foot in front of its jamb, then slid to the right along the building's white stucco wall. There was no visible rail system or hinges. Behind it, another metal door, sans the peeling paint and rust stains. This one was featureless and looked to be made of chrome or high-polished steel. It moved back into the building, then slid to the left until it was out of sight. Now, a black rectangle filled the Merc's windshield.

"What did it scan?" I asked.

"My brain's beta patterns," Stellan replied casually. "You can fake everything but those." He threw open the passenger door. "Let's go. We only have about a minute."

As we quickly walked toward the rectangle, I tried to get a sense of Stellan's age. He carried his body like someone who worked out a lot, but his face seemed older. Deep crow's feet and ragged worry lines suggested he might be in his sixties, but he had an energy about him like that of a man in his forties. His wavy hair was close cropped in a contemporary cut and lightly peppered with grey at the temples. He nimbly stepped though the doorway, and I followed.

Fluorescents automatically came on, and their hum filled the small waiting room where we now stood. Every surface was white, and we were facing another embedded chrome door. The front door slid silently back into place behind us. A faint sucking sound suggested we were sealed in.

"Stand still," Stellan ordered.

"Another scan?" I asked.

He answered with a crisp nod.

There was nothing to indicate that something was happening. No black camera domes in the ceiling like at ELT. No reader panels or ked pads. There weren't even any light switches or outlets. Just painted dry wall and white acoustic ceiling tiles. After a minute, the chrome door in front of us glowed slightly, then noiselessly slid back and disappeared to the left.

It was now abundantly clear that beyond this black rectangle was technology that was way off the books, and once I stepped through, there was no turning back.

"You're right, Dillon," Stellan said, eyeing the framed void. "There is no turning back." Then he faced me, and for the first time his expression was relaxed and filled with what I could only guess was empathy. "You don't have to, you know. I'm not like Chris." He pulled the lapels of his coat apart. "I don't have a Glock. And I won't force you to do anything you don't want to do."

How did this guy know everything? I glanced at my watch and thought of Irina, waiting back at my condo. She was probably watching some reality show. My media room had fascinated her, especially the big 60-inch Samsung. She actually squealed when the THX demo opened a movie we had downloaded. An image of her from this morning flashed in my head, and a deep passion moved through my heart. I had come out of the bathroom to find her sitting up in my bed, sheets clinging to her delicate breasts, hair tangled to one side from us making love, and wearing those dweeby black-framed glasses. The smile she fashioned had such a great mix of innocence and raw sexuality. I felt a hand at my shoulder.

"She'll be okay," Stellan said. "You'll be back there by nine. I promise."

I looked up from my watch, and the jerk from the park had somehow transformed into a man full of polite and sincere concern. His new act put me on edge a little. I started to say something, but his pat on my back cut me off.

"I know you do," he said. "It's written all over your mind. From what I saw, she's a great lady. It's no wonder you love her." Another pat. "Now, you want to see the future?"

How did he know I loved her? I didn't even know myself. I followed the guy through the door and into what felt like a large space. For a second it was pitch black, then overhead lights clicked on and cascaded down the room like ball lightning.

The space was enormous and droned with energy. It was at least ten times larger than the labs at ELT and tricked out with equipment that made Chris's lab in Russia look antiquated. The long rows of massive supercomputers that stretched the length of the huge room on either side of us appeared to be divided into color-coded sections, because the trusswork that supported the stacks were painted different colors. A command center that rivaled NASA's dominated the area between the supercomputers, and in the middle of all this impressive technology, a large two-story ring made out of what looked like the same metal as the security doors rose up on its edge like a shrine to some techno god.

"Shit." It was all I could think of to say.

Stellan walked up to one of the command consoles and faced me. "Everything you see in here doesn't exist." He ran a loving hand across the top of a flat screen monitor. "We're not on any corporation's books or in any defense department's budget. No Senate subcommittee knows we exist. No president has ever heard of us." He spread his arms proudly. "This is as black as it gets."

"What's that?" I asked pointing to the ring.

Stellan's eyebrows arched knowingly. "The chewy nougat center." He turned and started walking through the maze.

I quickly caught up, and we both maneuvered through the sea of stations. The computer terminals looked ordinary, but upon closer glance I saw that they weren't MAC or PC, but a kind of fusioned hybrid. The monitors were impossibly thin, and the keyboards were more organic and modular. At some stations, the keyboard was split into two separate pads, one for each hand, and between them a monitor was embedded into the counter. All the stations were dark and void of any electronic life.

The ring was standing on its edge and turned out to be a cross between a Star Trek surgical bay and an MRI on steroids, but not from any hospital I had ever been in. The machine's bed had an indentation for a person to lie down and intersected the open area in the center of the ring. The way it was set up, the person's head would rest in the exact center, and the whole thing was about 20 feet in diameter. There were no visible seams in any of the equipment, and it was all made out of the same chrome metal as the security doors. It was also extremely warm to my touch.

I walked around the device, occasionally leaning cautiously in, as if at any second it might come alive and bite my nose off. Stellan watched me with an odd satisfaction, arms folded.

"All this," I said gesturing around to the expanse. "For this ring?"

Stellan nodded. "Nothing but the best."

"Best isn't the word. This stuff is beyond—"

"Star Trek, I know. We get that a lot."

I eyed him for a long second. "I don't think I like you being in my head, when I can't be in yours."

"It's for security reasons, nothing else."

I continued around the machine and came up to Stellan's side. "You said something odd before about Irina."

He regarded me with slight trepidation. "Oh?"

"You said 'from what I saw.' Have you met her before?"

A new smirk played at the corners of Stellan's mouth. "Not exactly." He bent over the nearest console and passed his hand across its keyboard.

The station came to life, and the monitor brightened instantaneously. The counter, keyboard, and monitor all glowed with a pale green shimmer, and the surface of each was translucent enough to allow me to see the inner circuitry.

"Bring up file two five nine, case number DB Twelve," he commanded.

An image grew from the center of the screen and filled the monitor. On it was a freeze-frame of Irina eating in the dining area at the Russian radio tele-scope. It was a close-up view, as if the camera had been mounted on the table itself.

"Play the video, please," Stellan said as if he were addressing a slow child.

The video played soundlessly, and Irina silently talked and smiled and ate green beans. Occasionally she would glance into camera and say something, which was very weird.

My shock must have been apparent, because Stellan stifled a laugh.

"Pause," he said in the same monotone as before.

The video froze on Irina looking into camera, her glasses a bit askew across the bridge of her nose. She was leaning on the table with one elbow, about to bite into a forkful of mashed potatoes, and giving the camera that look over the rim of her glasses I had come to love.

"How did you get this video? It's remarkable. What did you do, hack into some security camera?" As I said the words, I knew that they couldn't have, because Chris would have never allowed it. Plus the angle of the shot was im-possible.

Stellan breathed out a sigh and leaned against the console. The translucency of the counter darkened against his slacks. "Dillon, this may seem hard to be-lieve, but this isn't from a video camera."

"Then how the hell did you get this imagery?" I pointed to the monitor.

"We got it from you."

I tried to process what he said, but couldn't. "Now what? From me? I don't follow you."

Stellan thrust his hands into his coat pockets and gave a nod to the ring. "This machine doesn't do what Debra and Chris's technology does. We're not concerned with something as archaic as listening in on someone's thoughts across the communications grid."

I was still lost. "Then what are you–?" My attention bounced from him to the paused image of Irina. The realization was overwhelming. "Oh my God," I barely uttered. "She's looking at me." I pivoted my disbelief back to Carter. "You got this from *me?*"

He pursed his lips and nodded. "Yes, Dillon ... we did."

"But how can you do that?"

Stellan came off the counter and walked to the ring. He patted the shiny surface of the bed like the loving owner of a pristine vintage car. "We call it Deep Consciousness Embedding. Think of it as going along for the ride."

"This is unbelievable."

"Not really." He folded his arms again. "Why can't the brain be computable? Why can't cognition be translated into an equivalent computation? Man has been on the verge of this for several years." He glanced around at the expanse. "We just accelerated the start point."

"No, I don't believe this." I shook my head, as if that would help me come to terms with the sheer abstraction of it all. "This is crazy."

"Is it, Dillon? Our kind's ability is the next genetic leap. And the nanos in your head are just the tip of the technological iceberg." He gave a nod to nearest supercomputers. "Each one of those can process way over a million yottaFLOPs per second."

"What the hell is a yottaFlop?"

"It's geek jargon for super fast computing. A ten with twenty-four zeros after it, times a million. It's like quantum computing, but different."

"What do you mean?"

"Let's just say it doesn't use silicon-based chips."

"How many of those do you have strung together?"

"They're not strung together. The whole *building* is the computer." He pointed to a section delineated by the color orange. "That section is motor function." He swung his finger to another section colored blue. "Short-term memory—"

"A brain," I said.

"Yes, Dillon. A brain. Each section represents an area of function. The color-coding makes it easier to differentiate the areas."

"Whose brain?"

"I'm sorry?"

"The techlepath's?"

"Oh, yes, the techlepath's. Interesting question."

My attention went to the long rows of matte black supercomputers that dominated both sides of the massive space. Each computer was the size of a shipping container, and both rows stretched the length of the building and disappeared into the unlit area. The whole thing reminded me of the Houston docks, where the shipping containers from cargo ships were stacked 20 high.

"You see, Dillon," Stellan said, touching my arm. "We're *inside* the computer."

Now it was my turn to lean against the counter. The ramifications pressed down like I was at the bottom of a distant ocean. "How does it work?"

"It's a bit difficult to explain. Let's just say that we can, for lack of a better term, digitize a techlepath's consciousness at the quantum level and imbed it into another person's brain. We use the communications grid, but through our own satellites. We have to packet the stream. It's similar to how Debra's group enhances our ability, but more complex."

The cluelessness must have been dripping off my face.

"Look, Dillon. I can have one of the lead techs tell you more later. For the moment, all you need to understand is that you'll be able to ride along and basically be the person we embed you in."

"So someone was … in me before. That's how you got those images of Irina, right?"

"That's correct."

"But I didn't feel anything," I said trying to think back.

"You won't," Stellan said. "Just like the people you listen in on don't."

My awe and disbelief was quickly turning into fascination. "But how can you have two personalities inside one human being? Wouldn't the mind, I don't know, short circuit?"

Stellan put his hands up. "I like that you're getting into it, but it's getting late. Besides, you need to get back to that Russian girlfriend of yours. We can continue this tomorrow, if you'd like. You can meet the team and ask them all your questions. Now come on, I'll walk you out."

I straightened unsteadily.

"You okay there?" he asked.

"Yeah, it's just a lot to process."

We started walking out along the path we had come. Stellan was behind me this time.

"I'll admit, it's a lot to take in at first," he said, scooting around one of the computer workstations. "But once you grasp the basic principles, it's really not that hard to understand."

"Easy for you to say. You're probably a neuroscientist or something."

"Something," he said, more under his breath.

I walked out in silence, but I couldn't tell if it was by choice or just the fact that I was still trying to wrap my head around the concept. And Stellan went quiet too, as if he was afraid of talking too much outside the walls of the lab.

The chrome security doors did their sliding aside trick, and when we stepped out into the parking area, I suddenly realized how cold it had been inside. The Merc chirped as we approached.

"Got to love technology," Stellan remarked.

"Hey, I need–"

Stellan was already pulling out his cell phone. I took mine out of my front pocket.

"Here," he said. "Give that to me." He held the two cell phones together, then handed mine back. "There."

"Nice trick." I started to thumb through my contacts, then realized I didn't even know who this guy was or what I was really getting into, for that matter.

I looked up, and the glow from my iPhone filled the space between us.

"So, Stellan. You got a last name, or are you like one of those one named celebrities?"

"Yeah, I got one," he said, regarding me with odd curiosity. "It's Bradford."

PAUL BLACK always wanted to make movies, but a career in brand design and advertising sidetracked him. Born and raised outside of Chicago, he is the international award-winning author of *The Tels*, *Soulware*, *Nexus Point*, *The Presence*, *The Samsara Effect* and *Cool Brain*. Today, he lives in Dallas, where he is one of the creative directors for global brand design at AT&T. In his off hours he feeds his passion for tennis and dreams of seven-figure movie deals. He is currently working on the next Dillon Bradford novel, tentatively called *Dark Slide*.

I would like to thank the following for their assistance, inspiration and patience: Lisa Glasgow, Bridget Boland, Brian Moreland, Pat O'Connell, and Max Wright. You all were there for me when I needed you.

For future trends in technology: www.socialtechnologies.com and its wealth of future forecasts and models of global trends. To NASA News and the Langley Research Center website for its white papers on the future of technology.

Special thanks to my editor and friend, Jay Johnson, for his faith in my talent, to Dr. Jerry Marlin, whose medical expertise was invaluable, and also to Irina Lykina Blocher, who graciously let me model Irina Tarasova after her likeness.

And to Trish, as always, with love.

Dallas, 2015

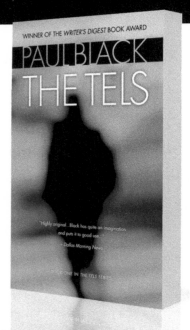

THE NEAR-FUTURE A new revolution has spread across the human landscape. The Biolution and its flood of technology have changed almost every aspect of life. Also changed, is the face of terrorism.

Throughout his life, Jonathan Kortel always sensed he was different, but never imagined how different, until two rival factions of a secret group called the Tels approach him out of the shadows of government. He has a gift that could change his life, and possibly the world, forever.

This is his story. A battle for the loyalty of a man who could change the course of human evolution. And the struggle inside this man as he comes to terms with his destiny. Deeply intriguing and powerfully suspenseful, Paul Black has created a future described as "mind-bending" by the *Dallas Morning News*. Part *X-Files*, part cyber-thriller, *The Tels* unveils a view of a world that could be just around the corner.

NOVEL INSTINCTS
www.paulblackbooks.com

Available at all online retailers including **Amazon.com** and **BN.com**.

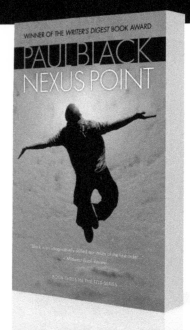

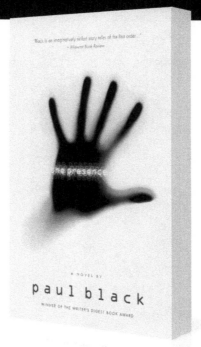

DEEP IN THE BASEMENT of the University of Chicago Biological Sciences Building, Dr. William Kanter is on the brink of developing a technology that will replace the MRI. Yet the images captured aren't of his brain, they're his memories. And they only take up only a small portion at the end of the scan. What Kanter discovers throughout the rest of the scan could rock the very foundation of humanity.

Across campus, child psychologist Dr. Trenna Anderson is reviewing a disturbing home video of a young Wisconsin farm boy who suffers from night terrors. After witnessing the boy become a Nazi prison guard, L.A. crack whore and Inuit native, Anderson suspects the eight-year-old may have multiple personality disorder. But when conventional psychotherapy fails, Anderson reluctantly meets with a maverick inventor named Kanter who's rumored to have created a revolutionary machine that might be the boy's only hope.

Kanter thinks his invention will help mankind, but there are forces at work that want to destroy a machine that threatens to expose the world's most precious beliefs. Soon Kanter and Anderson find themselves embroiled in a deadly and dangerous world of government espionage, corporate greed and religious fundamentalism. Is Kanter's invention capable of changing the world? And if so, at what cost?

NOVEL INSTINCTS
w w w . p a u l b l a c k b o o k s . c o m

Available at all online retailers including **Amazon.com** and **BN.com**.

CPSIA information can be obtained
at www.ICGtesting.com
Printed in the USA
FFHW020757110319
50946754-56372FF